APOCALYPSE Z THE BEGINNING OF THE END

Text copyright © 2007 by Manel Loureiro
English translation copyright © 2012 by Pamela Carmell
All rights reserved.

Printed in the United States of America.

Apocalypse Z: The Beginning of the End was first published in Spain by Dolmen. Translated from Spanish by Pamela Carmell. Published in English by AmazonCrossing in 2012.

Published by AmazonCrossing
P.O. Box 400818
Las Vegas, NV 89140

ISBN-13: 9781612184340
ISBN-10: 1612184340
Library of Congress Control Number: 2012910422

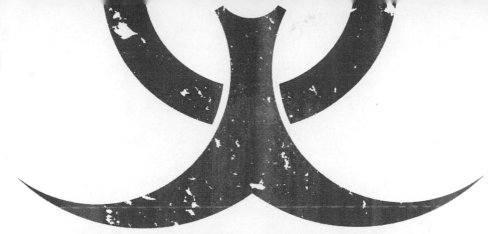

APOCALYPSE Z
THE BEGINNING OF THE END

MANEL LOUREIRO
TRANSLATED BY PAMELA CARMELL

When there's no more room in Hell,
the dead will walk the Earth.

—*Dawn of the Dead,* 1978

[T H E   B L O G]

ENTRY 1
Friday, December 30, 8:40 a.m.

Today's going to be insane. When I got up this morning, it was pouring down rain. It was still raining as I fixed myself a cup of coffee. I took a shower with the news blaring on the radio.

Some things never change. One day Spain's broke, the next day it's not. Today I have a meeting that could mean the difference between living like a king for the next six months or fighting with stockholders who have no idea what's best for them. It's their money, not mine, but if the merger goes through, I could kick back and live on my commission for the next few months. I need to relax, motor around on my little Zodiac, and do some scuba diving in the Ria Pontevedra...

I drank my coffee and looked out the window that opens on to the garden. This house was a good buy, but so many things still remind me of my wife. She chose it, she decorated it, she...I guess that doesn't matter now. I thought my doctor's advice to "unburden myself" to others would help me get over her, but time goes by and I still feel her presence everywhere. "Write a blog," my psychologist told me. "Talk about anything you want, any topic. Just talk." Well, that's what I'm doing right now, but it's not doing much good. What the hell. I'll give it a try.

The garden is green, damp, lush, and overgrown. It's been raining nonstop for three weeks here in Galicia. The humidity has permeated everything. If this rain keeps up, I'll have to cut the grass and clear the vines off the garden walls. It was her decision to surround the house with these high stone walls; water's trickling through them now. "We need privacy," she said. Now she's gone, and I feel like I'm living in a fortress.

I straightened my tie, grabbed my briefcase, and turned off the radio. The newscaster was talking about an explosive situation in a former Soviet republic in the Caucasus Mountains, someplace with a name ending in -*stan*. Something about a rebel group attacking a military base where Russian troops were stationed. Too bloody for me. I snapped off the radio. I had to get to the office. I was running late.

ENTRY 2: HOLIDAY HANGOVER
January 3, 1:15 p.m.

I haven't updated this blog for several days. The meeting with the company reps went great! Now I can splurge and take a nice vacation on what I earned last month.

On New Year's Eve, I had dinner at my parents' house in Cotobade, near Pontevedra. They moved there years ago, after they retired. In addition to my parents, my aunt and uncle were there, along with my sister and her boyfriend, in from Barcelona, where they work. She's a lawyer like me, although we work in different fields. She's lived there for years and has fit into life in Catalonia. I've always preferred Galicia.

During dinner we discussed the big story in the news: the conflict in the Caucasus. Apparently, a group of Islamic guerrillas from…Dagestan?…attacked a former Soviet base still under

Russian control there. My sister thinks they were looking for nuclear material. I hope she's wrong. That's all we need—another terrorist attack like in Madrid on March 11 but with nuclear bombs.

What few images there are on the news are hazy. The base that was attacked was top secret, and authorities aren't allowing anyone to take pictures. Reporters have to broadcast from the hotel roof, using images on file and street maps. They say hundreds have died, and Putin has put all of Russia on high alert. Images of soldiers and tanks occupying the streets are chilling. They must be afraid there'll be more assaults or attacks throughout the country. I'm glad I'm not there.

ENTRY 3
January 3, 7:03 p.m.

I'm watching TV. Channel 5 has interrupted its broadcast for a live report on the Russian Federation closing all its borders. All flights in and out of Russia have been canceled. The launch of a Soyuz rocket has been postponed *sine die*. On CNN they're discussing what this shutdown means—either the situation in Dagestan has gotten out of hand, or Putin wants to increase his power. A cautious analyst on some talk show is sure there's no cause for alarm; it's all a political maneuver. I don't know what to think.

The electricity came back on first thing this afternoon. I can't take the electric company's damn outages anymore. I'm living in a housing complex just a mile or so from Pontevedra, a city of eighty thousand people! "Problems with the power lines," they said. They estimated six months to fix it. They're not going to jerk me around anymore. Tomorrow I'm buying some solar panels and storage cells for the roof. And then screw the electric company.

ENTRY 4: GETTING WORRIED
January 4, 10:59 a.m.

I watched a news report about Russia on CNN this morning. Finally there are images of what the hell is going on in Dagestan. Putin's government continues to seal off the country. First they closed the borders; then they banned updates. Reporters based in Dagestan have been moved to Moscow to "ensure their safety," the report said.

Today they broadcasted a home video. You could see special units of the Russian army advancing down a deserted street in a town near the base that was attacked. At the beginning of the recording, they panned across the faces of the soldiers in a tank. They were young boys who looked pretty scared. When they jumped out of the tank, I was shocked to see that they were wearing gas masks, as if they were afraid of breathing something harmful. They started shooting like crazy at something or someone and then ran like hell back to the tank. That's where the tape ended. I don't know what to think about all this.

On Channel 3, they said it's possible that those rebel forces were from Chechnya and wanted to seize control of chemical weapons or nuclear material stored in the laboratories. The world is full of crazy people...

This afternoon I did some shopping. Three Kings Night is coming up. The mall near my house was packed with people buying gifts. I ran up my credit card buying tons of food, several five-liter jugs of water, a couple of powerful flashlights, and lots and lots of batteries on account of the damn power outages, and some electrical equipment, especially cable. If I'm going to install solar panels on the roof, I'd better be ready for some glitches. I also bought a ton of food for Lucullus, my Persian cat, who's been ignoring me lately.

Some girl kitty in the neighborhood must be in heat. Lucullus thinks it's his duty to shower her with his attention. He's constantly jumping the wall in search of adventure. That wall's ten feet high! What a guy won't do for a girl!

I went to the store that installs solar panels and bought a couple of BP Solar SX170 panels. They were pretty expensive. All totaled, including installation (they'll be here tomorrow to install them), it came to two thousand euros (storage batteries not included), but it's the best on the market. Each panel weighs about fifteen pounds, so they can be installed on the roof without caving it in. They're multicrystalline silicone cells guaranteed to last twenty-five years. With the two panels on the roof, I can charge two series of 24-volt storage batteries even in a place like Galicia where there's so little sun. That's crucial if I don't want food in the two freezers in the basement to spoil.

I don't have a lot of time to shop, so I stock up. That way I only have to go to the store every couple of weeks. These freezers are a great invention.

On the way home, I stopped at the liquor store and bought a couple of cartons of Fortuna cigarettes and a pad of paper, for when inspiration hits me. As I was waiting to pay, I saw a couple of guys in the gun shop across the street buying shotgun shells. It's hunting season, and there's a festival to kick it off. It'll be a long weekend for them.

When I got home, I put away my purchases and mowed the lawn as I listened to the radio. My backyard is only about five hundred square feet. I have a lot of privacy, with the wall around it. The house is brick and is in a development of forty identical brick villas, in rows of ten, on two parallel streets. Mine is in the middle of Street 1. It doesn't have a real name, since the development is less than three years old. These things take time. There's a house on each side of me and one in the back, facing Street 2.

A small backyard and a wall, about ten feet high, separate me from the villa behind me.

I don't know my neighbors very well, since I'm hardly ever at home. A very nice retired couple with a Pathfinder lives across the street. Next door is a doctor and his wife and two young daughters. A cool guy named Alfredo lives on the other side. He works construction and lives with his girlfriend. I live with my cat Lucullus, the horniest devil on the street. One of these days a hysterical neighbor will show up at my door with a box of kittens the spitting image of Lucullus, demanding an explanation. I have to do something with that cat.

On the radio they are still reporting news of Dagestan. It looks like the situation is spinning out of control. The Putin government continues the news blackout and sends in more and more troops and medical personnel. What the hell's going on?

ENTRY 5: SOMETHING'S NOT RIGHT
January 5, 1:54 p.m.

This morning a crew of guys installed my new solar panels. They're rated at 220W in optimal conditions of luminosity. The two rows of 24-volt batteries in the basement will give me about eight hours of electricity a day, more than enough to weather any power outage.

I called my sister in Barcelona to talk for a while. This weekend she's going to visit a friend in Girona. She said she's fine, and after some small talk, we hung up.

On TV they keep showing images from Dagestan. According to the latest news (what little there is, given the media blackout), Russian authorities have begun to evacuate the population. In the assault on the Russian base, Chechen rebels must have accidentally released some kind of chemical weapon stored there. On Channel 1, Lorenzo Mila, the highly respected newscaster from Barcelona, speculated it might have been sarin gas, what terrorists used in the attack in Tokyo. Channel 5 reported it might've been the hydrogen peroxide the Soviets used in their intercontinental missiles.

I don't think anyone knows for sure what's going on.

ENTRY 6
January 9, 10:23 a.m.

Something's really wrong in Russia. This weekend there has been a steady stream of news updates, statements, denials of those statements, blackouts, and violence. For the last forty-eight hours, nonstop on every channel, all they've talked about is the events in Dagestan.

On Friday morning they closed Russia's borders. That afternoon, Reuters reported that the raided base was really a biological research laboratory and that the substance accidentally released was some kind of pathogenic agent. Hours later, the Putin government categorically refuted that and talked only about a cloud of toxic chemical fertilizers. By breakfast time on Saturday, we learned that Russia had requested a team from the Centers for Disease Control (CDC) in Atlanta to come to Dagestan.

Now they're saying they released the highly contagious West Nile virus that was endemic in Egypt. A few years ago a mosquito transmitting the disease found its way on to a plane. Since 1995 there've been isolated cases in Europe and South America. That *sounds* logical, if it weren't for one small detail—there aren't many mosquitoes in the Caucasus Mountains in the middle of January.

On Sunday, things seemed to spin out of control. Just five hours after the CDC team arrived, just as they started to care for the poisoned—or should I say *infected*—people, two of its members had to be evacuated to the United States after some kind of incident with the patients.

Late that night, something similar happened to a team from the World Health Organization (WHO). They were rushed to the base at Ramstein, Germany. Some Internet sites are saying that members of the team were killed.

We don't have much information on the Russian medical teams, if they even have any, or the civilian population in the area. Home videos smuggled out of the country, mostly online, showed long convoys of people fleeing or being evacuated, some with pretty bad wounds, and lots and lots of ambulances. Army troops and Russian Border Guards in combat gear are headed in the opposite direction, toward what is now called the hot zone.

And this morning, the nail in the coffin. The Russian government declared martial law. All foreign journalists had to leave the country. No more freedom of assembly or the press. What's even weirder, they declared an Internet blackout across the country. Nothing can get in or out—in theory, anyway.

This morning our minister of health came on Channel 1 and said that the Spanish government will ensure that there are no outbreaks of West Nile in Spain. There's no cause for alarm. On Channel SER, the minister of defense said that a team of army medical personnel and construction engineers are headed to Dagestan to help control the situation. He emphasized that they won't be in danger. Blah, blah, blah.

Half of Europe, Japan, the United States, and Australia are sending similar teams. Something is happening in Russia. Something huge.

ENTRY 7: NEW IDEAS
January 9, 7:58 p.m.

I spent all afternoon trying out the solar panels. The power they generate is amazing. However, if I connected a lot of appliances at one time, energy consumption would soar and drain the batteries in a couple of hours. Using them with only a couple of freezers and the computer, for example, increases battery life to around fifteen hours. After that there's a lapse of about eight hours when the batteries can't be used because the voltage is very low and appliances could be damaged due to the difference in voltage. According to the manufacturer, in sunny climates you could use them for twenty-four hours, but it's winter in Galicia, so I can't complain. I won't have to put up with an outage of more than a couple of hours, not even during the worst winter storms. Overall it's a very smart investment.

Lucullus is kind of surprised by the strange hat his house is wearing. (I'm sure he thinks this is *his* home and I'm *his* pet.)

I listened to the radio all day—in the morning, on the way home from the office, and as I fixed dinner. The Spanish contingent took off from the Torrejón Air Base near Madrid, headed for a Dagestani town named Buynaksk, where they'll set up a field hospital. The Russians are dividing the international health groups among several locations. The region is very backward, and Russian health care seems to be on the verge of collapse.

In some refugee camps in neighboring republics, they're reporting new cases of what they insist is an especially virulent strain of the West Nile virus. But media sources are calling it Ebola. If that's true, the Russians are really screwed. Nobody seems to have organized camps for the refugees who were scattered to the four winds when the army expelled the healthy from their homes, along with the sick.

To make matters worse, many refugees have fled the country in little boats across the Caspian Sea to Iran, fueling fears that the disease will reach the Middle East.

I did more shopping, picked up some flu remedies, and went by my mother's house. I got her to write me a prescription for antibiotics. I'm a fanatic when it comes to colds.

ENTRY 8: MORE NEWS
January 9, 8:40 p.m.

Reuters reports that three of the WHO doctors evacuated to Ramstein have died. According to the medical report, this is a highly virulent hemorrhagic fever that causes disorientation, delusions, and acute aggression. The Ebola theory carries some weight.

ENTRY 9: TIPPING POINT
January 10, 11:01 a.m.

I write this during a break between meetings. I'm sitting on a park bench under my office window. With the new ban on smoking in the workplace, if I want to have a smoke, I have to go into exile, out in the cold. I can't even smoke in my own office! One good thing, I can pick up Wi-Fi out here so I can surf the net.

The news on several sites is very confusing. Almost all of it is disturbing. The situation in Russia appears to be completely out of control, just a couple of weeks after the Chechen assault. Martial law hasn't done any good. Chaos is spreading throughout the country. As you'd expect, the Internet blackout Putin ordered has been useless. Many Russian servers are located in countries outside the EU, so information is still getting out over the Internet. That's the only information besides official reports. Many bloggers report Russian military patrolling the streets, curfews, and indiscriminate shootings. Even cannibalism. With all the chaos this situation has triggered, many areas are totally cut off. In statement after statement, the Russian government has denied everything. The Russian minister of defense insisted that the riots were the work of Muslim extremists trying to destabilize the government. The truth is, the Russian government's credibility has plummeted, and the international press is highly skeptical of anything it says.

All we know for sure is that security around nuclear power plants and Russian missile bases has been strengthened, according to the US secretary of defense citing the CIA and images from its satellites. The US government has ordered the repatriation of all its citizens living in Russia. Apparently there are several dead and wounded among the US citizens working for NGOs in Dagestan, who arrived back in the United States this morning. CNN showed some of them being lowered out of the aircraft on a stretcher. They looked really bad.

North American troops are being withdrawn from Afghanistan back to the United States. There's a rumor they'll raise the terror alert to red. Most of those troops will have a layover at the base in Ramstein.

News flash: Cases of Russian West Nile, as they're calling it, have been reported in northern Iran and Iraqi Kurdistan. Internet forums are in full swing. Doomsday prophets are making a killing on blogs. This can't go on much longer. I'm sure it'll all turn out to be like the bird flu...

ENTRY 10: TIPPING POINT, PART II
January 10, 11:43 a.m.

About the bird flu. The United Kingdom just announced that it's suspending the Treaty of Schengen, which allows free movement around the EU. It's also going to set up health checkpoints at its borders. Countries on Russia's border—Denmark, Sweden, and Finland—plan to do the same. Our prime minister announced a press conference at noon to discuss measures Spain plans to take.

Radio stations are on fire. I'm surprised the pundits know so much about medicine. My sister called from Barcelona to tell me that the Catalan government is considering a mass vaccination. Vaccinate against what? Nobody has a clue, and everyone's trying to profit from someone else's misfortune. So what's new?

ENTRY 11: TIPPING POINT, PART III
January 10, 10:03 p.m.

The base at Ramstein has been quarantined, according to Google News. WHO members evacuated there out of Russia must have spread the disease to medical personnel. All US military flights are being diverted through non-EU countries.

Our minister of defense said on TV that the Spanish government has authorized North American aircraft to fly over our country. That may include using Rota as a support base.

Someone posted an image of Ramstein online. You can hardly see anything. Just two people dressed in what appear to be contamination suits talking at the door of a hut. There's something really disturbing about all this...

ENTRY 12: BREAKING POINT
January 11, 11:48 a.m.

Back on the park bench, having a quick smoke. Even a blind man could see that the mood on the street has changed. It's subtle, but there's no denying it.

Yesterday, at noon, the president gave a press conference, along with the ministers of health, interior, and defense. The message was basically "No cause for alarm." But people are more alarmed with each passing hour.

What adds to the alarm is that the opposition party's leader is demanding the immediate closure of ports and airports. COPE radio station in Madrid is calling for the army to occupy the borders. Just forty-eight hours after deploying soldiers to Dagestan, they've decided to bring them back.

I don't usually agree with talk show host Federico Losantos and his ultra-right-wing ranting on the radio, but maybe he's right this time. The situation seems to be completely out of control. In Russia, chaos has broken out for sure. Entire regions are incommunicado. No one's in control. News of looting, pillaging, and mass murder is spreading like wildfire across the Internet. Channel 5 broadcast French satellite images last night. You could see huge fires burning in Tbilisi, the capital of Georgia, only three hundred miles from its border with Dagestan. There's no word from the city, and no one seems to be fighting the fires. What the fuck's going on? Are they trying to burn the place down?

The WHO finally ruled that it's definitely West Nile virus and a strain of a disease similar to Ebola. Ebola. In every newspaper, on every radio and television station, they never tire of repeating that it's a hemorrhagic fever that affects humans and primates. Since it was discovered in 1976, they've identified five strains: Ebola Bundibugyo, Ebola Zaire, Ebola Sudan, Ebola Reston, and Ebola Taï Forest or Ivory Coast. Ebola spreads through contact with bodily fluids, primarily blood or saliva, and has a fatality rate up to 90 percent. But some sources have said this can't be Ebola, or at least none of the known strains. Rumors all over the place and not one goddamn bit of concrete information!

Deep down, I don't think anybody has any fucking idea what's going on. They're flying blind. The Swiss government has ordered the mass vaccination of its entire population with Tamiflu, to prevent bird flu. The United Kingdom has temporarily closed the Channel Tunnel and its ports, but they think there're already cases there, brought in by infected aid workers who rushed to evacuate out of Dagestan. Many came back wounded; some had been attacked by rabid animals. In Germany the situation is even worse. The Ramstein quarantine hasn't worked, and they've declared martial law. How long till Spain adopts similar measures?

I'm not sure what's going on in the rest of the world, but in Atlanta they're talking about a global pandemic. In the United States, apocalyptic sects are getting ready for an invasion of Martians or some crazy thing like that. Meanwhile, the

US president has announced he's raising the terrorism alert and creating an emergency cabinet.

According to the Ministry of Health, we've reached the "breaking point" in an epidemic, and a pandemic is now inevitable. It should hit Spain in a matter of days, if it's not here already. It happened so fast—just two weeks since it started. Judging from what the authorities have made public, it's still not clear how the disease is transmitted or what the incubation period is, or even what the symptoms are.

People are scared shitless. Today I saw two people walking down the street wearing masks. I was in a bar last night with Pablo and Hector when a guy started coughing loudly and was politely asked to leave. Some public activities have been temporarily suspended. The local government here in Galicia is considering closing public schools for few weeks. The government has not put restrictive measures in place, but people are starting to restrict themselves out of fear of the unknown infection. We're like animals, shrinking back in fear of a threat that a week ago was just a short piece in the newspaper.

My sister called me this morning. So far, life in Barcelona is going on as usual, but you can also sense fear on the streets. After rumors that hot air might be the ideal medium for spreading the disease, people quit using the subway. They eye everyone who looks Middle Eastern.

I took Lucullus to the vet. I got all his shots up to date, just in case. I also went by the dive shop to pick up a new regulator and a speargun and half a dozen spears, in case I decide to go fishing this weekend.

I need to get the car's oil checked. My Astra's not even a year old. I don't want it to suffer the same fate as my previous car. But that's really a long story...

ENTRY 13: BIRDS FALL FROM THE SKY
January 12, 1:19 p.m.

People are definitely starting to get nervous. This morning, the rain was falling in sheets. I left Lucullus licking his whiskers, nice and cozy next to a radiator. Fortunately I'd parked my car right in front of the house, or I would've gotten soaked. As I drove across town to work, I noticed a lot more people wearing masks. Maybe I should get one. Do they have masks for cats?

The news on the radio couldn't be more confusing. For eighteen hours, there's been no news of Dagestan. None. Not one word. What's more disturbing: bad news or the complete lack of it?

Fires like the ones in Georgia are burning in several cities in southern Russia, and no one's fighting them. The official story out of Russia is that the fires are mass cremations of bodies infected by the epidemic, but no one believes that. They're too large. Visible from space! They've destroyed entire city blocks, fuel depots, and ports. There aren't many, about a dozen, but they all started at about the same time.

The images of Germany are shocking. Highways are jammed with thousands of cars trying to leave the cities for the countryside, away from concentrations of people. However, only a small percentage has anywhere to go. Most people have stayed behind in the cities. They don't seem to be panicking, but you can tell they're worried. Martial law is in effect. Anyone out on the streets after 8:00 p.m. or outside rest areas on the highways will be shot dead, according to the German prime minister. They're not joking around.

I've saved the biggest news for last. Official information is flowing out in dribs and drabs. In Brussels at nine this morning, the presidents of all the EU countries held an emergency meeting, together with the ministers of defense, health, and interior.

They met until noon. When the meeting was over, they gave a joint press conference. That's when they dropped the bomb. From now on, all official information will be channeled through a single crisis management team throughout the entire EU. This team will issue an official report hourly to all EU countries. Individual governments will make clarifications they deem necessary only on domestic policy, health, and safety. The armed forces of all EU countries have been put on alert. They emphasized that that was to avoid widespread panic. Contradictory and confusing reports have created unwarranted alarm, the consequence of which is a mass exodus. They're referring to Germany, I guess.

That news gives me chills. Sounds dangerously close to censorship, right? The worst part was the faces of the prime ministers and presidents. They looked like they'd just come from a funeral. On TV, a political analyst said things must be pretty serious because as soon as the meeting was over, all the big shots headed straight for the airport and back to their countries. There's a constant buzz that Spain'll declare a state of emergency, like other European countries. For now, we've suspended all sports events this weekend "as a health precaution."

The United States has called up the National Guard. What you see on the satellite channel is amazing—armed troops patrolling New York, Chicago, Boston, and so on. Those Americans are crazy. What'll that accomplish? Scare the viruses? Are they going to shoot someone? They're overreacting, as usual. Speaking of the United States, there seem to be sick people in Atlanta, Houston, and Los Angeles, but no one's giving out any details or images. There are blackouts in the United States, too. All we know is that, over the last few hours, "vectors of contagion" have arrived on flights from Germany or the Middle East. The closure of all

American airports is imminent. The news from around the world is more or less the same.

The troops we sent to Dagestan are back in Zaragoza. There are reports of a lot of minor injuries. Some may have been killed, but information is extremely limited. We do know they've cordoned off a floor at a civilian hospital to care for them.

I called my parents. They're leaving Friday to spend the weekend in the little town where my grandparents grew up. That seems like a very wise move. I called my sister to see how she's doing. She says Barcelona has temporarily suspended subway travel. You can only ride the bus if you're wearing a mask. I bought a plane ticket to visit her this weekend. I hope I can convince her to come home for a little vacation.

Something will happen soon, but I don't know what. Fear travels faster than a dust cloud…and it's already in the wind.

ENTRY 14: …AND THE RIVERS WILL RUN RED WITH BLOOD
January 12, 7:28 p.m.

The lights went out. It's the first time this week. I phoned the damn electric company. They told me the power will be back on in a couple of hours, tops.

It's pouring down rain. The streets are totally dark, lit up only by lightning. The patio walls are dripping with water, but Lucullus and I are sitting comfortably on the couch watching TV, thanks to the batteries. If I turn on a lot of lights, the batteries will run down really fast. I don't feel like going down to the basement to hook up the second line of batteries.

The crisis team began issuing its official statements at three this afternoon, Spanish time. Apparently what's responsible for the epidemic is a mutated filovirus, or several filoviruses at once, that's still not clear. On Channel 3 they're now calling it the Marburg virus, whatever that is. Since seven this evening cases have been confirmed in Germany, the United Kingdom, Italy, France, Holland, Poland, Greece, Turkey…and Spain. At a press conference, the minister of health, with dark circles under his eyes that drooped all the way to his ankles, announced that three members of the troops sent to Dagestan were in the ICU at Zaragoza with symptoms of this disease. They showed pictures of the hospital. It's surrounded by fucking rioters and military police.

Worst of all is that the patients go through an acute traumatic phase and have paranoid, aggressive tendencies. There've been several attacks on medical personnel. More than one patient has run out of the hospital. I'm glad my mother's retired.

The disease seems to be highly contagious. They don't know exactly how it's transmitted. A hospital in Sussex, England, was quarantined after two patients ran around the facility for nearly an hour, attacking anyone in the halls. This was online a couple of hours ago. So far, no one has refuted it.

There's been absolutely no news out of Dagestan for twenty-four hours. There doesn't seem to be anyone there. The last report from Russia stated that Putin and his government have taken refuge in a Cold War nuclear bunker and the army is occupying the streets of major cities. Ukraine has declared a state of siege, but towns and cities on its borders haven't been heard from for hours.

A Russian blogger from a small town in North Ossetia–Alania, living in Moscow, reported on russiskaya.ru that he called his parents' number for hours but got no answer. Then he started calling all the neighbors listed in the phone book. Nobody answered. It's as if no one in a town of five thousand is still alive.

A little while ago someone closed down that website. Russian censorship is relentless.

What the hell's going on? Why aren't they telling us anything?

ENTRY 15
January 13, 11:10 a.m.

This morning as I got out of the shower, I sneezed really hard a couple of times. Normally I wouldn't give it a second thought, but with the psychosis spreading all over Spain, my hypochondriac side trembled in fear. Will the epidemic reach Galicia? Have I caught it, and this is the first symptom? Or is it just a cold?

During breakfast, I turned on the news. For the last few days, I've been glued day and night to the TV, the radio, or the Internet, along with three-quarters of Europe. We're all hoping the news will report that the epidemic is subsiding. It's just been one huge scare. But reality is ghoulishly stubborn.

Nothing from Dagestan for forty-eight hours. As impossible as it seems, there's been no news, official or unofficial, for two days. The republic's millions of inhabitants either left...or died. The southern Caucasus region (Georgia, Chechnya, Ossetia, Azerbaijan, Armenia, and so on) is as silent as the grave. Their TV and radio stations haven't broadcast for hours, and their websites haven't been updated for two days. Refugees from those countries en route to Russia, Iran, and Turkey are being held in huge "Safe Zones" guarded by the army, more prisoners than refugees. Censorship is ironclad.

In Europe, things are getting more complicated by the minute. In Italy, the army and special units of the carabinieri cordoned off the city of Cremona. No one can enter or leave, except doctors with escorts. They've quarantined the city; anyone who manages to get there is forced to turn back. France has declared a state of emergency. They set up roadblocks at major transportation hubs, and you need a special permit to travel from one province to another. In England the situation is more dramatic. Parliament decreed the Isolation Act, closing borders indefinitely. No one can enter or leave Britain, not legally, anyway. I have friends living in London. There must be tons of Spanish kids, students, living there. What'll happen to them? The epidemic is out of control in South Wales and parts of Essex. The *Herald Tribune*'s website reports riots and looting.

In Germany, the situation in some provinces is sketchy. In the north and along the border with Poland, they've militarized health and communication facilities, transportation, and nuclear power plants. In Japan there've been several mass suicides. Murders and disappearances have reached record numbers. It's as if their society has just crumbled.

In the United States, the situation is different, if you listen to speeches by the nation's secretary of state or watch satellite broadcasts from CNN or Fox News via satellite. It's a huge country. In some areas life goes on as usual; in others madness has been unleashed. The government claims to have everything under control. But Fifth Avenue in New York cordoned off by military trucks doesn't look as if they've "got it all under control." CNN has reported riots, murders, and a wave of kidnappings and disappearances all over the country. A revolution is brewing. Because of that, this morning they started withdrawing US troops from abroad. Not just hundreds of soldiers or a few units—all of them. Every last soldier.

A few weeks ago, that would have generated rivers of ink in the press. Now all it rates is a brief summary on the inside pages of newspapers. Things have changed a lot in the last two weeks.

Here in Spain, not counting the quarantine in Zaragoza, the changes are small, subtle, but clearly perceptible. Churches are packed. Supermarkets are running out of some items, especially any-thing imported and food that spoils quickly. Automobile factories have shut down their assembly lines due to a shortage of parts from abroad. This morning, as I was leaving for work, I saw my neighbors across the street, the retirees, loading up their Pathfinder. They told me they're going to a small town in Orense "until things calm down a little." I shut Lucullus up in the house so he doesn't knock up half the cats in the neighborhood. Then I drove to the office. The streets are strangely deserted. People hurry along with a furtive air, not stopping to talk. The vast majority are wearing surgical masks. At the office, our secretary handed me a mask. Boss's orders, she said. So here I sit in my office, in a paper mask, like a surgeon, helping my clients. I feel like a dickhead wearing it. Damn, what's next?

ENTRY 16
January 13, 7:34 p.m.

I write this in the smoking lounge at the Santiago de Compostela airport. My flight leaves for Barcelona in half an hour. I hope to bring my sister back with me. The situation is deteriorating by the hour. New cases of the epidemic have been reported in Toledo and Madrid. It so happens that the army unit just back from Dagestan is based in Toledo. Their most seriously wounded were sent to Doce de Octubre Hospital in Madrid. It doesn't take a rocket scientist to figure out where the "vectors of contagion" of the epidemic are.

The government's declared a curfew in Zaragoza, from 10:00 p.m. to 8:00 a.m. At noon today on Channel 4, I saw trucks and tanks carrying cleaning crews and firefighters, who were spraying Zaragoza's streets with medical-strength disinfectants. They say the whole town smells like a hospital.

Miguel Servet Hospital, in downtown Zaragoza, is completely sealed off. According to Europa Press, heavily armed SWAT teams entered the facility two hours ago. Shots were clearly audible throughout most of the city. No one knows if there are dead or wounded. The crisis team hasn't breathed a word, except to urge everyone to wear surgical masks. A blog, run by a nurse working in Servet Hospital, described crazed patients wandering the halls. It even claimed that security guards and doctors had been attacked in the morgue. There was so much traffic on that site that it crashed for a few hours. Now a message reads, "This blog no longer exists." Conspiracy buffs claim censorship. I don't think the blog was real—I'm sure it was a trick to scare the staff. That's what I want to believe, anyway. But people want to know what's really going on, so rumors are flying constantly. Some say it's nuclear fallout, others say it's the Black Plague, others say it's a gigantic toxic cloud from a Russian refinery. There's no shortage of people who claim it's a ploy by OPEC to raise oil prices.

Whatever it is, fear is about to give way to panic. It's scary to see the airport full of Civil Guard patrols armed with machine guns, wearing gloves and masks. One guy started to cough especially hard. Four friendly but firm agents hustled him off to an ambulance. His protests didn't get him anywhere. I can't stop thinking how I've been sneezing half the day on account of my cold. So I'm doing all I can not to cough.

I just got off the phone with my sister. She's picking me up at the airport, since they've closed the subway and moved all the buses downtown as backup. She says getting a cab these days is a heroic feat.

I left Lucullus with Alfredo, the construction worker next door. Lucullus glared at me, outraged at being left in someone else's home. I hope he won't hold it against me. It's just for the weekend.

It's last call for my flight. I hope everything goes well.

ENTRY 17: BOILING POINT
January 15, 6:03 p.m.

The last forty-eight hours have been an ordeal. I don't understand how things have gotten so out of hand. I'm no coward, but I'm scared. Really scared. It feels like the entire planet is about to jump the tracks, and no one can find the brake. I'm in a daze, confused, tired, and wondering what the hell we're going to do. But once again, I'm getting ahead of myself.

The flight to Barcelona on Friday was quiet, smooth. A routine flight, except that the flight attendants wore surgical gloves and handed out masks to all the passengers. The plane was half-empty, almost unthinkable at the start of a weekend. What I didn't know was that during the forty-five-minute flight, real social upheaval was taking place in Spain. When we landed, we were held on the plane for almost an hour and a half. Someone turned off the air-conditioning, and the temperature inside the plane was stifling. Passengers started to get nervous and murmur. Wearing paper masks didn't exactly help calm us.

They finally let us deplane, not down a jetway, but on foot across the runway. A minibus picked us up and took us to a room in the airport. We were told that, while we were in the air, the government had declared a state of emergency. All domestic and international flights would be canceled in twenty-four hours. Only those of us with a ticket could travel to our usual place of residence. My weekend in Barcelona was reduced to twenty-four hours. What's worse, I didn't think I could get my sister a ticket.

The Barcelona airport was a sea of people, but at the moment it was calm. The security presence was more pronounced. For the first time in my life, I saw troops patrolling a civilian facility in full combat gear. Impressive.

My sister and Roger, her boyfriend, were waiting at the gate. I was glad to see her. She's twenty-five, five years younger than me. She has lived in Barcelona for two years and is now completely at home in the city. When my wife was killed in a car accident two years ago, she was my shoulder to cry on. A while back, she gave me a little orange ball of fur named Lucullus who helped me climb out of the hole I'd fallen into Ancient history.

As we drove to Barcelona, they brought me up to speed. The king read a statement on TV, dressed in his military uniform, just like he did when he faced down an attempted coup in 1981. Military troops in Spain are on high alert. Within twenty-four hours all borders, ports, and airports will be closed. The fences at Ceuta and Melilla have been electrified. There've been outbreaks of the epidemic in Cartagena, Cadiz—and Ferol, which is less than a hundred miles from my house. How did the outbreaks get all the way up there?

The strangest part is the official secrecy surrounding the disease. No symptoms have been made public; neither has its incubation period, or how many people have died. Nothing. All we know is that it's highly contagious, it's very lethal, and it's spreading.

The outbreaks in Zaragoza, Toledo, and Madrid are still not under control. Zaragoza has started to evacuate all residents living within a half mile of Miguel Servet Hospital.

We finally reached my sister's house in Gracia, a quiet suburb near Barcelona. I took a shower with the radio news on. (These days no one ventures very far from a radio or a TV or computer screen.) The WHO will hold a press conference on Monday. In Barcelona, the regional police have detained suspicious foreigners. The government ordered widespread blood tests, but had to cancel the order after a few hours; the labs couldn't cope with their workload.

Roger told me that he was at a bus stop when a fight broke out between a very upset immigrant and a bunch of skinheads. When the police got there, they threw everyone into vans and took them God knows where. Fortunately, he gave them the slip.

We were going to have dinner with a friend who lives on the first floor, but given the state of affairs, we decided to stay home and eat dinner in front of the TV. Roger and my sister made it very clear that they're not coming to Galicia with me. Roger's parents have a farm in the province of Tarragona. They plan to go there next week "until this whole thing blows over." They've asked for time off work. Soon that might not matter.

They invited me to go with them. My sister casually mentioned that a friend of hers who lives there would be happy to see me. I'm tempted, but I've left Lucullus alone, and I have to work on Monday. Plus if I stay, I might not get back to Galicia for a while.

As we were talking, the venerable newscaster Matías Prats interrupted the program. With a long face, he reported that fifteen minutes before, there had been a thermonuclear explosion in Shanghai. It wasn't an accident or an attack. The Chinese government itself had wiped the city off the map. Our jaws dropped. The entire city? Is that the way to deal with a disease? My God, there must've been millions of people!

Germany has completely shut down all its nuclear power plants. They couldn't keep the plants running because workers weren't showing up for work. The United States, France, Italy, England, and Spain, too, it seems, are taking similar measures.

No one's heard anything out of Russia for hours. The army closed down their TV stations, and they finally managed to turn off the Internet tap. Many bloggers, very active until today, now show no sign of life. According to Reuters, large areas of the country are in darkness, with no electricity. I hope they took the precaution of disconnecting their power plants. That's all we need, another Chernobyl...

News of the plague has been reported from every corner of the planet. The epidemic is now global.

In the United States there are reports of looting, assaults, kidnappings, and widespread murder. In Europe we know almost nothing, because the crisis team isn't saying a word. There're plenty of rumors on the Internet, each one crazier than the last. Many witnesses agree on one thing: those infected sink into a state of deep confusion and become aggressive. From all over the world, there are reports of attacks by sick people. It looks like rabies. I don't know what to believe.

That night in Barcelona was very long. The sound of ambulances, army tanks, and police vans patrolling the streets kept me awake all night. I surveyed a section of the city out my window. The streets were deserted. No pedestrians. No traffic. The solitude was broken only by an occasional patrol car passing by, its spotlight lighting up doorways. Surely the situation will look different in the daytime when the curfew ends. For now, it's shocking.

ENTRY 18
January 15, 7:11 p.m.

I'm back home. I'm completely exhausted. The trip home was awful, unbelievable. Lucullus is back. I'm going to sleep for a long time. Today I saw them kill a man at the airport. I don't feel like writing.

ENTRY 19
January 16, 7:19 p.m.

Yesterday was really hard. Today's no better. When I got home late last night, I was completely broken emotionally. It all started at the El Prat Airport on Sunday afternoon. The tense calm on Saturday had turned into hysteria. By the time my taxi pulled up to the airport, all hell had broken loose—long lines of people shouting and pushing, exhausted children sleeping on piles of luggage while their parents tried to get a ticket to anywhere.

My flight was scheduled to leave an hour after I arrived at the airport. It was one of the last flights out of Barcelona. That same night, El Prat would be closed due to the state of emergency. Everyone who wanted to fly out of Barcelona was there. The problem was that the authorities wouldn't issue a ticket to anyone who didn't have proof he was headed for home. There weren't enough tickets for everyone. That was clear. Panic had seized the crowd. There was constant pushing, screaming, and racing around.

I made my way to the counter as best I could through a mob of hysterical people crowded together at the ticket windows. When I got to the counter, losing my coat along the way, I realized that the friendly counter clerks had been replaced by soldiers. Believe me, they weren't smiling.

I presented my ID card and the ticket I'd bought four days earlier. They told me I'd better head directly to the gate "for my own safety." That's when I noticed that a couple of the soldiers who'd impressed me so much when I first arrived in Barcelona were now standing at my side. For a second I thought they were going to detain me.

Then I realized that people were closing in on me, eyeing me, watching me like wolves. I had something they didn't: a plane ticket. After hours and hours of tension and struggle, any one of them was desperate enough to try to get the ticket from me. Those armed soldiers at my side parted the crowd as we headed for the gate. I felt dozens of eyes on me. I looked down. I couldn't meet their eyes.

Where the metal detector would normally be was a line of national riot police, in Kevlar helmets and body armor. Behind them was another line of civil guardsmen, armed with machine guns and wearing balaclavas. It was a horrible sight. A crowd was huddled in front of the row, pressing to get to the gate. The crush was incredible. When I reached the gate, two officers stepped aside to let me pass. They took me to a small room where searches are normally performed. An army medical officer asked for my ID and examined me while his assistants rifled through my carry-on. Although I'm a lawyer, I didn't protest. Where would that get me? It didn't seem like a very smart idea.

The doctor asked a lot of questions. Did I have a fever? Dizziness? Had I been out of Spain in the last month? Had I visited Zaragoza, Madrid, Toledo? Had I been bitten by an animal lately? Had anyone attacked me? I was about to say he was attacking me, but one glance at his face convinced me to keep my mouth shut.

As I left that room, that horrific event happened. In the front row, trying to get to the departure gate, was a guy in his forties, curly gray hair, unshaven, in a rumpled suit. He looked like an executive. He was very agitated, nervous, and red in the face. He looked like he was out of his mind, like he'd done more than one line of cocaine.

The crowd suddenly pressed forward, and panic broke out. The front row fell to the ground and was trampled by the people behind them. The line of riot police broke. Just then, the guy slipped through and ran to the gate. The civil guardsmen on the second line tried to stop him, but they couldn't reach him. Someone shouted, "Halt!" The guy ran down the corridor toward the plane and salvation. There was a burst of machine-gun fire. Red flowers bloomed across the back of the man's suit, and he collapsed. Hysteria erupted—screams, cries, shouts, shots in the air. The situation was out of control. One of the soldiers grabbed me by the collar and dragged me on to the plane while the rest of his unit formed a line behind us, retreating under the pressure from the crowd.

As I passed the body, I stared at his face. He was dead. Dead. I'm 100 percent sure. The soldier beside me stopped short. Unfazed, he pulled out a pistol and shot the body in the head. I was absolutely terrified. Why did he do that?

They shoved me toward the door of the plane, at the far end of the jetway. Very jittery flight attendants urged me to hurry in. The plane was packed. There were even people standing in the galley. Everyone was really on edge. They only relaxed when they shut the door and started to roll down the runway. As we started down the runway, the guy next to me whispered that there were only three more flights after ours. After that, El Prat would be closed for God knows how long.

I didn't say a word the entire flight. When I thought about what I'd just seen, I had to run to the bathroom. I couldn't stop throwing up. Hell, the soldier had blown the guy's head off right in front me!

Nobody handed out masks during the flight. I guess they didn't think it was necessary anymore. I don't know if that's good or bad.

When I got to Santiago de Compostela, the scene was the same as in Barcelona, but on a smaller scale. In the parking lot, a guy offered me his car in exchange for a flight to Zurich that was taking off in an hour. Our values have certainly changed.

I listened to the radio as I drove home. The situation is chaotic. More nuclear explosions in China. Are they trying to stop the epidemic with bombs? Or the carriers of the disease? Who knows. America is at DEFCON 1, whatever that means. Riots in Madrid, Valencia, Barcelona, Seville, Bilbao. The world's out of control. All the TV networks report that Spain could declare martial law within hours. No news from Russia. In Germany, in a statement broadcast three hours ago, Angela Merkel said, "Dresden is lost." Evacuation orders in Paris, Reims, and Marseille. In Italy, the carabinieri are ruthlessly taking a suburb of Naples. The world is shattered, and I still don't know why.

I picked Lucullus up and went home. This morning I called in sick. They said not to worry; the courts are temporarily closed. Only the military courts are open, and then only to try looters and anyone violating the curfew. I slept most of Monday. When I got up, I made some coffee and sat down in front of the TV. I'm writing this with Lucullus purring in my lap. I don't have a clue what's going on.

ENTRY 20: AT THE GATES OF HELL
January 17, 6:42 p.m.

It's official: we're fucked. At three this afternoon, the king came back on TV and announced that martial law had been declared all across Spain. The curfew is still in place from 10:00 p.m. to 8:00 a.m. Anyone caught on the street between those hours risks being shot, clear and simple. Travel between regions is prohibited, and the army is setting up checkpoints on all major roads.

Fifteen cities have been declared areas of risk. No one is allowed in or out of them. All the cities where there've been outbreaks of the epidemic are on the list, along with nine more.

Madrid and Barcelona are among them. I hope my sister moved up their plans and has already left the city. Fuck.

For now, Pontevedra has escaped the carnage, but who knows for how long. Ferrol and La Coruña, about a hundred miles away, are "areas of risk." They're cut off—in theory. But a friend who lives in La Coruña just called me on the way to his parents' home in Vigo. He made it out of town on two-lane highways and back roads. It's physically impossible to isolate a medium-size town, let alone a big city. The way things are going, the plague will get here soon. I should do something. But what?

I got in the car and headed downtown. The streets are half-empty, and the town looks like it's under siege. It's been raining nonstop for hours. On the sidewalks you can feel how uneasy people are. It's really cold. I passed several police cars and a couple of Light Brigade Airborne (BRILAT) troop carriers. Their barracks are located two miles from Pontevedra. They've been there for years, but I'd never seen troops stationed downtown until today.

I stopped at a service station to get some gas. As the Astra was filling up, I went inside to buy some smokes, the newspaper, and some magazines and a can of oil. (I should have gotten the oil changed a week ago. Damn!) The clerk told me that some gas stations were having problems getting gas, especially in remote areas. Now that the ports are closed, refineries have stopped production, and the government has militarized the existing supplies. That's just great.

Then I went to the mall. Something told me I'd better stock up. I was surprised to see the supermarket so crowded. A lot of people had the same idea. In the appliances and home repair department, I bought an ultrashortwave radio with a sweep dial. I've had my eye on it for a long time. I'd planned to listen to the Coast Guard channel when I went out on the Zodiac to dive around the wreck of the *Florita*. Its hull has been in the river for years, and it's in bad condition, so no one's allowed to dive down there. If they catch you, you'll get a heavy fine and lose your license, but it's worth the risk. Now I plan to use the radio for something entirely different.

When I got home, I brushed Lucullus and fixed him his favorite food. Then I tried the radio. After a while, I found the frequencies of the national and municipal police. Perfect. Now I can get information first. I also picked up a few amateur ham radio operators, but I didn't pay much attention to them.

Now I'm glued to the TV, watching images from the United States, taken from a helicopter, of a traffic jam on a freeway. Suddenly about two dozen people have appeared, shambling along the side of the road, and started to attack the drivers trapped in their vehicles. The scene is horrible. It lasts less than a minute, but I'm still trembling. I swear they bit the drivers. That's impossible. What the hell is wrong with these people?

Someone has opened the gates of hell, and you can feel the heat.

ENTRY 21: THE STUPIDITY OF MANKIND
January 19, 11:08 a.m.

I'm not a practicing Catholic, but the events of the last twenty-four hours seem like divine punishment for some gigantic, collective sin of mankind. Or a huge monument to our stupidity. Depending on how you look at it.

Yesterday was long. In the morning as I ate breakfast, the news reported that riots have spread globally. A pattern is emerging. First, the government says there's no reason to worry. Second, a quarantine is imposed. Next, panic ensues, and rioting and looting break out. Then they declare martial law. After that, there are more riots, but they seem different—stranger, more localized, heavily censored, with very little information and no looting. And finally, silence.

That's the pattern, but there are exceptions. In Chile yesterday morning, a general named Cheyre took advantage of martial law to mount a coup. A few hours later, a busload of Bolivian refugees was gunned down at the border, trying to get past a checkpoint. In retaliation, the Bolivian government shelled the Chilean border until Chile's air force reduced the Bolivian artillery to scrap metal. That's crazy. We're on the brink of the abyss, and all they can think about is starting a war.

The news of the day: a briefing by the WHO's Committee for Monitoring Compliance was broadcast worldwide yesterday afternoon. Every channel all over the world broadcast the same image. Not since man landed on the moon has there been anything like this. And there may never be again. Mind-blowing.

A committee of virologists appeared before the cameras. In a serious, guarded tone, they stated that the problem is a mutation of a filovirus transmitted by blood and bodily fluids (semen, saliva, and so on). They still don't know if it's transmitted through the air. The main symptoms are fever, disorientation, pallor, and, later, delirium and extreme aggression. If you see anyone with these symptoms, alert security forces. Under no circumstances should you try to make contact with the afflicted person, even if it's a relative or a friend.

That's it? What the hell are they getting at? What do they mean, "alert security forces"? Wouldn't it be better to call an ambulance? At the end of the day, these are sick people. Right? Are they going to cure them with bullets? Why do I have the feeling they're hiding something? I think there's a lot they haven't told us.

The Internet is a hotbed of rumors, each one more absurd than the last. An alien invasion, fluke parasites, mutants, the undead, mass brainwashing—take your pick. Let's be rational, damn it. It's a disease. Either you catch it or you don't. If you catch it—*bam!* You're done for. I'm still convinced there's something more, something really horrible. If not, then why this unprecedented censorship? This is crazy.

I'm really worried about my sister. I haven't been able to reach her since Saturday. Cell phone networks are overloaded. In some places they've shut down. After several repair crews disappeared, technicians refuse to travel without an escort. Private security companies are overwhelmed. The police, the army, and the Civil Guard are stretched thin on patrols, at quarantines, and at checkpoints. News of killings and disappearances are multiplying. In fact, they're no longer news.

The US president was on TV. He's at a presidential retreat. That's a bad sign. He delivered a speech to the entire country, asking them to obey the army's orders. He urged people to go to what he called Safe Zones. Safe Zones. Safe from what?

In Jerusalem, the pope, the chief rabbi, and the head Muslim muftis have come together to form one religious body. Any other time, that would've been moving, but they aren't granting any audiences to the faithful for "safety reasons." It isn't exactly reassuring to see religious leaders on the Temple Mount surrounded by Israeli assault troops.

Our president is back on TV, along with the king. They announced the creation of fifty-two security forces, one in each province. They will team up with the national police, Civil Guard, and local and regional police. Army generals will lead the teams and will have full military authority over their assigned areas. The army will supply the weapons.

I tried to go see my parents this morning. I took Lucullus with me because I didn't know how long it might take to get back. I put him in the passenger seat. His seat. Anyone who sits there invariably gets covered in cat hair. He can't stand riding in his carrier. I hadn't gone much more than a mile when I encountered an army checkpoint and had to turn back. I drove down a narrow country road that runs behind a housing complex and joins the main highway a couple miles later. Just when I thought I'd passed them, I came face-to-face with the local police at another checkpoint. Fuck! They know those back roads better than anyone. I tried to convince them to let me pass but got nowhere. They're really nervous and scared. Who can blame them? Their job is usually to catch petty thieves, regulate traffic, and tow away illegally parked cars. Now they're manning checkpoints, carrying army assault rifles with orders to shoot anyone who disobeys.

I'm back home now. I poured myself some whiskey, even though it's still morning. I watched some more TV with the volume off and listened to police broadcasts on the shortwave. I don't know what to think.

ENTRY 22
January 19, 6:58 p.m.

A helicopter's circling the area. They've been at it all afternoon. From my upstairs window, I saw a couple of police cars drive down the main road. They seem to be looking for something. Or someone. They're heavily armed. One police car even drove down the two short streets in our development to take a look. They shone their spotlight over all the walls, scaring the hell out of the woman in the corner house, who was outside at that time.

I went to the house of my neighbor, the doctor, to see if they were okay. His wife opened the door, her face haggard. She says her husband's been at the hospital for seventy-two hours straight. She hasn't heard anything from him since.

I went back in my house and double-locked the door, turned the shortwave back on, and listened to the police band. Usually it's full of routine messages, like "Patrol Twenty-Seven, zone fifteen negative, proceed to zone sixteen." There used to be some kind of funny ones, like the Civil Guard at a checkpoint ordering pizza. But now they were searching desperately for someone. All hell broke loose when a patrol reported a "hot spot," whatever that means. Ten minutes later I swear I heard shots. They didn't sound far off.

Twenty days have passed since this thing started. Today I heard shots in my city. Whatever this is, it's getting closer.

ENTRY 23
January 20, 1:40 a.m.

I was dozing in front of the TV when I heard brakes outside. I ran to the upstairs bedroom that looks out on the main road. A patrol car stopped the Civil Guard at the entrance to our street. Two guards with assault rifles got out and ran past my house to the embankment at the end of my street. Beyond that embankment are some houses, and behind them, a highway. I couldn't see where they were going.

Pretty soon they came back. A platoon of soldiers coming from the opposite direction was with them. They were nervous, and one soldier's sleeve was stained with blood or some other dark substance. They continued on in silence and disappeared down the other end of the street.

I heard it again. I can't swear to it, but I think I heard shots. And they sounded closer than before.

ENTRY 24
January 20, 11:22 a.m.

I went downtown to buy the newspaper or some magazines. There aren't any newspapers. The delivery van couldn't get through. On the way home, I noticed that most shops were closed. I found a small bakery open, so I bought some fresh bread. The worried-looking salesgirl whispered to me that last night she heard shots right next to her house, and something that sounded like "moans." When she looked out the window, she saw an army truck pulling up at top speed.

I saw skid marks at the entrance to my street yesterday. Now I know I wasn't dreaming.

ENTRY 25
January 20, 11:33 a.m.

I'm sitting in the garden, soaking up the winter sun, while I watch Lucullus, who's staring ecstatically at a lizard scurrying along the wall. The helicopter's flying tirelessly overhead again. The radio news reported that the government has created "Safe Havens" in the major cities, where they plan to concentrate people. They say around 80 percent of city dwellers can't (or won't) leave. Safe Havens. That's a fucking joke.

At all hours of the day, they repeat that under no circumstances should you try to make contact with any person exhibiting erratic, odd, or disoriented behavior, or who shows signs

of violence. Even if it's an acquaintance or relative. Yeah, right...
everyone knows how dangerous sick people are to healthy people.

On top of all this, Channel 3 stopped broadcasting their
regular programming. They're running movies and prerecorded
shows nonstop. Every forty-five minutes they broadcast a news
update. News anchor Matías Prats looks like he's been living on
the set for days.

ENTRY 26
January 21, 12:20 p.m.

On Friday afternoon I dodged the checkpoints in town to visit
Robert. We've been good friends since we were kids. Robert is
quiet, low-key, and methodical. He works as an accountant for
an import company. He got married two years ago and has a cute
baby girl only a few months old. When I got to his house, his wife
was packing their bags, and Robert was gloomily watching the
television. He said they were going to the Safe Haven downtown.
They don't know where they'll be staying or what they'll do there,
or anything, but they're still going.

I get it. I'm a single guy who lives with a cat, but he has a family
to look after. Good luck, Robert. I think we're all going to need it.

After I got home, I stopped to talk to my neighbor for a
minute. His house backs up to mine. Before all this started, he
was building on a deck. The smell of glue was pretty strong. Bits
of sawdust wafted over the wall separating our yards. Lucullus
sat mesmerized for hours, watching the dust twist and turn in
a light beam. A few days ago the carpenters didn't show up. I've
never had much contact with the guy, but I got up the nerve to ask
him for a couple of those heavy wooden posts to brace the gate
in my front wall. If looters show up, they'll have to jump over a

ten-foot-high wall or break down a wrought iron gate, reinforced with two wooden posts driven into the ground.

More than anything I need a project to keep my mind busy so I don't think about what's happening. Fuck.

On the official channels, there's almost no foreign news. People don't seem to care, either. It's as if each country has turned inward to survive. There hasn't been news of any kind out of Russia for days. Not even on the Internet. Zero. In northern Europe there are a few active blogs. Unfortunately I don't know Swedish or German or Polish, so I can't tell what the hell they're saying. I notice their blogs are full of capitalization and exclamation points, so I gather they are nervous. Or surprised. Or scared. Who knows.

CNN is the only US channel I can still get via satellite. CBS and ABC display blue screens with the channel's logo, and Fox News is broadcasting static. According to CNN, the population is being concentrated in the Safe Zones in each city's downtown. Authorities warn that they can't protect anyone outside those zones from "marauders." There's an unbelievable rumor going around on the Internet that the people in the San Diego Safe Zone—and maybe in those of many other US cities—have been massacred by marauding groups. From what I see, life is cheap worldwide these days. If you search for "dead" on Google, millions of links come up.

In Spain, the situation isn't any better. Safe Havens are being organized in cities with more than fifty thousand residents. Day or night, on every radio or TV station, they urge people to congregate there for their own safety. I'm not going. They don't allow pets, since space is limited. There's no way in hell I'll leave Lucullus. I'm not a nut case about animals, but after my wife died, having Lucullus around was all that kept me from doing something stupid. I owe him that. He's my pal, and I won't abandon him to get into some crowded ghetto and share a room with fifteen strangers. Fuck the government and its Safe Havens.

The king is back on TV, in his uniform again, with an update. But this time he's surrounded by generals. Come to think of it, I haven't seen any politicians on TV for days. The military has taken over. That sucks.

Now Channel 5, just like Channel 3, is only broadcasting reruns and a news bulletin every forty-five minutes. They're saying it's to ensure their employees' safety. Apparently their studio is located in an unsafe area. There are gangs of bandits, they explain.

Cell phones are dead. The three main providers have suspended service and "relinquished" their network to the Provincial Security Corps. Now it's going to be impossible to contact my sister. She's a smart girl; I'm sure she's okay.

I've got the shortwave radio on again, listening to the military evacuate people to the Safe Haven. Sporadic gunfire has kept up all day. Civilization is crumbling.

ENTRY 27: RIVERS OF SULFUR
January 22, 4:30 p.m.

I listened all night to the security forces' frequencies on the shortwave radio. It's mostly trivial chatter—progress reports from checkpoints, situation reports from patrols, and little else. Occasionally a "hot spot" flares up, and then the situation gets out of control. Although the media is constantly warning us about "disturbances," those are only a fraction of the incidents I hear about on the police band. Maybe it's because I live in a small town, but the number of looters seems very small.

However, I'm hearing more and more about the "others." A couple of days ago, you hardly heard anything about them. Their numbers seem to be growing by the hour. On the police band there are increasingly more reports of "incidents" involving what the soldiers call "those things."

Forty-eight hours ago, there were no cases in Pontevedra. What began as a trickle—a run-in with "those things" every twelve hours or so—is fast becoming a gusher of emergency calls, hysterical warnings from one unit to another, and a whole lot of movement by police and soldiers who seem unable to quell the situation.

What do they mean, "those things"? People infected with the virus? We all know that people who get infected are extremely aggressive, but why call them "those things," not the "infected people"? What does that mean, exactly?

A few hours ago, I heard on the military band that security forces in Pontevedra have been ordered to retreat to the heart of the city. The outlying areas must be evacuated. A few minutes later, on the city television station, a captain in the Civil Guard dressed in combat fatigues read a statement from the commanding general of the province, ordering the evacuation. I think we're under siege.

Just an hour ago, I heard a call to a patrol. Dispatchers reported an incident on some street and told them to investigate. The patrol (Civil Guard, I think) responded that they were already there. I haven't heard a word from that patrol since. Fifteen minutes later, I heard another call, this time to BRILAT troops. Dispatchers told them to go immediately to the same location. The fucked-up thing is that the address given is just half a mile from my house. I swear I heard two shots. Then nothing.

Whatever happened, there were only two shots.

In general, things look piss-poor. From what I can glean from all the crap on TV, radio, the Internet, and military frequencies, the situation is deteriorating by the minute. The security forces

seem to be overwhelmed by events that have skyrocketed expo-
nentially over the last twenty-four hours. There are police and
military casualties. Some units, especially those made up of city
police, are starting to desert. Something has gone fucking wrong.

A troubling rumor is preying on my mind. Of all the crazy
theories repeated endlessly on the net, one is gaining momentum.
People say that the sick are in a kind of suspended animation, or
that they come back from the dead. They swear that these people are dead but still walking around. Yeah, right. That's hard to
believe, but in the last few hours, so many strange things have
happened, I don't know what to think.

ENTRY 28
January 22, 7:59 p.m.

Just a few minutes ago, a troop carrier and a transport truck
stopped at the end of the two streets where I live. Soldiers got out
and went house to house, banging on doors. I was in the kitchen,
listening to the shortwave radio with all the lights off.

When they knocked on my door, I froze. I held the cat in my
lap and waited in silence until they went away. I had to see what
was going on, so I tiptoed up the stairs and looked out my window. I saw my neighbor's wife, whose husband, the doctor, had
disappeared several days ago, leave with her two daughters and
a few suitcases. The soldiers helped them into the truck. Several
of my neighbors did the same. They headed for the Safe Haven
downtown, where they've cordoned off some streets. In theory,
it's well protected.

The trucks roared off toward downtown. Before jumping
into the vehicle, a soldier painted a huge red cross on the pavement at the intersection. The trucks then turned the corner and

disappeared. The night was so quiet I could hear the convoy for blocks. I guess they had many more stops to make tonight.

Now the street is silent and dark. All the homes must be empty. If anyone's still in their home, like me, they're lying low. I went back to the kitchen and sat down with just the light over the stove on. I started to think. Clearly they're evacuating the area. Correction—they *have* evacuated the area. So from now on, anything goes.

ENTRY 29
January 23, 10:05 a.m.

The sun is up now. It was a very, very long night. Just a few hours after the convoy left, I was struck by the enormity of my decision. I'm alone. Nobody knows I'm here. I'm in an evacuated area. A no-man's-land.

After I blocked out that thought, I plunged into a project. I finished shoring up the front gate with the wooden posts. It's stupid, of course—sooner or later I'll have to go out that way. But it kept my mind busy, and I feel safer. Then I took stock of the situation. I have enough food for about three weeks, if I don't mind a steady diet of frozen food. I have about twenty liters of bottled water. I still have running water. Having solar panels means electricity isn't a problem. If I economize, I can be almost completely self-sufficient. That won't be hard. I don't plan on throwing a party any time soon.

Cooking gas is a problem. My kitchen has two ceramic burners and two small gas burners. The ceramic burners consume an alarming amount of electricity. For now, I have gas. Who knows how long that will last? Sooner or later they'll cut the supply to the evacuated areas to prevent the risk of explosions.

Overall, my arsenal is bleak. I went through the house from top to bottom and gathered all my "weapons" on the kitchen table: a scuba-diving speargun and six steel spears, a butcher knife, and a dull hatchet I chop firewood with. Great. I picked up my speargun, by far my most dangerous weapon. Besides the fact that I've never shot anything bigger than an eel, it presents a number of problems. It takes around twenty to thirty seconds to load. Its range is short, only about thirty feet. At a longer distance, its aim isn't very true. When all is said and done, it's not a precision weapon; it's only designed to spear an octopus at close range. If gangs of bandits show up, I'm screwed. My best option is to keep my head down.

The phone rang, and my heart nearly flew out of my mouth. It hasn't rung for days—I'd forgotten all about it. I almost didn't pick it up, but the need to hear a human voice is stronger than prudence, so I answered. It was my parents. I was so relieved I nearly passed out.

Tears ran down my face as I listened to my mother's voice. She'd been trying to reach me for three days. They're okay, there in my father's hometown with some neighbors. They begged me to meet them there. I convinced my parents that that option hadn't been feasible for days. I'm safer here than I would be traveling forty miles on roads clogged with checkpoints, with who knows how many maniacal gangs on the loose. Plus, Lucullus doesn't like the country, I tell my mother, trying to take the sting out the situation. She's really worried. My sister made it out of Barcelona before they sealed off the city and declared martial law, but my mother doesn't know where she is now. The last she heard, they were headed for Roger's place in the country.

There wasn't much news about the rest of my family. Most of them are probably at a Safe Haven, like 80 percent of the population. Human beings are social animals and tend to cluster in dangerous situations; only an insignificant few don't follow this pattern. I fall squarely in that latter group. With a kiss, I said good-bye to my parents, promising to call at least once a week, if I can get a line out.

That calmed me down a little and let off the emotional steam that's been building. My head is clearer. I've started thinking of practical things I can do.

First, the news. TV's disappearing. Of the eighty channels I used to get, almost every one has gone off the air. I can only pick up Channels 5 and 3 and one that now broadcasts where Channel 2 used to air. Scheduled programming has been reduced to the bare minimum; basically it consists of uninterrupted movies, prerecorded series, and a mini report every forty-five minutes that consists of telling where the Safe Havens are and the best ways to reach them. They insistently repeat that in no way should you try to make contact with the infected. If they attack you, avoid being bitten or scratched.

A tired-looking soldier has come on to say they can't guarantee the safety of anyone outside the Safe Havens. In case of attack, try to crush your attacker's head. "Use a stick, a machete, a bullet, anything—just smash their head. Nothing else works."

I was taken aback by that message, but things've been out of control for so long that nothing surprises me too much. Anyway, the news blackout seems to be relaxing. I guess there's nothing to hide. Or almost nothing. Gangs of thieves are now a minor concern compared to the main problem of those who are infected and extremely violent.

There's no agreement on those things' real physical state. Some say they're healthy, just deranged. Others say they're at death's door. More and more people claim they're dead, incredible as that may seem. I haven't seen any, but I guess that'll change in the coming hours. For now, I'll stay right where I am and take things as they come. I've gotten calmer since I realized that's the closest thing I have to a game plan.

The Internet is also coming apart at the seams. Hours ago Google and Yahoo stopped working. The servers must be down. The same goes for a lot of other websites. Of the over a hundred contacts I have, only two dozen are still active, almost all in Spain, where there's still electricity. Given what happened in northern Europe, the Internet won't last long here either.

Military radio frequencies crackle constantly, reporting more clashes with "those bastards." It sounds like there are lots of casualties. The fifty-two original forces have been consolidated into forty. The attacks are concentrated around the Safe Havens. Two Safe Havens, one in Toledo and one in Alicante, were attacked by hordes of infected people and have fallen. Tens of thousands of people died. Will thousands more die in the coming hours? You can bet your sweet ass I won't be one of them.

ENTRY 30
January 24, 3:03 a.m.

Sweat trickles down my back as I sit here, writing this. My hands are still shaking from the adrenaline rush. I'm scared out of my mind.

By midday, I realized I had to do something or I'd have a heart attack. I'd been cooped up for almost twenty-four hours, pacing like a caged animal. I had to do something. I had to get out of here. I had to take a look around. I had to know what was going on. Lucullus has been staring at me, wide-eyed, all day. He knows something's up. I don't know if his cat brain can grasp the enormity of the situation. The world's going to hell by the minute—if it isn't there already. Eventually it's going to grab up everyone in its path. It's not joking around.

I went up to my bedroom and put on heavy, thick-soled hiking boots. Winter nights in Galicia are wet and cold, so I bundled up. It was late; the curfew had been in force for hours. I didn't give a damn. I was going out. It wasn't like I was going to run into a cop around the corner. Forty minutes before, I'd heard several vehicles on the main road. From the upstairs window I saw a collection of police cars, army trucks, and armored vehicles pass by, filled with exhausted, frightened soldiers headed to the Safe Haven downtown.

It doesn't take a genius to figure out that those soldiers were the last line of defense against the infected people. They'd held their position until all civilians were evacuated. Now they were retreating. That means there's nothing between the Safe Haven and those things. They must be hot on their heels. I had to hurry.

I moved aside the posts bracing the door and cautiously stuck my head out. The street was deserted, the way it's been for the last several hours. Newspapers, plastic bags, and trash went flying down the pavement. In the middle of the street lay a beige sweater. One of my neighbors must have lost it in her hasty evacuation. Seeing that sweater brought it all home. They're gone for good. All of them.

I climbed into my car, which I'd parked right outside the door. As I sat behind the wheel, I remembered I hadn't changed the oil. The can of oil had been sitting in the trunk ever since I bought it. Shit. This was not the time to be a DIY mechanic, so I turned the key, hoping my car wouldn't leave me high and dry.

In the dead silence the motor sounded like a cannon. You could probably hear it for miles. I didn't care. No way was I going to walk. I drove to the main road and headed for the gas station about half a mile from home and just over a mile from the Safe Haven. The gas station was in the middle of the evacuated zone, but I hoped someone was still there. I realized I didn't have a decent road map. If I ever took to the road, I'd definitely need a map. Every gas station sells them. That's what I was after.

The absolute silence on the road was shocking. Not a living thing in sight. I could be the last person on earth.

When I got to the gas station, I let out a sigh of relief. The lights were on. It looked open.

I pulled up to the pump and went in cautiously. I'm not ashamed to say I was scared shitless. There was no one was in sight—no customers, no employees. Where was the fucking manager? The cash register was open. I could've reached in and made off with all the cash. I grabbed a couple of road maps and all the candy bars I could stuff in my pockets. I also grabbed some two-week-old magazines. Their covers reported things that now seem completely surreal. Everything seems so absurd in this chaos! As I left the money on the counter, I thought I heard a noise. My blood froze in my veins. Someone—or something—was out there. Fuck.

Trembling, I grabbed some snow chains hanging on a display. They weren't much of a weapon, but at least I had something sturdy in my hands. I spotted a man about a hundred feet from the station. He was too far away, and it was too dark to see him clearly, but he seemed to be staggering. I wasn't going to hang around to find out. I jumped in the car and headed for home. I looked in the rearview mirror and saw the guy stumbling along, trying to follow my car. Fuck that. I didn't want to know anything more about him.

A few minutes later, I was back home with the door secured again. My legs are still shaking. I was gone for less than twenty minutes and only went about half a mile, but I feel like I'm back from a tour in Vietnam. This is really fucked up. I thought I'd feel like the hero of an action movie. Truth is, I feel like prey who doesn't know where the hunters are.

I turned on the TV. There are only two channels left, Channel 3 and the public station, Televisión Española, which is

displaying the royal coat of arms and playing military marches. •
Very reassuring. There's static on all the other channels. CNN is
all that's left on the satellite; it's broadcasting images recorded
a few days ago. News scrolls across the bottom of the screen:
Atlanta has fallen. Denver. Utah. Baltimore. Cedar Creek, Texas.
And on and on…damn, the list is endless. "Do not go to the Safe
Zones. Seek safety elsewhere," the message says. Is that what will
happen here, too? Millions of "infected people" attacking millions of refugees in Safe Havens?

The Internet is almost nonexistent. Most servers are down.
The only search engine still operating is the Spanish affiliate of
Alexa. How the hell are they keeping it up and running? Backup
batteries, I guess. They can't last much longer, just a few days or
hours. People have left messages on my blog. I don't know how
they found it, but their stories terrify me. They say it's one of the
few sites still operating. My Internet provider is a cable company
based in La Coruña. How long before it goes to hell? How long
before *everything* goes to hell? They're coming—it's just a matter
of hours.

ENTRY 31
January 24, 8:56 p.m.

Today the power went out. A few minutes before six, the lights
flickered and then went out. At first I just sat dumbfounded in
the kitchen, in the dark. I've been spending most of my time
there, listening to military broadcasts and watching the last
two TV channels. After a while my eyes adjusted to the dark,
and I sprang into action. I grabbed a flashlight and went down
to the basement to connect the storage batteries. Those black
16-kilowatt beasts lay on the basement floor in two lines of

twelve. I was just about to throw the switch on the control panel when I froze. Before I connected anything, I made sure all the lights in the front of the house were switched off. The last thing I wanted was to call attention to myself with the only lighted house on the street. When I did connect the batteries, the bulbs' soft glow made me feel so safe. It was fantastic—I can't describe it. I never dreamed I'd be so afraid of the dark. I never dreamed any of this could happen.

I have a serious problem. They've cut off the gas, or maybe the pipes broke. Either way, I have no gas. That means the furnace isn't working. And that's nothing to joke about with the temperature outside down to 37 degrees Fahrenheit. I've bundled up, but the cold is still biting into my bones, and my breath turns into puffs of steam. Lucullus is indifferent to this cold. After all, he's a Persian cat, with long fur and a generous layer of body fat from years of living the good life.

I went outside to smoke a cigarette and think. I sat on the steps, staring at the walls around my yard, turning over and over in my mind the events of the last few hours. This disaster is picking up speed. It's like an avalanche—first they're just a few pebbles, then some boulders, and before you know it, the whole fucking mountain is sliding toward you at top speed. Shit!

On top of that, I'm more and more isolated. Channel 3 is dead; it stopped broadcasting around noon. During a repeat of *The Fresh Prince of Bel-Air*, the signal disappeared. *Poof.* As if someone unplugged the cable. I have no idea what happened. Spanish public television still displays the royal coat of arms and plays elaborate renditions of military marches. The news comes on every hour and a half, but the content has changed. They're no longer telling people to go to the Safe Havens. In some places, like Almería, Cádiz, Badajoz, and Mallorca, they warn it's highly ill-advised.

The Safe Havens were a logical idea—concentrate the population to defend it. But they turned out to be a disaster. The infected people are attracted to humans. Waves of them, maybe millions from all over the country, surround the Safe Havens. They overwhelm the defense forces with sheer numbers. Then chaos breaks out.

Not going to the Safe Haven was clearly a good decision. I think I have a better chance of surviving this chaos if I stay away than if I get herded there like everyone else. I felt a wave of relief for making the right choice. Then I was immediately overcome by grief; it was like a punch to the gut.

My parents. My sister. All my friends. Robert and his wife and child...I saw just them a few days ago. They were filled with worry as they packed their bags. All my friends and loved ones must be scattered among half a dozen of those damn Safe Havens. I don't know which is worse—knowing they're doomed or knowing there's absolutely nothing I can do about it. Bile rises in my throat. I'm choking with an anguish I can't describe, but amazingly I can't shed a tear. The situation is so overwhelming no tears will come.

Incredible as it seems, authorities all over the world now admit that somehow the infected corpses come back to life. The virus, or whatever the hell it was that escaped from the Russians in Dagestan, causes a total breakdown of the host's defenses, multiple infections, hemorrhages, and, within a few hours, death. After an undetermined amount of time, the deceased rises again. Not as he was, but as one of *them*. They attack every living being in their path. They don't recognize anyone and don't communicate in any way. Their only goal is to attack. There have even been cases of cannibalism. The only thing that seems to "kill them off" (pardon the sick joke) is destroying their brain.

I'm a rational, sensible guy. I should be roaring with laughter at this crazy theory, right out of a B movie. But I can't. The last few days have shown me that anything's possible. As wildly absurd as the report sounds, I believe it. The dead return to walk the earth and kill us. We're fucked.

Immersed in such happy thoughts, I thought I heard a noise outside the wall. I bolted up like lightning, completely terrified. It sounded like someone dragging something heavy. I had to know what it was. I grabbed the garden ladder and leaned it quietly against the wall. Then I climbed up slowly, careful not to make the steps creak, and peered over the wall.

I saw my neighbor sweating, dragging posts like the ones he gave me a few days ago. Completely absorbed in his work, he was standing on his unfinished deck, boarding up his house. He went inside, and then I heard hammering. When he came back out, I called to him. Now he was the one getting the shock of his life.

His name's Miguel. He's middle-aged, burly, slightly bald. I think he has a medical supply distributorship. He's divorced and lives alone with a small psychotic dog that barks at everything that moves. He says he "refuses to be crammed together with all those people at the Safe Haven." He thinks he'll be safer at home, and to some extent he's right. He's boarding up his doors and windows in case those things make it through the steel gate. He has a boat at the marina, so if things get ugly, we can escape in it. I said sure, but deep down I think it's a stupid idea. I know his boat; it's docked near my Zodiac. It's only sixteen feet long. We wouldn't even get out of the bay in it, assuming we could get to the port. We agreed to talk in a few hours.

Once inside, I breathed a sigh of relief. I'm not alone. There's another person nearby. Then I remembered: he and I aren't alone either. Somewhere out there are those things that aren't human anymore. And they're getting closer.

ENTRY 32
January 25, 2:36 a.m.

They're here.

Shit. I'm watching them out the window. There are dozens, hundreds, thousands of them. They're everywhere. God help me. For Christ's sake, how can this be possible? I think I'm going to throw up.

ENTRY 33
January 25, 6:38 p.m.

I'm calmer now. Last night was a real nightmare. In the light of day, the situation seems less terrifying. But I could clearly see the agonizing reality. In a few hours it'll be completely dark again, and I won't be able to see those things. (It goes without saying that the streetlights are out.) But I know they're out there. And somehow they know there are humans around somewhere.

It all started around one in the morning. I'd been talking over the wall to Miguel. We could have talked by phone and spared ourselves the bitter cold, but the need to see a human face was huge. I came back inside and then moved my headquarters upstairs to the front bedroom. I haven't slept in that room for two years. Now I have no choice. It's the only room with a window facing the front, and it's higher than the wall. From there I can see the entire length of my street and a small section of the main road. I brought up the radio, a laptop, a small TV, and my scuba-diving spear. I set everything next to the chair I'd pushed against the window, and sat down to wait.

At first I couldn't make out what was happening. The sound was the first thing I noticed. In the silence of the night, I heard a strange noise, like something dragging on the pavement, with an occasional groan mixed in. The hair on my arms stood on end. A moment later, I saw the first one: a man about thirty-five, wearing a blue plaid shirt and white jeans. He was missing a shoe. He had a terrible wound on his face, and his clothes were soaked with blood that was starting to get stiff. More followed behind him—men, women. Even children, for the love of God! They all had some kind of injury. Some even had gruesome amputations. Their skin was a waxy color. Their dark brown veins stood out against their pale skin like delicate tattoos. The corneas of their eyes were yellow. Their movements were slow, but not too slow. They seemed to have a problem with coordination. It reminded me of the way a drunk walks after a night of partying. Not bad, considering they're dead. Totally fucking dead. There's no doubt about that. Even though their wounds had been fatal, they walked around under my window as if those wounds were nothing. That's frightening!

Dozens, then hundreds, maybe thousands, I don't know. On the surface that multitude could have been a demonstration or a crowd at a concert, except it was plunged into a stony silence, broken only by shuffling feet and occasional moans. The fucking mob was headed for the Safe Haven. Tireless. Immutable. Unstoppable.

It's clear why they were headed there. I don't know how many people were crammed downtown, but any human crowd makes a lot of noise. In the silence, I could hear the crowd's noise more than a mile away. Loudspeakers, electric generators providing light and heat, vehicles. A magnet drawing this violent mob, eager for human bodies with a heartbeat. They would fall on the humans, and there was nothing their victims could do about it.

A few hours later, the shooting started, near downtown. First some isolated shots. Then the gunfire increased; for a while it was a loud roar. I swear for a moment I even heard mortar rounds. Although the BRILAT troops had withdrawn from several parts of Spain recently, there should still have been a sizable enough contingent to drive them away, no problem. The police band was jammed for hours with frantic messages from one unit to another. Distress calls, urgent requests for ammunition, surrounded platoons requesting backup, reports of casualties...*Fall back. They've broken through. They're overrunning us.* Then, little by little, silence. The sound of firearms gradually ceased. At dawn I didn't hear anything anymore. Radio frequencies were silent. Dead. A few of columns of smoke rose above downtown, marking where my city's Safe Haven once was.

We're screwed. A couple dozen of those monsters are walking up and down my street like automatons. One of them is beating monotonously on the door of the house next door, the doctor's house. I don't know why he's doing that. The house is empty. He keeps it up for hours, setting my nerves on edge.

It'll soon be nighttime again. I hope I see the light of day.

ENTRY 34
January 26, 5:57 p.m.

This has been a really long day. I'm writing this in the upstairs bedroom. I don't come out except to go to the bathroom or get something to eat. I have half a bottle of gin sitting next to my chair. It was full this morning. That doesn't make me an alcoholic. A couple of drinks helped me cope. Shit, my nerves are shot.

Today, when the sun came up, I was dozing in front of the TV. To save the batteries, I only turn it on once in a while. They're still displaying the royal coat of arms, but it's been hours since there was a news report. I woke up suddenly. Shooting. I heard gunfire close by. It went on for a while, then suddenly stopped. I don't know much about guns, but it sounded like a couple of pistols and some kind of high-caliber gun, maybe a shotgun. This tells me something important: there are other living people around! Or at least there were...

Miguel, my neighbor, is getting all worked up. He thinks staying here is suicide. The best thing to do is drive to the marina and get on his boat. I spent half the morning trying to talk him out of it. We don't know if his boat is still docked there. Most likely it's gone. Besides, the road will probably be closed in a dozen places, so we'd have to get out of the car and walk with thousands of those things everywhere. We wouldn't last a minute. I think I talked him out of it, but who knows for how long.

In a way, he's right. Either we improve our situation here or move on. Soon.

Those monsters are a constant presence on my street. When they heard the shots, hundreds of them headed down the main street toward the source of noise, including some that had been wandering around here for hours. The rest hung around here. Throughout the day, new ones showed up. From my window I see eleven of them wandering up and down. Four women, two children, and five men. One of them I named Thumper. He's been banging his palm against a metal gate for hours. They all have the same dazed, distracted look on their faces. Their clothes are torn and stiff with blood. Some are horrifically mutilated. One woman's rib cage is crushed, as if she'd been run over by a car. Her broken hip makes it really hard for her to walk.

However, the one that interests me the most is a soldier in the BRILAT special forces. He has a horrible wound on his neck, and he's missing a chunk of his cheek. I can see his teeth every time he goes slumping along under my window. The clotted blood has formed strange lumps on his jacket.

But the important thing is the backpack he's still carrying. And his belt, which has about a dozen pockets. And a gun. A gun! In a daze brought on by all the alcohol, stress, and sleep deprivation, I've feverishly plotted a dozen ways to get that gun and backpack. I need them. But all I've got is a scuba-diving spear.

Assuming I can bring him down, I'd still have to get everything off him. In the time that would take, the rest of the monsters would pounce on me. After a while I devised a plan. It's really horrible, but it's the best I've got.

I don't want to ask my neighbor for help. He's wound so tight, I can't rely on him. Plus, if something happened to him, my guilt would kill me. No. It's my plan, my risk, and my reward. I don't have the slightest idea how to use a gun, but it would make me feel a lot safer to have one. With it, I'd try to get out of here. And I won't hesitate to use it on myself to keep from turning into one of those things. That's for sure.

Now that I know what to do, I have to figure out when to do it. I'll wait a few hours. I want to be sure there aren't any more of those things out of my line of vision. I loaded the speargun and had some target practice in the garden. Pulling the trigger releases the tension in the band, and the spear shoots off like a rocket deep into the tree trunk. I sweated a lot getting it out. I couldn't get a grip on it. I won't have time to retrieve my spears. Since I only have six of them, I'll have to be a very, very good shot.

ENTRY 35
January 27, 11:25 a.m.

My hands are shaking. I needed a long, long break and another swig of gin to be able sit down and write. Dear God, my nerves are going to explode!

I started at the crack of dawn, when the light was good. Those things are deceptively slow; they can move really fast when they want to. I don't know if they see well at night, but one thing's for sure—I can't see for shit in the dark. And there're so many of them. I don't intend to find out how many, at least for the moment.

Thinking it through, I realize my plan is pure madness. But it's the best I've come up with over the last feverish hours. I need to do something to relieve the agonizing tension that's built up since those things arrived. Plus, the gun and backpack have become a symbol. I'll get them at any price.

All this excitement has infected poor Lucullus. He's been running around the backyard all morning like a wild animal.

After hours of watching those eleven monsters, I realized they only move when something gets their attention. At about seven this morning, a rat or a hedgehog or something was darting around at the end of the street. Several of those things headed after it but apparently didn't catch it. Six of them—two children, three men, and a woman—remained at my end of the street, about forty yards away, with their backs to my front door. When I saw that, I realized that my plan might have a fighting chance.

My entire plan hinges on the fact that there's only one way on to my street, where it intersects with the main street. On the other end my street dead-ends at the embankment where the civil guardsmen and soldiers headed several nights ago. It's steep, so I doubt any of those things can climb it. But I'm not 100 percent sure of that—one more unknown in my wonderful plan. I can see small groups of them wandering aimlessly on the main street. They don't seem to find my street especially exciting. In the last two hours, a couple of monsters walked a few yards down my street but went back the other direction after a while.

The soldier-monster is on the far side of the street, close to the embankment, swaying in the middle of the road. In addition to him and the six monsters with their backs to me, there are three women and one man, Thumper, who continues to haunt the house next door. One of the women is missing an arm and half her chest. She's standing in front of my house, less than two yards from my door, staring at the wall. Nothing has changed in an hour and a half, so I've decided to act.

I've racked my brain over what to wear. I don't want those things to bite me or touch me. I don't know if they sweat or if you can contract the virus through contact with their skin or their sweat. The sad truth is, I don't know shit about them. I just know they're dead, they're aggressive, and they're at my front door.

After a lot of thought, I decided to wear my wetsuit. It's superthick, top-grade neoprene—flexible and water resistant. I doubt they can bite through it. At most, I'll get a bruise under that layer of neoprene. Plus, it's completely smooth and thermo-sealed; there are no buttons or loose edges they could grab me by. It's like a second skin. I wasn't sure if I needed to cut the hood. It covers everything but my face, including my ears. Since it's so thick, I can barely hear. I have to be able to hear those things coming up behind me. It also limits my peripheral vision.

With a sigh I picked up the scissors and trimmed the hood. This baby cost me almost twelve hundred euros a year ago. I've taken it on many weekend dives, and now I'm destroying it. But what other choice do I have?

Next, I put on winter gloves and tennis shoes because they're flexible and—very important—quiet. I got a look at myself in the mirror. Jesus! I looked like some weirdo in my diving goggles, with the speargun and a handful of spears on my back. I don't know if I'll take down that soldier, but one look at me and he might die laughing. That is, if he has a sense of humor. Damn, I'm delirious!

I also grabbed an old umbrella and tore off the fabric and all the spokes. It had a mean ivory handle that must've weighed a ton. It'll do in a pinch.

I'm trusting my life to a speargun and a broken umbrella... great!

Time to get going. I'll leave Lucullus in the backyard. If something happens to me, I hope he'll have the sense to escape over the wall. My poor friend. He doesn't deserve all this shit.

Before I unlock the door, I pick up my secret weapon. My whole plan depends on a silly little toy I found when I was rummaging through a drawer. If it works, I'll have a chance. If not, I'll be really in big trouble.

ENTRY 36
January 28, 3:45 p.m.

Human beings are extremely complex. If you'd told me a month ago I'd be capable of what I did yesterday, I'd have laughed my ass off. And yet—I did it! And I'm still alive.

After I got my wetsuit on, I opened the upstairs window a crack to get an overview of my street. I shoved the speargun out the window and propped it against the windowsill. I toyed with the idea of shooting the monsters from the safety of my roof. What a stupid idea! There was no way I could hit a target the size of a human head thirty yards away with a speargun, even if the spear hit the target with enough speed and strength. I had to keep in mind I only had six spears. Only six shots...

I started laughing hysterically. I couldn't help it. I was thinking about shooting people from my bedroom window! It was all so absurd and ironic. Those things down there were clearly not human. Once upon a time, they had lives, family, friends. And now they're…whatever they are. The people they used to be had been either slower-witted than I was or not as lucky. That's all.

With a sigh I decided it was time to face the inevitable. I grabbed a roll of duct tape and pulled out my secret weapon: a little teddy bear with copper cymbals in its paws. When you press the button on the bear's back, it frantically bangs the cymbals and sort of hiccups. The noise is earsplitting. One of my young cousins, Laura, brought it to my house months ago. After chasing around an indignant Lucullus, getting chocolate all over my curtains, and breaking a picture frame, she finally fell asleep on the couch and left her teddy bear underneath it. I found it the next day and put it in a drawer until its owner could come to claim it. Now she may never be back.

For the love of God, she was only five years old! I hope she's okay, or if not, I pray she was shot in the head. Just not turned into one of those things…

I taped the bear to a spear, loaded it in the speargun, and aimed at the house at the end of the street, the one closest to the intersection. My idea was to nail the bear to the wood paneling that completely covered that house's upper floor. It would make a lot of noise and get those things' attention, giving me time to deal with the soldier as he passed by my door. A simple plan. A really shitty plan—a thousand things could go wrong. But it was all I had.

I took a deep breath, turned the toy on, aimed, and pulled the trigger. The spear took off like a flash, but the bear weighed too much and pulled the spear down. Instead of sticking into the wood, it hit the edge of the wall with a thud and fell into the trough on the ground that channels the rain away from the house. For a moment there was no sound. Just when I thought the plan I'd worked so hard on was a bust, I heard the cymbals clanging in the gutter. Laurita's bear hadn't let me down.

That sound electrified those creatures. They turned toward the sound and started moving in its direction. I had to hurry. I flew down the stairs and opened the front door, headed for the steel gate, and quietly pulled it open. It turned silently on its hinges (thank God I'd greased them three weeks ago). For the first time in days, I stepped out on to the street.

The mutants had all moved past my front door. Glancing to my left, I could see the backs of those creatures as they plodded slowly toward the trough and the sound. The soldier was the last in line, just a few yards away, with his back to me. My eyes darting in every direction, I loaded a spear in fifteen seconds. A record for me! I raised the gun and aimed. Less than three yards away. At that distance, I couldn't miss. If God still cares about this doomed human race, I hope he has forgiven me for what I did. But my life was at stake.

I squeezed the trigger. The spear took off with a faint hum and pierced the back of the soldier's skull. He stopped in his tracks and collapsed with a dull thud. I rushed over to the body. He seemed to be *dead* dead now, but I couldn't be too careful. I laid the speargun and the umbrella on the ground and started to wrestle with the loops of his backpack. Blood clots on the clasps prevented me from loosening the straps. Sweat was pouring down my back. I looked over and saw that one of those things had stuck its arm into the trough and was feeling around for the source of the sound. In moments, they'd grab it and tear it apart. Then I wouldn't stand a chance.

Something must have caught the attention of the woman with the crushed hip, because she turned in my direction. Had she heard me, smelled me? I don't know, but she saw me.

With that strange gait, she walked toward me, slowly because she was dragging one leg. Her balance was pretty shot. I only had a few seconds. I struggled clumsily to load another spear in the gun. Sweat rolled into my eyes as I pulled back the rubber sling. Four yards. I finally got everything set. Three yards. I raised the gun and aimed at the woman's head. Two yards. I fired.

The spear hit the woman hard. She stopped and fell forward like a sack. But the situation was deteriorating by the minute. One of the monsters had grabbed the bear and was shaking it. He'd managed to empty out its batteries, and its cymbals were silent now. The sound of the woman falling made everyone look in my direction. I had to hurry. Time was running out.

I grasped the soldier's body by the leg and started dragging it toward my open front gate, toward salvation. There was no time to loosen the clasps. I had to drag the body and the backpack with me. As I neared the gate, another one of those things suddenly came around a parked car. Shit. I hadn't seen that guy before. The speargun was hanging from my shoulder, but I didn't have time to load another spear. I let go of the soldier for a moment and steadied the umbrella shaft with both hands. With all my might, I struck the creature's temple with the ivory handle. I don't know if I killed it, but I do know the bone in its left temple cracked and it collapsed on the ground. I dropped the umbrella, grabbed the soldier's body, and made it through my front gate, slamming it behind me, just in time. They were just a few yards away.

I left the soldier's body in front of the front door and threw up. I've been drinking for nearly twenty-four hours. I'm drunk. Now these things know I'm here. But I'm alive. And if you're alive, you can fight to live another day.

ENTRY 37
January 29, 5:14 p.m.

If things keep on like this, I'll go crazy. They've been pounding nonstop on my front gate for hours. I can hear them no matter where I am in the house. It's horrible. And all that moaning! Jesus

Christ! They're destroying my nerves. I've been drinking too much, I know, but I don't know what else to do.

Miguel, my neighbor, isn't any help. Instead he's a pain in the ass. He's hung up on the idea that we should head to the marina, get his boat, and sail somewhere else. But he doesn't have the nerve to do it alone. He's driving me crazy with his constant complaining. He's insufferable.

I tried to get him to see things clearly, but he won't listen. The roads are either cut off or blocked by abandoned cars, accidents, collapsed bridges. It's insane to think about the trip as if everything were normal. Anything can happen. And the consequences could be fatal. You have to plan things out if you're going to survive.

Tonight I got up the courage to climb up to my attic. It's a small space under the roof, barely more than a closet. I haven't been up there for two years because it's full of my wife's stuff. The day after her funeral, my sister and her boyfriend put all her things up there. Until three weeks ago, when the technician installed the solar panels, no one had been up there. There's dust on everything. Over the musty smell, I can still detect a familiar scent—her perfume, which still permeates her clothes. My heart shrank, and I collapsed on an old couch with tears streaming down my face. I've been crying like a baby for hours, holding her old sweater. I miss her so much. Thank God she doesn't have to witness all this.

After a while I calmed down. Something's still broken inside me; I mourned for a while and vented. The stress I've been under is brutal. Taking refuge up here for a few hours was a good idea.

The technician's footprints in the dust went from the trapdoor to below the skylight. There were some bits of wire and a plastic bag of leftover screws. The remains of the installation. Silent witness that someone did his job what seems like a million years ago.

I wonder what became of that guy. Maybe he's one of those things wandering around.

I opened the skylight and let in some cold air. I tied myself to some buttresses and climbed very carefully onto the roof. The last thing I needed was to break my leg! Next to the skylight is a flat surface you can sit on. The roof slopes down from there and is covered by the iridescent solar panels. It's about a twenty-foot drop to the ground, where these things have tirelessly massed in front of my gate. Falling is definitely not a good option.

A few new creatures have arrived, drawn by the noise made by the things congregated at my door. Broken Hip's body is lying in a heap in the middle of the road. There's no trace of the other guy. The thump on the head I gave him mustn't have been enough to send him back to hell. Too bad.

Normally I had a spectacular view of the city at night. Now I was amazed at how completely dark it was. Most nights I could see thousands of lights, but tonight there was utter blackness. The electricity was definitely off. And they sure weren't planning to send a team in to fix it. I lit a cigarette and thought things over.

When all this started, people quit showing up for work. Power plant operators, too. So for two weeks now, those plants have been operating on automatic pilot. I tried to remember the way a friend's boyfriend, an engineer, explained it to me. A thermal power plant that runs on coal or fuel can only be set on automatic for twenty-four hours before its boilers run out of fuel. In theory, a hydroelectric or wind-powered plant could stay on indefinitely, but it requires skilled technicians to repair any damage done by around-the-clock use. It could last about two weeks before its systems started to fail. Parts would be tough to get now. It's horrifying to think of a nuclear plant operating with no one to make repairs. Chernobyl, the guy said with a sad smile, is an example of a nuclear power plant that wasn't maintained properly. I hope the report was true, that the nuclear power plants have been disconnected.

So I guess the whole country is dark, or soon will be. The electric company had a contingency plan if a plant or two failed, but all of them failing at once must have caused the entire system to collapse. In one fell swoop, they've sent us back to the nineteenth century. Except that we're struggling to stay alive, surrounded by walking corpses. That's a helluva picture.

I stubbed out my cigarette and went back inside. It's cold. I haven't looked through the soldier's backpack yet. I hope it was worth it. Let's see what I find.

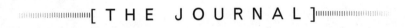[T H E J O U R N A L]

ENTRY 38
January 30, 6:38 p.m.

The last twenty-four hours have been a disaster. Just when you think nothing else can go wrong, reality sneaks up behind you with a new surprise.

As if I didn't already have enough problems with those monsters beating mercilessly on my door for the last two days, there's something new on the horizon. Because of the widespread power failure, the Internet has ceased to exist. Kaput. That's it. My blog's dead. So's the entire Internet. All I get is the white Explorer screen. The servers closed down days ago. That mine lasted this long was a miracle. It's amazing how much we depend on electricity for everything. We're back in the nineteenth century, with all its drawbacks. I don't know if I can handle it.

I'm going to keep writing entries in this journal. I need to record what I see and feel. I need to set my thoughts down on this blank page or I'll go crazy within a couple of months. This journal will speak for me; it's the only place where I can confide my experiences. If I really fuck up, at least there'll be a record of how I lived through these terrible times. And that's some fucking comfort.

I got up my courage and went back out to the front patio. I opened the door as stealthily as I could and peeked out. The soldier's body was lying where I left it, right inside the gate. Here, the noise those things made was deafening. I placed my hand on the steel gate and felt the vibration from their pounding. They know I'm on this side of the gate and are frustrated that they can't catch me.

I sat on the front steps and lit a cigarette as I studied the body. For the first time I got a good look at one of those things up close. It was starting to smell really bad. Putrefaction and rigor mortis must slow way down when they mutate into those monsters. Once they are *really* dead, that process seems to move at a normal pace. A sticky liquid flowed out of the hole in his skull and formed a clot on the tile floor. I didn't think I'd ever get that spot out, but I guess that doesn't matter now. His skin was yellowish, waxy, and his circulatory system was drawn on his skin like delicate lace. Combined with the terrible wounds on his face, the effect was chilling.

I got up my courage, put on the latex gloves I'd found in the medicine cabinet, and pulled a heavy, black, well-oiled gun out of his holster. On one side was the word "Glock," and on the other, an eight-digit serial number. I think it's loaded. That was the first time in my life I'd held one of those things. I studied it carefully. I felt much better having a real gun. I know it's psychological, but the feeling of security is wonderful.

On his belt were two cartridges that matched the ammunition in the gun. There were fifteen rounds in each, so when the gun was loaded, I had a whopping forty-five bullets. Now I'd have to learn to fire it without shooting myself in the foot.

In addition to the ammunition for the Glock, I found several cartridges that looked like ammunition for an assault rifle. Two of them were empty and still smelled of gunpowder. The poor guy lying at my feet had had time to shoot off at least two full magazines. Of course, there was no trace of that gun. When those things grabbed him, he must have dropped it. Who knows where it is now.

The backpack was a treasure. I found a sleeping bag, a large army camouflage poncho, a compass, a map with several battle plans noted on it (probably the defensive lines that contained those monsters during the evacuation), some smokes, a first-aid kit, including three vials of morphine and, best of all, some army rations. The cans are great. The reservoir in the bottom is filled with a reactive substance. Add water, and it generates intense heat so you can eat hot food without a fire or a kitchen. They'd come in handy when I had to get out of here. I'm coming to the realization that sooner or later I'll have to move. If I stay here, those things will finally get in, or I'll starve. The only problem is how to get out of here. And where to go.

I dug into one of the lower pockets and found the guy's wallet. That fucked up my whole day. His name was Vincent; he was only twenty-eight, from a small town just twenty miles from here. He had pictures of a girl (his girlfriend?) and a cute dog. A guy whose life they stole. A guy I drilled three spans of steel into to survive. Hell, I get sick thinking about it.

With a lot of effort and some throwing up, I pulled the spear out of his head. I put it in a pan of boiling water and left it there for about six hours. It took half a line of stored electricity to boil the water that long, but I wanted to kill any germs there might be on the spear. Then I put it back in the sheath with others. Now I have four spears. I can see the other two from my window, one next to the bear and the other stuck in Broken Hip. They might as well be on the moon for all the good they'll do me.

I don't know what the hell to do with the body. I don't see how I could throw it over the wall. Those bastards would see me. So I've wrapped it in a sheet of plastic for now. I'll think of something.

If that weren't enough, my neighbor's gotten all worked up. I suspect he's on something. I made the mistake of telling him about my adventure with the soldier. Now he thinks we can blast our way through the city to his boat. How do I make him see that reality is different? I risked my life to get just halfway down the street and kill only two of those things. Crossing the city with thousands of those monsters on the loose is something else again. We'd have to plan carefully, not go out with our guns blazing and a gram of cocaine coursing through our veins, not knowing what we'd find around a corner.

He's fixated on my wetsuit, and now he's wearing some overalls that look idiotic. He's sure to do something stupid if we don't get moving soon. I have to think. Fast.

ENTRY 39
January 31, 11:49 a.m.

I was sitting quietly in the kitchen when I heard shooting. It sounded like a shotgun blast coming from next door. My neighbor! What the hell was that asshole up to? Was he *trying* to attract all the walking dead in a one-mile radius? Jesus, you could hear those shots all over the fucking city!

I climbed the ladder to the top of my garden wall and peered into his yard. I didn't see anything but some posts he'd stacked there for a deck he'll never build. I called his name softly. No answer. Miguel, you idiot, what the hell did you do?

I could hear the noise those things were making on Miguel's side of the street. It sounded like they were pounding on a wooden door. They'd found a way to get through his steel gate, and now they were banging on his front door.

I was wondering how the hell I was going to climb down into his yard when I saw him through a window. He told me he was okay. He said he'd tried to get to his car so he could surprise me and pick me up at my front door. But there were dozens of those things on his street, so that plan hadn't worked. They were inside his front gate, too. "I killed two of them," he said with a huge grin. You asshole. Now there were at least a dozen of them out there, drawn by the noise he made when he shot those two monsters.

His overalls were torn and bloody. He told me one of those monsters tried to grab him by the neck, but he took him out, no sweat. All that blood belonged to "those shits," he said. He looked really pale. I sensed he was lying. Years of trying cases in court have taught me all about mankind's shortcomings. I'm good at picking up the little signals we give when we're not telling the truth. This guy is hiding something. There's got to be more to his story.

Now I'm in the kitchen, heating up a can of soup, thinking over the situation. Lucullus is curled up in my chair. I don't like it. Not one bit.

ENTRY 40
February 1, 10:58 a.m.

I went on a drinking binge again last night. Now, as I write this, I'm paying the price. This hangover's a bitch. I've never been much of a drinker, but since all hell broke loose, I've hit my liquor cabinet hard. I'm down to the dregs. That's probably for the best.

I haven't slept well for several nights. For a cocktail that'll blow your mind, mix together one part stress, one part anxiety, and a shot of that constant, merciless, monotonous pounding.

I considered taking sleeping pills, but I'm leery of chemically induced sleep. If those things got in somehow while I was under the influence of Valium, I'd never know what hit me. I'd be a nice, warm, sleeping meal served up on a silver platter. So, no thank you, no Valium.

I've thought about playing music, but if I turn it up loud enough to drown those things out, I'll attract hundreds of them straight to my door. Like a fucking pied piper. So that's out. I put on headphones, but I can't stand them for very long. Every couple of minutes, I think I hear them breaking down the steel gate and climbing up the stairs after me. In bed at night, I've ripped the headphones off, trembling, clutching a gun I really don't know how to use. I'm getting so paranoid. If I don't figure something out soon, I'll go crazy.

Since yesterday, three things have happened—one good, one average, and one bad. The good news is that when I was messing around with the shortwave radio, twisting the dials back and forth like I've done for days with no luck, I suddenly picked up a signal. It's weak, with a lot of static, but I clearly heard a human voice. I jumped for joy and hugged Lucullus so hard he glared at me all day. It's a military station that broadcasts news and advisories. Apparently, they still control the Canary Islands. The government and the royal family have taken refuge there. I heard a message from the king. I couldn't understand most of what he said, because of the static. But I'm absolutely positive it was him.

They said that the Canaries are completely full of refugees from the peninsula. They're running low on fuel, food, and water, so they urge people not to go there. Army units will divert any boat or aircraft attempting to reach them. Those bastards! They're like the *Titanic* survivors who used their oars to beat back anyone who tried to climb into their lifeboats. They're sitting pretty in their lifeboat and are afraid they'll tip over and sink if too many of us climb aboard. They're telling us politely but firmly to stick it up our ass. Hey! We're just trying to survive.

It's a huge relief to know I'm not the last survivor on the face of the earth. So to hell with them! If the Canaries are secure, there must be other places with people, food, conversation, heat, and hot water. God, I'd kill for a hot bath.

The fifty-two regional forces had already been reduced to forty, and now they've been consolidated into four main units. Their strength has been extremely reduced. The number of casualties is appalling. The poor guy wrapped in plastic on my porch could testify to that. There've been dozens of desertions and "lost" units. They have only enough resources to defend the few Safe Havens that have managed to survive, but they don't know for how long. Until the last bullet, I guess. The outlook is really bleak.

The average news is that I heard gunshots again today, coming from the southwest, somewhere between downtown and the road to La Coruña. It was nearly sunrise. A series of quick pops like pistols and then a series of hiccups I'd say were assault rifles. That went on for about half an hour and then suddenly stopped. Either there was no one left to shoot at, or none of the shooters survived.

The bad news is that for twenty-four hours I haven't heard anything from my asshole neighbor. He doesn't answer when I call to him over the wall. His evil, ugly mutt, Lucullus' sworn enemy, usually prowls around the wall, waiting for my cat to slip and fall. An hour ago I heard a horrible yelping inside his house. It sounded like someone was killing the poor thing. Then the yelping stopped. A little while ago, I peered over the wall. I didn't see the dog or its owner. Those posts Miguel stacked in the back-yard are the only witnesses to whatever's going on over there. I'm afraid I won't like it, whatever it is.

E N T R Y   4 1
February 1, 9:00 p.m.

Murphy's Law says when things can go wrong, they go really wrong. The jerk who wrote that book must be really happy with himself. If he's still alive. No one gives a shit about his ideas these days. Everyone has to cover his own ass in this new world of the "not living."

I spent most of the morning leaning over my garden wall, trying to get my idiot neighbor's attention without making a lot of noise. I finally gave up. I went back inside, feeling really uneasy. What if something happened to him? I ran through the list of all the accidents that moron could have suffered, everything from falling down the stairs to slipping in the tub. As I fixed a cup of instant coffee, I kept thinking that one of those things might've bitten him when he went on his insane outing. But I quickly dismissed it. Wouldn't he have told me? When I saw all the blood on him, it had occurred to me that he was hiding something. Would that idiot lie about something that important? I didn't want to believe that.

His lack of common sense could cause me loads of problems, but he was the only other living person around. Plus, he generously gave me the fence posts I asked him for. I owed him. I never dreamed I'd repay that debt by driving him through a city devastated by death and chaos to get to a boat that might not even be there. It was a really stupid plan, but he was obsessed with it. When I wouldn't go with him, he'd tried to go alone. He blew it before he even got to the corner.

But I didn't want to be left alone. I was panicking.

Maybe he was stoned out of his mind. Lately he'd been doing a lot of cocaine. Maybe he'd snorted one line too many, or maybe the shit his dealer sold him was cut with something lethal. My imagination was getting the best of me. I pictured him lying on his kitchen floor in his stupid striped overalls, blood running out his nose, dying twenty yards from me while I was scratching my balls. I set my cup in the sink and went in the backyard.

I went to the storage shed and dug out the rope I use to resurface after a deep dive. The rope has thick knots every eighteen inches to help me calculate the depth. That way I can surface slowly, decompress, and not get the bends.

Now I was going to slide down that rope into his yard. I tied one end to the chimney of my barbecue pit and unrolled the rope over the wall into my neighbor's yard. It was freezing cold. A soft blanket of frost covered his lawn and the piles of posts. Except for those things' constant pounding and their terrifying groans, it was absolutely still. Without a second thought, I climbed up the ladder to the top of my side of the wall, swung my legs over the ledge, and slid into my neighbor's yard.

When I reached Miguel's yard, it occurred to me I was only wearing a sweater and jeans. The only weapon I had was some cable cutters in my pants pocket. Yes, sir. You're really prepared… now that takes balls. I was just about to go back and get the right equipment when I heard a rustling inside the house. I'd look really stupid if I showed up in my wetsuit, speargun in hand, only to find him lying on the couch, drinking a beer, listening to music with headphones on. No, I'd rather risk it. I had my pride, after all.

I crossed his yard, stepping carefully onto the unfinished deck. The smell of sawdust and varnish was really strong. Tools and empty paint cans were scattered everywhere. Inside, the house was dark and gloomy. I gently knocked on the back door and called to Miguel. Nothing. But when I reached for the handle, all hell broke loose.

The window on my left broke. Out came that thing's arms and head. It wasn't Miguel, but it had been. Poor fool. He'd just wanted to "surprise me." Then one of those things had bitten him.

Now he was screwed. To make matters worse, he was trying to fuck me up. I ran like hell for the wall. I must have banged my ankle on some posts, because it's now the size of a tennis ball. When I got to the wall, I turned and saw Miguel trying to wriggle through the window frame. He must've cut himself. Dark, infected blood streamed down his left arm, soaking his clothes. I stood there like a dick, mesmerized. I snapped out of it only when he got all the way out of his house and started toward me. They might look slow, but they're really fast!

I started scrambling up the rope. It's not easy, especially when you know if you slip, you're dead. Or worse. He was right behind me. I think he touched one of my boots. When I reached the top of the wall, I looked down at him. He was angry, mean, covered in his own blood. He was one of them.

I went inside and grabbed my camera, an HP 735 digital camera. It was old, but it had a fantastic Pentax lens. I took a couple pictures of that howling thing down there so I could study it later and not be in any more danger.

Now I'm in the kitchen, looking at the pictures on my laptop. I can hear him scratching and banging on the wall. I need to do something about him, but I haven't come up with anything. I have to decide. Tomorrow.

ENTRY 42

February 2, 7:54 p.m.

I spent the whole day thinking about what to do about that thing scraping my wall. The decision got harder and harder to make. Most people would end his suffering. If he was suffering.

Did he know what he was? Did he perceive reality the way I did? Do those things think or feel emotions? Is anything left of their old self? Or is their spirit completely obliterated when they die and are reborn? Do they remember anything from their former life? Do they sleep or dream? Hell, all I know about those predators is that they want to hunt me down. Like all the other humans, I'm their prey.

Even knowing that, I had a hard time deciding what to do about Miguel. This guy was someone I knew. He was my neighbor, for the love of God. Although he was a complete moron, I couldn't imagine stabbing him in the head with a steel spear. I'm no murderer.

It took me three hours and half a bottle of gin to muster up the courage to end Miguel's life. His shouting was driving me crazy, and that tipped the balance. I could hear him all over the house. His voice, tirelessly demanding my blood, was getting to me. I was becoming hysterical.

Drunk, worked up into a frenzy, I grabbed the speargun. It took three tries to load a spear on the tightest setting. Stumbling, I climbed the ladder to the top of the wall and stuck my head over. As soon as he saw me, he shouted even louder, stretching his arms toward me, trying to grab me. He was just two yards away. Even a guy drunk on his ass could make that shot. I pulled the trigger, and the spear flew out with a sharp hiss. It entered his head with a *crack* right above his right eyebrow. He grimaced in surprise (or relief?) and collapsed like a sack.

Then the dam burst. I started laughing hysterically. I couldn't stop. Fat tears ran down my cheeks. A minute later, I was crying my eyes out, leaning against the wall, the speargun still in my hand. I'd murdered my neighbor from the top of the garden wall. I'd driven a piece of steel into his head. Just the day before, we were making plans and I was laughing at his lame jokes. Now I'd killed him. This is bullshit. I feel very alone. I'll go crazy if this keeps up.

I climbed down the rope into his yard, landing next to the body. When I put weight on the ankle I injured yesterday, pain shot through me. God, it hurts! I hope it's only a sprain and not a broken bone. I limped over to a pile of wood and grabbed a thick rubber tarp. I dragged the body to a corner of the yard and wrapped it in the tarp. I should bury him. I should pray for him. Fuck, I don't know if I'm still a believer.

I studied his house for a moment. The back door was still closed. The window Miguel had come through was shattered. Broken glass and clotted blood covered the ground. A bloodstained curtain was sticking out. The house was dark and silent. And empty.

I had to go in. I knew I should go in. I had to make sure there weren't any more of those things inside, and that the wood door was still braced closed. The last thing I needed was a couple dozen of those monsters in his backyard. Then I remembered that Miguel was a rep for a pharmaceutical company. He must have a ton of samples somewhere. I could use some painkillers. Most importantly, his house faces the other street. Maybe there was a way out there.

It was nighttime, and darkness obscured everything, so I couldn't go in. Miguel's house had no electricity. I wasn't about to go into the lion's den in the dark, drunk and without my wetsuit. No way. I'll leave that for tomorrow.

I climbed back up the rope and went home. I'm sober now, lying on the sofa in the dark, listening to the steady blows against my gate. I feel a dull, pulsating hangover coming on. I'll try to get some sleep. Tomorrow I'll go in that house and come up with some kind of a plan. I've got to get out of here.

ENTRY 43
February 3, 5:07 p.m.

I'm sitting in the hammock in my backyard. The last rays of the cold winter sun are falling on this small rectangle of grass, warming my bones a little. Lucullus is napping contentedly in my lap, dreaming whatever cats dream about. It's the most peaceful time I've spent in weeks. That's the truth. If it weren't for those things howling and pounding on the gate, I'd think it was a quiet Sunday afternoon. I almost feel like fixing hot chocolate and watching a movie. Unfortunately, it isn't Sunday afternoon, and my neighbors are among the undead out there, eager to kill me. Plus I've been out of milk for two weeks. Life sucks.

I slept until almost noon, recovering from my hangover. When I got up, I fixed myself a regal breakfast of a couple of cups of strong coffee and a bowl of beans out of a can and mayonnaise. My diet has become so monotonous over the last few days.

Today I have to face several problems. First, the soldier's body lying in front of the door. He's been decomposing all week, and he's starting to smell really bad. If I don't do something, it could make me sick.

I locked Lucullus up in my bedroom. All I needed was for him to jump on the body and then lick himself. After I wrapped the body in plastic, I dragged it out to the backyard, trying to keep from retching. The smell it left in the foyer, hallway, and living room was indescribable. I considered dousing the body with gas out of the lawn mower and setting it on fire, but that grisly idea made me stop and think. I don't know whether those things can smell or how well they can see. If they can see, then a column of smoke rising in a clear blue sky would draw them in droves. My only choice was to bury him in the backyard.

Resigning myself, I set to work digging a shallow grave in the corner of the yard, next to the barbecue pit. The ground was soft and muddy, so it was easy. I used a small spade, the only garden tool I could find. I slid the body into the hole and covered it. Then, dirty and sweaty, I sat down next to the mound. I lit a cigarette and considered the irony of the situation. This humble grave digging in my backyard was probably the most luxurious funeral held for weeks. Maybe the only one.

I threw the butt on the ground and went back inside. I washed up a little, wincing at the freezing cold water, then fixed some food for Lucullus and me. Today, more canned food. I'm down to canned sardines. That goofy cat is thrilled with this diet.

I got everything ready for the toughest task of the day. I pulled on my wetsuit and checked my speargun. I only had the three spears left. The fourth one was in my hapless neighbor's head. I didn't even have the umbrella handle; I'd left it lying on the street when I killed one of those monsters. The soldier's gun was my last line of defense.

The Glock felt huge and dangerous in my hand. I still wasn't sure how to use it, but at least I'd identified its parts: trigger, safety, magazine release, etc. It was loaded, but I'd try not to use it. I knew what those things did when they heard a noise. If I shot the gun, I might take out a few, but the noise would draw dozens more in minutes. I'd save it for another time.

After saying every prayer I knew, I climbed the ladder back over the wall and eased down into Miguel's backyard. Everything was the way I'd left it. His body was still in the corner, in a gray heap, wrapped in plastic. Warily, I went over to him, gave a couple of tugs, and pulled the spear out of his head. I must be getting desensitized because this time I didn't throw up. Interesting. If I survive long enough, I could become a textbook psychopath.

I left the spear on the grass and carefully walked toward the house. It was still dark and silent. I grabbed the doorknob and tried to turn it. Locked. I should have known. I'd have to go in the way Miguel came out yesterday—through the window. I slipped inside, careful not to cut myself on the blood-soaked glass. It was a disgusting scene. The damn dog, or what was left of him, was lying in a corner, ripped to shreds. He looked like he'd been attacked by wolves. The dog must've been concerned and gone over to his dying master, only to find he'd turned into a ruthless predator that tore him to pieces in seconds. Life's a bitch.

I quickly checked the house. I wasn't going to make that mistake again. It was empty and safe. None of those monsters had gotten in. The front door was armor-plated. They could beat on it for centuries, and it wouldn't budge. I went upstairs and glanced out the window. I could see the entire street and two cars parked out front. One was a delivery van with the logo of Miguel's company on the side. The other was a Mercedes, also Miguel's; the door on the driver's side was hanging open. There was blood on the upholstery and a corpse lying next to the car. Another one was not far away, lying halfway between the front door and the car. Miguel must have brushed against them. That's what cost him his life.

After I'd checked out the entire house, I breathed a sigh of relief. The size of my territory had doubled. What's more, that street offered some interesting possibilities. I might be able to get out that way.

I grabbed a box of powerful painkillers off a table and went home. It'd be dark soon, and I hadn't brought a flashlight. I didn't want to wander around a strange house in the dark. I'll come back tomorrow, when I can scavenge to my heart's content. That'll also give me time to come up with a plan.

E N T R Y   4 4
February 6, 5:57 p.m.

It's been days since I sat down to write in this journal. I'm really drained emotionally. Those monsters keep up their slow, steady pounding. They can't knock the door down like that, but they're shattering my nerves. If I stay here much longer, I'll be safe, but I'll run out of food. And I'll go insane. I need to come up with a plan—fast.

My sanity is the main reason I need to escape. Man's a social animal. He needs to interact with other people. I haven't spoken to another human, besides my neighbor, in weeks. I need to talk to someone. Pouring my heart out in this journal is therapeutic, it helps me let off steam—but it's not enough. I talk to Lucullus as if he were human. Lately our "conversations" have been too frequent. That's one more sign I need to leave.

I'm not using the solar panels and storage batteries in the basement correctly. They were designed to provide electricity in case of a power outage or if the voltage drops for a few hours, not to keep the electricity flowing all day. So it was probably inevitable that I would overload the system. At noon on Saturday, I turned on the microwave at the same time I was heating something up on the stove. The kitchen light was on, too. It was unforgivable; I wasn't paying attention.

We take electricity for granted. I simply forgot I was using up the dwindling reserves in the basement. The batteries were very low, since I'd run the electricity all night to boil tap water. When I turned on the microwave, the voltage dipped and burned out the fucking microwave...and the motors of the freezers in the basement. All my frozen food thawed in a heartbeat. I buried the food next to my neighbor's body, but not before stuffing myself with everything I could save.

My situation's even graver now. I didn't find anything special in my neighbor's pantry—some canned food, pasta, a couple pounds of moldy potatoes, and dozens and dozens of packets of powdered soup, freeze-dried coffee creamer, and minute rice. The only good thing about powdered food is that it's lightweight, so I can carry it in my backpack. But its nutritional value is questionable, and I need to build my strength up. Not to mention its "delicious" flavor...

I didn't find much else in the house. There were no weapons except a double-barreled Zavala shotgun. The only ammunition I found for it was lead pellets. They wouldn't penetrate a human skull, not even at close range. You have to get very close to the target, and that's too close when it comes to those things. Miguel could've attested to that, if he weren't buried in the backyard. And it's terribly loud. Still, I took it and the ammunition, fifteen pellets in all. You never know.

I tore the place apart looking for the keys to his boat. I don't have a clear idea what I'll do when I leave here. For now my plan is just to get out in one piece. I have no idea what to do after that. I can't rule out the boat, no matter how dangerous and far-fetched that idea is. Then it dawned on me where the keys were: in the most logical place. With a sigh, I went back out in the yard and started digging up Miguel's body. I'd just buried him four hours before. If this keeps up, I'll become an expert gravedigger.

Burying a person is hard, but digging him up is harder. He appears little by little—first his hands, then his body...and that awful smell. And it hits you he's really dead. Fighting the nausea, I checked the pockets of his overalls. There were his keys, along with his wallet and a bag of some white powder. Poor guy. He was a dick, but he didn't deserve to end up like this. No one does.

I covered him up again and went back into his house. The best discovery I made was that the house used bottled gas to heat water. One of bottles was still full. After twenty days with no hot water, a bath sounded like a dream. I filled the tub to the brim, grabbed a good bottle of wine from my house, and soaked all Sunday afternoon in a huge cloud of steam. I'd earned it. I got the feeling it'd be a long time before I did that again. The next few weeks will be intense...if I live that long.

I've halfway figured out how to get out of here and not get eaten alive before I get past the front door. My plan still has a lot of loose ends, but I think they can be solved. I've had almost three days to relax, eat well, and build up my strength. Now it's time to act.

ENTRY 45
February 7, 1:12 p.m.

It's hard to decide what to take when you know you won't be back for a long time. It's even more complicated when your life depends on what you take. Any extras were out. I piled my survival kit, everything I considered essential, on the living room floor. I have a sixty-liter water-resistant backpack I used to take scuba diving. It still smells like the ocean and reminds me of all the good times I had with my wife. I also have a sleeping bag and the heavy coat I got off the dead soldier. I took my laptop, the shortwave radio, some clothes, an extra pair of shoes, and the freeze-dried food from Miguel's house. I also threw in the army first-aid kit with the morphine, antibiotics, and analgesics; a five-liter jug of fresh water; a small toiletry bag; some photographs I couldn't leave behind; a notebook and some pens; my camera; and all the batteries in the house. The backpack was filled to the top. In a smaller bag that clipped on to the backpack, I packed all the Glock and Zavala ammunition and a couple of flashlights. One of the flashlights was filled with xenon. I used to use it on night dives. It devours batteries, but it's bright as a lighthouse. All that weighed a ton.

With all that weight, I moved at a snail's pace. I had to carry all this to my escape vehicle. I knew that the key to my survival would be agility, but I couldn't do without any of these things. On top of that, I had to carry the rifle, the pistol, and the speargun slung across my chest, as well as a carrier with a frightened Persian cat inside. I'd only have one hand free to fight off those monsters. It was going to be awkward. I sure as shit couldn't fight off a bunch of them.

Miguel's street was full of those things. Two or three dozen of them wandered up and down, attracted by the shots from the other day. The scene from my window was disgusting. About thirty bodies with ghastly wounds, their clothes stiff with dry blood, swayed aimlessly in the road. A handful of them banged on my door. I saw no way to clear the street of those monsters so I could reach Miguel's vehicles parked out front. There were too many of them, and they were too scattered for the clanging-bear strategy to work this time.

The scene on my street was slightly different. Out of the big group that had been milling around, I could only see four from my window. Most of them had gone to Miguel's street the other day when they heard him shooting. That's so ironic. I was getting a shot at survival, thanks to his pointless death. The four on my street were clustered around my front gate. I had to figure how to move them away from there. I thought I knew how to do it, but I'd only get one shot. If I failed, I was screwed.

Once everything was packed, I set the bags in the entranceway, next to the front gate. Lucullus was very nervous. It took a lot of scratching behind his ears and whispers to persuade him to get into his carrier. He's never liked it. He always sits in the passenger seat. But I couldn't risk carrying the cat in one arm with those things after us. Sorry, Lucullus. If those creatures caught me, it'd mean certain death for you, my little friend. You'd have no way to escape.

I pulled on the wetsuit and checked the three guns. I walked through the house one last time, my eyes gliding over everything that was so familiar. I might not ever see it again. My whole life was here. I was setting off for an unknown destination with no assurance I'd be alive in half an hour. It was crazy. My living room, my kitchen, my study (I never painted it a color I really liked), the couch my little roommate scratched up. I went up to the attic in tears and looked around. I grabbed one of my wife's old sweaters. When she died, I'd packed away all her things. Now I was abandoning them forever.

I wiped my tears and headed to the backyard to set my plan in motion. The next time I write in this journal I'll describe what I did. If I don't write any more…well, obviously, something went wrong and there's a new undead walking around town in a wetsuit. But I won't go down without a fight. I'm terrified—but I'm determined.

ENTRY 46
February 7, 9:01 p.m.

I'm alive. Exhausted, horrified, and in shock—but alive. Lucullus is fine too, even better than I am. We've taken refuge in a fairly safe place. I lost some supplies along the way, but I'm still battle-ready. My God, there are thousands of those things! I should write all about it right now, but I'm exhausted. I'll write some more tomorrow, after I've gotten some rest.

Today, I shot a gun for the first time in my life. I'm sure it won't be the last.

ENTRY 47
February 8, 12:39 p.m.

The winter sun in Galicia is really tepid. Some people would say it's weak. Its caressing rays aren't very strong on icy mornings like today, but at least it warms your bones a little. Better than nothing.

Lucullus and I are lying on the roof of our little makeshift shelter, hoping to get on with our journey. As we ate a breakfast of beans from self-heating cans, images of the terrible day we had yesterday replayed over and over in my mind.

It was unbelievably terrifying. Yet I feel more alive now than I have for three weeks. When I went over the wall into my neighbor's yard, I wasn't sure my plan would work. The further I got into it, the more doubts I had. But I couldn't turn back. I raced across Miguel's yard into his pitch-black house. Those things were all riled up. Somehow, they knew I was on the other side. A couple of them had even made it through the front gate and were pounding on the boarded-up windows downstairs. The noise was deafening. I carefully climbed the stairs and opened the bedroom window; I was sure they couldn't see me up there. Down below was Miguel's delivery van, parked right out in front. He had complained several times that junkies tried to break into it, looking for amphetamines or Rohypnol, the so-called date rape drug, even though he didn't distribute those drugs. So he installed a powerful alarm in the van. It woke me up many nights when he accidentally tripped it. I wanted to see how those things reacted to all that honking.

I gripped the Zavala rifle, loaded two cartridges, then calmly aimed at the van. The mob under the window kept on banging on the door, unaware I was right above them. I fired. The blast from the rifle sounded like a cannon in the morning silence, amplified by the sound of the van's windshield bursting into a million pieces.

The alarm went off immediately with honking, flashing lights, and a loud, steady siren. The effect on the crowd below was electric. Most of them surrounded the van and started rocking and shaking it. A few spotted me in the window. They crowded around below, stretching their arms toward me, looks of hatred in their glazed eyes.

So far, so good. I rushed back down into the yard. I didn't have much time. Between the gunshot and the alarm, all the monsters in a one-mile radius would be drawn to this area in minutes. It would become a hot spot. I scrambled down the ladder like a monkey back into my yard. When I put weight on my poor ankle, a stabbing pain shot up my leg all the way to my eyes. For a moment everything went white and I almost passed out. No time to stop. I went in my house and upstairs to my bedroom to take a quick look.

I sighed with relief—my plan was working. Three of the mutants on my street were shambling toward the van. That blaring noise drew them like moths to a flame. For some reason, the last creature left on my street decided to cross the embankment at the end of the street. He'd probably fall, but that didn't matter. He wasn't close enough to stop me from getting to my car.

Breathing hard, I ran to the foyer, slung the backpack on my back, and crossed the speargun and the small bag over my chest. Then I knocked down the wooden posts that braced the gate and poked my head out. The coast was clear. For the second time in a month, I ventured outside. Only this time, I was setting off on a journey, and I didn't know if I'd survive.

Clutching Lucullus's carrier and the Glock, I crossed the road slowly, heading for my car, keys dangling from my wrist. I grabbed the keys and pressed the release button. My first mistake. With a double beep and a flashing light, my car opened, but that got the attention of the creatures on all sides. They turned and headed right for me. Shit. I had to move fast. I opened the driver's door and threw the backpack in the backseat with so much force that the bag flew open and some of my gear fell out. Out of habit, I went around the car to the passenger side to settle Lucullus in his seat.

My second mistake. As I came around the car, I saw a man in his twenties with long hair and goatee. He had on a filthy, torn black shirt and was missing both legs below the knees. I wondered how he'd lost them. He was lying on the ground, right behind the car. I don't know when he crawled there or how long he'd been waiting, but he startled me. I took a step back, but he still managed to grab my ankle (my good one, thank God) and sink his teeth in.

It all happened so fast. I stepped back so fast he couldn't get a good grip on my ankle. Plus my wetsuit was too thick and pliable for his bite to pierce it. He did leave visible tooth marks in the fabric. With disgust mixed with pure terror, I dropped Lucullus' carrier and grabbed the gun with both hands. I aimed right at his head, less than three feet away, and fired.

I'm no expert marksman, but I couldn't miss at that distance. I was really nervous, so I shot him in the head several times. It was a gruesome sight! I still shudder at the memory. It's not like in the movies. A bullet doesn't make a small hole; it opens a gaping hole. Blood clots, bits of brain, and bone fragments flew everywhere.

Trembling, I leaned on the car, trying to catch my breath, but time was running out. The rest of the creatures were less than thirty yards away, approaching very, very fast. I grabbed Lucullus's carrier off the ground and tossed it in the car. The poor guy meowed uncontrollably, scared to death. Before I got into the driver's seat, I aimed at the things coming from the main street and fired. My third mistake. I didn't have a clue how to shoot a gun, even at just thirty yards. All I did was empty the clip and make even more noise. Well, that was the least of my concerns. Every monster in the town must've heard the racket I was making.

I tossed the empty gun to the floor of the car and jumped behind the wheel. When I turned the key, the Astra coughed a couple of times, then started up. My blood ran cold. It hadn't been started up in several days. For a moment I thought it was going to stall—then I'd be screwed for sure. It's a good thing Opels are tough. Nothing fancy, but tough. I put it in first and drove toward the end of the street. I swerved to keep from hitting three of those things (I've prosecuted drunk drivers, so I know what a human body can do to a windshield and chassis upon impact) and turned on to the main street. The sight blew me away: a tide of nonhumans, hundreds of them, coming from downtown.

From the other side, there came several dozens more, eager for prey. I only had one way out—a country road at an intersection about twenty yards away. I floored it, made the turn, and—

ENTRY 48
February 9, 3:09 p.m.

As I was writing yesterday, with Lucullus in my lap, I heard a noise on the ground floor of our strange shelter. I climbed down the stairs with my stomach in knots, gun in hand. I looked all around but didn't find anything. False alarm. Maybe stress and exhaustion are starting to play tricks on me. Or maybe I'm hallucinating. Or worse—battle fatigue.

Back to my story. When I was in the car at the intersection of my street, the situation was not encouraging. Hundreds of those things were coming from downtown with that strange gait, deceptively slow looking but really fast, taking up the entire street. It was the grisliest sight you can imagine.

For the love of God! All those bodies—with wounds and amputations, covered in blood, pale, that awful look in their eyes—headed for my car, with a bloodlust, a longing to catch me. Damn it! You have to see a walking corpse in person to understand how terrifying it is. The sight of hundreds of them trying to catch you would make even the most laid-back person's hair stand on end.

The situation was no better at the other end of the street. There were fewer, but too many for me to drive through them without hitting one. If the crash didn't kill me, those things would. I only had one way out: the country road.

I live in an area that's been developed relatively recently. There are still some narrow country roads that wind through old farms, though they were being transformed into streets with buildings or town houses like mine. I knew there was one of those roads straight ahead. I didn't see any of those things on it, so it was my only choice.

I floored it and turned on to the smaller road, bouncing over a huge pothole. In the rearview mirror, I could see that a mob had gathered and was following me. To my horror, I realized that the engine noise would attract dozens of these creatures anywhere I went. All I could do was drive so fast they couldn't catch me, and they'd lose my trail. Sounds easy in theory. Fucking hard in practice.

That road was not exactly a highway. It was wide enough for one car. In places, its surface was just a bed of rocks and huge potholes. On top of that, I didn't know where it led. If it was a dead end, I was in serious trouble. I drove slowly, about fifteen miles an hour. I had to stop often and maneuver around a pothole, so those things never lost sight of me. Lucullus meowed plaintively in his carrier with each jarring bounce the Astra made. I was terrified and knew just how he felt.

I gripped the wheel really tight. The car lurched along. Once I heard a terrible creaking sound coming from the motor. That didn't bode well. I drove too fast through an especially narrow point and left both mirrors and the rear bumper lodged between two stone walls. I didn't give a shit. I had to get out of there no matter the cost.

A moment later, I ended up on a wider country road and had no idea how. I braked hard, throwing up a cloud of dust. There was nothing in sight. Not a soul, living or dead. I could see Pontevedra off in the distance, sitting on the banks of the Lérez River, silent, unchanging…dead. Here and there, columns of smoke rose from burning embers. I stared at long black scars where entire streets had burned to the ground.

I guess when the electricity failed, transformers and substations broke down and started the fires. There was no one to put them out.

I shook my head in disbelief. The only sound was the hum of the motor. As the dust cloud settled, I righted Lucullus' carrier in the passenger seat and whispered a few words of reassurance. No time for petting; he was going to have to tough it out for a while. I had to decide which way to go now.

Suddenly I knew where I was—the damn secondary highway I'd tried to use to get out of town almost a month ago. The one where I was stopped at the checkpoint. Well, I wasn't likely to run into a checkpoint now. If by some chance I did, I'd cover them with kisses as long as they took Lucullus and me into their custody. I'd played the Lone Ranger too long.

I rolled along the deserted road for a couple of miles. Not a soul was in sight, aside from two bloody figures staggering around in the distance on the edge of a cornfield. A small river between them and the road would stop them from following me, but it was only a matter of time before more of those things showed up. I finally came to the checkpoint. Cement blocks were the only memorial to the troops stationed there. They'd been put there to cut off the road, but someone cleared them away later. You could see the scrape marks they left on the cement as they dragged the blocks across the road. I don't know who moved them, what they did with the cement blocks, or where they went.

I continued for a mile or so, getting more and more worried. It wouldn't be long till I came to the main intersection. That would mean more homes and more cars blocking the road. And more of those things—a lot more. The county road ran through an undeveloped part of the belt around the city, but it was the exception. The rest was densely populated, so there were probably thousands of bodies wandering around. I couldn't forget the huge crowd following me. Many would get lost down other roads, or they'd stop. However, I felt sure a few would reach that spot.

Plus, the sun was setting. Nighttime is as dark as a well in an urban area with no electric lights. It would be suicide to continue. I had to find a place to hide. Fast.

Just when I thought I'd never find shelter, I came upon the perfect refuge on a small hill in the middle of a field thick with prickly broom plant. I spotted its little orange roof and sighed with relief. I know that kind of building well: substations along the pipeline that pumped oil across Galicia from north to south, to major cities. It would do nicely.

I eased on to the road leading up the hill. It grew narrower and narrower, overrun by vegetation. I almost ran into the high mesh fence. I could only see the gate. The rest of the perimeter fencing was completely covered by a thick layer of vegetation at least 150 feet high. You couldn't reach the fence without hacking through that jungle with a machete, and I seriously doubted those monsters could do that. The only access to the substation was down this road. It was a great place to spend the night.

Fortunately, the fence had a simple bolt, not a padlock. Wire was twisted around the bolt to hold the gate closed. It was pretty sloppy, but complicated enough to stop anything that wasn't human.

I drove through the gate and closed it behind me, then stopped in front of a hut. It was very small, roughly the size of a bedroom, but solid, with no windows. Its metal door locked with a key. After a few minutes, I finally forced it open with a crowbar I had in my trunk.

It was dark and dusty inside, lit only by a skylight and light from the door. In the middle of the room were some pipes, gauges, and valves used to purge air from the lines. I don't know if there's still gas in them, and I don't plan to find out. I'm not going to touch that stuff for anything in the world. The last thing I need is to gas myself or blow myself up.

I settled in and slept for almost twelve hours, then slept all day today, too. This is the first time in weeks I've been able to rest, without that constant pounding and moaning. It's great. I could stay here forever. But it's not especially comfortable. Plus, I'm down to about half a liter of water, and I'm getting thirsty.

ENTRY 49
February 10, 8:11 p.m.

Before all this started, I didn't believe in fate. I thought signs and omens were just old wives' tales. This morning, as I study the keys to Miguel's boat, I'm not so sure. Maybe his plan to head to his boat was a sign. Signs from the gods may not be irrational when the whole world has gone to hell in this merciless apocalypse.

I am sitting on the substation roof, soaking up the morning sun. The temperature has gone up a little over the past few days, but the skies are cloudy, so any time the sun comes out I'm grateful to soak it in after days of being cooped up and scared.

I have a plan. I'm going to do exactly what I told Miguel was impossible: head for the marina on Orillamar Avenue, get on his boat, and set a course for any place that's safer, with electricity, water, food, and people. In a word—paradise.

Pontevedra is situated at the far end of the ria—that is, an inlet—of the same name. It's only a mile or so from shore to shore at its widest point, with Tambo Island in the middle. Over the centuries the island has been a Celtic settlement, a religious site for the Germanic Swabian tribe in the 400s, a medieval monastery, a lazaret where they quarantined lepers, and, most recently, for many years a weapons depot for the naval base in the nearby town of Marin. Deserted since the 1970s, the island is now a nature preserve, one of the last tracts of pristine land in the densely populated area around Ria Pontevedra. That's my destination.

When everything started going to hell, more than one person probably thought of taking refuge on Tambo Island. There are military buildings, barracks, and warehouses on the island. It's accessible only by boat and is surrounded by strong currents. I'll bet the military took control of it. It may be the safest spot for miles. It's perfect. There was just one little problem—finding a boat that could reach it. That wasn't going to be easy. My idea was kind of risky, but it might work.

In a dusty corner of the substation were two large blue watertight plastic barrels. Judging from the labels, they once contained chemicals, but now they're empty. It took some work, but I finally fit them into the Astra by laying the backseat down flat. That left just enough room to squeeze in the backpack and the cat carrier. I left behind the shotgun ammunition, since I'd lost the rifle back on my street. Now my arsenal was reduced to four spears and a Glock with only thirty rounds after my futile shooting spree.

When I turned the key, the motor made a scary grating noise. My harrowing escape down that tortuous, bumpy little road has definitely damaged something. All the blood rushed to my feet, and I felt faint. If the car wouldn't start, I was a dead man. I wouldn't make it very far on foot in a populated area. I turned the ignition again and again, cursing under my breath. Oh, Jesus, let the motor start. Come on, come on, let's go, let's go!

With a muffled explosion, the motor started up, gasping and panting. Shouting for joy, I put it in first and rolled toward the main road, without a backward glance at that odd refuge. When I reached the county road, I headed for the main highway. Once I got there, things would get dicey fast. I figured it was about half a mile to the next turn.

The road proved to be even shorter than I thought. When the intersection came into view, I laid the loaded Glock on the passenger seat and floored it. Speed would be crucial. With squealing tires, I turned and headed north. The road looked deserted, but looks can be deceiving. Several of those creatures hovering around some houses nearby perked up when they heard my motor. With a roar, I sped away from them. I just had to go one mile. Just one damned mile. In a hundred yards, I encountered my first problem. An accident. A blood-splattered two-car pileup took up almost the entire road, leaving only a narrow passage on the left shoulder. I maneuvered around the wreck carefully so I wouldn't get stuck.

Suddenly, there was a sharp blow on the passenger window. Out of nowhere appeared two hands, followed by a battered body. The thing slapped the window and wailed over and over. My heart almost flew out my mouth.

Trembling with fear, I managed to drive away from that thing as I calculated my next move. Half a mile more. I passed several more abandoned or crashed cars. Some were splashed with blood; others must've been deserted in panic or madness. More of those things everywhere. Not a single living person in sight. Five hundred yards to my turnoff. Almost there. Three hundred yards. Two hundred.

Two more of those things, a woman and a man, popped up in the middle of the road. I didn't have time to swerve, so I ran into them. The man's body bounced off my bumper and slammed into the windshield, shattering it. I hit the brakes. I couldn't see out my broken windshield. Inertia propelled the man in front of the car when I braked. I think I ran over the woman.

The car stalled. I tried to start it, but the motor was completely dead, the dashboard a constellation of red lights. There was nothing I could do. It was kaput. An absurdly funny thought came into my head—now I didn't have to change the oil.

I got out of the car. Just a hundred yards to go. I could almost see it. I strapped on the backpack and grabbed the cat carrier. Glancing all around, I opened the trunk and hauled out the two barrels. The hundred yards were all downhill, so the two barrels would roll there on their own. I sent them flying with a kick and started to walk. Just then the man got back up. He was about seventy, and he looked even more horrible after I'd run over him. I didn't hesitate. He was about thirty yards from me. Before he got too close, I raised the Glock and fired. The first bullet went through his sternum, even though I'd aimed for his head. My second shot was at point-blank range and hit him in the face. That scene will haunt me for the rest of my days. I don't even want to think about it. Once the body fell, I turned to the woman. She was still lying on the ground; it looked like she had a broken spine. I didn't hang around to find out.

I ran down the hill, almost tripping, and finally caught up with the barrels at my destination: the dock on the Lérez River. It was deserted, but I'd counted on that. In the summer there was a boat rental service, but that wasn't what I'd come for. From there, the river flows downstream through Pontevedra and then empties into the inlet, right at the marina. My salvation. All I had to do was jump in the water and let the current drag me to Miguel's boat. Those creatures couldn't catch me in the water, and I could travel through the city without any danger.

With lightning speed, I threw the backpack and the gun in one of the barrels and sealed it up. I put the carrier with Lucullus in the other barrel. He was meowing uncontrollably, upset by all those hardships. With a spear, I punched holes in the top of the barrel. A little water would get in, but at least he could breathe. I tied the barrels together with a rope and dragged them to the river's edge. The water was dark and unfriendly.

The monsters were right behind me. With a deep breath, I leaped into the water, dragging the barrels along with me. I nearly screamed when I hit the icy waters of the Lérez. Hell, it's February. It must be about 39 degrees Fahrenheit. It's a good thing I was wearing my wetsuit. Even so, my body temperature plunged.

The current slowly dragged me down the river as those things watched helplessly from the dock. A couple of them fell into the water but didn't float back to the top. Either they stayed on the bottom or the current dragged them off—and away from me.

My hand is cramping up as I write this, and Lucullus is demanding food. He and I are still recovering from that adventure and getting settled in our new home, the *Corinth*, a beautiful boat that appeared out of the blue.

ENTRY 50
February 11, 3:49 p.m.

The cold is the worst feeling you can have in the water. Your muscles contract, your fingers gradually stop working, and you feel thousands of pinpricks all over your body.

It seemed like an eternity since I'd cut holes in the hood of my wetsuit. It never occurred to me I'd wear it in the water again. Icy river water poured through those holes and down my neck as Lucullus and I glided downstream. The wetsuit's thick layer of insulation was severely compromised.

The river was slow and lazy at that point. I hadn't realized that, this close to the mouth of the river, the combination of high tide and the river's back current would slow me down. I'd calculated that the trip would only take a few minutes, but in reality it was an hour-and-a-half ordeal. Still, I figured I was getting close. I accidentally swallowed water a couple of times and noticed that it tasted briny—seawater and river water mixed together. I was getting close to the mouth of the Lérez River.

My main problem was that darkness was falling over the water. In Galicia the sun sets early in the winter, around six. Visibility was getting worse.

Floating through the city in the dark, I ran the risk of not seeing the marina and overshooting it. If that happened, the tide and the current would sweep me into the heart of the inlet. That was a death sentence. With the low water temperature and no one to rescue me, I'd be a frozen corpse by the time I reached open water, or lying numb and helpless on a riverbank at the mercy of whatever awaited me there. I didn't have the slightest fucking idea what to do about it.

Darkness crept up the riverbanks. At least I wouldn't be visible. I grabbed a plastic bag floating next to me and covered my head with it. From the shore I'd look like a couple of barrels tied together with a plastic bag stuck to their side. Drifting trash. Nothing interesting. The perfect cover.

I was approaching the bridges that connected the two shores of the Lérez as it flowed through the city. The first bridge worried me the most. It was the nearest to the water, since the river was at its highest point there. If one of those creatures was standing on that bridge, it wouldn't have far to jump to trap me. As I floated under the bridge, I didn't look up. If something or someone was up there, it didn't see me.

As the river rolled on, its banks transformed into an urban landscape with buildings slowly rising around me. Its wide streets were deserted except for those things, hundreds of them, covered with blood, mutilated or intact, roaming up and down the streets.

The scene was shocking, especially the silence. The total, absolute, dismal silence. Nothing but the sound of water flowing around me. The city was dark and dead. The impact of this bullshit crisis was everywhere. Cars abandoned in the streets with their doors hanging open. Traffic accidents people had just walked away from. Some stores were open; others had their gates closed. Tons of paper, plastic bags, and trash were blowing down the empty streets. Dead traffic lights, broken streetlamps. The wind whistled through that ghost town. A void. Devastation. The apocalypse.

My vision grew increasingly limited. After a few minutes, the outlines of that canyon of buildings had become a blur. The anxiety was wearing on me. I've never liked being in the water at night, not knowing what's around me. I clung to the barrels and tried to peer through the darkness to make out any threat lurking there.

My fevered imagination raced along unbridled. At least thirty times, I thought I'd passed the marina, and each time it was a false alarm. Suddenly the ghostly form of the yacht club came into view, dimly lit up by the moonlight. I'd made it!

The Pontevedra Yacht Club was built on stilts on the banks of the Lérez River. Trying to splash as little as possible, I kicked my numb legs and swam for those posts. I planned to climb onto the pier, bypass my Zodiac, and head for Miguel's boat. Piece of cake. Three minutes, tops.

Hoisting myself up onto the pier took a titanic effort. After two hours in the water, my arms were asleep. When I finally got up, I lay on the pier, gasping like a fish, totally exhausted. If one of those monsters had showed up right then, I would have been a snack in seconds. I couldn't move a finger, let alone defend myself.

I stretched out with my eyes closed and listened hard. I couldn't hear a thing. So far, so good. I struggled to sit up and wrangle the barrels onto the pier. But first, Lucullus. I took his carrier out of the barrel. With numb fingers, I struggled to unlock the latch. The poor guy was scared, confused, hungry, and wet, but alive. My little friend deserved a prize. He'd endured a river journey, barely complaining, terrified but stoic.

I walked toward the boat, backpack and carrier in hand. When I got to the main dock, I froze. I couldn't believe my eyes. There were no boats. Not a single one. Not even my Zodiac. Every boat had disappeared. But how?

I sank to my knees, too tired to think, my mind a blank. My worst fear had come true. There were no boats. When the Safe Haven fell, the terrified survivors must've run to the docks, hoping to escape on anything that floated.

The masts of two sailboats stuck out of the water; the rest of those boats sat on the bottom of the river. Too heavy a load or lack of expertise, I guessed. They hadn't gotten far. Gradually I noticed more. My heart stopped. Blood and bullet holes were everywhere. Signs of a fight on the pier. A fight to the death over a boat. Survival of the fittest. A scene from hell. My God…

Suddenly it hit me. Maybe all was not lost. I remembered I'd seen sailboats on the other side, anchored far from the pier. Boats on the waiting list for a slip. A pain in the ass for their owners, since every time they wanted to take their boat out, they had to be ferried to them in a Zodiac. Maybe the mob hadn't boarded them. Maybe there was one left. I stuck Lucullus back into one barrel and my backpack into the other. As quietly as I could, I dived back into the dark waters of the Lérez.

I swam just a few strokes, but it felt like I'd swum the English Channel. My hope was fading as I swam closer. Nothing…but… wait! In the distance, with Venus reflected in the waters, I could see a swaying mast. There was one left!

Using my last ounce of strength, I splashed up to the sailboat. It was forty feet long, with graceful lines and a polished transom bearing its name, the *Corinth*. My new boat. My salvation.

I grasped the gunwale in the stern and dragged myself on board. I figured out why no one had taken this boat—and what I'd have to do to sail it.

ENTRY 51
February 13, 11:26 a.m.

It's pouring rain. The morning sky is a leaden gray. Violent gusts of wind are blowing out of the north, sweeping sheets of rain against the portholes in the cabin as the *Corinth* rides out the waves. The wind is whistling through the rigging, and rain is pounding the deck. I'm holed up in the cabin with a steaming cup of coffee, trying to get my thoughts together and plan my next move. There must be a powerful storm raging out on the open sea. Its undertow is rocking the boat. *My* boat. My new home.

When I boarded the *Corinth*, I wasn't thrilled with what I saw. Someone had tried to seize the boat but had failed. The pieces of the puzzle were coming together.

Dried blood was splashed across the deck. Splintered fiberglass and an ugly scar on the boom backed up my theory that someone had fired a weapon. I could picture the scene. Night fell at the Safe Haven. A tide of creatures broke through the lines of defense. The civilians panicked. Hundreds of people rushed to boats moored in the harbor, looking for a way out. There wasn't room for everyone, so it was dog-eat-dog. Proof of that struggle was everywhere. From the looks of it, they took the fight to the decks of the boats as they shoved off, overloaded, half-sunk, fleeing the doomed city.

The river must have dragged down many bodies that day. The image makes me sick. But something went wrong on the *Corinth*. On closer inspection, I figured out what.

The *Corinth* is forty beautiful, sharp, aggressive feet long. The deck is trimmed in chrome and teakwood. A real beauty. The interior is wide and spacious, comfortable yet compact, what you'd expect in this type of boat. I couldn't understand how anyone could have bypassed this gorgeous sailboat. Even the harbor's security boat, an old wooden barge, had been requisitioned.

The *Corinth* was anchored not at the pier but at the mouth of the river, tethered to the muddy river bottom. Instead of the usual nylon rope, it had a chain on its anchor. These days, chains are almost never used on sailboats because of their excess weight. Most sailors prefer the very high-tensile-strength rope mountain climbers use.

The previous owner of the *Corinth* must have been old-fashioned. To raise that heavy anchor, you had to use a small electric motor located next to the hawse hole in the bow. The chain is drawn up through that hole. On the horrific night the Safe Haven fell, a large number of people must've boarded the boat, hoping to escape out to sea. Some of them shot at other fugitives (and were shot at, judging from all the blood and bullet holes), while someone tried to weigh anchor. That person had no clue what to do. He didn't know the anchor was attached to bolts sunk deep into the silt at the bottom of the river. Instead of slowly winding the chain up, thereby releasing the suction that held the anchor at the bottom of the river, he ran that motor at top speed. It overheated and burned up.

The guy must have been too terrified with what was going on around him to realize he was overloading the winch. By then it was too late. With the motor burned out, there was no way to weigh anchor. Someone had tried to chop off the bracket with an ax (it was still in the hawse hole) but only succeeded in stripping the finish off the fiberglass. They couldn't cut the chain, and time was running out. A boat that couldn't sail served no purpose, so they must've abandoned it for another boat. End of story.

Now I was on the deck of the *Corinth*, trying to figure out how to free the anchor. I had to get the boat going at any cost. There was a way, but it meant getting wet again.

I dried Lucullus off and settled him in the cabin. Then I dived back into the dark waters of the Lérez and swam toward the yacht club. Once I got there, I headed for a protected corner where I could check out the main entrance. The gate was locked. Monsters were wandering around on the other side of the gate, unaware I was there. Signs of fighting were everywhere. The survivors must have locked the gate behind them to keep those things (or other survivors) from attacking them. Great! That meant I probably wouldn't encounter any walking dead on the premises.

I headed for a door at the back of the building, the warehouse where oxygen bottles were refilled. I'd been there many times. I even knew where they kept the key to the front door. Now I hoped to find equipment I could use to dive to the bottom and release the bolt that joined the chain to the anchor.

Just as I thought, the key was under a buoy next to the entrance. I slowly opened the door. In the dark, the room was terrifying. I thought I saw a figure looming in the background and fired a spear. Then I discovered it was a wetsuit on a hanger. Smooth move.

In one corner, covered by a tarp, was some diving equipment. It wasn't new, but it would do fine. I checked the oxygen level in the tank and the regulators and put it on my back. I slipped on the flippers and looked around for a mask, but there weren't any. Great. I'd have to dive into the murky waters and remove the pin in the dark with no mask. Once I had what I needed, I swam back to the *Corinth*. When I reached the chain, I dived down to the anchor. The bottom was about twelve feet down and dark as oil. I groped around and discovered that the anchor had caught on a rusty piece of metal sticking out of the river bottom. That's why the engine had burned out. I patiently wiggled the brass bolt, gradually loosening it. Just as my fingers went completely numb, the bolt suddenly came out. I barely had time to grab on to the chain as the *Corinth* glided into the inlet, carried out to sea by the tide.

I climbed up the chain onto the deck and took off the diving equipment. I dried off for the first time in hours and dropped the small emergency anchor through the hawse hole. When the boat was secured, I staggered into the cabin, collapsed on to a berth, and slept for twelve hours. I've been anchored here for days, waiting for the storm to pass so I can head for Tambo.

E N T R Y 5 2
February 14, 6:38 p.m.

Tambo Island is no longer an option. That sucks.

This morning, I dropped anchor fifty yards off the island in one of the small coves. From there, I could see some mutants wandering along the shore. Just a dozen or so, but that was enough. The island—and whoever had been on it—had fallen. Who knows when? I didn't have a clue. And I had no idea if there were any survivors.

This was a tragedy. I'd watched the island's familiar outline grow as the *Corinth* approached. Dozens of times over the years, I've sailed within a hundred yards of the island. I landed on it a few times, even though that's banned. But I'd never headed there with so much enthusiasm. That made my disappointment even more painful.

I was about twenty yards from shore, considering how to reach land without running aground, when I saw a sailor come out from behind some trees, wearing a white uniform and a flat cap. Apparently he didn't see me, because he headed back into the forest. I ran to the bow, waving my arms like a madman. Just then he stumbled on a rock and almost fell, revealing his left side. He was missing half his face, and his once-pristine white uniform was the rusty color of dried blood. His eyes were empty, lost, like the eyes of all those damn things. My shout of joy died in my throat. They'd found a way there. That's fucked up.

I slunk back to the cabin and got drunk on cheap wine, my hopes fading as I gazed at the shore. So close and yet so far. I couldn't even land. I counted at least a dozen of those things, but there had to be more. I wasn't familiar with the island, so I didn't know what surprises I'd find there. I had no backup if something went wrong. It'd be suicide.

I cried bitterly. I cursed and spat over the side in anger. Those monsters roamed along the shore, unaware that a few yards away, on the *Corinth*, fresh meat awaited them. They can kiss my ass.

That afternoon I made a decision. I weighed anchor and coasted along the western end of the island until I reached a spring-fed creek I knew of. A small path was all that connected a steep cove to the rest of the island. I didn't know if those things could maneuver down that winding path, but at least it would slow them down. Relying on that, I rowed ashore in the small inflatable dinghy stored on the *Corinth* and filled the water barrel I'd found on board. It held about fifty liters, more than enough for the journey I was planning.

Not a single creature showed up while I was at the spring. For a moment I toyed with the idea of hiking up the road and taking a look around, but I decided against it. I was no trained commando. I was barely armed. It cost me part of my sanity just to keep myself safe, let alone play the hero. If there were people in trouble on the island, I felt sorry for them. They'd have to fend for themselves. In this new world, only those who protected their own ass would live to see another day.

I rowed with some difficulty as I towed the filled barrel to the *Corinth*. Taking one last look at the island, I raised the anchor and set a course for the mouth of the inlet. To my new destination.

ENTRY 53
February 15, 2:19 a.m.

It's a miracle I'm still alive.

The last few hours have been exhausting. As the *Corinth* approached the mouth of the inlet, conditions at sea grew worse. A powerful storm must've been raging near the Azores archipelago in the Atlantic Ocean, hurling wave after wave against the coast of Galicia. Typical winter gales. No one in their right mind would sail out in this shitty weather. But I had no other choice.

As I sailed away from Tambo Island, my head was reeling. My grandiose escape plan had just been to sail for the island and let the military, or whoever was in charge, take care of me. Discovering that the island was one more slice of hell was a huge blow. I had no idea what the hell to do next.

As I hoisted the water barrel on board with a pulley, I spotted the port of Marin on the southern shore of the inlet. It was completely empty. There too anything that floated had been used to escape. Even the docks at the naval base were deserted. Normally two or three navy frigates and even an aircraft carrier were docked there. Now it was a scene of devastation and chaos, with dozens of figures staggering around aimlessly, covered in blood.

Where the hell had all the people sailed off to? They couldn't have just scattered to the four winds. They must've gone ashore somewhere. Maybe another Safe Haven. Or maybe they set a course for Vigo. It's one of the largest ports on the European Atlantic coast. And it's just twenty nautical miles away.

That's it! The Safe Haven at Vigo must still be holding out! Anyone with a boat would head there, confident they'd be safe. With those thoughts percolating in my head, I quickly pulled up the anchor and set off for my new destination.

Maybe it was fatigue or the excitement of getting under way. Maybe I was so anxious to get out of there, I wasn't paying attention. In any case, my mistake was unforgivable. I've lived my whole life by the water. I know when conditions aren't right for sailing. This time I didn't pick up on them. All the clues—dirty gray waves, seagulls flying low, wind gusts out of the north— should've set off alarm bells. But my mind didn't register them. All I could think about was getting out of there as fast as I could.

After three or four hours, it became crystal clear that the sea was going to be very choppy. Fifteen-foot-high waves shook the *Corinth* like a nut in a shell. Curtains of water crashed onto the deck, drenching me as I clutched the tiller, stubbornly trying to make it to the mouth of the inlet. If the storm was this fierce in the inlet, what was the open sea going to be like?

The wind blew mercilessly. The seaworthy *Corinth* sliced through the waves like a knife as I peered at the coast through the foamy spray. It was clear I wasn't going to make it very far. I decided to head to a little port named Bueu, a couple of miles from the mouth of the inlet. I'd hunker down there until the weather improved.

Convinced I was doing the right thing, I made the second mistake of the day. No matter how much experience you have at sea, never get overconfident. That's exactly what I did. As I turned

toward the coast and angled the *Corinth* into the wind, the spinnaker started to flap. I left the cockpit in the stern and went to the
bow to tie it up. Suddenly a wave struck the hull and knocked me
off balance.

In the blink of an eye, my entire body was hanging overboard,
with one ankle caught in a loop in the line. I was slammed against
the boat as we headed for shore with no one at the helm. My head
and shoulders hit the hull hard. I blacked out for a moment but
came to fast with waves breaking right on my face, nearly drowning me. The situation was really dangerous. If I couldn't get back
on board, I'd either drown upside down or I'd fall and be set adrift
as the boat crashed onto the rocks on the shore. Lucullus certainly
couldn't sail the boat. Cats make lousy sailors.

After a few anguished minutes, a sudden change in wind
tilted the *Corinth* to the other side. Suddenly lifted up and hurled
against the gunwale, I grabbed one of the cleats and hoisted
myself back on board. Soaked and dazed, I pointed the *Corinth*
toward the port of Bueu. The ship slowly responded to the wind
and gradually stopped shaking. In seconds, we were speeding for
the port with the wind at our back.

I started trembling violently. I'd almost lost my life. I could've
been injured or killed in a ludicrous way or set adrift, which was
the same thing. My stomach was churning so badly that I stuck my
head over the side and threw up all the salt water I'd swallowed.

I'd just learned an important lesson. The undead weren't the
only things that could kill me. Accidents, disease, hunger—all the
normal causes of death—were just lurking in the shadows, waiting for their chance. If I weren't careful, they'd catch me. I'd only
been thinking about my stalkers. I'd forgotten something very
basic: man is a fragile being.

I'm now anchored in the port of Bueu, a safe distance from
the dock, while the storm rages on. The coast is dark and silent,

jolted by flashes of lightning that light up the buildings' ghostly silhouettes. The roar of thunder shakes the entire boat.

I know they're there, on the shore. I think they know I've arrived. But that's not the worst part. I've realized I need something basic. To get it, I'll have to go ashore tomorrow. Right where those things are. Into the mouth of the wolf.

ENTRY 54
February 16, 10:13 a.m.

I've never liked rain. That's a pretty futile way to feel, since rain's a regular part of life in Galicia. However, as I watched the rain fall on the small fishing village of Bueu, I decided, in the end, it was not so bad. It might even help me.

The storm lasted for nearly twelve hours. Rain and wind lashed the coast. The sea, shaken and stirred, was an ominous steel gray. Normally the fleet would stay moored in the harbor and sailors would drink a hot toddy in the bar. But as far as I can tell, there's no fleet and no sailors. Not living, anyway.

Despite being sheltered behind the Port Bueu breakwater, the *Corinth* pitched violently in the remnants of the powerful storm. The wind shook the rigging and dragged sheets of rain across its deck. The scuppers could barely keep up with all the water. I could just make out the buildings onshore. Five minutes out in that storm and you'd be soaked to the bone.

Yet this weather gave me the edge. The wind and rain would cover up any noise I made on land. And visibility was really low. This time, the weather was my ally.

I had to go ashore. I badly needed nautical charts. The fugitives who attacked the *Corinth* couldn't get the boat out of the harbor, so they looted anything they thought they could use, including the charts. Without them, I risked hitting a shoal or debris in the water. Plus in their flight they tried to start the GPS built into the control panel. All they'd accomplished was to break the LCD screen. It was of absolutely no use. Although I only had to sail along the coast to Vigo, my experience at Tambo taught me not to take anything for granted. After Vigo, my path might lead me someplace else, and I needed to be prepared.

Besides, my supplies were getting really low. I could stand a couple of days on half rations, but Lucullus looked at me indignantly each time he got a whiff of the meager rations I served him.

I don't know what Lucullus thinks of all this, but I'm sure what really bothers my little friend more than being scared and bounced around and getting wet is the catastrophic state of our pantry. I don't want a cat mutiny. I'll give him credit, he's holding up like a champ. He's the only company I've had for almost a month. If it weren't for him, I'd be half out of my mind.

I'd made a decision; now I had to come with a plan. The prospect of going ashore was really frightening. I didn't know what I'd find beyond what I could see from the deck. So my plan was just to reach the shore, get what I needed with as little hassle as possible, and get the hell out of there. I'd have to wing it the rest of the time.

I put on my wetsuit and grabbed the Glock, its two magazines, the speargun, and four spears. I strapped on the empty backpack and climbed down into the *Corinth*'s lifeboat. The rain and pounding waves nearly drowned me. I ignored the cold rising up my legs and rowed cautiously toward the dock on the deserted shore.

As I rowed, I noticed that the usually muddy, oily water at the port was strangely clean. The environment had changed amazingly fast after just a couple of weeks with no humans. I hardly saw any animals except birds. There are hundreds of them, especially gulls.

I shuddered when I recalled that, besides eating fish, gulls are scavengers. Lately they must've had all the carrion they could eat.

I finally reached the steps to the dock. I tied up the lifeboat and quietly climbed the stairs. I glanced around. The storm was still raging over the deserted dock. The pounding of the rain and the wind whistling through the streets combined with the rhythmic din of thunder. The wind lashed my face, dragging rain across my eyes. I couldn't see or hear anything more than five yards away. It was perfect.

I crossed the dock on high alert. When I reached the fish market, I pressed my back to the wall and poked my head around the corner. I saw two of those creatures, a young man and an elderly woman. They stood stock-still in the middle of the walkway, looking strangely desolate. The pouring rain plastered their clothes to their bodies. After nearly a month out in the elements, their clothes were starting to wear out. Now they really looked like something out of a horror movie. As if they hadn't before.

Flattened against the wall, I started forward, with the speargun and Glock ready. I came within four yards of them, but they didn't see me; the storm, the growing darkness, and the rain hid me. Yet I was sure they sensed I was there. As I passed them, my nerves taut as piano wire, they snapped out of their trance. They began to stir, turning in every direction, trying to get a bead on me. Their senses may have diminished when they crossed the threshold of death, but they'd developed another "sense" that allowed them to detect beings. They knew I was close. Very close. It was just a matter of time before they located me. I had to hurry.

Slithering along walls, crouching between cars abandoned in the road, I made it to a nautical supplies store I knew of. Then I realized two things. First, the store's wrought iron gate was down. I'm such an idiot. I hadn't thought about that. How the hell was I going to get through the gate with no electricity and no key?

Second, about a dozen of those things were coming down the street toward me.

I needed a solution. Fast. Suddenly, I saw it. Parked in front of the store was a delivery van. I crawled across the hood of the van onto its roof. The rain was harder than I expected, and I almost slipped a couple of times. I became hysterical as those things got closer. Shit!

I finally managed to climb onto the roof of van. From there, the second-story balcony was less than three feet away, right above the store. I took a deep breath and jumped. Almost slipping on the moss growing on the ledge, I let myself fall inside the railing. The glass balcony door was locked, so I broke it with the handle of the gun. The pouring rain muffled the noise of breaking glass.

The balcony door opened quietly and smoothly. Inside the enclosed balcony, I could make out heavy wooden furniture. A musty smell assailed my nose as I stepped inside.

I eased up to the bedroom door. I reached for the glass doorknob, took a deep breath, jerked the door open, and jumped back.

Nothing. Just a dark room. Fumbling around in the backpack, I pulled out a flashlight, lit up the hall, and entered the dark room. A monstrously large antique canopy bed loomed out of the dark. The place smelled musty from the damp and from being closed up. But behind that smell, in the background, I detected a faint smell of decay. I pictured the worst.

I heard rain pouring through the downspouts in the background. From time to time, a powerful clap of thunder shook the house. The storm was right on top of the town. I admit I was scared to death.

Next was the dining room. On the other side of the room a staircase led downstairs. I figured this house and the nautical supply store on the first floor had been owned by the same person. As

I started down the stairs, I heard a noise totally unrelated to the storm. It was a constant, rhythmic beat accompanied by…bells?

Bam, bam, bam, bam, bam, bam! Then suddenly the noise stopped. Then it started up again, with those damn bells in the background. It was maddening.

The noise was coming from the floor I was on, not downstairs. From the back of the house. I could have ignored it and gone downstairs, looted what I needed, and left the way I came in. But I'm human. Besides being irrational, stupid, and unpredictable, humans are really curious. I needed to know what the hell was making that noise. Shaking, scared shitless, holding the Glock in my right hand and the flashlight in my left, I walked to the other end of the house.

I walked through a small living room with a TV, a couple of sofas, some two-month-old magazines, and a lonely kneesock left on a table. I came to another door at the other end. The noise was louder here. I was getting closer. When I reached the door, I looked through the keyhole. I didn't see anything, but the smell of decay was more intense here. Holding the flashlight in my mouth, I jerked the door open, only to find a shorter hall with two doors.

Bam! The banging got louder, clearer, more intense. A whiff of rotten air stung my nostrils. *Bam!* I walked cautiously down the hall, trying not to throw up. *Bam! Bam!* I shone the flashlight all around; the hall was clear. All I saw were some lithographs of nautical scenes and the two doors. One of them was half-open and led to a bathroom. I carefully pushed the door. It opened with a creak as I flashed the light around the room. Empty.

Bam! Bam! Bam! Bam! The creak of the bathroom door caused the jingling and blows to increase. No machine made that sound. Whoever it was, he'd heard me. Holding my breath, I planted myself in front of the door.

I still had time to turn around and leave. Whatever it was, it knew I was there, but it hadn't come out. Either it couldn't come out or it wasn't interested in me. And I wanted nothing to do with it. But I had to know what the hell it was, so I grabbed the knob and yanked open that damn door.

Jesus, I still shudder. That godforsaken room must've been the master bedroom. A quilt covered a huge bed. Lightning filtered through the half-closed blinds. At the foot of the bed, giving off an infernal odor, lay the body of a woman whose age I couldn't determine. Clutched in her hands was a shotgun, pointing up. She'd stuck a gun in her mouth and pulled the trigger. The top of her head was gone. She'd been dead for weeks. Shining the light on to what was once her face, I saw fat white worms protruding from what remained of her mouth. I gagged and threw up in a corner for what seemed like an eternity. My small contribution to the hellish scene.

Bam! I got to my feet like a bolt of lightning, a trickle of vomit dangling from my mouth. I shone the flashlight and saw him. A little boy about three or four, strapped into a high chair, barefoot and wearing overalls.

He was one of them.

When I shone the flashlight on him, he started to squirm, and the high chair bumped into the wall, making the pounding sound I'd heard. Rattles attached to the front of the chair jingled and shook as he looked at me with empty, dead eyes, his little arms outstretched, trying to catch me. What a sight!

Disgusted, I backed into a corner and watched that little monster. The woman who lay at my feet must be his mother. When the little boy contracted the virus, it was too much for her. She saw what he'd become and didn't have the courage to kill him, but she couldn't go on living either. Trapped in the house, desperate, alone, she shot herself. That monster must've been strapped in that chair for weeks, unable to break free and search for warm-blooded, living beings.

That little monster never stopped swaying, agitated at the sight of me. With what little cool I had left, I raised the speargun and aimed at his head. A weak, threatening growl came from his dark, foul-smelling mouth. Trembling, with tears running down my cheeks, I pointed the speargun at the boy. I closed my eyes. And fired.

I know I did what I had to do, but I can't help thinking he was practically a baby. It's the most horrible thing I've ever done. It will haunt me for the rest of my life.

I pulled out the bloody spear and wiped it clean on the woman's clothes. I stumbled out of that room from hell. I had to get a hold of myself. I'd come here with a purpose. I had to work fast so Lucullus and I could live another day. I wiped away my tears and headed down the stairs to the store.

It was dark. Fucking dark. The stairs were black as a tunnel. In the halo of light from my flashlight, I could make out the steps and the wrought-iron railing, which twisted and turned in a complicated pattern. I was still trembling and had the bitter taste of vomit in my mouth. My tongue was dry as straw. I could've killed for a glass of water.

I started down the steps cautiously. They creaked and groaned. Outside, the storm raged, the wind blew with a fury, and lightning lit up the scene. It was an eerie scene, right out of a horror movie. But this was not a fucking movie. I was in the middle of all that shit. Suddenly, I felt the urge to run away as fast as I could and cower on the *Corinth*, but that wasn't a viable option. Not anymore.

I finally reached the landing. The door was locked, but the key was in the lock. It turned with a loud *click*, and, presto, it opened.

Very carefully, I poked my head in and shone the flashlight on a shelf with fishing rods and reels lined up in neat rows. I was inside the sailing shop. Great. Gaining confidence, I took a few steps and swung the light across several shelves, my mind racing through my shopping list. I shouldn't linger. In one corner I saw some sailboat harnesses. After the incident on the way here, I thought that would be a good "purchase." I set the gun and spear on a nearby shelf and, pointing the flashlight toward myself, got engrossed in choosing a harness in my size. It almost cost me my life.

There was a roar, and a stack of fishing rods collapsed next to me. A pair of waxen white arms shoved them aside. The rest of the body followed. He was a man about forty, pale and ghostly, with dead eyes, his mouth ajar. One of them.

He closed in on me fast. Before I knew it, he was on top of me. My weapons were too far away to do me any good. His claw-like hands grabbed my arm, and his momentum pushed me backward, off balance. I stumbled and fell back against a display case, dragging the monster with me.

With a loud crash, we landed on a pile of compasses. The monster was on top of me, his entire weight pressed down on me. Somehow I got hold of his arms. With one leg bent between us, I kept his mouth away from my face. His expression was absolutely crazed; his jaw snapped open and closed, biting the air like a rabid dog. One bite nearly ripped off my nose.

As I held him off, my mind was racing. The bastard was so strong. I didn't know if those things got tired, but of course I did. My arms cramped up. The situation was becoming desperate.

With one last effort, I rolled onto my right hip. The thing's body crashed into the display case. Its steel corner dug into the base of his spine. A human would have writhed in agony, but he wasn't fazed.

Now we lay side by side, like lovers entwined in bed, but I was certainly not feeling sexy. One of his arms was trapped under my body. Through my wetsuit, I felt his fingernails raking across my back. Fortunately the neoprene was too thick and the position too awkward for him to get a firm grip.

But now I had one arm free. Amid the confusion, the flashlight had fallen off the shelf, so we were in complete darkness. I ran my free hand over the nearest shelf above my head, groping around for something, anything. I grasped a heavy, cylindrical object and, with all my might, slammed it down on the creature's head. It didn't slow him down. I hit him again. Nothing. I knew you couldn't knock out those sons of bitches with a blow to the head, but knowing that wasn't going to save my life. Then something happened as I took my last swing.

A slippery, greasy liquid poured down on me. At first I thought the thing was bleeding, but it was too sticky and thick to be blood. Then I thought he'd vomited on me. I was disgusted, and I drew strength from that thought. I lowered my other arm and, with my bent leg, kicked his body and pulled away. I slid away surprisingly fast and crashed into another row of shelves.

The blow made me see stars. A million white, green, red, and blue dots danced before my eyes. Slipping and sliding, I stood up as I heard the thing fall less than three feet from me. Leaning on the display case, I realized it was the same one I'd set my weapons on. I groped around for my gun, praying the flashlight hadn't fallen on the floor. Behind me, that thing struggled but couldn't get to his feet.

Beads of sweat rolled down my forehead. Suddenly, my fingers found the butt of the Glock. I turned and fired into the dark.

The shot sounded like a cannon in the confined space of the store. My ears ringing, I tried to grasp what I'd seen in the flash of light from the first shot. Correcting my aim, I fired three more times.

The roar of gunfire and the smell of gunpowder engulfed the room. The thing just stopped moving. Gasping for breath, I swung the Glock in all directions, squinting in an effort to see in the darkness. I bent down and felt around for the flashlight. Finally I found it and shook it, relieved that it wasn't broken. I turned it on and surveyed the scene.

It looked like a hurricane had hit the place. Display cases were lying on the floor, overturned in the struggle. The creature's body was leaned against a wall as if he were asleep. Blood was gushing out of a huge black hole in his forehead.

The floor was covered with a thick, oily substance. I bent down to inspect it. I realized I'd hammered on his head with a can of boat motor oil. It had split open and spilled all over us. Thanks to that, I was able to slide free, and the monster had slipped several times, giving me time to find my gun. A simple can had saved my life. The irony isn't lost on me.

I was covered in motor oil from head to toe. I must've looked pretty grim, standing there amid the devastation, the dark, sticky oil running down my body. As the adrenaline roared through my body, it sank in that I was still alive. If it hadn't been for that can of oil and a lucky shot, that bastard would be snacking on me, and I'd be one of them. I felt sick to my stomach again, but I had nothing left to vomit up.

He must have been the child's father. Now I understood how the little boy got infected. His wife had locked her husband down here in the store when she saw what he'd become, and run back upstairs with her little boy, not knowing he was doomed too. That sucks.

The metal gate was locked in place, and there didn't seem to be any more creatures in the store. But the sound of gunfire had drawn a small crowd that was banging on the other side of the gate.

I had to do three things: secure the area, find what I'd come for, and figure out how to escape this madhouse. And I had to hurry.

ENTRY 55
February 22, 6:15 p.m.

Was it Roosevelt who said, "The only thing we have to fear is fear itself"? But he was never locked in a store in the dark, pumped full of adrenaline, covered in motor oil, with dozens of eager monsters banging on the gate six feet away, determined to kill him. I'm sure he would've been afraid. Fucking afraid.

As I looked at the pile of rags lying at my feet, the magnitude of the situation hit me. I collapsed, exhausted and trembling, on to a pile of rain slickers and stared at the gate, which shuddered with every blow.

There were no other noises, not even thunder. The storm had dissipated after venting all its fury. The gurgle of rainwater streaming through the gutters was all that remained of the storm that had raged over Bueu while I was fighting for my life.

I leaned against the shelf and struggled to sit up. I looked around, every sense alert. I quickly checked out the store to make sure there were no more surprises. There was no other exit, just a small bathroom and a storeroom with neatly piled merchandise. Nothing out of the ordinary, except for a rust-colored bloodstain in one corner. That must be where the guy had gone through his transformation, alone in the dark, lying on the floor like a dog. I shuddered at the thought.

I didn't have much time. In a matter of minutes the place would be surrounded, and I'd be done for.

I rushed around, shoving half the store into my backpack: two complete sets of charts of the Spanish and North African coasts— one drawn by the Spanish Navy and one by the British Admiralty (still the best), a high-quality GPS with a plotter connection, a couple of compasses, dozens of flashlight batteries, signal flares, a telescopic fishing rod, a box of hooks and fishing line, a safety harness, a spare wetsuit, two high-tech spearguns, and two dozen long, ominous, molten steel spears. Three loaded spearguns were definitely better than one.

I stuffed all that into my backpack. As I climbed the stairs to the top floor, I started laughing hysterically and couldn't stop. With those spearguns, my backpack, my torn wetsuit, my body covered in oil and blood, I must've looked like some wacko slasher.

Once upstairs, I went into the kitchen for some provisions. The last thing I wanted to do was run around town, dodging monsters, looking for a store that hadn't been ransacked. When I left home, I'd toyed with the idea of going to the shopping center for some groceries and supplies. But it dawned on me that, in the last days of the Safe Haven, loads of people must've had the same idea. The armed forces had probably plundered every store in the country to feed the multitudes in the Safe Havens.

Fortunately, the pantry was really well stocked—pasta, canned goods, tomato sauce, rice, and flour. I also took some bags of sugar and five pounds of coffee. I was about to leave when I discovered a large supply of baby food. I stood there looking at all those jars lined up, knowing I'd killed the baby that food was intended for. The thought turned my stomach.

With tears in my eyes, I packed up the baby food the little boy's mother had so lovingly stored away. Not for me, but for Lucullus. He'd love it. On my way out, I discovered a wet bar. I took a couple of bottles of gin and half a carton of Marlboros. Great! I planned to have a smoke when I got onboard to help me sleep. And forget.

My backpack wasn't completely full, but it weighed far too much, considering I had to dodge that howling crowd all the way to the dock. I peeked out the front window. There was no way out there. About two dozen ghostly, soaking wet undead had packed into the narrow street in front of the store.

I tiptoed back to the kitchen. The window opened onto a narrower street. It was deserted. I stuck my head out and looked to the left. I could see the sea. That would be my escape route. I went back down to the store and cut about ten yards of the heavy-duty rope used on boats. Back in the kitchen, I tied one end of the rope to a radiator and cast the other end out the window. All I had to do was climb down and make it to the end of the street before those bastards saw me. Piece of cake!

But first I had to raise the blinds. They were rain-soaked, so I had to yank them up with all my might. It sounded like a machine gun in the dead silence of the street.

I shimmied down the rope and landed carefully so I wouldn't aggravate my injured ankle. I ran toward the end of the street, easily dodging a couple of those creatures along the way, one at an intersection and another behind a telephone booth on the opposite side of the street. I kept running and didn't look back. I didn't dare. In my fevered mind were images of a horde of bodies filling the road, following me in silence, cornering me in a blind alley, and finishing me off.

Fortunately, the street wasn't a dead end. It ran parallel to the one I'd come in on and ended at the port. I stayed out of sight, crawling along the breakwater, slowly approaching the lifeboat. This return trip took almost three times as long. I slipped on the rocks, got all banged up, and nearly cracked my head open. By the time I reached the boat, I was soaked and scared out of my wits. In a normal world no one in his right mind would crawl over algae-covered rocks pounded by the last waves of a storm with the wind furiously pushing against him. But this is no longer a normal world.

Darkness was falling when I finally scrambled onto the dock and made my way to the little boat. As I paddled gently through the swell toward the *Corinth*, my blood froze. Something was moving on deck! Those bastards had gotten out there somehow!

Suddenly, the shadow on the deck stood perfectly still, as if it had spotted me. A howl greeted me. Lucullus! My poor cat, confused and upset at being left alone for so long, had gone on deck, looking for me. It breaks my heart to think about it. As I approached the *Corinth*, I could see the little guy, drenched and shivering, but proud, at the ship's rail. He'd kept watch on deck, riding out the storm, waiting for me. Atta boy.

With the last of my strength, I climbed on board, hauled up the lifeboat, and emptied out the backpack. I took a long shower and dried Lucullus off (he never stopped purring), then we sat down in the cockpit to eat, staring at the silent, dark streets of Bueu, where just hours before I'd nearly lost my life.

It would be dawn soon. After an unimaginable week, the storm had subsided. It's time to continue our journey. To our next destination. To hope.

ENTRY 56
February 23, 6:00 p.m.

Good thing the only mirror on board was the little one above the minibar. I was spared the look of excitement on my face as the *Corinth* approached Vigo.

The last few hours have been intense, exhilarating, and liberating. At first light, I raised the anchor and let the boat slide lazily away from the dock to the center of the inlet, riding the tides and the current. The silence was broken only by screeching gulls and cormorants as the *Corinth* drifted away from shore. The morning was cool and bright, with no trace of the terrible storm. A perfect day for sailing.

Before this hell, fishing boats would be heading out. You might even see a sailboat zigzagging in between tankers headed for the port of Marin. But yesterday morning I didn't see a soul as I stood at the stern, bundled up, a cup of strong coffee in my hand. I guided the boat to a windier area. I looked all around, but the landscape was completely dead. I felt like the last man on earth. It's really disturbing.

When I thought the breeze was strong enough, I let out the genoa sail and a small jib. The *Corinth* sprang forward, quick and high-strung as a horse that's spent too much time in the paddock. Before I knew it, we were sailing at a good seven knots.

As I watched the whitecaps we left in our wake, Lucullus came on deck. In one agile movement, he stretched and jumped into my lap. Ever since he was just a little ball of fur, he's been very independent, like all cats. But with all this chaos, I can hardly get rid of him. Maybe he senses, in a feline sort of way, that the world has changed. He wants to be near the only part of his universe that hasn't disappeared. Me. I welcome all the affection, but sometimes it's too much. Way too much. Still, he's a charmer. And my only companion.

Throughout the morning, the wind brought us closer to the end of the inlet. I scanned the silent towns on both coasts with binoculars, hoping to catch a glimpse of some sign of life. Bueu, Combarro, Sanxenxo, O Grove, slid slowly by. All I saw were dark, silent buildings, abandoned cars, and lots of those things wandering aimlessly. Somehow they'd made it to places that were evacuated before the Safe Havens fell.

I have a theory that those mutants retain some memory of what they were in life, and that draws them to where they used to live. That's probably bullshit, but since I seem to be the only man alive, my theories are the best in this part of the world.

That led me to wonder if anyone else was still alive in one of the thousands of homes overlooking the river. What must've gone through his mind when he saw a boat cutting through the water toward the ocean? If I were trapped a mile from the sea and I looked out and saw the *Corinth* sail by, I'd die of anguish.

I prayed no one signaled to me from the coast or the surrounding mountains. There was no way I could rescue anyone, but guilt would've made me try. Attempting something that stupid would surely have led to my death.

With that thought, I put the binoculars away and stopped scanning what I was leaving behind. Time to focus on something more productive. Lucullus and I had eaten canned or packaged food for nearly two months. We needed some variety in our diet. I baited a hook and set the fishing rod on the stern. Then I sat down with a cigarette to enjoy a morning of fishing and sunbathing. After just twenty minutes, I had half a dozen mackerel flopping around in a bucket, ready to grill. For a few hours I forgot those monsters, the end of the world, and my anguish at being separated from my family. For a few hours it was just me, my cat, my boat, and the sea.

But when I went in the cabin to get a knife to gut the fish, a cloud marred that perfect day. Hanging in a corner was my dirty, torn wetsuit. It had saved my life so many times. Now it swayed to the rhythm of the waves. It was a reminder of all the evil wandering along the shore, waiting for me, as if it were saying, "Sooner or later you'll have to come back down to earth." Shit.

At least the fish I grilled up on deck was delicious—the first fresh food I'd eaten in months. Seeing Lucullus quivering with excitement by his bowl as I served him a mackerel made me understand the phrase "lip-smacking good."

Things changed as I came around the tip of Morrazo Peninsula at the southern end of the Ria Pontevedra and the northern edge of the Ria Vigo. Although waves six to ten feet high shook the *Corinth*, it proved extremely seaworthy. Unfurling the spinnaker, I got up to an amazing nine knots. The bow cut through the waves, sending up big plumes of spray. I yelled and screamed like crazy with a wild look on my face as cold seawater washed over the cockpit, soaking me. It was great!

Nighttime was a different matter. I couldn't sleep, so I mulled over the sailing route. The last few hours have been exhausting, but great. The *Corinth* stayed right on course and entered the Ria Vigo via the route laid out on the chart. After nearly twenty hours of sailing, I anchored off a deserted beach and settled down for a good night's sleep. At dawn, I'll cover the latest few nautical miles to the huge commercial port of Vigo. I plan to dock at the section of the port owned by the Citroën car manufacturer. I hope somebody gives me a warm welcome.

[V I G O]

ENTRY 57
March 5, 5:38 p.m.

|||||||||||||||||||||||||||||||||||||||||||||||||||||||||||||||||||||||||||||||||||||||||||||||||||||||||||||||||||||||||||||||||||||||||||

It's been days since my last entry. Up till now, my captors haven't allowed me to board the *Corinth* to get this book and my personal belongings.

Ten days ago I sailed into the port of Vigo and dropped anchor. The *Corinth* rocked gently in a breeze blowing off the port. The waves at ebb tide splashed lazily around its long, thin hull. Without sails, the mast swayed gently, with an occasional *clink* as steel clips struck the aluminum wheel. There I was, in the midst of that bucolic scene, propped up on the deck, slumped against the hatch, a half-empty bottle of gin in my hand, eyes brimming with tears.

Vigo was dead. Totally, absolutely, horribly dead. A corpse. Kaput. Not a living soul in sight. I was anchored two hundred yards from the docks of what had once been a city of a quarter of a million people. The docks were crowded with those mutants, in numbers I hadn't seen before. Amid unprecedented devastation, they wandered up and down the port.

The port looked like a battlefield. Charred vehicles, large warehouses blown apart by some powerful explosion, even a couple of amphibious Army personnel carriers with all their hatches open. It was a really creepy landscape. Thousands of bodies lay burned, decomposing everywhere. Walking around, oblivious to everything were the victors in that battle: the undead.

I was right. The Vigo Safe Haven had held out to the end, the last refuge of southern Galicia. But I'd gotten there too late.

The scariest part of that hellish landscape was the main docks. The masts and antennae of dozens of half-submerged boats protruded out of the water. Here and there you could see a half-drowned ship, and even some hulls belly-up, indecently exposing their propellers.

To complete the chaotic landscape, dozens of bodies hung like ripe fruit from cranes in the port. Some kind of hellish circus, right out of Dante's *Inferno*, must've played out on those docks. There were signs of gun battles and fire everywhere. Pescanova, one of the largest fisheries in the world, was nothing but a charred heap.

Earlier that day, as the metropolis came into view, a chill ran down my spine. Through my binoculars, I could see ugly scars all across the city, made by huge, devastating fires. No firefighters were battling the still-smoldering embers. Storms had put out the flames. As I drew near the port, I was sure I wouldn't find anyone alive.

For hours I sat there, leaning against the hatch, too stunned to react. I didn't know what to do, where to go. Terrible dark thoughts crossed my mind. That scene was too shocking to be true.

After a few hours, a lot of alcohol, and tons of self-pity, I was able to focus on the one thing that stood out in that scene. Six hundred yards from shore, anchored peacefully, was an old freighter, painted red and white. Wide bands of rust were visible at the waterline. It had been through hard times, but was still in one piece. It was the only boat I'd seen afloat since I left Pontevedra. Its presence defied all logic.

I got up the courage to approach, since I had nothing better to do. Without much enthusiasm but with a gentle breeze at my back, I raised the anchor and let the *Corinth* drift toward that hulk, imagining how to board it and loot some supplies.

I finally made out its name and home port: *"Zaren Kibish—Nassau,"* it proclaimed in huge white letters. It was flying a limp, frayed Spanish flag and a piece of cloth so faded and wrinkled it could've been the flag of any country in the world. Next to that was the radar mast with its rigid antenna.

As I got closer, I could barely make out, in the glare of sunlight, a strange bracket incongruously hanging over the side. I wondered what the hell it was. Just then, the "bracket" jumped up and ran down the deck, yelling. For a moment I thought I'd gone crazy. It took me a second to realize that what I'd taken for a piece of steel was actually a person's legs dangling over the side. A living being's leg! Dear God!

An electric current ran through my whole body. I let out a whoop and rushed toward the bow, waving my arms and jumping up and down. The first figure multiplied into two. Behind them appeared another half dozen.

Tears ran down my cheeks as I brought the *Corinth* alongside the *Zaren Kibish*. They were the first humans I'd seen in weeks.

They threw me some lines so I could tie the *Corinth* by the bow and stern. Then they unfurled a rope ladder, which I scrambled up like a monkey, anxious to get on deck and embrace my new friends.

The first thing that greeted me when I stepped on deck was the black barrels of assault rifles aimed at my face. Behind them was a group of glowering, foreign-looking guys. I was not well received on the *Zaren Kibish*. Something was horribly wrong.

ENTRY 58
March 6, 5:26 pm

The sun beat down on the deck of the *Zaren Kibish* and bounced off the hulls' steel plates. I didn't move a muscle, waiting for the crew to make the first move. Sweat was running down my back. I couldn't say if it was from the heat or from fear.

Those men were really puzzling. Half of them looked Asian; the other half looked like a UN delegation on a world tour. I cautiously raised my hands and said a timid "Hola." Not one of them grinned. I introduced myself in English, Galician, Portuguese, and French, exhausting all the languages I knew. No one even raised an eyebrow in response.

The situation was getting ridiculous. A dozen people on deck, boiling in the midday sun, staring at each other, not moving a muscle. Worst of all, I was on the wrong end of their rifles, and my arms were cramping after five minutes with my hands in the air.

Suddenly, pushing through the sailors, a heavyset middle-aged man appeared. He looked Slavic and was wearing a heavy wool jacket; leftover food studded his bushy gold beard. From the respect the sailors showed him, I surmised that he was the captain of the *Zaren Kibish*. I was becoming sorrier and sorrier I'd boarded.

He came over to me and stood with his hands on his hips. He looked me up and down for a good couple of minutes, deep in thought. Finally he must have made a decision. He barked a couple of sentences in a language completely unknown to me, and the guys lowered their weapons.

Taking a couple of steps forward, he held out his ham-sized hands and crushed mine, regaling me with a huge smile. The atmosphere on deck relaxed. I was so relieved, I almost couldn't speak.

The big man introduced himself in English with a Slavic accent. His name was Igor Ushakov, from Ukraine, captain of the *Zaren Kibish*. He welcomed me to that floating heap of junk. Before I could react, the sailors surrounded me, clapping me on the back, flashing huge smiles, speaking half a dozen incomprehensible languages. Fortunately Captain Ushakov barked some orders in his booming voice and saved me from being crushed by their displays of affection.

Questions raced through my head as they led me inside the ship. A couple of sailors climbed down to the *Corinth* to get Lucullus, who was meowing desperately.

When we got to the captain's quarters, I realized I'd interrupted his lunch. With a sweep of his hand, the captain invited me to sit at his table. Before I knew it, I had a plate of something that that might loosely qualify as beef stew and a glass of cold beer. As I wolfed down the food, Ushakov kept looking at me, deep in thought. After I'd finished the surprisingly tasty stew, he started asking questions. Who was I? Where did I come from? Where was I going? Had I met many people along the way?

Leaning back, stuffed, I related the story of my life over the past two months. He seemed more interested in the current situation at the mouth of the inlet than in my close calls with those monsters, but he listened politely to the end. Then it was my turn to ask questions.

The ship was the *Zaren Kibish*. It sailed under a flag of convenience from the Bahamas, but its owner was a Greek woman, and her business partners were Estonians. It was loaded with forty thousand tons of steel spools. It had been anchored in Ria Vigo for over a month. As on most international carriers the majority of the crew was Filipino or Pakistani; the rest were from a mix of Third World countries. The only trained sailors on board were the captain and his first officer, another Ukrainian. He commanded the crew in a mixture of Tagalog and Urdu, with the Pakistanis or Filipinos acting as interpreters. The rest were cheap labor, wet behind the ears. They wouldn't have passed even an extremely lenient inspection. A floating garbage heap, like thousands sailing the waters around the world—or that used to.

With a grunt, Captain Ushakov got up from the table, went to a cupboard, and took out a bottle of Ukrainian vodka and two delicate little crystal glasses. He poured two generous shots and handed me one, scratching his head as if he were rummaging through his sonorous English for the words to continue his story.

"We sailed into Ria Vigo right before the European Union closed all the ports," he began. "They hadn't ordered everyone to gather at the Safe Havens, so we saw nothing out of the ordinary. Vigo was the first port we'd seen in almost two weeks, so we were eager to go ashore and find out what the hell was going on."

"Two weeks?" I interrupted. "Where the hell had the *Zaren Kibish* been?" I couldn't believe it. While the world was going to hell, this man and his crew sailed halfway around the world, oblivious to it all.

"Port Pusang, South Korea. Our destination was the port of Rotterdam, but we had to dock at Vigo because the drive shaft was damaged after we sailed through a storm near the Canary Islands." He shrugged and poured another round of that explosive vodka.

"And you've been here ever since?" I asked, astonished. "Why didn't you get the hell out when you saw what was happening? Maybe head for the Canaries?"

"We couldn't," he replied laconically.

"Why not?" I said, stunned.

"I can't change the boat's course without the boss's approval. Company policy."

"But your company doesn't exist anymore!" I replied, amazed at his stubbornness.

"Out of the question," he replied stubbornly as he poured himself another drink. "I'd lose my job."

End of discussion. He was loyal to the company, and that was that. Their boat had broken down. He'd anchored in the harbor to wait for instructions that never came. He wouldn't dream of moving an inch.

In vain I explained it was highly likely his bosses were now wandering around somewhere in Estonia or Greece, turned into monsters like the ones on the shore, but there was no way to change his mind. Ushakov had been a captain in the Soviet navy and joined the civilian fleet when the Soviet Union fell apart. He still thought like a soldier. Without orders, he wouldn't move a muscle. He was convinced there was still someone making the decisions. What if no one was in charge? Unthinkable!

Then I heard the frightening tale he had to tell. Reluctantly he began the story of the last days of Vigo's Safe Haven to explain why they were still alive.

The military and civilian authorities thought the best place for the Safe Haven was the free trade zone at the port of Vigo. It seemed ideally suited to accommodate large crowds. It had a fence around the entire perimeter, large warehouses and store-houses stocked with nonperishable food, a desalination plant, and access to the sea for receiving supplies. The astonished crew of the *Zaren Kibish* watched two hundred thousand people mob the port. In just a few days, the multitude reached numbers they'd never dreamed of.

A place they thought would never fill up couldn't handle this human tide. The overcrowding got out of control, as refugees from all over Galicia and even neighboring northern Portugal joined the original refugees. The Safe Haven was soon at maximum capacity, but refugees kept thronging to its doors. Plus, no one dared leave the Safe Haven. That'd be suicide, since the undead already roamed the area.

The Safe Haven was supposedly commanded by a civilian committee made up of the mayor, a representative of the provincial government, and two *conselleiros* of the Xunta of Galicia who happened to be trapped there. But the commander of a navy frigate docked in Vigo and an army colonel really ran the whole show. Together they directed the military forces defending the Safe Haven.

Ushakov stopped abruptly and looked up from the bottom of his glass. "Here's where the story gets *unpleasant*." He studied me. "Sure you want to hear the rest?"

I swallowed hard and nodded, unable to speak. With a sigh, Ushakov continued.

ENTRY 59
March 7, 6:42 p.m.

At first, everything went according to plan. The military forces at the Vigo Safe Haven—about six hundred men from various units of the army, navy, and Civil Guard, along with what remained of the local police—maintained the integrity of the perimeter. They had plenty of combat equipment, including several armored personnel carriers and a couple of helicopter gunships. Docked in the harbor were a navy transport ship and an F-100 frigate, fresh from the shipyard, equipped with a modern Aegis missile system. The civilian and military command center for the entire region was based in Ferrol, in northern Galicia.

"Their defenses easily took out the first waves of undead," continued Ushakov. "They were well entrenched and had enough firepower to keep the undead at bay. But more and more came, and ammunition grew scarce."

"How do you know all this?"

"During that time I went ashore with some of my men," he said with a shrug. "One of my crew was in the hospital they'd set up in a warehouse. He fell and broke his hip during the storm. We visited several times."

"Why not stay on land?"

"I couldn't abandon my ship," he replied, giving me a that's-a-no-brainer look. "The Safe Haven authorities wouldn't let us stay more than a few hours." He poured another glass of vodka. "Their supplies were running low, and they didn't want any more mouths to feed." As the days went by, the Safe Haven filled to overflowing. Two hundred thousand people became 350,000 as groups from other Safe Havens and isolated survivors arrived. It was the only place humans controlled for 250 miles around.

From the start, there were problems with supplies and disease. A crowd that size consumes several tons of food every day. The supplies they thought would arrive by sea never came despite promises from authorities. There were no supplies to send.

The commanders quickly organized looting parties. Every day, columns of armored trucks, escorted by soldiers and volunteers armed to the teeth, left the Safe Haven and returned at nightfall with pounds and pounds of food. But that plan soon failed. Once they'd looted the shopping centers downtown, the expedition had to go farther and farther, with increasingly discouraging results. On a good day, they brought in about thirty tons of food, not enough to feed all those mouths. So they started rationing.

"Rationing," I whispered, stunned. "How can that be? The malls around here are huge. There should've been enough food to last for years."

"My dear boy," Ushakov said, shaking his head. "Think about how much food three hundred and fifty thousand people eat every day. The biggest shopping centers could only feed a crowd like that for a week. Tops. Then supplies ran out, and there were no delivery trucks to replenish what they'd consumed."

I was speechless, stunned. I pictured how desperate the looting parties must've felt, crossing the dead city, surrounded by thousands of those things, forced to strip every little corner grocery store, risking their lives for less than two hundred pounds of food. Damn, they must've been demoralized.

"Food was not the only problem," continued Ushakov mercilessly. "Three hundred and fifty thousand people shitting and pissing generate a lot of waste. The plumbing system couldn't handle it all. Soon the port smelled like a sewer." A smile lit up his sad face. "Life aboard the *Zaren Kibish* looked like a dream to that mob of people on land."

I couldn't speak. The pressure in my chest tightened as the story unfolded.

"Disease quickly followed the filth, the way it usually does in situations like this. The port had maybe one or two thousand bathrooms. That's an average of three hundred fifty people per crapper, *nyet?*" Ushakov was talking louder now. "Typhus and other diseases spread like wildfire."

"Other diseases?" I uttered in a hoarse voice. My throat felt like sandpaper.

"*Da*, other diseases. Those in charge didn't take that into account. Even in a crisis, people were still people. They had cancer or high blood pressure, children came down with childhood diseases, women gave birth..." He frowned deeply. "There were outbreaks of botulism from eating spoiled food." He sighed. "A sailor on this ship came down with it. Diseases began to take their toll. Part of the port was turned into a cemetery. You can see it from our deck. In a few weeks several hundred mounds covered it." The vodka bottle was almost empty. "They were the lucky ones."

Ushakov snorted, hoisted up his huge bulk, and went to the cupboard for a second bottle. Then he continued. "Things spun out of control. Desperation and the law of the survival of the fittest undermined the Safe Haven. There were fights, thefts, and murders as people fought for food. The military declared martial law. Dozens of murderers and thieves were hung from cranes in the harbor as a lesson for the rest. Only the crows and gulls benefited from that as they feasted on the eyes of the hanged."

The situation was dire. The need for food was overwhelming, so the fighting continued. The survivors had two choices: live in purgatory at the port or face the hell outside. They'd come to the end of the road.

"When things got ugly, a boat loaded with soldiers boarded the *Zaren* and searched for provisions. They couldn't find anything, of course." Ushakov winked at me. "We'd hidden most of our food in the hold with tons of steel coils. Thanks to that, we never went hungry."

My first reaction was that he'd been incredibly selfish. Then I realized he'd made the logical decision. I'd have done the same thing. As I studied the pensive Ukrainian staring at the wall behind me, it struck me that this guy was devious. And very smart.

"What happened next?"

"Then things got really nasty. One dark night, the frigate and the military transport weighed anchor and quietly left the harbor. On board were all the navy personnel, civilian authorities, and two or three hundred people with connections, influence, or money." He shook his head. "I don't know where they were headed. The Canary Islands, maybe. Some place the infection hadn't reached. They just took off and left everyone else in the lurch," he said, knocking back another shot of vodka.

As I sipped my vodka, Ushakov told me that the next day, when the crowd discovered that the military vessels were gone, all hell broke out. The most surprised was the army colonel who commanded the three hundred soldiers left at the Safe Haven. He and the navy commander had crossed swords. The confrontation got so bad, no one let him in on the escape plan. Colonel Jovellanos was a strict disciplinarian in every way. The tense situation and the responsibility for the safety of all those people rested too heavily on his shoulders. It weighed on him so much that he lost control.

When the crowd discovered that the warships were gone, they went crazy trying to board any boat in the harbor. A rumor spread that the frigate was headed for the Canary Islands, the only place in Spanish territory the plague hadn't reached. Any boat accompanying it would be allowed to dock. Jovellanos knew this rumor wasn't true. To make matters worse, 80 percent of the boats in the port couldn't make a journey of thousands of miles on the open sea, so he did what felt was right. He dispersed the crowd with bullets. It was a real massacre. Then he gave the order to shell all boats in the harbor and sink them. If there was no way to escape, survivors at the Safe Haven would have to fight to the end. What he didn't know was that all hope for the Vigo Safe Haven was gone.

The *Zaren Kibish* was saved from being sunk because it was anchored quite a distance from the port, and its broken drive shaft prevented it from sailing off. Still, every day dozens of desperate people swam to the freighter, begging to be allowed on board. Ushakov was very strict and ordered his men not to even come out on deck. The *Zaren Kibish* couldn't afford to host dozens of starving, sick, desperate survivors.

"That was the situation at the Vigo Safe Haven when it happened."

"When what happened?" I asked.

"The day the Vigo Safe Haven fell," he replied, ominously.

ENTRY 60
March 8, 5:13 p.m.

Thick clouds rolled in as we talked in the stiflingly close air of that unventilated cabin. A storm was brewing, but it was nothing compared to the earthquake inside me as I listened to Ushakov's story. I couldn't tear myself away from that story. I needed to hear it. I needed to know everything.

"Things really fell apart about a week after the boats sailed away." His eyes clouded up. "That was to be expected."

"Why was that to be expected?"

"Think about it, Mr. Lawyer. When the ships sailed off, all naval personnel were on them, plus a few lucky soldiers. That left the overwhelmed Colonel Jovellanos with only three hundred men to defend the entire perimeter of the Safe Haven and the hundreds of thousands of men, women, and children crowded into it."

"Yeah, so?" I admit that all the vodka I'd drunk had clouded my mind. I didn't see all the implications. Ushakov, like any good Ukrainian, was used to the poison and didn't seem affected.

"Well, that's obvious!" He snorted. "They were so short of troops, he had to recruit volunteers from among the civilians huddled like rats in the harbor and equip them with combat gear." He paused. "That was the only way he could continue to control the perimeter. Considering how low their spirits were, that was a recipe for disaster."

Through my alcohol-induced haze, I grasped the situation as Ushakov mercilessly reeled off the events he witnessed from the deck of the *Zaren Kibish*. Jovellanos recruited several hundred civilians, armed them to the teeth, and had them patrol the perimeter or sent them on looting missions outside the Safe Haven.

But they weren't soldiers. They were just armed civilians dressed like soldiers, with no notion of urban warfare and survival. Add to that, they were desperate and hungry. Casualties mounted dramatically. Every time a volunteer fell, his equipment was lost, so the defense capability was slowly but inexorably reduced.

"That's when the captain started talking to himself. By now there were tens of thousands of those creatures mobbing the fence around the harbor. I could see them through my binoculars. It was a horrible sight—thousands of those *prvotskje*, packed together, silent, with their horrible wounds, all dead yet still walking." His brow furrowed. "It is a punishment from God, I have no doubt."

"What happened then?"

"What happened was what had to happen. Those monsters overran the port."

"But how?"

He glared at me. "How? What difference does that make? The fact is they got in. That's what matters. It could've been anything. Maybe some of the civilians on mission outside the perimeter got infected and weren't brave enough or disciplined enough to report it until it was too late. Maybe those things found a breach in the perimeter. Or maybe one night someone forgot to lock a gate or didn't double-check a padlock." He spread his arms and shrugged. "They got in…and then it was chaos."

I could picture the scene as Ushakov described it. Some infected creatures slipped inside the perimeter and wreaked havoc. Panic broke out. An avalanche of humans rushed aimlessly from one side to another, trying to escape those things. That chaos was their downfall. If Jovellanos had had more soldiers, he could have done something, but he didn't stand a chance with his cobbled-together civilian militias and the remnants of military groups. The units he sent to restore order were trampled by a panicked crowd that wouldn't listen. The few professional soldiers that remained tried to wade into the crowd and confront the undead. Since there so few of them, the crowd kept them from acting quickly.

"No matter how much firepower you have, if you're alone on a battlefield filled with enemies, you're screwed." He scratched his head, looked at me gravely. "We learned that in Afghanistan years ago. It was the same here."

The few surviving soldiers were cut off from the rest of their units. They put up a heroic, desperate front against the growing number of undead. Finally they were swallowed up by that tide. From that point on, the fate of thousands of refugees was sealed. They were unarmed, trapped, panicked, and helpless. The die was cast.

"Those who were crushed to death or suffocated by the crowd were the lucky ones." Ushakov's voice was almost a whisper. "At least they didn't see what came next."

I hardly dared to ask. But I had to. "What happened?" My voice broke.

"When the colonel saw all was lost, he applied his own type of 'final solution.' Weeks before, his men had placed explosive charges filled with highly volatile chemical fertilizers in the warehouses and barracks in the port. He reasoned that if everything went to shit, he'd drag all the fucking monsters he could to hell." Leaning his hulk back, Ushakov rubbed his eyes and blinked. "But it went terribly wrong."

"What happened?"

"He miscalculated the impact of the explosions." He pulled a crumpled pack of cigarettes out of his jacket pocket and handed me one. I grabbed it, eager to have the taste of something besides alcohol in my mouth.

"Many people had taken refuge inside the warehouses. When the charges went off, the roofs crashed down in flames on their heads." He lit the cigarette and exhaled a plume of smoke. "They were burned to death or crushed almost immediately. They were very lucky."

"Why do you say that?"

"For the thousands still on the port, running from one place to another, there was no escape." His gravelly voice quivered. "Picture the scene that night. In the dark, lit up by just the glow of the fires, thousands of people ran nonstop, terrified, not knowing if the group behind them was human or the undead. From the *Zaren* we could hear the shouting, moaning, howling, and a few shots. The smell of smoke and charred flesh hung thick in the air. You wanted to throw up." He bowed his head, looking feverish. "It was a window right into hell."

I shuddered. I imagined the horror and utter despair those people must've felt, trapped in the port, cornered by those things. When they were bitten, those former refugees were now hunters, joining the pack of the undead, attacking their friends or relatives. The eerie glow of roaring fires lit up that madness.

"There's not much more to tell. The carnage continued for thirteen or fourteen hours. We couldn't see the shore because of all the smoke. Finally, all the noise stopped. We didn't hear another thing except the occasional crackle of a charred building collapsing or the low moan of one of those things." He paused. "Well, and that sound, of course."

"Sound? What sound?"

"At first we didn't know what it was. We were used to the racket hundreds of thousands of people made. Now the port was strangely quiet, the way it is now," he said, pointing out a porthole.

"The silence took us by surprise. That's how we were able to hear the noise."

"You still haven't told me what the noise was," I protested.

"You keep interrupting me!" he snapped. "As the dense smoke lifted, we figured out the source of the sound." He shuddered. "It was the sound of thousands of feet, in shoes and barefoot, shuffling across the pavement." He looked at me. "The feet of all the refugees who didn't die before they got infected and became undead."

I was horrified, crushed by the thought of hundreds of thousands of innocent people bitten and maimed, rising again, turned into monsters. Jesus, it was shocking. I felt dizzy. I needed some air.

"Evidently, not all the refugees succumbed. The most resourceful, the hardiest, a handful, maybe even a few hundred, found a way to survive that terrible night. They hid in the ruins of the port until the vast crowd of undead scattered. When only a few hundred undead remained on the pier, they fled in every direction, alone or in small groups," concluded Ushakov.

"Yeah?" I looked at him, glassy-eyed. "How do you know?"

"Simple." He smiled, gesturing theatrically. "One of those survivors is on board the *Zaren Kibish*. I'll introduce you to him," he said. He stood up and headed for the cabin door.

I got to my feet to follow Ushakov. But as soon as I stood up, I felt nauseated. I realized that my delicate Western stomach couldn't handle the combination of vodka, damp heat, the gruesome conversation, and the smell of food and motor oil. I pushed aside some chairs, threw open a porthole, and left a lovely pattern of vomit on the hull of *Zaren Kibish*. Terrific! I was making a great impression on my new friends.

I wiped my mouth, turned, and headed back to Ushakov, who was watching me from the cabin door with an ironic look on his face. He must've thought I was a wimp, but at least he didn't say so. He simply nodded for me to follow him.

We walked down a short hallway crowded with pipes and cables and lots of doors. Overall, the ship was a complete wreck. It was amazing to think it had traveled tens of thousands of nautical miles from Southeast Asia. We came to a hatch at the top of a staircase that led down to the bowels of the ship. The damp, musty smell was stronger there, but I seemed to be the only one who noticed.

Through the open hatch, I saw a cabin laid out like the captain's cabin, but smaller, with narrow cots instead of a wide bed. Sitting on one of the bunks was a heavyset man in his fifties. His face was very wrinkled, and his beak of a nose was covered with broken capillaries, on account of his fondness for alcohol. Across from him sat another man in front of an upside-down wooden box with a chessboard set up on it. He was about forty, short, muscular, blond, with piercing blue eyes and a droopy mustache. He reminded me of the comic-book hero Asterix the Gaul.

When we entered, Asterix and Drunk Nose were engrossed in the final moves of a game of chess. They jumped to their feet when they saw us.

Ushakov exchanged a few quick sentences with them in Russian. He pointed to me several times during the conversation. I felt very ill at ease. Ushakov and Drunk Nose were having a heated discussion about something. Asterix merely looked at them sadly and occasionally gave me a resigned look. Finally, Ushakov turned and beckoned me over.

"Mr. Lawyer." I didn't like the sound of that. It had a disrespectful ring. "May I introduce you to the first officer of the *Zaren Kibish*, Mr. Aleksandr Grigori Kritzinev," he said, pointing to the man with the red nose.

I shook his hand cautiously, as Ushakov introduced me in a torrent of Russian I couldn't decipher.

"My first officer is old school. He says he's sorry he hasn't mastered any language but Russian, so I pass his greetings along to you."

"Tell him I'm happy to be aboard this ship and to meet all of you."

"Such formalities aren't necessary between friends, *nyet*?" Ushakov replied in a tone I was starting to dislike. "Let me introduce Mr. Viktor Pritchenko, Ukrainian like Alexander and me, and survivor of the Vigo Safe Haven."

I studied the little blond guy with the mustache as he shook my hand and tried to keep the surprise from showing on my face. What the hell was a Ukrainian guy doing in Vigo? What a strange coincidence. I was totally blown away when the Ukrainian guy addressed me in halting, rudimentary Spanish.

"Nice to meet you, sir. My name, Viktor, Viktor Nikolaevich Pritchenko."

"You speak Spanish?" I replied, astonished. He wasn't what I expected.

"*Da*, I living in Spain for six months. I live in Spain several times before, since four years. I come Spain every year," he answered, with a sad look in his clear eyes.

"What brings you to Spain?"

"I work. I work many years for Siunten."

I was too stunned to ask what or who the hell Siunten was. There'd be time for that later. I realized a few things as I looked at the little man and his honest blue eyes. He wasn't lying to me. But he was terribly afraid. Something had terrified him, and they'd kill me if I figured out what it was.

I could see that Ushakov, who didn't speak Spanish, was uncomfortable not knowing what we were saying. He abruptly cut off our conversation, barking a couple of orders to his first officer and sending him and the Ukrainian guy up the stairs. He beckoned me to follow him. As we climbed the flights of stairs, he told me the rest of Viktor Pritchenko's story. The night of the slaughter at the Safe Haven, he swam to the *Zaren Kibish* and shouted for help. When Ushakov heard him speaking Russian, he decided to take him aboard. He's been there ever since. In the port, he worked as a longshoreman or technician or something like that.

Ushakov's story made me suspicious. He wasn't telling me the truth—at least, not all of it. What was he hiding? And why?

When we reached the top of the stairs, I was surprised to discover we were headed for the bridge. When we got there, Ushakov sat at his captain's chair, his eyes boring into me.

"What's going on?" I asked, more and more confused.

"Let's see, Mr. Lawyer. If I remember correctly, you told me you're from a town near Vigo, *nyet*?"

"Yes, Pontevedra, twenty miles away," I replied, not sure where he was going with that.

"So, you know this city pretty well, right?"

"Well...yeah, sure." I was more confused. I didn't understand where those questions were leading, but something was in the air.

"*Da*, perfect." He thought for a moment. Then out of the blue he blurted out, "Know where the main post office is?"

"Sure. What the hell is this about, Captain Ushakov?"

"Oh, come on. I'm sure a smart guy like you has figured it out. I need something from there."

My expression must have been comical. From the post office? What was he up to?

"Two months ago, I received the last communiqué from the company," he began wearily. "When we docked in Vigo, right after the storm, the first thing I did was phone the company's agent in Spain for instructions. But the phones weren't working in Estonia, and no one answered in Greece." He stretched out in his chair. "He promised to mail me complete instructions from

Madrid, but the evacuation to the Safe Haven prevented us from picking it up at the post office."

"Why are you telling me this?"

"Isn't it obvious, my young friend? I need that package. Someone has to pick it up. Someone who knows where the post office is. That someone is you."

I just stood there, staring at him. Was he joking? This guy was asking me to go ashore, cross a city infested with thousands of undead, as if I were just going out for a loaf of bread? He wanted me to find the post office and deliver his damn package like some postman? The vodka had definitely addled his brain more than mine.

"Captain, you can't be serious. I'm sorry about your package. As far as I'm concerned, if it's in that post office, it can stay there till the end of time. You don't know what you're asking. I've been around those things. Let me assure you they're monsters." I was getting all riled up. I couldn't help it. "It's sheer madness! It's absolutely impossible for a person to set foot in that city without those hellish monsters getting him! I'm dead serious!"

"Oh, you won't be alone. My first officer and some of my men will go with you." He smiled mischievously. "That package is from my employer, and you're a stranger, so we don't know if we can trust you. Your only job is to guide them there and back."

He was nuts. I had to get far away from there.

"I'm sorry, Captain, but count me out," I said as I stood up. "I appreciate your hospitality, but I think I'd better go. So, if you don't mind—"

"Oh, I'm afraid you've got it all wrong," he interrupted. "I'm not asking you. I'm ordering you. If you don't agree in five minutes, you'll be floating in the water with a bullet in your head. You don't have a choice." That son of a bitch leaned back in his chair, looking very pleased with himself, and glared at me. We both knew he had me by the balls.

I swallowed hard. My blood turned ice cold at the sight of Ushakov comfortably seated in his captain's chair, watching me. That bastard thought that was funny.

"Come, come, *tovarich*, don't take this so seriously." He leaned forward and whispered right in my ear, "After all, I'm just asking a small favor in exchange for another favor, *nyet*? I brought you on my boat. In exchange, you bring me the one little thing I need. That's all."

"You have no idea where you're sending us, Captain. We could all die for one lousy package sent by someone who's probably dead," I said, forcing back my anger.

"I'm counting on your expertise to bring everyone back. You've made it this far without a scratch, *nyet*? I'm confident you can take that little trip without anything bad happening."

"Do I have a choice?" I asked, grimacing.

"I'm afraid not."

"I guess appealing to your good nature or your humanity would be pointless, right? You're a real bastard, pal! Fuck you!"

The words were barely out of my mouth when Ushakov leaped out of his chair as if he were on a spring and grabbed my neck with one of his big, beefy hands, lifting me up against a wall. He caught me completely off guard. Who knew that such a big guy could move so fast? He held me a few inches off the ground and pressed his now demonic mask of a face right up to mine.

"I've been stuck in this hellhole on this goddamn boat with my crew for a month, understand?" he shouted, red with rage. "I've waited for someone in charge to send me that package. Know who came? No one! Absolutely no one!"

I was choking, spots dancing before my eyes. That psychopath was going to strangle me. He must've noticed my strange color, or maybe he realized if he killed me, he'd have no postman.

Whatever it was, it broke the spell, and he let go. I fell to the ground, gasping for air.

"I need that package! I need it! A week ago I sent a team ashore, and we haven't heard from them since. I can't afford to lose any more men." He sat back down, glaring at me. "You *will* get that package for me. And if you think about straying even a couple feet off the path, I swear to God I'll put a bullet in your head. So don't try to fuck me over. Understand, Mr. Lawyer?"

I nodded, unable to speak, as I struggled to get up off the floor. That fucking nutcase was capable of killing me if I refused. On top of that, I couldn't go anywhere. From the bridge I could see a couple of sailors relaxing on the deck of the *Corinth*, smoking, with AK-47s lying across their laps. And I didn't know where Lucullus was.

"Okay," I said, when I could get the words out. "You give me your word that if I bring you the package, you'll let me go on my way?"

"Absolutely. You do your part, and I'll do mine."

I'll believe that when I see it! And as a parting gift, a couple of blondes in bikinis and a keg of beer!

I had to be pragmatic and get control of the situation before it got completely out of hand. Taking a crushed Marlboro out of my pocket, I leaned against the wheel and fixed my gaze on him through a column of smoke. My mind was racing at top speed.

"Okay, but I have one condition. On shore, I'm in charge. Your guys will do what I tell them and won't fuck me around. Agreed?"

"I totally agree."

"I don't know why I even care. They'll probably kill us before we've been ashore ten minutes. Besides, I don't know a word of Tagalog or Urdu. How the hell am I going to make myself understood? In Morse code?"

"Don't be a smart-ass. Mr. Pritchenko speaks Spanish. My first officer will go with you. You can talk to everyone through them."

"Why not just send Pritchenko? Didn't he live in Vigo before all this started?"

"Pritchenko never lived in Vigo," he replied laconically.

"But you said—"

"Enough of this crap. You've got a lot to do," he interrupted, and motioned for me to follow him.

ENTRY 61
March 9, 11:00 p.m.

I'm still alive. Banged up, bruised. My wetsuit's in tatters. But I'm alive. I'm still trying to get over the shock. It was one very long day. All I want now is a few hours' rest. This mission or "journey"—I don't know what to call it—was doomed from the start. From the moment we set foot on land, things have spiraled out of control. We have no plan. We're flying blind.

Right now we're hiding in a ransacked mom-and-pop grocery store. The metal gate, or what's left of it is, is off its hinges. We've braced it up from the inside with two steel shelves. The other survivors are crowded together, sleeping in the light of a kerosene lamp. Shafiq is standing guard, nonchalantly nibbling on a candy bar. I can't sleep. Images of the last twenty-four hours are racing through my mind. I have no one to talk to about all this, no shoulder to lean on. I'm writing to keep from going crazy. I don't want to wake up tomorrow and think this was all a bad dream and I'm losing my mind. Hell, I don't have a clue where to start. At the beginning, I guess.

For two weeks I was under heavily guarded "freedom" aboard the *Zaren Kibish*. The captain and his first officer spent all their time getting ready for the trip. I only left that wreck of a cabin to go to the bathroom, take a shower, and make quick trips on to the *Corinth*. Except for Ushakov, I only saw the cook, a pimply-faced, pockmarked Filipino who doesn't speak a word of Spanish. So I had plenty of time to think about how off the chart things were.

I was in the middle of writing when Ushakov himself came to my cabin and motioned for me to follow him. We climbed down the stairs to the deck where the rest of my "team" was waiting: Viktor "Asterix" Pritchenko, whom I hadn't seen since I first came on board, so I guess he and I are both prisoners; the first officer, with a huge pistol hanging from his waist; and four Pakistani crew members. They were all wearing heavy navy-blue uniforms, with crammed backpacks on their back. They all carried AK-47s, except for Viktor, who was unarmed. He gazed at me, half-resigned, half-terrified. He was as fucked as I was.

"You volunteered, too, right?" I asked and laid a hand on his shoulder.

"What?" he replied, confused.

"Nothing. Forget it." Clearly he didn't get my sarcasm. I turned to Ushakov. "What about my weapons?"

"You won't need weapons, my friend. My men will protect you. Just guide them to the post office and bring me that package," he replied and handed me a piece of paper. "The receipt for the package."

I grabbed it with one hand and adjusted my wetsuit with the other. They all looked at me, astonished. They were probably asking themselves if I'd lost my mind. Did I think we were going surfing? When I read the receipt, I didn't feel like joking anymore. Shit! No wonder the last team never came back. That package wasn't at the main post office, which you could practically see from the harbor. The fucking receipt was from the VNT office, a local courier company. At the other end of town.

Resignedly I shook my head and put the receipt in the small, empty backpack they gave me. Clearly I wasn't the one who'd carry the package back. I adjusted the straps and leaned on the railing to study the dead city. It looked grim and bleak. Beyond the devastated port, I could see the streets of Vigo, filled with abandoned cars, trash, dirt, paper, and plastic bags fluttering in the wind. In the midst of all that, those creatures wandered along a never-ending path. A damn Dead Zone. And we were headed right into it. I shuddered and turned to Ushakov.

"It's getting dark. We'll leave tomorrow morning, when there's enough light."

"No, Mr. Lawyer. You leave right now, under cover of darkness."

"Do you know what you're saying? We won't be able to see!" I replied, agitated. I couldn't believe it.

"They won't be able to see you either," said Ushakov, disdainful.

End of discussion. I couldn't convince him that "they" didn't need to see us to know we were there. Maybe he thought I was trying to delay our departure. Ushakov was a soldier, and he still thought like a soldier. In his mind, you had to infiltrate at night to have any chance of success. He was sending us off on a moonless night to a place filled with monsters. Things just got better and better.

A large Zodiac waited, tied to the side of the *Corinth*. As we were boarding, I saw one of the sailors clutching Lucullus. The guy had a couple of deep scratches across his cheek. My cat wasn't happy with his captors either. As soon as he saw me, he let out a long, desperate howl and twisted around, trying to run to me. But the guy had anticipated his reaction and was wearing thick gloves. He skillfully moved his right hand and got my poor cat in a choke hold, immobilizing him. An inch more of pressure and he'd break his neck. Lucullus meowed plaintively as I looked on helplessly.

I saw red and took a step toward the guy. Someone shoved me hard toward the gunwale. Next thing I knew, I was climbing down into the Zodiac. As I took a seat at the bow, Ushakov leaned his huge hulk over the rail and cupped his hands.

"Hurry back, Mr. Lawyer! My Filipino cook hasn't had any fresh meat for weeks. His culture has many recipes for cat!" He laughed. "I don't know how long I can hold him off!"

The Zodiac's motor started on the third or fourth try. We took off with a mighty roar. His threat rang in my ears. Fucking son of a bitch…

The light was fading fast. It'd be dark soon. As we approached land, I could make out the shore more clearly. I'd almost wished I couldn't. It was a preview of what awaited us just a few hundred yards away. Suddenly I noticed the silence in the Zodiac. I turned around and looked into six pairs of expectant eyes. Drunk Nose barked at Viktor in Russian. He nodded and turned to me, his eyes round as saucers.

"Officer Kritzinev asks where get off, where land. He says you must guide."

I nodded. Okay, I was in command, at least for the moment. I had to calm down. I had to think, if I wanted to get out of this nightmare in one piece and get my cat and my boat back. I got up the courage to scrutinize the shore, searching desperately for a safe place to land, a path, a sign…anything!

Suddenly I saw a place near the shore. Fuck it. It might be our only chance. I turned back around and signaled to the Pakistani at the tiller where to head. it was a crazy idea, but we didn't have many options.

After so many days at sea, the feeling of solid ground underfoot was weird. As the shadows grew, I tried to make out the shape of the buildings around us. Behind me I heard the Ukrainians and Pakistanis rushing around, unloading the equipment. I breathed deep and instantly regretted it. The nauseating smell of decay, garbage, feces, and burned flesh was mixed with another, more subtle scent. I couldn't describe it, but I'd noticed that smell for weeks. I think it's their smell. Do they have their own smell? Or am I going crazy?

The Pakistanis and the Slavs were ready to head out. They seemed to be a pretty competent and well-trained team, except for Viktor, who seemed lost in his own world and resigned. The way they handled their weapons told me they weren't just sailors. Damn. Those guys were pros. Who the hell were they? What were they really doing here? And what was in that package? Was it worth risking the lives of seven people?

We'd landed at the far end of the Safe Haven, between some huge industrial warehouses and the gigantic lot where the Citroën factory parked its new vehicles. From there the cars would've been loaded on to the tankers and distributed all over the world. Now hundreds and hundreds of cars sat on the lot, abandoned in the dark.

Nearby I could make out a long row of brand-new Xsara Picasso luxury compact sedans, their seats still covered in plastic. They were dirty and neglected. I ran my hand over the nearest one, leaving a deep swath. After sitting there for weeks, it was covered in a thick layer of dust and more. With a shudder I realized they were covered with ashes from the fires. Maybe even human ashes. Jesus Christ!

I turned away from the thousands of vehicles that would never drive along a sunny highway. That was the past. Now all I could think about was being smart enough to survive until the next day.

The corner where we landed had a special feature: a small, squat building sitting next to a narrow esplanade entirely surrounded by a high brick-and-concrete wall. What had drawn us there wasn't the wall or the esplanade. We were interested in the huge Seguritsa sign on the building. It was the headquarters of an armored truck company. With hundreds of businesses operating in that tariff-free zone, it was logical they'd have a branch there. The port's fish market alone moved a million euros a day. Someone had to guard all that dough and drive it to the bank.

The building was a veritable fortress. Those monsters couldn't have climbed over the wall. If I was wrong, we were fucked. But we had no other option.

With a sharp wave, I communicated to Viktor that we should approach. I whispered that we should check the perimeter of the building. Nodding, the little Ukrainian slipped like an eel into the group that was hiding in the increasingly thick shadows. He relayed what I said in Russian to Kritzinev, who in turn gave instructions in Urdu to the Pakistanis. Quick as deer, they ran past me and melted into the shadows.

I felt uneasy about how complicated it was to pass along orders. They had to be translated several times and could've been misinterpreted at any point. The slightest mistake could send all of us to our grave. That's just great! We handful of survivors made the UN look like a bunch of neighbors.

After five torturous minutes, one of the Pakistanis materialized out of nowhere, right in front of us, signaling that everything was okay. As we moved stealthily toward the building, I studied those odd guys. They were all in their twenties, thin and sinewy, with huge black mustaches and copper skin. They were very good at what they did.

When we reached the wall, we stuck to it like leeches. It was dark as the mouth of a well.

Although none of those things was close by, I could hear the noise their dragging feet made. That sound gave me the creeps. Something like *rasssssssss-thump, rasssssssssssss-thump*, repeated over and over. I could feel my balls shrink in sheer panic. Those things were on the other side of the wall we were leaning against.

I walked quietly to the door of the building. As I expected, it was a huge steel doorway with slits on the sides. I grabbed the doorknob and turned. The door didn't budge. It was locked up tight.

For a moment I didn't know what to do. The possibility that that door would be locked hadn't crossed my mind. We'd come to a fucking impasse. We couldn't go back, we couldn't get into the building, and we couldn't move on.

All eyes were fixed on me. Turning to Viktor, I shrugged to say, "What do you think? I haven't got a fucking clue." Kritzinev stepped forward, raised the AK-47, cocked it loudly, and aimed at the lock. Before he could go on a shooting spree, I grabbed the muzzle of the gun, aimed it at the ground, and raised a finger to my lips. Shooting this door would only advertise our presence. I pointed to the corner of the building and the parking lot. It was our only option.

We walked along quietly, trying to melt into the wall, in complete darkness. I don't remember if the moon was out, but the sky was clouded over. The starless night made the situation even more unnerving.

I was beyond terrified, but in my defense, I wasn't the only one. I felt some satisfaction when I saw the fear in their eyes. Fuck them. It's one thing to watch the bullfight from the sidelines, quite another to jump into the ring.

When we reached the corner, I cautiously stuck my head out and saw absolutely nothing. The darkness was so thick I couldn't see more than a few yards in front of us. We had to turn on a light, so I signaled for a flashlight. A huge Polar Torch flashlight, the kind the police use, appeared in my hand as if by magic. I grabbed it with sweaty palms and pointed its polarized lens into the blackness. For a moment, I panicked. What if I turned it on and spotted dozens of those monsters lurking around, with the light reflecting off their dead eyes? What if the light attracted hundreds of them? I hesitated. My finger was on the switch, and sweat was dripping down my back. Kritzinev nudged me. He whispered something Viktor didn't have to translate. Something like, "What the fuck're you waiting for?"

I was up shit creek. I pressed the switch, and a huge beam of light lit up the scene. All I saw was a huge, empty parking lot and a wall with a large metal gate on sliding tracks. It was still closed. I breathed a huge sigh of relief and realized I'd been holding my breath all that time.

We quickly crossed to the heavy gate. I looked at it in despair. Too large for us to force open. We'd come to a dead end. I stood there, stunned, staring at that huge gate, wondering what the hell to do. I knew the others behind me were waiting for me to make a decision. I had no idea what to say. Viktor walked up to the door and inspected it carefully. I just stood there, watching the Ukrainian in surprise. He ran his fingers along the edge closest to the wall. I tapped him on the shoulder. He turned, smiling, sweat beading on his forehead, and whispered a single word: "Broken."

With a creak as loud as a gunshot, the door moved an inch. It wasn't locked! I suddenly remembered I'd seen that kind of door when I visited a client in prison. It was a high-tech model that used electromagnetic locks. As long as there was electricity, it was impossible to force the lock. In a power outage, the battery could keep the operating system armed for days. But even the smartest manufacturer couldn't have planned for a power outage that lasted several months. So the lock was turned off, and you could push it open with one finger.

How the hell had Viktor figured that out? Who was this guy?

The door slid smoothly on its tracks, and we got a look at the street outside the compound. The street. The outside. Where those things reigned unchallenged. But when we cautiously poked our heads out, we didn't see any.

Feverishly I swung the light left and right, afraid I'd catch a glimpse of one of those monsters. I swear to God if I'd seen one close up, I'd have slammed the gate shut and never come out, not even at gunpoint. Now I almost regret that didn't happen. We'd have been spared what came next.

Just when I thought I'd swept the whole street, I aimed the flashlight to the right and my heart almost stopped. A huge red eye, evil and bright, was staring at me, unblinking, less than three feet away. It was terrifying. I was suddenly mesmerized. When I snapped out of it, I jumped back and almost dropped the flashlight.

At least I didn't scream. I was spared the embarrassment of explaining why I'd screamed like a girl over a beam of light bouncing off a piece of glass. What I'd taken for a huge eye was just the door reflector of a van parked partway up on the sidewalk.

The rest of the group hung back in the doorway, covering both ends of the street while I nervously approached that huge hunk of metal. Halfway there, I realized I was completely unarmed. If any undead were inside that vehicle, my health would be seriously compromised in seconds.

It was a yellow armored van with SEGURITSA written in bold black letters on the side. The passenger door was open. The reflector on the door lit up when you opened the door. I'd mistaken that for an enormous eye. I definitely needed a huge bag of pot. And a vacation in the Caribbean.

I inched up to the van, the way Lucullus approached a dog, ready to run my ass off. It was a huge armored van and must've weighed several tons. I placed my hand on the hood. It was completely cold. It must have been sitting there for weeks, even months. I stuck my head into the driver's side. Empty. I eased into the plush leather seat and tried to think.

That van wasn't parked. It'd been abandoned on the sidewalk. The driver must have been in a hurry. He hadn't even bothered to close the door. The keys were still in the ignition. With a shudder, I pictured a couple of security guards in the backseat, turned into undead, closed up in that small space, their rotten teeth pressed to the dividing window that they smashed as they reached out to grab me…

I turned around, bracing myself, but the backseat was empty and dark. Shining the flashlight around, I saw bags with the company logo, covered in dust, tossed on the floor. I sighed with relief. False alarm. There was no one in the van but me. Those bags were filled with the euros people had coveted not long ago, before those monsters came on the scene.

On the floor was a folder on a metal clipboard. I picked it up and glanced over it. The guy's last route was dated late January. Based on the number of bags and the markings on the side, the driver was near the end of his route when he saw something that made him shit bricks and race back to base. I could think of no other reason to leave behind a van loaded with millions of euros, its door ajar, in the middle of the street and the keys still in the ignition. I didn't have to be psychic to know what that poor man saw. Where was he now…and in what condition?

That van just might get us across the city. There was plenty of room for all seven of us. It was armored, sturdy, and weighed enough to keep a pack of those things from overturning it. The more I thought about it, the more perfect it got. But one look at the ignition quashed my enthusiasm. The key was in the on position, but the motor was off. The driver had stopped the car so abruptly he'd left off the motor running. It idled for weeks until it ran out of gas and died. I had the perfect vehicle to cross a city of the undead, but not a drop of gasoline. And I didn't know what shape the battery was in.

Just then, Kritzinev and Pritchenko stuck their heads inside the van, alarmed that I was taking so long. I almost fainted from shock. When I told them the van's possibilities, they smiled.

E N T R Y   6 2
March 10, 12:02 a.m.

False alarm. Those young guys out there have just been on edge a bit.

The situation couldn't be any bleaker. We're trapped in this shithole of a store, exhausted and hounded by those creatures. I tried to fly under the radar, but Kritzinev whispered a couple of times that this was all my fault and gave me looks that weren't exactly reassuring. But I'm getting ahead of myself.

When we determined that the van was in good working condition, we got ready to set out. The more we thought about it, the better that vehicle sounded. An armored van is as close to a tank as you can get in civilian life. We had one parked right in front of us, with the keys in it, beckoning to us to get in. The problem was that its gas tank was dry as dried tuna. After idling for God knows how long, it was completely empty.

We came up with a solution, thanks to Shafiq, one of the Pakistanis. He's a wiry guy, very dark skinned. His monstrous black mustache makes Viktor Pritchenko's mustache look puny.

When we discovered the tank was dry, Kritzinev muttered a string of words in Urdu to this kid. While another Pakistani went back to the Seguritsa parking lot, Shafiq shrugged off all his gear and stripped down to his shirt and shorts with the ever-present

Kalashnikov strapped across his back. Viktor and I were sitting with our backs against the wall, slightly amazed at the scene. The remaining Pakistanis kept an eye on the street through the half-open metal gate, watching for any unwanted visitors.

After a few minutes, the guy returned from the lot with a long piece of rubber tubing cut from a hose. Taking the rubber tube and a five-liter plastic jug, Shafiq headed back to the Zodiac, not saying another word. He untied the boat and paddled quietly toward the Citroën depot about fifty yards from us, disappearing into the black night. We could only hear his rhythmic paddling in the distance.

As I sat there, dying to light a cigarette, I could imagine the scene: Shafiq crouched down, running up and down the rows of cars ready to be shipped to the four corners of the world, the keys in the ignition and a couple of liters of gas in the tank, just enough to drive on to the boat and then the tractor-trailer. A trip they'd never make.

The plan was simple. He'd empty that gas into the jug and then fill the van's tank. Since the jug only held five liters, he'd have to make at least a dozen trips. But we didn't have any other containers, except for our canteens. The job would take a while. At least we'd have a vehicle to safely cross the city in. We wouldn't have to walk. And we'd be setting out in daylight. Call me a coward, but I'd rather see what's around me than head into a dark ghost town full of mutants.

As I settled down for a break, thousands of paranoid thoughts raced through my mind. What if he mixed regular gas with diesel? What if the cars only used regular gas? (The van, of course, took diesel.) What if the cars had already been cannibalized by the Safe Haven survivors? What if a former employee of the factory, now changed into the living dead, was wandering around? What if it snuck up on Shafiq as he worked? More and more fatal errors went through my mind. With each new terrifying thought, I felt less and less confident and sweated more and more.

All my fears were unfounded. Shafiq returned with a jug of amber diesel gas, wearing a huge smile. He didn't make a mistake. He only got fuel from the diesel vans. Yeah, someone had already emptied a lot of the vehicles, but there were dozens more that still had gas. He'd have to go a little farther, but that was no problem. The area was empty.

I relaxed and leaned back against the wall as Shafiq set off again. It was strange. For those guys, being in complete darkness, an assault weapon in their hands, risking their lives, was the most normal thing in the world. It was their daily bread.

It occurred to me that the epidemic had hit the more advanced countries harder. In Spain only the army, security forces, and a few thousand people had guns. That's how advanced Europe used to impose order, law, and comfort. In places like Pakistan, Liberia, Somalia, or God knows where else, even a child at his mother's tit had a gun hanging around his neck or something more serious at the front door. There, you shoot first and ask questions later. There, having no electricity or running water has never been a problem.

Now the most advanced parts of the civilized world are defenseless, devoured by their own citizens. Maybe the undead haven't had as much luck in more remote, primitive, isolated areas. Maybe they haven't even made it that far.

It's ironic. The poorest, most underdeveloped areas of the world are now humanity's last hope. The rest of the world is one huge hell where a handful of scattered survivors are trying to escape.

The sun was slowly rising. The tank was filled just as the sun peeked over the horizon. Poor Shafiq, drenched and exhausted, was starting to stumble with the jug. Another Pakistani, Usman, ventured to the end of the street, where a Volkswagen Beetle with two flat tires was parked. He looked around the corner and came back to inform us that a few of those mutants were walking back and forth about ten yards away, unaware of our presence. The guy looked terrified. That was the first time he'd seen those things up close. I knew only too well that it was not a pretty sight. Hard to believe I was the veteran of the group.

When the tank was full, we got in the van. I was surprised when they gave me the driver's seat. I guessed I was supposed to lead them in everything. With a sigh I got in and closed the heavy door. Kritzinev, Shafiq, and I crammed into the front seat, while Pritchenko and three other Pakistanis climbed into the compartment in back. I adjusted the seat and mirror and turned the key.

The starter didn't even turn over. I tried again. Nothing. And again. Nothing. Kritzinev's face told the whole story. Mine too. I leaned back, my mind racing. What the hell was wrong? My eyes swept across the dashboard for a clue. I looked down at the dashboard. The light indicator was on. Shit. The driver had not only left the motor running, he'd left the lights on too. They'd been on for weeks. The battery was dead.

I imagined the scene: the yellow flashing headlights all that lit up that dark street. The battery dying as hundreds of undead surrounded that van, abandoned on the road to the Safe Haven.

I had to think of something. I focused on the Volkswagen at the end of the street. It was less than three years old, so its battery was probably in good condition. I considered telling Kritzinev to send Shafiq back to the Citroën parking lot to look for a brand-new battery, but I was sure he'd say no. The sun was getting higher, we were behind schedule, and the Ukrainian was getting impatient. Besides, in daylight the Citroën parking lot might be too dangerous. And he wouldn't want to waste any more time dragging the van next to the Volkswagen. There was nothing to do except get the battery out of that little round German car.

I turned to Viktor and whispered through the little window in the barrier what to tell Kritzinev. After a quick exchange in Russian, Viktor turned pale and looked at me with despair. I understood instantly. Kritzinev had ordered him to get the battery.

He quickly corrected me. He'd ordered both of us to go. Shit.

We got out of the van, amid the Pakistanis' mocking jokes. Almost tiptoeing, we approached the Volkswagen; its lemon-yellow color was like a beacon amid all the dirt on the deserted port. It was parked at the very end of the street, near the corner of the wall. Cautiously poking my head around the corner, I saw half a dozen of those things standing at different spots along the road, as if in a trance. Who knows, maybe they were sleeping. One thing was clear—they were close. Too close.

Viktor was struggling with the handle of the Volkswagen. It was locked. Not everything would be easy, after all. Wrapping his fist in his thick peacoat, Pritchenko drew his arm back and, before I could stop him, slammed his fist against the driver's window.

The window vaporized into a million little pieces, making an outrageously loud noise that set the undead in motion. We had to hurry. With the agility of a car thief, the little Ukrainian slipped into the car and popped the hood. I propped the hood up, one eye on the street corner, waiting for those monsters to show up.

A bunch of wires stuck out of the battery. I jiggled the battery, but the clamps slipped again and again in my sweaty fingers. Pritchenko looked at me expectantly as the Pakistanis knelt on the ground beside the van, calmly watching the show.

When the copper connector slipped out of my hands again, Viktor Pritchenko lost his patience. He gently pushed me aside and leaned over the battery, grabbed hold of the connectors, and yanked them off. Then he tugged on the handle of the battery and pulled it out of the engine well. He smiled and muttered some-thing that sounded like "Better fix things old Soviet way."

Just in time. Around the corner appeared the first undead, rocking along, drawn by all the noise we were making. It was a middle-aged woman, covered in blood. Her thick torso was bare, exposing one of her drooping breasts. Where the other breast should've been, there was only a gaping, bloody hole.

Pritchenko and I stood there paralyzed, staring for a few sec-onds. No matter how disgusting they are, a walking corpse inevi-tably awakens a morbid fascination in a person, a fascination as dangerous as a swaying cobra. I've written many times in this journal that those monsters are fast, damn fast, even if they are crawling. They'd be on us in less than twenty seconds.

The next guy was wearing just a bloody, dirty hospital gown tied in the back. The wind ruffled his very long hair. From his arm hung what had once been a drip. When he saw us, he stopped, stretched his hands toward us, and uttered a guttural, horrifying growl.

That broke the spell for me. Pritchenko still stood there, bewildered, leaning on the hood of the car with the battery in one hand, his jaw hanging open. We had to get out of there before they grabbed us, or we were done for. I grabbed his arm and whis-pered louder and louder, "Run…run…RUN…*RUN!*" We turned and ran like hell to the van. Those things were so close you could almost feel their breath.

The three hundred yards to the van looked like a hundred miles. A wetsuit is not exactly the most comfortable thing when you're running like a deer. Two hundred yards. Pritchenko was like a soul running from the devil. Even his mustache was bris-tling with horror. It was a comfort to know I wasn't the only one who was screwed. A hundred yards. I could see Kritzinev's and the Pakistanis' faces. My heart dropped when I saw them raise their guns and aim at us. For a second I thought we'd be executed on the spot. Fifty yards. We were almost there when they started shooting.

The sound of five AK-47s firing all at once is deafening, especially when it's right next to your ears and you've never heard it before. I collapsed, panting, at the foot of the Pakistanis, next to a contorted Pritchenko, watching a barrage of bullets rain down on those undead. I watched with horror as the men shot into their bodies. I knew that didn't faze them. I stood up like a crazy man and shouted to them to shoot them in the fucking head, but I realized I was shouting in Spanish, and those Pakistanis from hell didn't understand me for shit.

Pritchenko jumped up almost in front of the AK-47s and shouted, "*Head, head!*" like a man possessed. It was a miracle they missed him, but he got the message across. The Pakistanis corrected their aim, and in less than a minute a dozen undead lay on the ground, definitely dead now, with some ragged holes in their heads.

I'm really hardened. Just a month ago, the sight of carnage like that would've made me vomit my guts out. Now I looked on the scene as detached as a child tearing the wings off a fly. It's natural, but I don't like it one bit.

Time was running out. That shooting spree had gotten the attention of every ghoul in the vicinity, and they were headed right for us. It was just a matter of time before they'd congregate there. I got into the driver's seat, while Pritchenko and one of the Pakistanis tried to jump the van's motor with the Volkswagen's battery. I don't know if it was an easy process or if Viktor was forced to reapply the "old Soviet ways," but he suddenly signaled for me to turn it over. The van's motor sputtered a couple of times and stalled, but at least the dials were lit. We had a battery, but something was wrong with the fuel.

I could hear a violent exchange in Russian and Urdu across the hood. They couldn't understand each other, but they finally came to some agreement. They looked up at the same time and signaled for me to try again. This time the motor started with a powerful roar that echoed through the narrow street. They slammed the hood and raced into the van. We were ready.

Just in time. An enormous mob was pouring around the far corner. I shuddered to see that that mob had closed off all our escape routes, while the engine sounded increasingly uncertain. If I turned it off, we were done for, trapped in the tight space in the van forever.

The sight was terrifying. The street was three hundred yards long. A high brick wall on one side and the back wall of a huge warehouse on the other formed a corridor about six yards wide. At the far end of the street, near the Seguritsa gate, an armored van, crammed with seven people, sat panting after sitting for more than month and a half. The other corner of the street was packed with undead. In a word, hell.

Shots from the AK-47s had saved Pritchenko's and my lives, but the noise they'd made had drawn all the undead around. A tidal wave of hundreds of those creatures was headed down the narrow street right for us. The motor's backfire drew them like a moth to a flame.

The din was deafening inside the van. The four Pakistanis chattered nervously, nonstop in Urdu, pointing at the mob headed our way. Pritchenko was pale, crouched in a corner staring, beads of sweat on his forehead. I'm no shrink, but I'd guess he was recalling his last moments in the Safe Haven. This time he had nowhere to hide. Kritzinev sat next to me, pale as wax, his eyes wide as saucers; the veins on his nose stood out like a map. Seeing those things through binoculars from the safety of the *Zaren*'s deck was one thing; it was quite another thing to be there with nothing to keep them from coming at you. I was scared, very scared, like everyone else. Fuck 'em all, I couldn't help thinking.

Kritzinev shook my arm, shouting fast and furious in Russian. I shrugged. I had the same panicked look on my face. I wasn't sure what to do. You're never prepared for something like that. I released the handbrake, put the van in first gear, and let it roll slowly toward that roiling mass that took up the whole street.

The van's engine panted noisily as the wall of flesh, bone, and bloodlust closed in on us in the middle of the street. At a hundred yards, we saw the first undead. We could guess at the mass behind them. It was like trying to clear a path through a demonstration or drive through an audience at a concert.

My mind worked feverishly. Adrenaline and panic urged me to charge the crowd. It was an obscenely inviting idea—floor it and mow down row after row of undead and then drive someplace where no one's ever seen those things, not even in a picture.

The rational part of my mind got me back on track right away. Charging that shambling crowd wasn't an option. A body projected against a windshield, no matter how dead it is or how shatterproof the windshield is, was still a 150-pound bundle thrown against glass. It could do a lot of damage to a vehicle. When I say a lot, I mean a lot. A broken window in the middle of that crowd was a death sentence.

I recalled forensic reports I'd read about people struck by cars. In most cases, the victim died, but not before doing serious damage to the undercarriage, suspension, tires, and steering of the vehicle that hit him. Real life is very different from movies. Cars aren't indestructible; they break down easily and suffer serious damage, not to mention flipping over or crashing.

We had one option, but it required cool heads. I let the van move slowly toward the crowd just twenty yards from us as I quickly explained my plan to Viktor. We'd move through the crowd, practically idling, at the speed of a person walking. I was sure we'd gently part the crowd of undead. If any of them fell under our wheels at that slow speed, I didn't think it would do any damage, considering we weighed more than three tons. To the van, that is; damage to the fallen creatures was another story.

The downside was that we'd be surrounded by those monsters for a very long time. I speculated that they'd hit the sides and windows of the van many, many times. If it weren't for the armor on the vehicle, we couldn't do it.

At that moment, those mutants—hundreds of them—engulfed us. Seeing their faces plastered to the glass was deeply disturbing. I assumed it was high-security glass, impossible to punch through. Still, I shuddered every time a fist hit the windshield. They saw us clearly, and that drove them crazy. They surged toward the vehicle with a hungry look in their dead eyes. The smell of urine filled the van. Someone had pissed himself in fear. Not a surprise. It was the most terrifying experience imaginable.

Purring softly, the van slowly penetrated the crowd until we were surrounded on all sides. We'd bet it all on that card, putting our trust in the weight and the armor of our vehicle-shelter. In there we were safe and secure. For a moment, I even felt a little confident.

The dense crowd plagued us from all sides. From time to time, we felt a jolt as we ran over one of those things that didn't move fast enough or didn't have room to get away and ended up under our wheels. It was gut-wrenching.

I noticed my vision was blurred. I rubbed my eyes and realized I'd teared up. I was crying out of sheer terror. We were going three or four miles an hour down the middle of a huge crowd of corpses in varying degrees of decay. They were all ages and all kinds. I saw middle-aged women, young men, the elderly, children...they were the most unsettling.

A girl about eight years old, with a dark stain on her torn Bratz T-shirt and a deep cut on her head, her dirty blonde hair plastered down with blood, stayed glued my window for about ten minutes. With one hand, she gripped the rearview mirror, and with the other she hit the window, moaning furiously. Up close like that, we got a good look at her dark mouth and her pale skin, riddled with dark, broken veins. After a while she started hitting her head against the glass. She seemed frustrated to be so close yet not able to reach me. At one point I heard the *clack* her teeth made against the armored window. God, I still shudder when I remember that moment.

ENTRY 63
March 10, 1:05 a.m.

I feel better, calmer. I want to leave a written record of every moment I've lived through, but some situations come back so strongly, it makes me nauseous. That half-hour ride in the van is one of them.

I was talking about the little girl. After ten minutes she let go. Maybe because she got tired (do these beings get tired?) or because a huge, muscular guy about thirty years old pulled her away. That bastard was right out of a nightmare. Half his body was burned and blistered from a fire. He was missing three fingers on the hand he pounded against the windshield as he clung to the hood with the other. With each blow, he let out an inhuman bellow. He hit the windshield with such fury that after a while his arm turned into a mass of red pulp that clouded the window. The bastard finally turned loose when the truck shook and squashed one of those things. Thinking about him made my hair stand on end long afterward.

Those are just two examples. I remember twenty or thirty more and could describe them perfectly, but I just can't face it right now. It's too scary. Hundreds of those creatures were all around us, shouting, wailing, and beating on every inch of surface of the van. The shouting outside contrasted sharply with the deathly silence inside the van, broken only by the monotonous, guttural whisper of the Pakistanis praying in Arabic. I was amused by the idea of praying to God when we were in hell, but I kept that thought to myself.

Kritzinev, his eyes bulging, clung to his flask like a drowning man with a life preserver. From time to time, he knocked back a long, deep gulp that made his Adam's apple bob up and down. Pritchenko was pale and scared, but behind his huge blond mustache, he calmly studied the scene. I concluded he was the only guy in that van I could rely on if I wanted out alive.

All went well for about thirty minutes. Each time the vehicle threatened to go belly up, it put the fear of God in me. If the vehicle overturned, we'd be as good as dead. Either those mutants would kill us, or we'd die of hunger and thirst in the van, surrounded by an impassable crowd of undead. The best solution would be a shot to the head. Frankly I didn't relish ending my life in a modern-day version of Numantia. At least in 133 BC those early Iberians were fighting noble enemies, the Romans, and not some freakish undead.

Occasionally the van rocked violently as several undead were crushed at once. More than once we nearly tipped over, but we managed to continue our slow, tortuous pace. Until we reached the tunnel.

It wasn't really a tunnel, but a passageway under an intersection. I remembered driving through it on the way to a meeting. It was three hundred yards long and very narrow, with a lot of support beams. And black as midnight. I didn't know what was inside. If it was blocked, I'd have to back out in the dark with that crowd around me. I'd probably crash into a beam, and we'd be stuck there forever with a snowball's chance in hell of surviving. I wouldn't go in there even if Kritzinev held a gun to my chest.

So I told Pritchenko to translate that to Kritzinev. While Viktor talked, I watched the first officer's reaction out of the corner of my eye. He shrugged and mumbled something in Russian, not taking his eyes off the crowd howling around us, pounding on the windows nonstop. Kritzinev was too out of it to make a decision. I gave the orders here. That made me feel more confident—maybe too confident.

If we didn't drive through the tunnel, we'd have to use the overpass that was just two hundred yards away. The crowd had thinned out a little. For the last mile or so, we'd been able to speed up. We were driving on wider streets, dodging abandoned vehicles. That worked in our favor. Our pursuers had to maneuver around those obstacles. That slowed them down and gave us some time before they reached us. But they'd catch up with us in a few minutes.

We drove onto the overpass until we came to the middle of the bridge.

I braked hard. Across the middle of the road was a car crashed into some concrete blocks that had once been a roadblock. Some poor devil had driven too fast, fleeing God knows what, and been hurled into those blocks, wrecking his car. There were bloodstains around the chassis and the footprints of someone or something who'd splashed through puddles getting away from the car. If the guy had survived the accident, he soon suffered something truly horrible.

Kritzinev shook off his stupor when he discovered we weren't surrounded by all those undead. He roared something to Viktor, who rushed to translate for me. "Ram that abandoned car," that thug said. I shook my head. I told him he'd seen too many movies. It would destroy our van. He roared again, getting red in the face, spewing frothy saliva, screaming, choking. A drunk, scared, angry Ukrainian is a sight to see. That Ukrainian was calling me names that were anything but pretty. Viktor deftly edited out the worst parts and told me to change seats with Shafiq. He'd take the wheel.

I don't make a habit of arguing with someone pointing a gun at my chest, so I gave my seat to Shafiq. In the process of switching seats in that narrow cabin, he and I got all tangled up. I ended up sitting in the middle seat of the van, with Shafiq on one side and Kritzinev on the other. I barely had time to turn around and tell Viktor to hold on tight, then turn back around. I fastened my seat belt just in time.

The Pakistani floored it and launched the three-ton van against the abandoned car, like a ram butting its head against a wall. I braced myself against the dashboard. The impact was terrible. I figured someone in back was thrown forward violently. There was a hard blow against the partition, followed by a long howl of pain.

I didn't have time to find out what had happened. Putting the van in reverse, Shafiq disengaged from the wrecked car, which had moved about twenty inches to one side, and rammed it again. I held on tight as the heavy van lurched forward.

This time, the blow was accompanied by the sound of iron grating against concrete. The car spun around like a top, leaving a space open. Shafiq let out an excited shriek that drowned in his throat a second later. In the impact, the van veered to the left and skidded against the railing of the bridge. With a nasty crunch, the heavy vehicle splintered the aluminum railing and hung for a second from the bridge's parapet, swaying. After a few agonizing seconds, the van fell twenty feet to the pavement.

Most trials involving traffic accidents have something in common: the injured parties narrate the incident in great detail. They say, "It felt like everything happened in slow motion." It had always sounded like a cliché before, but when the Seguritsa van skidded out of control toward the railing, I experienced that feeling firsthand.

The aluminum railing tore like paper when the van skidded into it. One of the tires exploded as it ran over an uprooted post. Sparks flew off the concrete as the van swept along the bridge, dragging fifteen feet of the railing. It struck one of the concrete beams and came to a stop, swaying, its rear end suspended in the air.

The van stayed in that position for just a few seconds. It felt like time stopped. Slowly, it started to tilt backward under the enormous weight of its armor plating. I tried to reach over a dazed Shafiq to open the door, but it was too late. With a creak and the gut-wrenching sound of scraping metal, the van slid into the void.

The impact was mind-blowing. The van fell on its rear end from a height of twenty feet. When it hit the road, there was a massive crash of crushed metal and broken glass. It slid sideways, then came to rest on its roof in a thick cloud of smoke and dust.

For a couple of minutes, I hung upside down, strapped to my seat, too stunned to react. Colored lights flashed before my eyes, and there was a ringing in my ears. When I finally tried to move, I felt a heart-stopping whiplash. We'd fallen backward, and the rear of the van had absorbed most of the impact, but the front of the van had taken a brutal hit too. The seat where Kritzinev and I sat had come loose and been thrown against the bulkhead. The iron bolts that anchored it had absorbed most of the impact and been twisted beyond recognition, so he and I were miraculously unhurt.

I couldn't say the same of the other occupants of the van. Shafiq was unconscious. His head had flopped to one side, and blood trickled from the corner of his mouth. In the rear compartment someone was screaming in pain. Along with the urine smell there was now the stench of vomit and blood. I had to get out of there.

Slowly moving my arm, I felt for the end of my belt and released the latch. Then I crawled over the unconscious body of Shafiq and pressed the button to open the door. When the lock on the driver's-side door clicked open, I felt a profound relief. I couldn't imagine how I'd have forced open that armored door, which was seriously dented by the crash. I placed both hands on the door frame, got some momentum going, and pulled myself out of the vehicle. I stood on top of the wreck to take a look around.

It was a disturbing scene. The van had folded like an accordion in back, reducing its length by about a third. The right front wheel was missing, and fuel was leaking out in a growing puddle. The road we'd fallen on to didn't intersect the one we'd come from or any other road I could see. It was deserted, but it wouldn't be for long.

Gravel fell next to me, pinging against the van. I looked up and saw a half dozen undead leaning into the gap we'd left in our wake. They seemed stymied by our being on a different level from them. For now, they weren't jumping down, but I didn't know how long that would last. We had to hurry.

Kritzinev was dragging himself out of the van, his eyes clouded over, a deep gash on his right arm. A guy his age and physical condition wasn't up for this. For a second I felt sorry for him. Then I remembered the smug look on that bastard's face when the sailor almost strangled Lucullus.

I let him struggle out of the cab on his own. I went to the side door and pulled the handle, praying it would open. The handle turned, and I pulled the heavy door open. The sight was terrifying. One of the Pakistanis lay on the floor, his neck at an unnatural angle; blood poured from a deep gash in his forehead. He was dead. His brains were splattered against the barrier window. That explains the vomit I smelled.

Another Pakistani, Usman, was holding his arm, screaming like a madman. It had broken in the crash, and splintered bone protruded through his skin. It looked like he had another joint between his elbow and wrist. That must've hurt like a son of a bitch. The last Pakistani, Waqar, was still strapped in his seat. He didn't look hurt but his mouth was bleeding profusely.

Pritchenko was struggling to get out of his seat. That lucky SOB. Several money bags had cushioned his fall. The little Ukrainian was floating in a sea of fifty-euro bills, making that the most expensive airbag in the world. He just had a bump the size of an egg in the middle of his forehead. He gave me a big, toothy smile. Now he really did look like a cartoon character.

There was no time to stop and admire the scenery. We got Usman and Waqar out of the backseat. Viktor then helped a still dazed Shafiq out of the driver's seat.

After a couple of minutes we headed downtown. Pritchenko carried the dead Pakistani's AK-47, and I carried the gun belonging to the guy with the broken arm. But we were just porters. Kritzinev had ordered them to take out the ammo.

The light was fading. The place would be packed with undead as soon as they found a way to reach the road. After we'd walked for ten minutes in the heart of that ghost town, we realized we couldn't go any farther. Waqar's mouth was still bleeding, and he was getting weaker. The rest of us were dead tired and stiff. We needed some rest. Kritzinev was the first to spot the little shop.

It was a small neighborhood grocery store. Someone had rammed a massive armored personnel carrier into the door and then looted it. Piled up around the store were dozens of rotting corpses, all shot in the head. Someone had held those monsters at bay while a team from the Safe Haven searched for food.

It looked like a good place to spend the night.

The light was growing dimmer, and rain was starting to fall. As the rain splattered, soaking everything, we went cautiously through the gaping hole, single file.

My heart sank when I saw the inside of the store. The looting party had thoroughly trashed the place. Empty shelves and torn boxes were tossed everywhere, and broken display cases lay on the floor. It was a deeply disturbing sight.

I took a closer look and noticed some telling details. The looting was systematic, yes, but rushed—not surprising when you consider how quickly those creatures gathered when they located a human being. Packets of noodle soup had been torn open in the shuffle; the entire floor was covered with little stars. I don't know why, but that image jolted me like an electric shock, more than any other atrocity I'd witnessed.

I collapsed against a wall, exhausted, eyeing all that pasta on the floor. I remembered how my mother and I had fixed soup on rainy days. That memory was intense and painful. I'd stored away that anguish, but now it flooded me in an unstoppable torrent. I mourned silently, big tears rolling down my face.

I hadn't heard from my family for months. That was something I didn't want to face. Now an overwhelming pain and emptiness filled me as I wondered what had become of my parents and my sister. I tried to imagine where they might be, wondering if their shelter had been safe enough. But this chaos was too powerful. No coping mechanism could have held up more than five minutes in all this madness.

They could be anywhere. They could be living; more likely they were dead. God forbid they were one of those things wandering around. I shuddered at the thought. If I came face-to-face with them, I don't think I could defend myself. Not against them.

All the pain I'd accumulated over the last few weeks was unleashed. One of the Pakistanis sneered at me when he noticed I was crying. He must've thought I was weak or scared. I didn't really give a damn what he thought. All I wanted was to get out of there alive and get my cat and my boat back. Then maybe I'd find a way to contact my family. In this apocalypse, I've learned that your plans have to be short term. The pain'll always be with me, not just now but in the weeks to come. It can't get any worse. Surely it will fade, like an ember. That's enough talk about sad things.

We braced the battered iron gate with some display cases and shelves, and settled down to spend the night. I lit a cigarette. Pritchenko fixed dinner on a kerosene stove while Shafiq and Kritzinev set Usman's broken arm.

Shafiq grabbed his countryman from behind, and Kritzinev stuck a wooden stick in his mouth. Then he grabbed the guy's broken arm at both ends. With a sudden flick of his wrist, he set the bone in place with a crunch that made my hair stand on end. Usman's eyes rolled back, and he fainted. The rest was easy. They improvised a splint with a metal bar and a roll of bandages. It would hold the arm in place, but it wasn't the right way to set a fracture. If a doctor had gotten a look at that botched job, he'd have been hopping mad. That kid's arm was going to be fucked up forever.

In this new world, where the Health Department no longer exists, we're at the mercy of accidents, just like the cavemen were.

Waqar's injury had gotten worse. The guy was really pale, and he was coughing up blood. The severe pain in his abdomen was constant, and he was getting weaker. He must've had an internal injury. Probably his spleen. That was very bad, considering there was no hospital nearby. We didn't know what to do. Even if we did, we had no way to help him. Only a properly equipped hospital with a trained staff could help him. Unfortunately, in the entire continent, there wasn't much of either.

The smell of a stew soon filled the room. We left Usman, unconscious, lying by the gas lamp. Propped up against the wall, Waqar refused to eat. Kritzinev, Shafiq, Pritchenko, and I dug into that warmed-up stew and listened to the raging storm outside.

The meal was sad and somber. In general, our "mission" was in the crapper. We didn't know where we were, we had no transportation, we'd lost a member of the team, and two were wounded, one seriously. It was a joke.

Just then Waqar struggled to his feet and headed for the bathroom at the back of the room. That guy was looking worse by the minute. I felt sorry for him, so I got up to help him, since he was having a hard time moving. He was just a couple of yards ahead of me. On the bathroom door hung a colorful poster of a bunch of fat guys in nineteenth-century clothing. They looked like they needed to take a piss and were frantically banging on the bathroom door. Below that was written "Wait Your Turn" in huge red letters. The owner of the shop had a real sense of humor.

We'd made a huge mistake when we first arrived—no one had checked the bathroom. Waqar reached out and turned the doorknob. As he did, the door slammed open. Waqar fell on the floor with a cry of pain as that thing hovered over him.

I reacted instinctively. Waqar was lying on his back, trying to pull away from that monster that was biting the air, going for his throat. He was a young guy, in army fatigues that were too big for him and hair too long to be a soldier. A volunteer from the Safe Haven, I speculated as I sprinted the two yards between us. He'd gotten infected somehow so they left him locked in a bathroom.

They couldn't shoot an old friend; they weren't that cold-blooded. They figured no one would open that bathroom door again.

I grabbed that thing by the back of his jacket and struggled to pull him a few inches away from Waqar. The undead are like junkies all strung out on cocaine or pills. It's very hard, if not impossible, for one person to overpower them. Not to mention that if they bite you, you're screwed. Waqar took advantage of this break to roll over and escape from his clutches.

In the process, I lost my grip and fell backward, giving that monster a chance to stand up and turn around. The son of a bitch saw me lying helpless on the ground and gave a grunt of triumph before pouncing on me.

Shots rang out, and the guy's head exploded like a ripe watermelon, leaving a strange pattern of brains on the wall. His knees buckled, and he fell in slow motion.

I turned my head toward the door. There stood Sharif, the barrel of his AK-47 still smoking, looking at me with more respect than he had just a few minutes earlier. He'd saved my life. But the gunfire doomed us. They knew we were there.

ENTRY 64
March 10, 2:35 a.m.

Something's horribly wrong with Waqar. I'm no doctor, but I swear that the internal bleeding, or whatever he has, is getting worse. Blood isn't seeping out of his mouth anymore, but he's deathly pale. His groin is very hard, and his skin is as taut as a drum. He also has a huge bruise on his chest, a deep scratch on his right arm, and a high fever. All we have is some Tylenol and a box of Clamoxil, a medium-strength antibiotic. We have absolutely nothing to relieve the pain. I gave him a couple of Tylenol and forced him to drink lots of water. Pritchenko puts wet compresses on his forehead every ten minutes. We're the only ones caring for this poor kid.

Kritzinev found a case of wine, so now he's completely out of it. The other two Pakistanis are praying and looking at us with anguished faces. Beyond that, they're no help. From time to time they say something to us in Urdu, but neither Viktor nor I understand them. I feel absolutely powerless.

Outside there are plenty of monsters. We don't know exactly how many, because the shutters—which fortunately are holding up well—are down. But we can hear their pounding and their enraged roars. We haven't found any other way out. We're trapped.

I'm worried about Waqar. He'll kick the bucket in a few hours if we don't get him out of here. It baffles me how completely irresponsible these people are. Coming to shore without even a basic first-aid kit, just a few odds and ends of medications! Our provisions are running low, too, I noticed when I rifled through the Pakistanis' backpacks.

I guess they thought this would be a walk in the park: reach the VNT office, grab the package, and get back on board. Idiots! This is hell on earth, and in hell, any problem can become a tragedy in a heartbeat.

Like now.

It's 2:46 a.m. I'm so exhausted I can't sleep. Waqar's starting to rave.

ENTRY 65
March 10, 2:50 a.m.

I don't like this one bit. Waqar's semiconscious. He's still raving in Urdu, but from time to time, he goes into a kind of trance and has seizures. The wound on his arm is swollen and red and is leaking a clear liquid with a repulsive smell. When I tried to wipe it with gauze, he came to, screaming in pain, blindly pulling away from me. That reaction isn't normal for someone with internal bleeding. I studied the wound more carefully. It's more like a deep scratch on the inside of his arm, about eight inches long.

I can't help thinking the worst. I don't remember seeing the scratch when we pulled him out of the van. He must have gotten it later, and I can only think of one way. I looked up from the wound. Viktor's blue eyes were wide, watching me intently. I didn't have to say anything. He knows what I'm thinking. It's just a scratch… could it be enough to change him? Waqar passed out again.

ENTRY 66
March 10, 4:30 a.m.

About twenty minutes ago, Waqar started death rattles. The gruesome wound on his arm is still oozing smelly pus. His insides must be getting worse. A reddish fluid is flowing from his intestines; he lost control of his bowels a long time ago. His panting sounds like a steam freight train climbing a mountain. He stops breathing suddenly, then gasps for breath as if he were drowning. His agony has put everyone on edge.

I take some comfort in knowing that he lost consciousness a couple of hours. If he were awake, his suffering would be horrible.

I feel absolutely helpless. A human life is ending before my very eyes, and I have no drugs or knowledge to prevent it.

Usman and Shafiq recite *suras* monotonously, clutching a Muslim rosary. If this is hard for me, it must be terrifying for them. They're thousands of miles from home, watching a friend die. I saw disgust in their eyes when Waqar started shitting blood.

Violent death isn't a pretty sight like in the movies, where the hero falls with a smile and some last words for his beloved. Death is terrible, dirty, and very painful, if you've got what Waqar has. Those guys don't seem to know that. I didn't know that either a few weeks ago, but I saw a few dead on the way here, and that hardened me.

Viktor and I have a very serious problem. We know, or suspect, what will happen to Waqar in a few hours, but we've decided not to do anything for now. In the first place, we're unarmed. That severely limits our possibilities. In the second place, neither Usman or Shafiq will shoot Waqar. Not surprising. He's their friend, after all.

I laughed bitterly at that. The group from the Safe Haven must've felt the same way when they left that poor devil locked in the bathroom. Now, thanks to their "love for their fellow man," we have this freak show on our hands.

Kritzinev is totally drunk and out of it. He keeps mumbling incoherently in Russian. From time to time, he laughs, doubled over with tears running down his cheeks into his beard, as if someone's told him an extremely funny joke. At one point he screamed like a madman at the gate, where the undead are still pounding away outside. He pulled out his gun, but Pritchenko leaped up like a deer and grabbed it before he could shoot. Kritzinev glared at him and then collapsed, unconscious, drunk as a skunk. Just as well.

Now we have a weapon. Neither Usman or Shafiq made any move to take it away. That's something.

The undead are still out there, mercilessly beating against the door. It's an awful, grating sound. I think their numbers are growing, but I have no way of knowing for sure.

Waqar's death rattles are becoming more frequent, one every ten minutes or so. The end is near.

ENTRY 67
March 10, 7:58 a.m.

The sun is coming up. Faint rays of sunlight filter through slits in the metal gate. From time to time those things' shadows block the light as they wander back and forth. The store smells of blood, shit, sweat, fear, and pus. Waqar died ten minutes ago in terrible agony. Usman and Shafiq are reciting a funeral oration that sounds like a mantra. They keep watch on the body with one hand on their AK-47s and the other on a Koran. Pritchenko and I are keeping watch, too, but for other reasons.

Waqar will rise again any time now. Or something that looks like Waqar. There are no words to define our anguish as we wait. My hand is trembling as I write this in my journal. It looks like a six-year-old's handwriting.

Viktor and I are breathing fast, and our hearts are racing. We know we'll see one of those things born from a comrade-in-arms, if not a friend. When he returns, he'll be the predator, and we'll be his prey.

Waqar's agony has been horrific. Two hours after he lost consciousness, small purple spots, the size of a dime, spread all over his body. Waqar's circulatory system failed. It couldn't send oxygen throughout his body, so he slowly suffocated.

Three hours later, something creepy happened. Delicate capillaries and veins in Waqar's circulatory system became visible on his skin. You could trace them perfectly, like in a med-school drawing. I had no way to measure his blood pressure, but I'd estimate he was running hot. His heartbeat was wildly irregular. Sweat poured off him, but I wouldn't let Pritchenko dry him off without gloves. If the Ebola virus is transmitted by contact with sweat, this disease must be too.

The sad truth is, nobody knows shit about this disease. In another time, in a better world, this kid would've been fighting for his life, quarantined in an ICU, monitored by a regiment of doctors and nurses. Now he lay there in agony, in his own excrement, on the floor of a looted, dirty store in the middle of a city abandoned and dead. Like all of Europe and the whole fucking world.

At three and a half hours, his veins became visible; the vena cava and aorta were like thick cables. Excessive blood pressure burst the small, delicate veins under his skin. Waqar was starting to look an awful lot like the things that have tormented me for months. By now, we all knew, even the Pakistanis, that Waqar was becoming one of them.

After four and a half hours, he lost consciousness and started bleeding profusely from the mouth, ears, and eyes, and I suspect the anus and penis (no one had the courage to check). Except for Kritzinev, who was passed out, we watched that terrifying spectacle, frozen, not saying a word, too scared to react. In the background, a chorus of groans and thumps against the increasingly weakened gate greeted the birth of a new member of the legion of the undead.

At four hours and forty minutes, Waqar shook with spasms that looked like an epileptic seizure. His body arched to incredible heights, and his limbs flailed away on the ground. His head pounded rhythmically against the concrete. We couldn't do anything. With each contraction, with each jolt of his limbs, he sprayed blood mixed with pus and excrement into the four corners of the room. Unless I'm mistaken, if even a drop of that goo came in contact with an exposed part of the body, it could be lethal.

I ordered Pritchenko and the Pakistanis to stay back in the front room while I used an old Plexiglas display case as a shield and observed this horrible death. I don't know if Waqar could feel anything, but I prayed his mind was long gone.

Four hours and fifty-five minutes into the coma, Waqar's body lay still. Even after ten minutes, I didn't dare leave the precarious protection of Plexiglas to approach the still-warm body. He didn't seem to be breathing. I wasn't sure. I decided to get a little closer, just six feet. The body lay motionless in a pool of red liquid. The smell was nauseating. I squatted down beside the body to see if he was breathing (not for all the gold in the world would I have knelt in the middle of that mess). He wasn't.

Suddenly, Waqar's gummy, bloodshot eyes flew open. He opened his mouth and let out a deep death rattle. I got the fright of my life. With panicked scream, I jumped up, took a couple of steps back, and fell on my ass on the concrete. I was terrified that Waqar's body would get up.

But nothing happened. As I tried to calm the runaway beat of my heart, Viktor, Shafiq, and Usman peered through the door, drawn by my unmanly shriek. I didn't feel one bit ashamed. Anyone in my place would've been scared shitless.

I sat up and scanned the body again. That had been his last gasp. It was so violent and unexpected, I nearly died of fright. Waqar was dead. But for how long?

That was the least of our problems. The only way out of this place was the front door, and that crowd of monsters had no intention of leaving. That door would give way sooner or later.

ENTRY 68
March 10, 8:26 p.m.

I write this by the light of Victor's flashlight. The last twelve hours have been worse than when those things turned up at my house, a million years ago.

Twelve minutes after Waqar's last gasp, his body did a number of things that definitely weren't natural. His chest wasn't moving. I guess those things don't breathe. His entire right arm shook. He was dead, and yet his arm twitched. It was incredible.

If that weren't enough, his gummy, bloodshot eyes flew open and started moving spookily from side to side, not focusing on anything. The tiny broken veins in the whites of his eyes gave him a ghoulish look.

The tremor in his right arm spread to other limbs. After a few minutes, his entire body vibrated as if an electric current were running through it. In an ominous way, its body was coming alive. I say "its body" because Waqar's soul, spirit, or whatever you call it had flown far away. A monster inhabited that body now.

We watched that unnatural spectacle, mesmerized. Usman was terrified. Tears rolled down his face, and he sobbed loudly and soulfully as he clung to his AK-47. The guy was about to lose it. It was too much for him.

Shafiq seemed unwilling to accept that reality and stubbornly bobbed forward and backward, sort of catatonic, obsessively reciting prayers from the Koran in a muffled chant that gave me the willies. In the background, we could hear the sound of hell—undead roaring and pounding at the gate.

Viktor gripped the huge gun he'd taken from Kritzinev with both hands. With a determined look on his face, he took a deep breath, cocked the rifle, and aimed at Waqar's head. The thing was wobbling as it attempted to stand up. I shook my head and grabbed his arm to lower the gun. I wanted to see. I needed to know. Will he recognize us? Can we talk to him?

Kritzinev suddenly appeared at the door, staggering around, half-asleep. That crazed scene took him completely by surprise. He'd come to take a piss. On the way to the john, he came upon his two hostages now armed, two of his men totally overcome by the situation, and the third mutating into one of those things.

For a moment he didn't grasp the situation. Then the light went on. He ran over to Shafiq and snatched his assault rifle. By then, Waqar had managed to sit up and was looking around, dazed and bewildered. A new monster had been born, twelve minutes after he died. It was scary. Kritzinev went up to Waqar and aimed, his hands trembling. His voice cracked as he shouted something in Urdu. Waqar didn't respond and continued to try to stand up. He shouted again. This time Waqar, the monster, glared at him and let out a terrifying groan, revealing a dark mouth filled with blood and pus.

That was too much for Kritzinev. He took a step back and pulled the trigger. The AK-47 was set on automatic, and it jumped in his hands, unleashing a hail of bullets. Waqar's head was instantly turned into red pulp, like a watermelon hit by a truck, soaking Kritzinev with brains and blood.

All hell broke loose. One of the Pakistanis threw up noisily. Waqar's body fell backward, convulsing. Kritzinev was enraged. He jumped over Waqar's body and pointed the gun at our heads. For a second I thought he had the DTs from all the alcohol he'd drunk and was to going to blow us all away. That would be an absurd, ironic end: survive the apocalypse and hundreds of undead, only to be killed by a hallucinating drunk in the back room of an abandoned grocery store.

Fortunately, Kritzinev got a hold of himself and didn't fire, but he kept the gun pointed at us. Barking at Pritchenko in Russian, he forced us against the wall. He snatched the gun from the Ukrainian, who made no effort to resist. Smart move. Hearing the gunfire, both Pakistanis snapped out of their catatonic state and stood behind their boss, guns in hand, glaring at us, ready to pull the trigger if we made the slightest hostile move. The best thing was to look innocent and roll with it.

Kritzinev pounced on Pritchenko and violently punched him, sending him crashing against the wall. With a look of sadistic satisfaction, he turned to me and raised his arm, ready to give me my share. I cringed, bracing myself.

At that moment, the unsettling sound of ripping metal ricocheted through the store. The gate had given way. Kritzinev forgot all about punching me. He shouted something in Urdu to the Pakistanis and rushed to the front door with them right behind him. I hung back with Pritchenko. I heard them drag shelves over to build a barricade.

I helped Prit stand up. He had a bruise on his cheek and spat out some blood, but nothing that would kill him. No time to think about that. I went up to the storeroom door. The Pakistanis and Kritzinev had barricaded themselves in behind the metal gate, which was coming loose on one side. Each time the crowd hit it, plaster and rubble fell from the door frame. Some monsters had already stuck their arms through the cracks on the side and were pushing against the shelves. One of them even tried to push its head through. That gate would only hold for a few minutes.

Kritzinev turned, pointed his rifle at us, and ordered us back to the storeroom. He clearly didn't trust us and didn't want us in the middle at that fight. I didn't want any part of it either. The Pakistanis were chanting what sounded like a hymn of martyrdom in Arabic. Shafiq had tied a piece of green cloth around his head and seemed calmer.

I shook my head. Fuck. It was getting ugly. Two guys who aspired to martyrdom and a crazy, drunk Ukrainian. I waved Pritchenko back to the storeroom and desperately looked for a way out. There was nothing. No window or back door or vent! Nothing!

Once again, life wasn't like the movies. There were no back doors or windows that opened onto vacant lots or secret tunnels or trapdoors. Just a grocery store with brick and concrete walls too thick to kick in. We were trapped.

Suddenly Pritchenko dragged me behind a counter. Above a heavy table was a trapdoor built into the wall. Leaning a chair against the table, I climbed up and slid the door open in the foolish hope of finding a tunnel out of there.

Toilet paper. Dozens and dozens of rolls of toilet paper and paper towels neatly stacked. This was where the owner had stored items that wouldn't fit on the shelves. I frantically pulled down package after package of paper as we heard the first shots in the front of the store. The final assault was starting.

It only took thirty seconds to empty the whole storage area and another thirty seconds for us to climb inside a space that was claustrophobically small, but safe and hidden. We had a liter-and-a-half bottle of water, two flashlights, a chocolate bar, and my journal. Absolutely nothing else.

We stretched out a bit. Viktor fit perfectly; he's only five foot two. I was a little cramped, but comfortable. A small hole in the door allowed us to breathe and gave us a partial view of the storeroom. All we could do was wait.

From the front room came the clatter of AK-47s and the howling of the undead. The gunfire grew more intense. Three guns firing simultaneously in a confined space made a lot of noise. We smelled the gunpowder. I don't know what the firepower of those weapons is, but in such an enclosed space it had to be devastating.

But the enemy outnumbered them. After a couple of minutes we heard piercing howls, and one of the guns stopped firing. The fighting moved closer to the door. A crazed, bloodied Kritzinev appeared, walking backward. He threw down his AK-47 and drew the pistol at his waist. Pursued by at least a dozen of those creatures, the Ukrainian emptied the clip, but for every one that fell, two more appeared.

Kritzinev realized the battle was lost and pointed the gun at his temple. Before he could shoot, an obese young guy in a striped shirt, covered in dried blood from head to toe, bit his neck and tore off a piece of flesh the size of a fist. Kritzinev dropped the pistol, uttering a cry of pain and surprise with anger in his eyes as he disappeared under a mass of those creatures. I don't want to replay the sounds we heard.

Twelve hours have passed. The shop is quiet and dark. Oil lamps lying on the floor have burned out. There're no words to describe the smell. We can't leave the crawl space because a few of those creatures are still here, walking in the shadows, relentless. We have no idea what to do.

E N T R Y 6 9
March 11, 9:38 p.m.

The human mind is amazing. After more than twenty-four hours locked in a tiny storage space the size of a closet, with no lights and hardly any sound, I started to hallucinate. I was sure I heard a TV. I could even make out the ads. It was agonizing. I knew perfectly well they were just in my mind, but they sounded so real. Oh, God. I covered my ears, but I could still hear everything clearly.

That closet was my undoing. I was sliding down the slippery slope of madness. I couldn't take any more fatigue, terror, and pent-up stress after seventy-two hours of light and food deprivation. I couldn't take it anymore. I was suffocating in there. The walls were closing in on me; the space seemed even smaller, crushing, squeezing me. The darkness was thick as oil; even the air was dark. I couldn't breathe; my lungs pumped air like crazy but got no oxygen. I was choking. I had to get out of there!

I scratched at the door, desperately groping for the handle. Then two hands, hard as steel, grabbed my arms. Pritchenko whispered something in Russian, trying to reassure me. He had immobilized me with the strength of a karate black belt. He didn't let go until my breathing calmed down and I regained control. That fucking Ukrainian's looks are deceiving. He's so small, and his huge blond mustache covers half his mouth, but he has an iron spirit and amazing resilience. He hadn't collapsed under pressure; I'd been about to send us both to hell in an attack of claustrophobia.

I started to cry in silence, like a real idiot. I'd had enough. We'd been shut up in that closet-size hole for an entire day. I was hungry, thirsty, and sleepy. I had excruciating cramps and was completely disoriented. It was fucking hell, but there was no neon sign pointing to the exit.

With all that movement, I'm sure we made some noise. Fortunately those monsters were making far more commotion as they moved around the wreckage in the storeroom, stumbling over fallen shelves and the remains of our team. For the moment, they hadn't noticed us. I peered through the little hole in the door. All I could see was half of the storeroom and the hallway that led to the front of the store. A little light was coming through the front door.

I could see the shadows of at least eight of those things still in the room. I knew there were plenty more in front of the store and out in the street. Those bastards hadn't left when they finished off Kritzinev and the Pakistanis. They just stayed out there, searching for something...or someone.

For the first few hours, that room was crowded with the monsters drawn by the gunfire. Now, something (instinct?) told them there was still fresh prey in the vicinity. As time passed, most lost interest and moved outside.

Somehow they knew there were humans nearby but they didn't know exactly where. Was it the heat we gave off? Electromagnetic fields? Some other sense that eludes me? They restlessly prowled around, frustrated that they couldn't find what they were sure was there.

For four terrifying hours, a tall, gangly monster with a big gash on his back stood in front of the crawl space, slamming his fists at the bottom of the sliding door and roaring. We froze. We thought that bastard had discovered us, and that was the end of the line. But finally the guy lost interest and went back to wandering around the room, then retreated to God knows where.

Those things are strong and have a kind of sixth sense, but they aren't very smart or persevering. Their coordination and ability to concentrate are limited; their motor skills are worse. After a while, they seem to get bored or distracted, except when a strong stimulus, usually a human, gets their attention. Then they're relentless.

All this is just a guess. To my knowledge, nobody has any idea of how those creatures think. The epidemic spread too fast for anyone to do any scientific studies. If anyone is doing research in a bunker somewhere, he must be miles underground. A lot of good that'll do us, surrounded by them.

And it wouldn't fix my hallucinations: I thought I heard a siren.

Pritchenko squeezed my arms so hard I nearly howled in pain. He'd heard it too! It wasn't a hallucination!

There were three long blasts, a pause, and three more long blasts. It was the hoarse, deep sound made by a powerful steam turbine coming from far off. A ship's horn! The *Zaren Kibish*. Ushakov was trying to contact us. He must be getting worried, wondering what was taking us so long. We needed to answer, let him know we were alive. But that would have to wait.

The siren riveted the monsters packed inside the store. The room emptied out as they stumbled out the door, one by one, headed for that new sound only a human being—prey!—could make.

All but one. For some reason, an undead woman in her fifties wearing sparkly earrings, her face streaked with makeup and dirt, kept walking around in the storeroom. Maybe she detected human prey more intensely than the others. Or maybe she was dull-witted. Who can say? She just stood there watching, waiting. This was the chance we were waiting for. Pritchenko and I didn't have to say a word. I shoved the sliding door aside and jumped onto the counter, Prit following.

The woman looked up, surprised. With a mad roar, she walked toward us, dodging the mangled remains of furniture and rotting corpses on the ground.

I tried to stand up, but my legs didn't respond after a whole day tucked into that tiny crawl space. I just couldn't get up. There was an unpleasant tingling in my legs as circulation was restored, but for all intents and purposes, I was helpless as a puppy.

Again Pritchenko rose to the occasion, drawing strength from somewhere. He crawled forward and grabbed the empty AK-47 Kritzinev had thrown down before he died. Using the rifle as a cane to help him stand up, he leaned against the wall, then grabbed the rifle by the barrel like a club and squared off against that harpy, whose breathing whistled softly between her teeth. That guy sure had some balls.

Prit didn't have to wait for that creature's response. She wobbled toward him. When she was within reach, he raised the AK-47 over his head and brought it down with all his might against the woman's skull.

There was a loud *crack* as her skull split open, exposing her dark, infected brains. She rocked back and forth and staggered. Pritchenko leveled a second blow. Her head burst like a ripe melon and she fell to the ground. He bent over her, hitting her skull again and again until it was a mass of red pulp.

I struggled to my feet and grabbed Viktor's shoulders as he gave the corpse the umpteenth blow. He had a maniacal look in his eyes and that woman's brains all over his arms and chest. When he felt my hands, he spun around like a cobra. For a moment I thought he was going to whack me too.

His expression slowly returned to normal. Finally his weak legs couldn't hold him any longer and he collapsed to the floor, dragging me down with him. Now he was the one sobbing convulsively, venting the tension that had built up over the last twenty-four hours, as adrenaline roared through his veins.

I wrapped my arms around his shoulders and helped him sit up. We didn't have much time. We had to get out of that hellhole right away. Regaining his composure, Prit sniffed loudly and picked up Kritzinev's gun. He said wearily, "We're finally out of the closet."

I burst out laughing as the Ukrainian gazed at me, wondering what had gotten into me. Every time I tried to stop laughing, the puzzled look on Pritchenko's face made me laugh even harder. With tears in my eyes, I explained the slang meaning of what he'd said. Then the Ukrainian laughed too. That was liberating. For the first time in weeks, we laughed uncontrollably, as stress flowed out of us. Any silly comment would set us off again. It was fantastic. We were still human. We were still alive. We could still put up a fight.

We didn't glean much from the gruesome scene. Kritzinev's pistol was our only weapon. We found the AK-47s, but couldn't locate the ammunition. Usman and Shafiq had had the ammunition belts, but there was no sign of them. They were probably wandering around, mutants now, packing dozens of rounds of ammunition. Fuck.

Before we left, I bent over Kritzinev's corpse. The undead's fury had been over the top; they'd ripped the poor bastard's body to shreds. There was no way he was coming back to life. Part of his brain was missing; an arm and both legs and his stomach were torn apart as if a wild animal had attacked him. What a gruesome death. I reached into his jacket pocket and pulled out the blood-stained receipt. I hadn't forgotten about that fucking package. It was the only way I'd get Lucullus back.

We left the store, stepping around a huge mound of putrid bodies piled up at the door. The sun was blinding. As Pritchenko and I walked out of the store, I glanced around. I saw a couple of those things about four hundred yards away. They'd spotted us and were heading our way. Time to get a move on.

We ran up the street, limping, drained from lack of food and water. We wouldn't get far in that shape. As we walked along the deserted street, more and more of those things came out of unex-pected places to join the chase. Thousands of them! They were closing in on us.

Suddenly Pritchenko and I stopped dead in our tracks. Spread out before us was a gruesome scene. We were at the edge of a swath of Vigo charred by fires that had raged out of control. I'd seen those fires from the *Corinth*. The street we were on dead-ended in an area where scorched, collapsed buildings had fallen every which way. The city looked like it'd been bombed.

This was our chance. Prit and I climbed onto the ruins, crawling over piles of rubble and twisted, blackened beams. The undead couldn't follow us into this shattered land. They weren't coordinated enough to climb that rubble. That landscape looked as dead as the moon, riddled with holes, covered with beams, piles of rubble and mangled remains. It wasn't much easier for us, given the shape we were in, but the important thing was, we could climb and they couldn't.

After twenty minutes of wandering around in that hell, Pritchenko and I collapsed, panting, into a deep hole in the middle of the devastation. At the bottom of that hole was a large pool of rainwater. We drank like camels, then lay down to catch our breath, with the sun on our faces and a breeze in our hair. Spring had arrived in all its glory. We were glad to be alive.

ENTRY 70
March 12, 10:41 p.m.

I'm sitting next to a small campfire. A tasty chicken vegetable soup is bubbling away. Across the flames, I can see Pritchenko's familiar silhouette wrapped in a blanket, snoring so loud he could wake the dead. For the first time in weeks, I'm in such a good mood I can even joke about this.

Yesterday we left that burned zone after languishing there for three days. Prit and I were completely exhausted. Fortunately, the Ukrainian had quickly spotted a place to take shelter and recuperate, which undoubtedly saved our lives.

It was hot at the bottom of that hollow. The sun in a cloudless sky beat down mercilessly as we lay like lizards next to a pool of rainwater that was evaporating before our eyes in that stifling heat. It was so hot the air vibrated. Debris seemed to tremble. The silence was complete, broken only by occasional snaps and pops from the ruins and crumbling buildings and the drone of flies. Once we heard dogs barking in the distance, but the barking stopped after a few minutes.

Prit and I tried to build a tent out of a torn sheet, but we had nothing to prop it up with. We were too weak to perform any feats of engineering.

Bottom line, our situation was pitiful. We were alone, essentially unarmed, lost in an abandoned, half-destroyed city, exhausted, hungry, with just dirty water to drink, surrounded by thousands of undead. Not exactly a tropical vacation.

We were sweating like pigs in that torrid heat. I walked to the edge of the puddle of water, made a bowl with my hands, and drank some water. I smiled ruefully at my reflection. Pritchenko and I looked strikingly alike. After all we'd been through, we both had beards; our hair was matted and dirty; our clothes (in my case, a swimsuit and a ragged shirt, since I'd stripped off my wet-suit in the storeroom) were in tatters; our skin was greasy and smeared with soot; our hands were dirty; our nails were broken; we had that sharp, bony, hungry look and, I suppose, a foul smell. A beggar from before the apocalypse would look like a movie star next to us.

I told Prit that if a client could see me like this, he wouldn't recognize me. Laughing, he said that Siunten probably wouldn't hire him looking like that.

A while back, I'd considered asking him what the hell Siunten was. That company didn't sound familiar. I hardly knew anything about my friend, except that we'd spent three terrifying days together, and twice he'd saved my life. Just as I started to ask, the *Zaren Kibish* sirens thundered again, breaking the silence of the dead city.

That hoarse blast spread throughout the city. It's amazing how sounds travel in absolute silence. We city dwellers are surrounded by thousands of sounds, so we don't realize that. In such silent surroundings, the sound of an engine or a radio could be heard miles away. They probably heard the ship's horn all over Vigo and in neighboring towns. The fools on the *Zaren Kibish* kept mindlessly blowing the siren. Bad idea. They'd draw all the fucking undead in the entire region right to us.

We had to move on. If we stayed where we were, we'd starve or die of sunstroke or God knows what. My questions for Pritchenko would have to wait. We dragged ourselves to our feet and crawled back over all the rubble and the charred remains of cars and buildings.

The smell of burned flesh hung over everything. Occasionally we saw piles of scorched bodies, but there was no way to tell if they'd been humans or undead, trapped in the voracious fires that devoured parts of the city.

I was stopped in my tracks by the terrifying thought that the VNT office might've been burned to the ground. If it was, we could kiss that mysterious package good-bye unless it'd been wrapped in an asbestos box. I tried to calm down. I reminded myself that when I scanned the city from the *Corinth*, the part of the city the office was in looked to be intact. Still, that was even more reason to hurry to our destination. Although it would only take a few hours to get there, we couldn't travel at night, of course.

As the afternoon wore on, the temperature dropped. Soon Prit and I were shivering. Spring nights in Galicia can be chilly, no matter how hot the days are.

Prit and I hesitated at the edge of the burned-out zone. Before us stretched a wide two-lane street covered with dust, dirt, and soot, but unscathed. Maybe because of rain or a sudden change in the wind, the fire had stopped there and hadn't continued down the street, devouring the city. From that point on, the rest of Vigo was intact, but dirty, abandoned, and infested with undead. Walking among the ruins had been torturously slow and difficult, but at least we were sure we wouldn't encounter any undead. Now the road would be easier, but considerably more dangerous.

We had no choice. We stepped on to the street, trying to pass unnoticed. I couldn't read the street sign; it was covered in soot. Night was falling, and the light was fading.

Although we were just a few blocks from the VNT offices, we had to stop and hide. It would be suicide to walk around, unarmed and unable to see where we were, in an unfamiliar area infested with those creatures. We hadn't come this far just to fuck up as we turned a corner. Plus, we'd pass out if we didn't get something to eat. Our growling stomachs would scare a bear.

Suddenly, a smile lit up Pritchenko's face. He stopped and pointed. I breathed a sigh of relief. It was turning out to be a good day. He'd had found a great place to spend the night.

It was a small tavern sandwiched between a ransacked bank and a video store with bloodstained windows. Its facade was covered in dirt and soot. Hanging over the door was a rickety Coca-Cola sign with the bar's name painted on it: THE OLD VINE.

To call it a corner bar would be generous. It was really a dump. Before the apocalypse, I wouldn't have given it a second glance. The door was secured by a hinged gate that reached all the way to the ground and had a large, rusty padlock. Between the gate and the door was a pile of old, yellowed newspapers dating from before the epidemic and a lot of flyers, faded from months of exposure to rain and wind.

That hole-in-the-wall must've closed long before everything went to hell. It was unlikely we'd find undead in there, but we wouldn't know that till we went inside. Our options were dwindling fast. It was getting dark; soon we wouldn't be able to see past our noses. The sky was clouding up; a storm was about to break. There wouldn't be any moonlight. Every minute we stood in the middle of the street increased the chance that unwanted company would track us down.

The door to the bank had been blown off its hinges. Judging from the scrapes on the wall and pavement, someone had dragged the ATM outside with a powerful vehicle. Probably looters during the chaotic days at the end. One thing was for sure—we'd be no better off sleeping in that bank than in the street. I wasn't crazy about entering the video store, with all the blood on its windows. And I certainly didn't need to rent a movie.

So our best alternative was the bar. While Prit fiddled around with the padlock on the gate, I peered in the window through ads, faded posters, and a list of local soccer matches. In the dusty, dark interior, there were bottles were lined up neatly behind the bar. Suddenly, I was obsessed with the idea of drinking a frothy beer, sitting quietly at a table. We had to go in.

Walking a few yards from the demolished area, I picked up a piece of cement rubble that weighed about ten pounds. I gathered my waning strength and threw it at the window. The thud startled Prit, and he jumped to one side as shards of cement rained down on him. I gave him a sheepish look, silently apologizing. The Ukrainian shook his head, still shaken up. The window was shattered, but not broken.

Safety glass, but bad quality. If it'd been high-quality safety glass, I could've thrown that boulder a hundred times and it wouldn't have scratched the surface. But this was a seedy bar, not a jewelry store. After few well-placed blows, what Pritchenko called "the old Soviet way," the window finally gave way, leaving a gap big enough for Prit and me to slip through.

There was dust everywhere, and the place smelled musty. I laughed at myself when I automatically reached out to turn on the light. Some habits never die. Prit leaned a table against the window to cover the hole, transforming the bar into a fortress against the undead. I slipped behind the bar to take stock while some light still remained. The cash register was empty, and the moldy carcass of a lemon was rotting in a bowl next to a rusty knife. I found a Bic lighter. Pritchenko pulled some heavy curtains across the window to block the view from the street. Perfect.

By the light of that lighter, we looked through the drawers and finally found a couple of candles. Once they were lit, we opened one of the refrigerators. In less than two minutes, Pritchenko and I had chugged half a dozen bottles of water and a couple soft drinks, sitting with our backs against the bar. You could almost see all that liquid running through my body, reviving me. My tongue rehydrated with each bottle of water, and I could feel my cells soaking up that blessed liquid up like a sponge.

Once we'd quenched our thirst, hunger became our next priority. As I was writing some lines in this book, I heard Prit tinkering in the little kitchen at the back. I was too weak to help. After a few minutes, he reappeared, smiling, carrying a huge pile of cans. The kitchen was pretty well stocked and relatively intact. It wouldn't feed an army, but it would feed a couple of survivors for a few days.

That night we slept soundly for the first time in a week. When we awoke, sunlight was filtering through the curtains. After we washed up a little with bottled water, we assessed the situation. After some discussion, we decided to stay in the bar for another day to get our strength back. Through the curtains, we saw plenty of undead moving down the street, headed for God only knows where.

ENTRY 71
March 13, 7:30 p.m.

This morning we finally ventured outside again. The street was drenched. It must've rained during the night. As the Ukrainian and I traveled along the sidewalk, hiding behind abandoned cars, a weak sun began to emerge. Wisps of steam rose off the pavement as the humidity burned off. It promised to be another sultry day, but right then it was still nice and cool.

Pritchenko carried a huge kitchen knife hanging at his waist. I'd grabbed a small meat cleaver. It wouldn't do much good against a horde of those creatures, but it made me feel a lot more confident.

To be honest, we got overconfident, and it nearly cost us our lives. We were less than ten minutes from the address on the receipt when we turned a corner without taking the time to scope it out and stumbled upon the girl.

She was in her twenties and quite tall. She had a spectacular blonde mane halfway to her waist and a nice figure. She wore a top that left little to the imagination and skintight jeans that fit really well. Her features were delicate, and she wore enormous rhinestone earrings. She was very pretty. A really great-looking girl. The only thing marring her beauty was the ugly wound that ran along her shoulder blade, leaving a messy trail of blood down her bare back. That and the fact she was a damned undead.

I didn't see her coming, and before I knew it she was on top of me, struggling to bite me. Her saliva dripped on to my chest as she locked me in a deadly embrace. I shuddered. If she scratched me, I'd end up like the Pakistani guy. I cried for help from Pritchenko.

Prit coolly situated himself behind the girl, who had me backed against a wall. With a quick, expert gesture, he grabbed the girl by the hair with one hand and began to methodically execute her with the knife in the other hand.

It was a scene out of Dante's *Inferno*. Black blood gushed from the girl's neck as Pritchenko methodically sawed through muscles and tendons. When he reached the trachea, the knife made a scraping sound as it tore the cartilage. He was like some mad butcher. Blood gushed all over Prit and me. I couldn't get free of her deadly arm, which held me against the wall. The woman twisted around, trying to attack Pritchenko, but now it was my turn to grip her tight. I could clearly see the hole in her esophagus through the blood clots. I was mesmerized.

When Pritchenko's knife reached the vertebrae in her neck, it hit bone. He pulled out the blade and stood back while I shoved the girl's bloody, trembling body into the middle of the street. Her head hung at an impossible angle on her back.

It was my turn. I hauled back and brought my cleaver down, trying to hack through the remaining piece of the thing's neck. Her body swayed backward, and the blade struck her collarbone. Now she was bouncing around wildly in the middle of the street, her head hanging by a thread, her arm half severed. It was something out of a gory movie.

I whacked her neck a second time. My aim was true this time, and her head rolled on the ground. Her convulsing body collapsed.

Pritchenko picked her head up by the hair and gazed at it, deep in thought. It was creepy. That fucking head was still snapping its mouth and gnashing its teeth. It made no sound since it had no larynx or lungs, but if it could, it would've been screaming with rage.

With all his might, Prit threw it down the road. The head flew through the air in an arc, hit the ground with a thud, and rolled into a corner. If no one touched her, she might stay there until…when? How long can these beings live? Are they eternal? Questions and more questions and not a fucking answer.

Pritchenko and I were bathed in blood.

That episode gave me something new to think about. Prit had meticulously, patiently beheaded a girl in cold blood. His pulse didn't even seem to rise. Calm and professional. I asked myself: Who the hell is this guy? A bit uneasy, I studied the Ukrainian as we got back under way.

The VNT office was just around the corner. I was sick of it all. I wanted to get out of this damn city as fast as I could.

Fifteen minutes later, we were surveying the wide street that stretched out before us. Plastic bags fluttered wildly on hot, thick air from one end of the street to the other while dust swirled in intricate patterns. Separating the two lanes was a median where nature was urgently reclaiming its place. The flowering plants that once grew there had succumbed to weeds. Vines, ferns, and brambles coiled around trees no one would prune again. Shoots of grass were poking up through cracks in the pavement.

Dozens of vehicles were parked on the shoulder or abandoned in the road. There were a lot of cars, some vans, and even a couple of huge, heavy trucks. The cab of a monstrous eighteen-wheeler was embedded in the window of a women's clothing store. Dried blood trailed from the driver's door.

Tattered curtains flapped through open windows. Windows in every building were shattered, and the pavement was covered by a thick layer of broken glass. The huge explosion at the port must have blown out all those windows.

There was no sign of life apart from dozens of rats and countless gulls hovering overhead. It's funny. Since all this began, I've seen dogs, cats (my Lucullus), rats, and gulls, but not a single pigeon or horse or sparrow or any other animal. I wonder if this epidemic affects other living beings. One more question to add to the growing list.

Prit and I had taken up a position on the cab of a massive dump truck. It had a busted windshield and four flat tires and was parked partway up on the sidewalk on the corner. It had a perfect view of the street.

There wasn't a single monster around, but drag marks in the dust on the pavement were unmistakable. We spotted a few tottering figures about two hundred yards away, at the far end of the road. Too far for them to see us, but still too close.

The ground was covered with trash and dirt, along with dozens of rotting corpses, all with gunshot wounds. Pritchenko thought they were the undead killed by the raiding parties from the Safe Haven. I didn't know what to think. I was starting to suspect that the collapse of law and order in large cities like Vigo had been more terrible and chaotic than in small towns. Thousands of civilian sightings of the undead must've overwhelmed the security forces. Then it was every man for himself. Those bodies might be proof of that.

Across the street was VNT's home office. It was in a medium-size building with a glass door and a huge window on one side, where the offices were located. On the other side, a large black metal gate with the company's gold logo painted on it sealed off the van parking garage. The place appeared to be closed up tight and deserted.

In the back of the eighteen-wheeler was a huge load of building materials. On its last trip, they must've been planning to install a pipeline; about fifteen PVC pipes, four inches in diameter, were stacked in the truck bed. Behind the cab were a number of tools, including a crowbar. We could use that to open the office door.

Several months ago, our firm defended a small-time thief. He gave us a detailed lesson in the art of breaking and entering. The guy was a real pro who'd been caught *in flagrante* after he'd cleaned out at least a dozen apartments, so we couldn't get him off. He was probably in jail when all this hell began. I wonder what's happened to that poor thief, and everyone locked up in prison. I shudder at the image of entire wings of starving prisoners. Even though they were criminals, I hoped at least some of them survived.

Grabbing the crowbar with both hands, I quietly crossed the road, Pritchenko on my heels, to try out what the thief had taught me. Knowledge never goes to waste.

It was easier than I expected. I struggled briefly and took a couple of chips out of the door frame. Then the door sprung open with a loud *crack* that chilled me to the bone. The sound probably didn't carry more than ten yards, but in that silence it sounded like a gunshot.

We entered the lobby of VNT. We'd reached our destination at last. The customer service department was located behind a wooden counter, badly scratched by countless packages sliding across it. In one corner sat the dust-covered skeleton of a houseplant. Months-old newspapers and magazines were piled on a coffee table framed by two armchairs. The stale smell of cigarette smoke hung in the air, faint but perceptible. Someone in that office had smoked a lot, although nobody had lit a cigarette there for a long time.

That wasn't the only odor. Partly masked by the smell of cigarette smoke was the intense, sickening smell of decay. The smell of death.

Prit and I were immediately on alert. Brandishing the butcher knife, I inched up the swinging door that led to the back of the store. Prit stationed himself in front of the door, aiming Kritzinev's assault rifle. Sweating like crazy, I looked over at him. At his signal, I kicked the door open and leaped aside, giving him a clear shot.

I cringed, bracing myself for the blast of the weapon, but all I heard was Ukrainian's ragged breathing. I looked over and saw Prit's expression change. I turned around to see what he was staring at. I gagged as vomit surged up my throat.

A half-rotten corpse hung by a rope from a ceiling. The guy had looped the rope around his neck and hanged himself. He wore VNT overalls rolled down to his waist. The maggots covering his face looked like a beard.

It was a revolting sight. The body was decaying, and a stream of smelly liquid dripped from his body, forming a thick, dark puddle. The body was swollen with gas and looked obscenely fat. A thick purple tongue stuck out of his open mouth; dozens of green flies were buzzing around it. His eyes had receded into their sockets, and his swollen, bruised fingers looked like a cartoon character's fingers after he'd been crushed. The stench was awful. Pritchenko and I covered our noses and mouths and went in, trying not to look at that grim spectacle or brush up against him. A quick look around the store told the whole story.

That poor guy had been stuck there from the beginning. He must've seen the first undead go staggering down the street. He reacted like most people: he locked himself in until help arrived. Unfortunately for him, help never came. That was the start of that poor devil's personal hell. An empty snack machine, its glass broken, was proof that his only source of food soon grew scarce. Dirty laundry and some well-thumbed girlie magazines were piled up on the floor. He had sense enough to use one of the vans as the john and drink the water in the toilet, but that must've run out too. Poor bastard. After a while, he just couldn't take the hunger, thirst, loneliness, and madness any more.

I shuddered to think I could've met the same end if I hadn't left my house. I shook my head to drive away those dark thoughts. There was no time to grieve for a stranger. We had to look for the damn package.

And we found it—a black steel Samsonite briefcase, sealed with red plastic tape. Prit and I spent the afternoon in the stifling heat, digging around in that damn store, but we finally found it.

I can't believe we've got the package. Thoughts whirled through my mind as we decided what our next move would be. My first impulse was to try to open the damn case to see what was inside. But a reinforced steel Samsonite briefcase wouldn't be easy to break into, even if I did what that thief taught me. Only the key holder or a real thief could open it. Unfortunately Prit and I don't qualify as either.

We got used to the smell of rotting flesh after a while. I suggested we take down the body and wrap it in a blanket, but the Ukrainian talked me out of it. Given the condition of the corpse, it'd probably burst in our arms and shower us with rotting guts. Better leave it there, in his words, "drying like a cured ham." I was creeped out, wondering where the hell he'd learned that, but I didn't ask.

I've saved the best for last. That Ukrainian is full of surprises. What I learned about him today amazed me.

While I was rummaging through an office drawer, looking for the keys to some cabinets at the back of the store, I absent-mindedly set some government forms to one side and opened another drawer. Just then Pritchenko walked into the office and collapsed in the desk chair, stretching and yawning loudly. His eye fell on the forms lying on the table. He casually pronounced one word: "Siunten."

I stopped in my tracks. I looked at the Ukrainian's impassive face and his huge blond mustache and then at the forms on the table. I couldn't hold back any longer.

"Siunten? Siunten?" I asked, excited, pointing to the forms. "Is this Siunten?"

"*Da*, yes," Prit replied, surprised at my reaction.

I had good reason to be surprised. Those forms weren't important. The really interesting part was the logo in the corner of the file folder.

"Siunten" was Pritchenko's distorted Slavic version of *Xunta*. The Xunta de Galicia. The Galician government.

A light came on. I understood everything. Not many Ukrainians worked for the Xunta de Galicia, and Pritchenko was one of them. Now I knew exactly what my friend did. An excited shiver ran down my spine. What an idiot I'd been.

I turned to study Prit's affable profile.

I felt completely drained all of a sudden. We'd spent five terrifying days together to retrieve that damn case lying on an old wooden table. At least five people had died on account of whatever was inside. But we were still alive. We'd come within a hair's breadth of losing our own lives a couple of times. Natural selection had been ridiculously harsh over the last few months. We survivors are the most skilled, the fittest…or we just haven't made many bad decisions. All that was in the past. We had the case.

Now we had to get out of that fucking store, thanks to Prit. He didn't know it, but he was one of the most valuable people left in that part of the world. Not even Ushakov, the *Zaren Kibish*'s captain, knew who Prit was. Otherwise, he would've exploited his skills, not blithely sent him ashore to almost certain death.

Prit was worth his weight in gold. Sitting beside me, quietly smoking a Chesterfield, his huge blond mustache drooping over his mouth, was Mr. Viktor Pritchenko: the only living helicopter pilot for hundreds of miles around.

Wildfires plague Galicia during the summer. Because the area is so heavily wooded, voracious fires destroy acres and acres of woodlands every year. Combating those fires takes enormous efforts, materials, and human resources.

The early 1990s were very dry years, with particularly large fires. The Galician government was overwhelmed. Using military aircraft to fight the fires didn't cut it. Firefighting crews couldn't get to the affected areas fast enough on the ground, and seaplanes weren't very reliable. They decided to hire pilots from Eastern Europe.

The majority of those pilots were former Russian, Polish, and Ukrainian soldiers who were kicked out on the street when the Eastern Bloc fell. After paying ridiculous sums of money in bribes to save their planes and helicopters from the scrap heap, they earned a living in emerging Eastern European nations by giving air shows or transporting people and goods more or less legally from one country to another. They were experienced, tough, cheap, and had their own helicopters. The perfect solution.

They quickly proved they were worth every penny. Plunging into a forest fire was child's play for those pilots, especially the ones with combat experience in Afghanistan and Chechnya. Where the terrified Spanish civilian pilots refused to fly, the former Soviet soldiers dived in with a recklessness bordering on madness, losing their lives on more than one occasion. What's more, their old Soviet helicopters were tough, easy to maintain, and had a larger cargo capacity than their Western twins, making them ideal.

Since then, pilots from the East and their old workhorses fought fires in Galicia year after year, from March to October. In the winter they went back to Eastern Europe, loaded down with Western goods they resold on the black market.

Prit related all this in a monotone, lighting one cigarette after another. He was from Zaproshpojye, a tiny village in northern Ukraine, but he was a Russian citizen. He joined the Red Army when he was only seventeen. After basic training, he was assigned to a company of transport helicopters. He fought in the final days of the war in Afghanistan, where he was shot down once, and in the Second Chechen War, transporting Russian troops to the front. He had a bright future in the army. Then he married Irina.

He took a crumpled photo of Irina out of his wallet. His voice trembled, and tears welled up in his eyes. Irina was gorgeous, a little Slavic doll with blonde hair and huge green eyes. He met her on leave, and they got married a year later. Little Pavel came along a year after that, complicating the couple's lives. A Russian military pilot's salary was terribly low compared to what he could make in the West. Plus the Chechen war was getting more dangerous and out of control. Prit had a family to support, so the decision was easy.

Three months after getting out of the army, Pritchenko was working for a shady German transport company. He first came to Spain as a forestry pilot in 2002. He'd returned, year after year, while his family settled in Düsseldorf, Germany. He'd been considering bringing them to Galicia to live when the apocalypse started.

Prit was now sobbing. He hadn't heard a word from his family since late February, when they took refuge in the Düsseldorf Safe Haven. He was sure they were dead. I didn't dare give him any hope. What good would that do?

The question was on the tip of my tongue, but I didn't dare ask it as Prit wept bitterly on my shoulder for people who'd been killed or turned into monsters months ago.

When he'd calmed down, I blurted out, "Prit, where's your helicopter now?"

"Where I left helicopter two months ago, maybe," he replied, his breathing still ragged. "At forest camp. Mount Facho, twenty miles from here."

"What about the other pilots? Where are they? What did they do?" The questions shot out of my mouth.

"Oh, when everything kaput, they go. I don't know where."

My heart sank. Had Pritchenko's helicopter disappeared in the chaotic days before the fall of the Safe Havens, or been stolen by another pilot or seized by the army? To my surprise, the Ukrainian shook his head.

"Not possible," he said. "Helicopter damaged. Need cog tail rotor. Part small, but very expensive. Mailed from Kiev to Vigo."

My temples throbbed as I guessed the rest. "Where's that piece, Prit? Do you have it?"

The Ukrainian shook his head again. "*Nyet.* VNT make mistake. They know that part for a Ukraine, but give to wrong Ukraine."

I plopped down in a chair, thinking at top speed. Ushakov or Kritzinev must have gone to the VNT office to pick up their fuck-ing package. The employee couldn't read the label in Cyrillic, so he gave him the package with Pritchenko's part. The situation at the time was chaotic. A scared employee anxious to get the hell out and head for home wouldn't have bothered to check IDs. The package was from Ukraine, and Ushakov was Ukrainian. When Prit showed up for his part, they discovered the mistake, but by then it was too late. The world was falling apart.

This is great. I have a pilot and a helicopter at my disposal. That changes the situation dramatically. I only need two things: a small helicopter part and a cat. And I know where they both are. On the *Zaren Kibish.*

ENTRY 72
March 14, 7:36 a.m.

The sun's coming up. It's really cold in the VNT warehouse. Prit and I plan to leave in fifteen minutes. The Ukrainian is checking the bat-tery and tires of one of the delivery vans parkcd in the garage. They aren't as safe as that ill-fated armored van we came in, but at least we've got four wheels to drive to the port. Or as far as we can get.

I'm jotting down these notes as my friend tunes up our trans-portation. We changed out of our torn, filthy clothes and into gray-and-black VNT coveralls we found in a dressing room. We couldn't take a shower since there's no water, so our odor and appearance still leave a lot to be desired. At least we don't look like fugitives from the law anymore.

We talked at length about how we could swap the briefcase for Lucullus and the helicopter part. We finally had a plan. We spent hours working out all the details, but I think it'll work.

This'll have to be fast. Pritchenko's just started the van and is signaling for me to raise the garage door. The engine sound will soon attract a mob of those creatures, and we still have to make a stop along the way.

I hope everything goes well. The next time I write in this journal I'll have Lucullus.

Time to go. We're off.

‖‖‖‖‖‖‖‖‖‖‖‖‖‖‖‖‖‖‖‖‖‖‖‖‖‖‖‖‖[I N F E R N O]‖‖‖‖‖‖‖‖‖‖‖‖‖‖‖‖‖‖‖‖‖

ENTRY 73
April 11, 2:14 p.m.

I surrendered the driver's seat. I didn't want to argue with Prit about his ability to "drive any heap on four wheels." Truth is, the Ukrainian is a damn good driver, but he puts the fear of God in me.

Traveling from the port to the VNT office had taken nearly a week. We made it back to the port in just thirty-five minutes, ten minutes of which we spent trying to back out of a café window where we'd gotten stuck. A hair's breadth from killing ourselves, the way I saw it. According to the fucking Ukrainian, just a small mental fuckup.

The fact is, we were just a few yards from the entrance to the port, almost back where we started. The tall buildings at the port hid the *Zaren Kibish* and the *Corinth* from view, but they were close by. And we were ready with a plan.

With a screech that set my teeth on edge, Pritchenko shifted gears and set off for the entrance to the port.

There's an old military saying that a plan only works perfectly when you try it out on the enemy. We'd find out very soon that our plan was no exception.

The entire port gave off the pungent stench of rotting flesh. In the light of day, you could see that the entire Safe Haven was one big graveyard. Everywhere we looked were mountains of half-burned, rotting corpses.

The chuffing of the van drove away hundreds of gulls and fat rats with glossy coats. I shuddered when I thought about their diet. From time to time, a few staggering figures came out from between the wrecked warehouses and headed for our vehicle, but they were too far behind us. We were moving too fast for them to be a threat.

The Darwinian principle of survival of the fittest seemed to be working. Gradually only the toughest, fastest, or biggest sons of bitches were left. Or the luckiest, Prit said acidly. I was more and more convinced we'd get out of this alive. The mere fact that we were moving at top speed through an area full of those creatures would've paralyzed me with fear a few months ago. Now it just seemed like an everyday occurrence.

I told Prit what worried me most was not that there were so few survivors, but that there were so few *female* survivors. He thought for a moment, then started to tell a lurid tale about a girl from his village named Ludmila, nicknamed the Firefighter. Just as he got to the part about the straw, he hit the brakes. I almost flew through the windshield. We'd come to the Seguritsa alley, a few yards from where we'd landed what seemed like a million years ago.

Prit parked the van alongside a wrecked Beetle, leaving no way to get through, not even on foot. That makeshift barrier wouldn't hold them for long, but it would give us time to carry out our plan. Let the dance begin.

ENTRY 74
April 12, 1:07 p.m.

As the Zodiac approached the *Zaren Kibish*, adrenaline roared through my veins. The salt spray soaked my hair as the freighter's hull loomed ahead. With my right hand on the rudder, I clutched the black steel Samsonite briefcase with my left. A familiar bearded figure was leaning over the railing, staring through binoculars. Ushakov.

I closed my eyes and took a deep breath. The salty air, the familiar scent of algae and burning fuel, took me back to better times. I opened my eyes, with the childish hope it had all been a nightmare. Instead I saw the ladder hanging over the side.

Gripping the briefcase, I started up the ladder to the *Zaren*'s deck. When I got to the rail, an eager Filipino hand reached for the case. I slapped the hand away and hit another sailor in the chest with the briefcase as I stepped on deck. I didn't plan to let go of that briefcase. Not yet.

Ushakov pushed through a group of sailors and planted himself in front of me, his hands on his hips. There was a deathly silence on the deck.

On one side was Ushakov, surrounded by half a dozen burly sailors aiming Kalashnikovs at my chest. On the other side, there I was, dirty, unshaven, covered in cuts and bruises, wearing VNT overalls two sizes too big, bone tired, clutching a shiny black steel Samsonite briefcase. A real duel of Titans.

"Well, well, Mr. Lawyer!" Ushakov boomed. "You look awful! Where's the rest of group?"

"They're not here," I answered laconically.

"Kritzinev?"

"Dead."

"My crew?"

"Dead."

"Pritchenko?"

"He's dead, too." My voice cracked. "I'm the only one left, Comrade Captain."

Ushakov's face turned gray. I guess he hadn't expected me to return. His greedy gaze was fixed on the case.

"Is that it?" he asked in a trembling voice. "Is that the briefcase?"

"That's it, Ushakov," I said quietly. "Check the label."

I carefully placed the briefcase on the ground, the label clearly visible, and took a couple of steps back. Ushakov stared at the label and muttered something in Russian as he grabbed the Samsonite with both hands.

"I've fulfilled my part of the deal, Ushakov. Now it's your turn. Give me my cat and let me go."

Ushakov was mesmerized by the case. For a moment, I thought he hadn't heard me. I was about to repeat myself when Ushakov snapped out of his trance. Glancing briefly at me, he turned to one of the sailors armed with an AK-47.

"Kill him," he said matter-of-factly.

The Filipino cocked the rifle and aimed it at my chest. I had a split second to get out of that mess. It was now or never.

"I wouldn't do that, Captain," I said in a trembling voice. When I'd planned that, it seemed much easier. That was because I hadn't had the barrel of a gun pointed at my chest.

"No? Why not, Mr. Lawyer?" Ushakov said with a wicked gleam in his eyes. "I have what I wanted, thanks to you. And I've decided I don't want a lot of people to know about it. I don't know if I can trust you to keep your mouth shut, so I'll shut it for you. So…bye-bye!" He smiled.

"Can you be sure you have the right case, Ushakov? Don't be in such a hurry."

Ushakov's face froze in a grimace as he looked from the case to me and vice versa. "You're lying."

"I'm not lying, Ushakov. Take a look."

I walked over to the side of the *Zaren Kibish* and waved toward the shore. Prit's familiar silhouette appeared from around the corner. The bastard was smiling from ear to ear. He lifted a shiny black steel Samsonite briefcase over his head so it was clearly visible from the boat.

Ushakov's face was quite a sight. The crew looked confused. Nobody knew what was happening.

"That briefcase you're holding is full of old newspapers, Ushakov. You don't have shit, you fucking maniac."

"But..." he stammered. "How?"

"Oh, come on! Vigo's a big city. It has several luggage stores. It wasn't hard to find a case like that one, Ushakov." I smiled.

"But the label..."

"Ripped off the other case. Consider it a show of good faith, proof that the other case is the real thing, Captain. As soon as you give me what I want, Pritchenko will leave the bag on the shore and we can all go our merry way. Now, don't fuck with me. Let's talk this over like good little boys, right?"

"What do you want?" Ushakov muttered, as he approached menacingly. Sparks of anger shot from his eyes.

"Very simple," I said quietly. "My cat, my boat, and Mr. Pritchenko's package. One of those AK-47s, and food for a week," I ticked the items off on my fingers, as Ushakov's face got redder and redder. "Oh! And a carton of Chesterfields."

Ushakov yelled something unintelligible as he squeezed his fists tight. He stared at the shore for several seconds that seemed to go on forever. "What's stopping me from killing you and going after your friend onshore and killing him too? Tell me."

"Simple," I replied, acting more relaxed than I felt. "If I'm not back in fifteen minutes, *alone*, Prit will run like hell with the briefcase and hide in some corner of that godforsaken city. You won't find him in a million years, Ushakov. Think it over."

Ushakov thought for a moment. Suddenly he turned to a sailor and began barking orders in Russian. After that, he strode toward me menacingly.

"All right, Mr. Lawyer. I'll give you what you want, but you'll regret this. I swear."

Some people say lawyers are sons of bitches. I won't argue with that. But when it comes time to negotiate, it's great to be a lawyer.

ENTRY 75
April 13, 11:57 a.m.

Sometimes the craziest memories hit when you least expect them. A strange image kept coming to mind as I stood on the deck of *Zaren*, waiting for them to bring me my stuff.

I was six or seven, and my parents had taken me to the circus. I was watching the knife thrower. I remember I was impressed that the girl standing in front of the target was so brave that she let a man hurl knives at her. My mother always told me knives are very dangerous and they can cut you. The smiling, relaxed face of the surprisingly calm girl was etched in my mind at that tender age.

At that moment, I wished I had the same presence of mind. The truth is, I was scared shitless. One false step, a wrong word, a miscalculation, no matter how small, and someone might get nervous and shoot me between the eyes. I knew Prit would be all right on his own, but I didn't want to die that morning.

Ushakov was pacing like a caged bear, shooting me murderous glances. I had to be careful. The bastard must have had an ace up his sleeve to fuck me over with.

A furry blur appeared through the ship's hatch, attracted by the noise on deck. My heart raced. Lucullus! Instinctively I stepped forward but stopped short when I realized my mistake. It wasn't Lucullus but a brown female cat, with a bell around her neck and wicked green eyes. She slithered sinuously between the sailors' legs, then sat on a roll of cable to groom herself, giving everyone the withering look only a cat can.

This cat brought to mind Lucullus with a painful intensity. Suddenly, bouncing out of the same hatch, a couple of steps behind, came another ball of fur, this one a familiar shade of bright orange. Lucullus!

He must've sweet-talked the ship's cook while I was gone, because he was fatter and his hair was glossy. He smugly approached the brown cat, purring, doing what my sister called "the Lucullus move," twitching his tail seductively and roguishly wiggling his ears.

Typical. I dragged my ass through an abandoned city full of monsters, dying of hunger and thirst, risking my life at every turn, while he spent the whole time stuffing his face and romancing that green-eyed doll.

I opened my mouth, but no words came out. I cleared my throat. The noise was enough. Lucullus looked up. As soon as he saw me, he forgot all about the gorgeous feline at his side and rushed to me, meowing so pitifully you could've heard him all over the city. Before I knew it, he'd planted himself in my lap and was purring with delight, rubbing against my neck.

I grabbed my cat and felt a strong sense of relief. Not only had they not killed him, he was great shape. I'd been afraid I'd never see him again.

I looked up to find Ushakov watching, with contempt tinged with anger. I didn't give a rat's ass what he thought of me. I just wanted out of there. Who cared if the bastard was furious? But he was calm—too calm, when you consider I'd just fucked him over royally, showing him up in front of his own men. No, the guy was planning something, and I didn't know what it was.

Time passed very slowly, as boxes of food were piled at my feet. One of the sailors brought me a package addressed in

Cyrillic. I checked the part to make sure it matched the description Pritchenko had given to me. A Pakistani handed me a loaded AK-47 and a box of shells.

All that stuff weighed a ton, but no one was helping me load it onto the *Corinth*. I raised an eyebrow at Ushakov. He replied with a half bow and barked some commands to two sailors, who carried the boxes to the sailboat. Shit. Too easy. I didn't like that.

Something vibrated in my pocket, accompanied by two short beeps. Before the astonished eyes of crew and captain, I pulled out a small blue walkie-talkie we'd taken from a blood-soaked patrol car, abandoned on a side street.

That car was a real mystery. It was perfectly parked near a ransacked hardware store, between some smelly trash cans and a car with flat tires and broken mirrors. After more than a month and a half of neglect, all the vehicles in the street were covered a thick layer of dust and dirt, but that patrol car was nice and clean, as if it'd just come from a garage. That was what made us stop and take a look. Inside it was empty; the driver's seat was covered with dried blood. There were no traces of blood on the sidewalk or tracks leading away from the car. The street was completely deserted. A ghostly wind whistled through the dirt and abandoned vehicles. The car was spotless, as if it had just been parked there. It was so unnatural and mysterious, my hair stood on end. Prit and I found a pair of police-issue walkie-talkies in the car, as well as a high-powered flashlight. Not a single piece of paper or a weapon, not a clue, not a trace. Nothing. A complete mystery.

Now one of those walkie-talkies crackled in my hand. I pressed the button, knowing Prit was on the other end.

"Talk to me," I said in Spanish, fairly certain no one else on board spoke Spanish.

"How's everything going?" The Ukrainian's voice was staticky.

"Well...too well," I said, not taking my eye off the sailors. "They're up to something."

"Don't look, but we have problem on bridge," Pritchenko said quietly in his Slavic accent. "A guy with RPG-7 is hidden behind top rail. I see him perfect."

A cold sweat rolled down my back. An RPG. A fucking rocket launcher. I should've guessed. Anyone with a TV has seen an RPG. The poor man's artillery. Virtually all guerrillas and Third World armies had thousands of those things, mass produced in the former Soviet Union. The black market was rife with them. They are so simple and effective. You just insert the grenade at the end; a tube serves as a launcher. So easy to use, even a child-soldier from some remote African country can learn to shoot it in ten minutes. So lethal that when the Russians invaded the Chechen capital of Grozny in 1994, they lost dozens of tanks to Chechen guerrillas armed with those lethal tubes.

Their plan was clear. Once we'd left the suitcase in the harbor, that bastard Ushakov would fire the grenade launcher at the *Corinth*, at Prit, Lucullus, and me. If one of those things could blow up a tank, imagine what it could do to a fiberglass sailboat like the *Corinth*.

The sailors climbed back on board the *Zaren* after loading the *Corinth*. I swear they had a sadistic expression on their faces. They were looking forward to the fireworks.

With a twinkle in his evil eyes, Ushakov approached me and stuck out me his hand. "I hope you keep your word, Lawyer. Leave the case on the dock. Then it's every man for himself. No hard feelings."

"Of course. No hard feelings," I said as I bowed my head, ignoring his outstretched hand.

Ushakov slowly lowered his hand. "We live in difficult times, Mr. Lawyer. Things are changing fast; only the toughest will prevail. I don't expect you to understand. I act the way I do for very powerful reasons."

I stopped, half my body hanging over the side, and looked hard at him. "You'd kill me over a fucking briefcase?" I snapped. "Tell me. What the hell's in it?"

Ushakov looked at me with a frightening grimace. "Good luck, Mr. Lawyer," he said with a smirk. "You're going to need it."

I climbed down the ladder to the *Corinth*'s deck, Ushakov's laughter floating down around me. Once I'd set foot on the familiar teak deck, I untied the ropes, with everyone's eyes on me.

The *Corinth*'s engine roared to life, and I gradually pulled away from the huge bulk of the *Zaren Kibish*, headed for the port where Prit and the briefcase waited. The second part of the dance was about to begin.

ENTRY 76
April 14, 9:40 a.m.

Water lapped quietly between the side of the *Corinth* and the black stones of the dock. As I approached the shore, with Lucullus nestled against my chest, purring nonstop, I thought about our next move. With a slight pressure on the rudder, I maneuvered the *Corinth* alongside the pier, next to the bollards, and tied it up.

I smiled, satisfied. I was relieved that the auxiliary motor, which I'd hardly used, responded perfectly. I would have been embarrassed to be stuck just a few hundred yards from shore, with sails furled and the crew of the *Zaren Kibish* looking on.

I passed my hand lovingly along the teak beam. The *Corinth* was a superb boat. She had sheltered me and saved my life. Now I must abandon her forever.

Before I jumped to the dock, I ran to the pulley wheel in the bow and grabbed the tip of the line. I kicked the sail locker open, jumped down in it, and waded through a lot of bunched-up fabric with the line in my hand. The locker smelled of Dacron, stagnant salt water, and rotting seaweed. The *Zaren* crew had carelessly gathered up the *Corinth's* sails and piled them every which way.

On a bottom shelf, I found what I needed—the spinnaker, the huge-bellied sail used on the bow. It was normally only unfurled at sea with the wind aft, but I was confident no one aboard the Russian freighter had a clue how to sail.

I hooked one end of the upper ring of the spinnaker, then crawled on deck and turned the hand-cranked pulley wheel. With the familiar click of the winch, the spinnaker slowly ascended to the top of the mast, swelling slowly as the soft south wind brushed against its fabric. The huge sail spread open with a loud flutter. It didn't stretch all the way, since I'd taken the precaution of leaving the bottom sheets loose.

The huge sail hung along the length of the ship, slack like a gigantic curtain. Any sailor watching the *Corinth* would wonder what kind of freshwater rat had hoisted that sail in such a weird way. Had any strong gusts of wind blown through as I was putting up the spinnaker, it might've torn the sail and taken part of the rigging along with it.

All that went through my mind as I hurriedly adjusted the lines. The sail would only have to stay in that position for a few minutes, long enough for Prit and me to carry out our plan. This was the last service the *Corinth* would provide me.

The fluttering sail caused the hull to rock and bump against the dock. Each crack that scraped the fiberglass and chipped the wood pained my soul. It was a crime to treat the *Corinth* that way, but I had no time to put the side shields in place.

I dived into the cabin and rushed around filling my backpack with everything I'd salvaged off the dead soldier, my other wetsuit, which still dangled on the hanger, and one of the spearguns with a dozen spears. Some sailor from the *Zaren Kibish* with nothing better to do must've taken the other speargun as a souvenir.

A familiar mustachioed face appeared at the cabin hatch. I started passing all the bundles to Prit, and he set them on the dock. We worked feverishly and quietly. We had to empty it all in three or four minutes, or they'd figure out what we were up to on the *Zaren Kibish*. The huge sail blocked the view of the sector of the dock where we set our supplies, and disguised Prit's trips back and forth. All they could see was a sailboat next to the dock, swaying in the breeze.

We were sweating like crazy as we hid our stuff behind the spinnaker, out of sight from the *Zaren*. Finally, I pulled on my wetsuit as Prit dragged a life-size male mannequin out of the back of the van, courtesy of a fashion boutique downtown. He dressed it in a yellow slicker, drawing up the hood as a finishing touch.

Not three minutes had passed from the moment I unfolded the sail till we set up the dummy in the cockpit of the *Corinth*. While Prit slipped back around the corner, I cut the line that held the *Corinth* to the dock.

In one smooth motion, the sailboat began to slide toward the harbor entrance. The rudder was locked in place so it would hold its course for a few minutes—more than enough time. Trying not to make noise, I let myself down into the water between the *Corinth* and the dock. The water was really cold, but I didn't even notice. As the hull slid up against me, I took a few deep breaths and dived.

Diving relaxed me completely. I could make out the black silhouette of the *Corinth* as it pulled away, and beyond that, through the rushing waters of the port, the *Zaren Kibish*'s waterline.

I gently began to swim for shore, trying not to create lots of bubbles. Less than ten yards from the shore, I ran out of air. Angry with myself, I kicked a few more times. Finally, about to pass out, I surfaced at the dock, right where we'd tied up the Zodiac the first time. Prit was waiting to hoist me out of the water.

Breathing hard, we ran to the imposing Seguritsa warehouse. Dripping wet, I peered around the corner of the deserted dock, to where the *Corinth* had been just minutes before. At the edge of the dock, sparkling in the midday sun, lay the black Samsonite briefcase, the object of so much trouble.

Swaying as if a drunk were at the helm, the *Corinth* sailed slowly toward open water. Before getting off the boat, I'd caught up the sheets in the most visible way possible, trying to draw the attention of the sailors on the freighter. Now I was afraid I'd tightened them up too much and the sail would rip.

It was too late to worry about that. A barrage of automatic weapons fire from the *Zaren*'s bow splintered the *Corinth*'s deck into a thousand places. The dummy's head rocketed through the air. Wood chips and pieces of carbon fiber flew everywhere as hundreds of bullets pierced the boat's hull and rigging. A man stood on the bridge with an RPG-7 on his shoulder. The *Corinth* swayed and drifted less than two hundred yards from his position, making it an easy shot.

With a roar, the grenade hit the sailboat in a cloud of smoke and a blinding flash. The impact was devastating. A huge column of fire shot up through the hatches of the *Corinth*. The hull disintegrated into a million pieces.

As thousands of gallons of water flooded the injured vessel, another shell hit the deck. A jet of fire and smoke rose from the bowels of the *Corinth*, now a roaring inferno. A piece of mast spun in the sky and fell back into the water. With a gurgle, the battered hull sank to the bottom amid the explosions.

Pritchenko and I didn't hang around to watch the show. We ran like hell down the alley to the idling van. As the last explosions on the *Corinth* thundered all over the port, Prit gently accelerated and headed for the exit.

In the backseat, a fat, happy orange cat was perched in a mesh cage, contentedly eyeing his owner and a small mustached man who drove as if the devil were carrying him to hell.

Prit and I smiled. Not only had we danced with the devil, we'd gotten out alive. Nestled between the two seats sat a black Samsonite suitcase sealed with red tape, identical to the one we'd left on the dock.

ENTRY 77
April 15, 9:08 p.m.

Everything was going too well. And that was the problem. We got too confident. We let our guard down. We acted like heroes out of a damn action movie, and we paid the price. The world today is dirty, mean, tough, and terribly dangerous. If you play with fire, you're going to get burned. Burned. Fuck. That's ironic. But I'm getting ahead of myself again.

When we drove away from the rubble of the port, we were euphoric. We were alive, healthy, with a car full of supplies and weapons. And we knew where a helicopter was, so we could get out of that hole. Everything was going smoothly.

Prit drove like a madman through the deserted streets of a Vigo suburb. Out the window I saw luxury villas, most of them locked up tight. Some had boarded-up doors and windows. Those safeguards suggested that it was one of the first neighborhoods evacuated in an orderly and systematic way.

After several months of neglect, the area was starting to look really bleak. The houses peeped out from behind overgrown bushes and weed-choked gardens. On one driveway, a fire-engine-red tricycle lay on its side, gradually being consumed by hedges. With all the humans gone, nature was reclaiming its place. Almost no cars were abandoned on the shoulder. Maybe their owners had fled in them, trying to escape the inevitable.

There were dozens of undead in that area. Their occupation of the city didn't seem to follow any pattern. There were wide avenues where you only saw a couple. Then, around a corner, you stumbled upon dozens, even hundreds, of them, wandering around or staring off into space, waiting for prey. What motivates them or draws them to one place or another is a mystery to me.

That neighborhood was a hot zone. There were dozens of those things at every intersection, in every garden, some in good shape, others horribly maimed or disfigured. I've gotten used to them; their smell doesn't even disgust me. I know what they are, and they know what I am. Period.

Prit zigzagged, dodging undead. He drove awfully fast, as usual. With each turn, the tires screeched, shaking us around like peas in a can. The undead appeared in greater and greater numbers. Prit performed heroic feats behind the wheel to keep from ramming them. We had to slow down, and the mob pursuing us was more abundant. It didn't look good.

Out of the blue, a middle-aged guy appeared suddenly in the middle of the road. He was about fifty, heavyset, his shirt open to the waist, wearing lots of gold chains around his neck. Half his face was a bloody, tattered mess; he was deathly pale like the rest of them. We didn't have time to dodge him.

Just seconds before, Prit had swerved to avoid a group of undead crowded together in the middle of the road. What happened next was inevitable. He didn't see the guy until we were on top of him. With a loud thud, the monster's body struck the front of the van and was thrown to the side, completely limp, leaving a clump of putrid blood on the windshield. Prit swerved like crazy, trying to regain control, but the heavy van skidded out of control, dragging several of those monsters in its path as ominous noises came from its engine.

Doing a spectacular 360, our car finally stopped in the middle of the road, enveloped in the acrid smell of burning rubber. For a moment there was silence. I exhaled; I didn't realize I'd been holding my breath. Once again I was glad to have the very talented Ukrainian at the wheel. He'd kept us from crashing and made sure the van didn't stall. That would have been absolutely fatal.

But the motor sounded like it was falling apart. A thin trickle of steam wafted through a gasket mangled by the impact. The radiator had a leak—and not a small one. That motor's days were numbered. It was a miracle it was still running.

Slowly putting the van in gear, Prit got us going again, this time more slowly. We weren't laughing it up anymore. If the engine broke down in that infested area, with all the houses closed up tight, we'd be doomed to a certain death in seconds.

The next twenty minutes were endless. Both tires on the right side had blown out, so we inched along through the subdivision, wrapped in a cloud of smoke, with the temperature light on. We were forced to slow down to a lousy ten miles an hour as dozens of hands pounded on the sides of the van.

Suddenly my window exploded into a million pieces. It had been cracked by a previous blow, so a punch from one of those things shattered it. A young woman tried to climb through the smashed window, trying to grab me. She reached in and touched my face. Her touch was cold. Cold, wet, and dead.

I panicked, almost like when this whole nightmare started. Paralyzed with terror, I could feel her trying to slip inside the vehicle as Prit shouted hysterically in Russian and Lucullus hissed inside his carrier, baring his teeth.

When she put her hand on my thigh, I finally shook off my stupor. I grabbed the AK-47 and bashed her temple with the butt. She raised her head and hesitated for a second, staring at me with dead, bloodshot eyes. I hit her in the face again. The woman slipped back out the window, unable to hold on, her face completely mutilated.

Drenched in sweat, grimacing, I turned to Prit. One look around told me that either we got out of there immediately or we'd be dead men in minutes. The resilient Ukrainian nodded and wrung a little more out of the damaged, groaning engine.

Once again, our luck held out. Just five hundred yards away, half-hidden by the weeds, was a sign pointing to a ramp to the nearby highway. Just a little farther, and we might be saved.

With one last push, Prit turned on to the highway. There, the van picked up speed, though the damaged motor was still making some very scary sounds.

At last we were on the highway. We felt relieved. We didn't know the worst was yet to come.

The highway looked like a ghostly lunar landscape. I'd made this trip a million times, every time I had business in Vigo. Back then this stretch of highway had been packed with traffic. Now, it was deserted.

With the van making a deafening noise, we drove as fast as that battered motor allowed. We passed a few cars abandoned in the strangest positions. Some of them were ringed with blood. Others looked like they'd rammed into something—or someone. Aside from a couple of corpses rotting in the sun, we saw no sign of humans.

I tried to imagine the scene. In the first days of the epidemic, dozens of undead turned up suddenly, staggering down the middle of the road. Startled drivers tried to dodge them. Some couldn't avoid running over them, and they crashed. Some caring people, unaware of those monsters' true nature, must've stopped to help what they thought were badly injured pedestrians. Either way, the drivers' fate was fucking awful.

A mile or so down the road, we came upon the first serious accident. A Nissan SUV had slammed into the concrete median, knocking it down. The Nissan had bounced back into the middle of the road and collided with a couple of cars and a small delivery truck. All those vehicles were now a huge pile of bloody plastic and steel lying in the middle of the road, blocking all the lanes. We stopped, stunned by the scene. Rising off that mass of iron was the foul, sickening smell of corpses that had been rotting in the sun for several months. The smell of death.

Those people had been in a brutal accident and no one had come to their aid. They hadn't even removed the bodies. My God!

A small space on the left allowed us to continue on our way. Prit drove deftly through the narrow gap, leaving some of our paint behind in the process. I wondered whether that lane was there by chance or whether another survivor had been there before us, moving the wreckage aside.

After two or three miles, we saw another major accident in the opposite lane. It was a huge pileup of about forty or fifty cars, buses, vans, and trucks. They had collided in a chain as they sped along, running from those things or just trying to dodge them. As a gauge of how hard the impact was, I saw a small Smart car folded like an accordion under the cab of a truck.

Those who weren't killed in the collision had died in the fire that followed. The heat was so intense that pieces of asphalt had melted. A couple of blackened skulls stuck out from the charred frame of a car. The scorched remains of several more bodies were visible here and there. A shocking scene, right out of hell.

This was not a highway. This was a graveyard.

Six miles later, we saw undead again, reeling down the road. Prit said this meant we were getting closer to an urban area, so we'd better be prepared. My frowning friend ordered me to buckle my seat belt, and then he floored it. Bad idea. Something under the hood exploded with a thunderous bang, causing a sizable dent. Thick black smoke poured out of the engine. My heart almost flew through my mouth.

The Ukrainian looked at me, chagrined. "A rod," he said laconically, as we came to a standstill. "The engine kaput." He let the dying van roll slowly down an exit ramp.

I couldn't read the highway sign, so I didn't know where the hell we were. For the first time, I was totally disoriented.

We were wondering how the hell we were going to make it without the van when chance smiled on us again. The ramp was steep, so the van coasted to the bottom of the hill, right in front of a small industrial park with fifteen or twenty warehouses. There, in front of us, as if it were expecting us, was a huge car dealership with the familiar logo of the three-pointed star enclosed in a circle.

This was fucking great. I smiled and asked Prit how'd he like to drive a brand-new Mercedes. The Ukrainian's beaming smile spoke volumes. We'd be traveling in style.

Momentum had carried us about 150 yards from the dealership. We could see several undead in the distance, but we'd passed by them unnoticed, since we'd driven the last half mile in neutral.

We got out of the battered, smoldering van and grabbed everything we could carry in one trip. We couldn't risk coming and going, drawing unnecessary attention. I put the soldier's knapsack on my back and the speargun across my chest and held Lucullus's carrier tightly in my arms to keep him from escaping. The last thing I needed was to chase after my cat through an unfamiliar industrial park full of monsters eager to sink their teeth into me.

Prit carried the AK-47, the heavy box of ammunition, and some of the food from the Russian ship in one hand and the notorious briefcase in the other. The rest, unfortunately, we had to leave behind.

Loaded down like that, we didn't think we'd ever reach the dealership. When we finally got there, we were out of breath. In the shade of the huge entrance gate, I collapsed exhausted against the giant glass window. Prit glided along like an eel, pressed against the building, searching for a way in.

As I waited, I took a swallow from the canteen and rummaged around in the backpack. At the bottom, I found a pack of crushed Chesterfields. I remembered putting them there when I left home. Kicking back a little, I lit a cigarette. After all this time, the first puff was like a shot of heroin to a junkie. Everything seemed simpler.

The muffled sound of breaking glass shook me out of my trance. I jumped up like lightning, the blood pounding in my temples. I gripped the speargun, braced for whatever might come next.

Suddenly I heard the metal door open behind me. I was terrified. But then I saw Prit's amused smile. He'd slipped inside through a bathroom window. Hot damn!

I lumbered through the entrance to the dealership, loaded down like a mule, with Lucullus scampering around at my feet and Prit standing guard. Once we got inside, he closed the gate again and threw the bolt to secure it.

Prit and I stood still for a long minute, trying to determine if anyone—or anything—was in there.

I stood there dumbstruck. The interior was dark and cool. Somehow, this dealership had been spared by looters. I could make out neat rows of vehicles in the shadows. I smiled. Time to go shopping.

That darkness felt really good. After a long day on the run, my muscles relaxed for the first time in hours. I'd started the day on the *Zaren*'s deck staring down the muzzle of an assault rifle. Now I was lying on a leather couch in a Mercedes dealership, puffing on a cigarette, thinking how wonderful it would be to sleep for three days in a hotel bed. And drink a cold beer. And get a foot massage from ten girls in sexy lingerie…I'm not shitting you. I sat up with a groan, every muscle pinging. I'd never been so tired in my life.

We quickly checked out the dealership. Nothing. All the doors and windows were closed and barred, except for the bathroom window Prit had broken. It was too high and narrow for those things to sneak in, but we wanted to take every precaution.

We wrestled a panel from one of the cubicles against the broken bathroom window. It wouldn't withstand a heavy blow, but it would do for the short time we'd be there.

Bone tired, we collapsed in a room that adjoined the manager's office. It was a room with no windows, stacks of files, a tiny bathroom with a shower and, surprisingly, a fold-out bed. What the hell was that bed doing there? Prit snooped around the room like a bloodhound. He picked up something from underneath the cot. With a sly smile, he held up some wadded-up lacy burgundy panties.

Well, well. This must be the manager's bachelor pad. Way to go, you bastard. It'd been some time since that guy got laid. If he were still alive, he had better things to think about.

Overflowing with newfound energy, Prit tossed every drawer. I stepped into the bathroom and peered into the mirror. Out of habit I turned on the tap. To my surprise a stream of rust-colored water gushed out, popping with all the air built up in the pipes.

I figured the dealership had its own water tower, so it still had running water. Running water! If there was water, there had to be a gas or battery-operated water heater somewhere. I went back to the bachelor pad, where Prit was stretched out on the bed, leafing through a pile of old magazines. I left my friend comfortably settled there and started my search, armed with a flashlight.

Behind the hallway that connected the offices to the garages were some steep stairs that disappeared into the darkness underground. I got up my courage and started down the steps, my back pressed to the wall, a cocked speargun in one hand and the flashlight in the other. The basement was cold and dry. It looked like a very old repair shop that had been completely renovated.

Surrounded by a thicket of cobwebs and tons of boxes of old brochures was a large modern water heater hooked up to an orange bottle of butane gas. Once I was sure the basement was safe, I climbed down the rest of the way. I shook the bottle. Empty. The pilot light had been on for weeks and used up all the gas in the bottle.

Disappointed, I turned around in the dark. As I started back up the stairs, I hit my knee so hard I saw stars. I shone the flashlight on what I'd run into. It was a mesh cage containing half a dozen sealed bottles. Fucking great!

Parting the cobwebs, I replaced the empty bottle with one of the full ones and pressed the button to purge the system. When I pushed the power button, a flickering blue flame appeared. I shouted for joy. We had hot water!

I raced up the stairs as Prit came walking out of the office, carrying a box full of keys to the Mercedeses. In a cheerful mood, we went into the showroom, where dozens of vehicles waited, neatly parked, ready to drive out the door.

As we strolled around looking for our new car, Prit and I had a little argument. He had his heart set on the fire-engine-red CLK cabriolet. He said it was a rocket, perfect for escaping at full speed. I finally convinced him that even though that convertible was fast, it wasn't the wisest choice for driving on roads infested with undead.

I pragmatically chose a huge GL, the largest SUV Mercedes made, with four-wheel drive and lots of horsepower. We could drive off road in that beast if we encountered an accident blocking the road. Plus, it could push aside more undead than the sports car.

Prit grumbled and accepted my reasoning, casting a longing look at the convertible. We set to work and exchanged its battery for a brand-new one we found in the garage. Then we loaded our stuff, including an increasingly restless Lucullus.

A sudden, loud noise made us jump out of our skin. I threw myself on the floor, feeling around for my speargun, as Prit cocked the AK-47. We looked around for the origin of the sound. A couple of yards from us, beating on the armored glass window, were two undead, watching us with empty eyes, roaring with rage.

It was a gruesome sight. Since I'd offed my poor neighbor, I hadn't had an opportunity to study those monsters up close when I wasn't running or fighting for my life. I eased up to the glass, an arm's length away. That drove them nuts. They wanted me. They wanted my life. My blood. Fucking bastards.

Something dawned on me. A newly transformed undead, my neighbor for example, had *pallor mortis*, thousands of burst veins visible on its skin, bloodshot, vacant eyes, and homicidal behavior. The two men outside, though covered in bumps, cuts, and scratches, looked exactly the same. Those guys showed no trace of putrefaction, unlike a normal corpse. No rigor mortis, no decomposition…nothing. Amazing. They were dead. No doubt of that. The terrible gash in the neck of one of them was proof. But something kept then moving…and stalking.

Clothes worn thin from months outdoors was all that indicated they'd been that way for a while. I was sure their appearance hadn't changed one iota since they were attacked. That had some disturbing implications. Over the past few weeks, I'd entertained the hope that over time these bodies decayed or even "died."

That didn't seem to happen. The passage of time didn't seem to affect those monsters. I didn't know what to think. Maybe they stay that way for months, even years. Maybe they're eternal. How the hell should I know? I'm no scientist. I don't have any data on their condition. I just know they're somewhere between life and death. If I didn't want to end up like them, I had to keep on the run and not get caught.

A bitter taste rose in my throat. As a species, a race, a planet, we were really screwed. I punched the glass in rage, right on one of those monsters' faces. He didn't flinch.

Prit watched me in silence, guessing my thoughts. Finally he came over and tried to calm me down. He said that when we got his helicopter, we'd find a place the monsters hadn't gotten to.

I shook my head bitterly. Nice words. We had a long way to go before I'd feel completely safe.

We parked the SUV in front of the gate. Prit checked the tire pressure while I took my first hot shower in many weeks. It was heaven. The jet of water hit my back and my head. Clouds of steam curled around my body. I stood there for about twenty minutes, enjoying that wonderful feeling. Then, with scissors and new razor blades I'd found in a bathroom drawer, I shaved the beard I'd had for weeks. I didn't look like a bum anymore. Something so ordinary before the apocalypse was now a real treat. That's how far things had slipped.

ENTRY 78
April 16, 10:24 a.m.

When I got out of the shower, I found Prit in the manager's office, hard at work. He'd cleared off the desk and set the black Samsonite case on it. He'd discovered a ton of tools in the garage, including a battery-operated grinder and a blowtorch. The Ukrainian was determined to open the damn case come hell or high water.

With my hair still dripping wet, I joked that if he found smokes in that case, he'd better share them with me, or else he'd wake up dead the next morning. Prit laughed and threw a piece of red tape at me. He said to make myself useful and find some gas for the SUV.

I left the office, listening to Prit singing softly in Russian, his voice drowned out by the shriek of the grinder.

It took ten minutes to find a gas can and five more to find a rubber tube to siphon the gas into the tank. As the tank filled up, I petted Lucullus. Every time I'm out of his sight, he goes nuts. I think he's afraid I'll leave without him. My poor cat.

I was wiping off my hands when a violent explosion shook the dealership. A huge white flash came out of the office, followed by a cloud of smoke and a burning smell. For a moment my ears whistled. Then I heard screams of pain. Prit.

I raced into the office and saw Prit lying on the floor. His hands were badly burned, and he had wounds on his chest and face. He was writhing in pain, howling like a wounded wolf. I crouched beside him and took a look. The face and chest wounds were superficial, but his hands looked awful. They were completely burned. I could only see three fingers on his left hand; the right hand wasn't much better. He was bleeding heavily. Blood also trickled from his ears.

I scanned the table for something to staunch the bleeding. My eye fell on the briefcase. Or what was left of it. That fucking case must've had a pyrotechnic device inside to keep any unauthorized person from gaining access. The device exploded when Prit forced the case open. He was lucky it didn't blow him to bits.

I stared, absolutely helpless, as Prit's cries of pain echoed in my ears. Whatever was in that case now burned with a fury, its valuable and mysterious contents quickly becoming a pile of ashes.

ENTRY 79
April 17, 6:37 p.m.

I was in shock and scared to death, more than at any other time during all this shit. Prit was hurt badly, and I didn't know what to do. His hands looked terrible. All that was in our little first-aid kit were some mild painkillers, antibiotics, and sunblock.

I struggled to get him on his feet and to the bathroom, then washed his hands and forearms as best I could. What a fucking mess! His right hand was raw, burned all over. They looked like second-degree burns to me. His left hand was worse. He was missing his little finger and middle finger; the bones of the ring finger were sticking out. He also had a deep gash in his left palm that wouldn't stop bleeding. Fuck. I rummaged through the dealership's medicine cabinet and found some gauze and a gel for burns. I smeared his right hand with the cream and put a lot of bandages on both hands to stop the bleeding. It was a pretty sloppy job.

I had to do something fast. Soon all the undead in the area would be on top of us; they'd surely heard the blast hundreds of yards away. Plenty were groaning outside already.

I settled Prit in the SUV, between waves of pain. Dozens of undead were crowded around the dealership. I'd only have a few seconds to open the gate and climb in the SUV before those things swarmed all over me. I wouldn't have time to close the gate. Those monsters would then invade the dealership. One less refuge.

I needed bandages, analgesics, and especially antibiotics. In the best-case scenario, I'd find a doctor to tend Prit's wounds, but that wasn't going to be easy.

Xeral Hospital was a mile or so away, in downtown Vigo. I didn't really think anyone would still be there, but I hoped I'd at least find the medicine Prit needed.

I had no choice. I set off the alarm of one of the sports cars at the other end of the dealership. That cleared the door just enough so we could get out. Prit was losing blood by the minute and couldn't bear the pain much longer. I had to get to that fucking hospital no matter what shape it was in.

ENTRY 80
April 18, 11:02 a.m.

I was an idiot. I let Prit suffer in pain for more than an hour before I remembered there were several injectable vials of morphine at the bottom of the soldier's backpack. They were hard to miss. They were in a box with a red cross against a white background on one side and "Morphine" printed in big letters on the other. Any lamebrain could've figured out what that was. I completely forgot about it until I took a curve too fast. The backpack shot across the backseat, hit a window, and spilled out its contents. But I'm getting ahead of myself again.

We beat a quick retreat out of that dealership. Given the jam we were in, that was the best news. The car alarm drew most of the howling mass to the opposite end of the building. I knew the sound would attract many more of those things, but it was the price I had to pay. No matter what, we were getting the fuck out of there.

I walked up to the huge metal gate and pried open the door's security latch. I pressed the red button to open it. Of course, nothing happened, since there was no electricity.

Pressure and stress were playing tricks with my mind. Cursing under my breath, I surveyed the device, looking for a manual switch. There it was! A small lever next to the coupling of the cable drew the door open.

When I activated it, it made a soft *clank*. When the counterweights in the door started to move and the huge gate folded back (faster than I'd expected), I ran like crazy for the SUV idling in front. As I climbed in, I realized that, with no electricity, the only way to close it was to drag it manually with a pole located somewhere at the top. I had no idea where the hell that was. Anyway, what did that matter now?

When I stepped on the gas, the GL leaped forward and burned rubber. I think I bumped against a couple of those things. I recall a middle-aged woman in a pearl necklace and big hair splayed out against the back of the SUV. Otherwise, the entrance to the highway was relatively trouble-free. I noticed that the broken-down van we'd come in was surrounded by a dozen undead; some had gotten inside.

What attracted them to the abandoned vehicle? Did they detect our scent or body heat in it? They may have lost "human" qualities, but they've compensated with more subtle senses. More dangerous to us.

After a couple of miles, I noticed that the GL had a small screen on the dashboard. I finally realized it was a GPS, standard in a high-end model like that. I pressed the button and prayed the thing still worked.

The screen lit up with a flashing blue light as it connected to satellites in geosynchronous orbit. I sighed with relief. Society had collapsed, and the undead had taken over, but satellites continued on their silent, unflappable paths in the solitude of space, indifferent to the chaos unleashed thousands of miles below. They were still working, and they'd go on working for a long time, until the lack of ground control or some other incident rendered them useless forever.

The GPS was an expensive model with a touch screen. Keeping one eye on the road, I quickly searched through the menu for nearby hospitals. From time to time, I had to swerve around a wreck or dodge some undead, but in general the road was clear.

With a beep, the GPS told me that the nearest medical center was Meixoeiro Hospital, not Xeral, and mapped out the shortest route. Fantastic! That saved me from having to reenter the rotting carcass that had once been the city of Vigo.

Engrossed in the screen, I almost didn't see the pileup. Suddenly, rising up before me was a twisted mass of at least fifteen wrecked vehicles. I hit the brakes hard and desperately turned the wheel to the right, trying to avoid the inevitable.

Its tires screeching, the GL skidded sideways for a few yards and came to a stop just inches from the first vehicle. All of its flashers emitted a loud *click-click*. Everything else was silent.

I wiped off my sweat, grimacing. If it weren't for all the safety features like minibrake assist and other technical marvels, I'd have plowed into that wall of twisted scrap metal. End of story.

I shuddered. We live on the razor's edge, and we don't know it. There're no police, army, doctors, or anyone to help us if something happens.

We're screwed.

We're alone.

All alone.

I put the SUV in first gear, raced on to the shoulder, and drove off the highway. Engaging the four-wheel drive, I plowed through the low barrier at the outer edge of the highway that had kept animals off the road in the old days.

After ten minutes of violent bouncing off road through abandoned farms on weed-covered roads, I stopped under a clump of trees. It was cool, sheltered, and, above all, out of sight. There was not a soul around for hundreds of yards. Not human or undead.

A broken-down old washtub lay abandoned beside the road, almost hidden under blackberry bushes. A jet of cold water gushed from a pipe. I got out of the SUV and plunged my hands into the water. It was cool, almost cold, in contrast to the searing afternoon heat. It was delicious. I drank like a camel, filled up the canteen, then wet Prit's dry lips. Half conscious, he wouldn't or couldn't drink.

I touched his forehead. He was burning up. Either he was suffering from shock or his wounds were starting to get infected. Whatever it was, he needed antibiotics immediately. I gave him a shot of morphine to ease the pain and got back in the car, leaving that brief moment of peace behind.

We peeled out in a huge cloud of dust. We still had a long way to go.

About thirty minutes later we had to cross a small stream. It wasn't too deep, but the Mercedes, though luxurious, was not built to ford streams. I couldn't keep water from coming in through the door seals and air vents. We were going to get a little wet.

The sky was clouding up, so we were going to get wet one way or another. After days and days of heat, we were due for a big storm. Lucullus was really agitated, something that only happens when there's a storm.

We got on to a back highway about three miles from the hospital, according to the GPS. The muddy SUV skidded a little on the weeds growing on the shoulder, but thanks to its four-wheel drive, we made it back on to the deserted highway. I stopped to take a look at Prit. He was delirious on account of the morphine, fidgeting, half asleep. I looked up and down the highway. I didn't see a single living being, not a fucking soul. Some weeds poked up through cracks in the pavement. No one had been down that highway for weeks. In a few months, the weeds would completely swallow it up.

I shifted into first and headed for the hospital. After a few minutes, I relented and turned on the lights. It was just six in the afternoon, but it was almost dark. A storm was on its way, and I couldn't see for more than thirty or forty yards. Distant thunder rattled the SUV's windows.

I concede I was spooked in the dim light, but the fright I got five hundred yards ahead still nearly gives me a heart attack. When I swerved around a small eucalyptus tree growing right out of the road, the headlights lit up a grinning skull, wrapped in a pile of rags, lying on the pavement. I was almost right on top of it, so I braked hard. I heard a *crack* under the front wheels as I drove over that pile of bones. I stopped the SUV and wiped the sweat off my face. The wind was rising. The first gusts of the storm were whistling through the trees. I was sure there was something huge right in front of the car, but in the dark night, I couldn't see what it was. There was something sinister about that place.

I cocked the AK-47, painfully aware of how little I knew about firing it, and got out. The purring engine was the only sound except for the roar of the wind. I walked cautiously in the space lit up by the headlights. My shadow projected before me as I approached the black figure at the back.

I held the rifle tight. My hands were sweating, and my heart was pounding wildly. That shapeless mass took up nearly half of the road. I still couldn't figure out what it was. The hot wind enveloped me like a blanket. Then the smell hit me. My God.

Stacked in front of me were dozens, maybe hundreds, of rotting corpses slowly decomposing, at the mercy of the weather and vermin. I leaned against the barrel of the AK-47 to keep from falling down. Oh, Jesus. My legs failed me, and I had to sit down. I couldn't tear my eyes away from what I saw in the headlights.

The figure I'd spotted in the shadows was a pile of huge spools of reinforced concrete and some kind of metal container with barbed wire stretched in front. It was an abandoned checkpoint.

All the bodies had bullet wounds. The ground around the checkpoint was littered with shiny copper casings as far as the eye could see. It was a huge graveyard, reminiscent of Rwanda during their civil war in the 1990s.

I could guess what had happened. It was an army checkpoint in a strategic place, by the hospital. Suddenly hundreds of undead had converged on the road, attracted by human presence. Security forces fought them desperately, taking out hundreds of those creatures, frantically calling for reinforcements.

What happened next was clear. The dried blood splattered against the walls and a couple of assault rifles lying on the ground told me everything I needed to know about the fate of the checkpoint's defenders. The undead had made it through. Just like in Pontevedra. And Vigo. And everywhere else.

I headed back to the SUV, tears streaming down my face. As I climbed into the car, lightning lit up the grim scene. In the space of a few seconds, the SUV crushed hundreds of rotting bones as I drove over that heap. I drove through the checkpoint and didn't look back. We had to keep going.

ENTRY 81
April 19, 12:37 p.m.

The lightning was so bright that for a few seconds the whole horizon turned a sickly blue. Thunder rattled the SUV's windows with
a gruff, deep, terrifying rumble that lasted seven or eight seconds.
Lightning and thunder followed each other about every minute
and a half. The rain hadn't broken yet, but the air had a strong
smell of ozone. A helluva of a storm was coming.

Startled by the roar of the GL's engine, a flock of crows and
fat, glossy gulls flew up in the air. Over the months, I've learned
to sort through all the haunting images, blocking out the ones
that disturb me the most (too many, sadly). But I saw what those
scavengers had been feeding on—another pile of lifeless bodies. The image of the half-decayed body of a little boy about
three years old with empty eye sockets and pecked cheeks gut-
punched me. I was fucking sick of being sick. True, all that bullshit is making me harder, but I can tell I'm getting crazier by the
second.

According to the GPS, the county road abruptly intersected
with a much wider and better-cared-for road half a mile from
the hospital. The area was wooded; a dense mass of eucalyptus
and pine trees was shaking wildly, whipped by the wind. The road
was strewn with twigs, tree bark, and piles of rotting corpses. The
undead had been through there in droves, but resistance must
have been tough. I was coming to the scene of a disaster. I started
to feel light-headed.

A half a dozen wobbly figures stepped out of the shadows,
headed for our SUV. I couldn't stay there any longer. I turned on
to the main road and approached the hospital slowly, dodging
fallen branches and the occasional passersby who tried unsuc-
cessfully to claw the car.

Then, something caught my attention—a couple of undead wandering on the road, dressed in tattered hospital gowns. I shuddered with terror. If Meixoeiro Hospital was infested, we were really screwed.

I rounded the last bend in the road to the top of a small hill; from there I could see the hospital. I hit the brakes and stopped for a moment. I held my breath. Fuck.

Meixoeiro Hospital is a huge conglomeration of modern steel, glass, and cement, a gigantic maze built in several stages, with miles of corridors and rooms. It had been one of Galicia's premier hospitals. It was cutting edge, equipped with the best, most modern human and technical resources. Thousands of people used that facility daily. A real temple of science, pride, and human health. Something to behold.

Now it looked like something out of a nightmare. Every window facing north was shattered. Torn, faded curtains stuck out of the dark recesses of those broken windows, flapping wildly in the wind. A sewer pipe on the fourth floor must have burst—dried, smelly black slime covered part of the wall.

What was really frightening was the total absence of light, sound, and movement. The huge building loomed up like a dark monolith, devoid of life. The tunnel to the emergency room was shrouded in shadows, like the entrance to a deep mine.

Around the building I could see evidence of hectic activity. Dozens of civilian cars, police cars, Civil Guard tanks, and ambulances sat abandoned every which way, many with their doors flung open. Some were covered with a rust-colored crust that could only be dried blood. Stretchers and medical equipment were scattered here and there, as if they'd set up a field hospital on the front lawn to take care of the overflow.

A city bus, its windows streaked with dried blood, was parked on the lawn, as if a drunk driver had left it there. On the rear doors of the bus you could see bloody palm prints. God only knows the story that bus could tell.

A double row of sandbags and concrete barriers surrounded the perimeter. Some places were reinforced, so I assumed they'd been checkpoints. As I'd seen on the road and so many places for miles around, shell casings and rotting corpses were everywhere. There were far fewer around the hospital than I expected, though.

I quickly corrected that thought. When the horde of undead arrived, the defenders must've been decimated, exhausted, almost out of ammunition. Those monsters easily overpowered them. Then came the carnage.

The bitter taste of bile filled my mouth. I pictured a hospital full of the wounded, refugees, medical personnel, women, children…then hundreds of these things broke in. Oh, blessed Christ.

The place was filled with pain, death, and despair. That dark, silent building was a huge grave…or worse. But we had to go in. Prit needed medical supplies.

I rolled the SUV up to the tunnel to the ER, virtually silently. Drenched in sweat, I looked in every direction, hesitating. On one hand, if I went in alone, I could move faster. If I ran into trouble, I could defend myself better. On the other hand, I didn't dare leave Prit, semiconscious and alone, in the parking lot, at the mercy of those things, as I walked through the bowels of that building.

And besides, there was Lucullus. Fuck.

The *ka-boooooom* of a giant clap of thunder startled me out of my wits. Time was slipping away. A big raindrop splattered against the windshield with the force of a bullet. Then another and another, in quick succession. Scattered raindrops turned into a downpour. The storm had reached us. The thunder was drowned out by the roar of millions of drops hitting the ground.

I calculated we were no more than twenty yards from the tunnel. I couldn't go any farther in the SUV. Reinforced concrete blocks and lots of sandbags lying across the road made it impassable. In better days, a guard would've waved me on from a entry box a few yards to my left, but now it was abandoned. That empty landscape, lit up by lightning, gave me the creeps.

I put the backpack on and cinched the straps tight. Between Prit and Lucullus, I wasn't going to be very mobile, so I distributed the weight as evenly as I could. I didn't want all that weight to drag me to the ground right under an undead's nose.

I took Lucullus out of his carrier and cradled him in my arms for a moment before setting off. My little furry friend purred happily, comfortable, dry, and warm on my lap, watching the rain fall. I scratched behind his ears, gazing at him fondly. Since he was a tiny ball of fur, he'd liked to curl up on the radiator and watch the rain fall in the garden.

The memory of my house, my life, my whole world, pierced my heart like a dagger. I missed my home. I missed my job, my friends, my life—but most of all I missed my family. I hadn't heard from them in months, not to mention the ton of friends I have (had) all across Galicia. I've tried to keep my mind occupied with my own survival and not think too much. Every time I thought about my past, I tried to tell myself they were comfortably holed up in a Safe Haven, somewhere those monsters hadn't reached.

Now I know that's all a lie. Those monsters from beyond the grave are everywhere. There's no safe place, and no one's safe. All the survivors are drowning in a sea of suffering that goes on forever.

I could feel tears flooding my eyes. I took a deep breath, rubbed my face, and shook my head, trying to blank it all out. If I started crying, I wouldn't be able to stop. If I collapsed, I was screwed. The survival instinct kicked in again. Something deep in my hypothalamus secreted enough endorphins to get me going. Still, the pain was buried deep inside me, oozing emotional pus. Someday, I'd have to face it and wrench it out of my heart. But not now. Not yet.

I pushed the door open cautiously, making as little noise as possible. As I stepped out of the car, a violent gust of wind blew a curtain of water in my face. The thunder and lightning overlapped each another. It was almost completely dark. I closed the door behind me and crouched down for a moment, my back to the SUV.

I didn't see anything that looked threatening, but instinct was telling me just the opposite. To be honest, instinct screamed at me to get the fuck out of there.

About six yards in front of me, I could make out the half-decayed body of a civil guardsman in riot gear. His distinctive blue uniform had faded in the sun. In places it was a blackish oxidized color from bloodstains and body fluids. From the waist up, the body was a pile of torn, stinking flesh. No trace of the head.

I shrank back. I didn't know if scavengers or the undead had disfigured that body, but it looked like the work of a demented butcher. I gagged but didn't vomit. Amazing…I was getting more macho or deranged, depending on how you look at it. None of this shit affected me anymore.

I approached the body. Holding my breath, I pulled a shiny black pistol from the holster on his right hip. It was larger and heavier than the Glock, but I didn't have time to study it any more than that. I unlaced the guy's combat boots. His feet were black and rotten from fluids that had pooled there. It smelled really foul, so I hurried as fast as I could. When I'd pulled out the shoelaces, I had a cord about six feet long.

With the gun and shoelaces, I went back to the SUV, soaked to the skin. I grabbed the surprised Lucullus by the belly and tied one end of the cord to his collar and one end to my wrist. Then I hung the AK-47 and the speargun across my chest and dragged Prit's unconscious body out of the car.

The downpour brought the Ukrainian around. His groans signaled he was still alive but hurting like hell. Draping his arm over my shoulder, I started walking toward the access tunnel, holding the gun with my free hand and dragging Lucullus, who was indignant at being treated like a dog on a leash and at being soaking wet.

Our progress was painfully slow. Prit could hardly walk, and I was loaded down like a mule. Those few yards seemed like miles. The cat viciously yanked at the cord, trying to take cover from the rain. Every time he leaped forward, the bootlace dug into my wrist, sending waves of pain up my arm.

What a surreal picture we made! It occurred to me if an undead popped up, I'd have a hard time defending us, with both arms immobilized. That thought made me pick up the pace.

We reached the access tunnel in a matter of seconds. The glass roof over our heads amplified the heavy downpour. I twisted around, pulled the flashlight out of my pocket, and shone it toward the end of the corridor.

I leaned my shoulder against the emergency room door, and it opened with a soft hiss. I poked my head inside. The huge admitting room was in the shadows. A soft light filtered through large rectangular windows that ran all the way up to the ceiling. There were two bullet holes right in the middle of one of them.

The lobby looked like an abandoned slaughterhouse. Rust-colored blood was splattered across floor and walls. In some places it looked like someone had dumped large buckets of blood. The sweet, nauseating smell of dried blood mingled with the smell of decaying food…and stale sweat. It was subtle and faint but unmistakable. Human sweat. Someone had been sweating in that space, but I couldn't determine whether it had been hours or months ago.

Everywhere, lying every which way, were cast-off clothes, used bandages, stretchers stained with dried fluids, and even a couple of defibrillators with their paddles dangling. It was not a welcoming sight, to say the least.

The most upsetting part was the dozens of bloody handprints and footprints crisscrossing every inch of that corridor. Many feet (and I mean a *whole* lot) had traipsed through pools of blood, leaving an erratic trail. There were large and small footprints, including children's little steps, long strides, dragging feet…a complete collection. But no one was there. I couldn't say for sure that the tracks were made by the living.

I settled a nearly unconscious Prit in a wheelchair and untied Lucullus from my wrist and tied him to a radiator. Tying him up like that hurt his feelings. He was dying to explore that new place, but I couldn't turn him loose, not knowing what we'd find.

There were bodies on the floor, of course, but fewer than outside. By some miracle, I avoided stepping on a woman inflated by the gases of decomposition. Most of those unfortunate people weren't undead, just innocent victims the monsters had maimed so savagely they were beyond resurrection. The lack of corpses there was surely because most of the patients were now part of the giant brotherhood of the undead.

A sudden, loud metallic sound paralyzed me. Someone had run into a filing cabinet or a cart, then let out a drawn-out groan. The sound seemed to come from a couple of floors up, close enough to give me chills.

We weren't alone.

I wasn't about to walk around a dark, deserted hospital full of corpses just to identify the source of a noise. Whoever or whatever it was could have the whole place to himself. I was scared shitless just standing at the entrance. I couldn't imagine heading into the bowels of the building.

I walked by the nursing desk. A dust-covered stethoscope lay abandoned on a pile of medical records. I couldn't resist hanging it around my neck. When I was little, I used to "borrow" my mother's stethoscope. I loved those things.

Suddenly I could picture myself in an episode of *ER*. What the hell would those characters think if they saw a guy holding an AK-47, wearing a wetsuit and a stethoscope around his neck, prowling around the ER?

I giggled hysterically. My God, all that shit was starting to go to my head. Next stop: schizophrenia.

Beside the check-in desk, next to some cubicles with the curtains drawn, was the emergency medicine cabinet. The door was caved in. I entered cautiously, treading on the broken glass that covered the floor.

It looked like a bomb had exploded in there. The steel cabinet where they kept morphine and opiates was shredded into what looked like flower petals. Someone had opened it the hard way, with an explosive, maybe a grenade off a dead soldier. The explosion had reduced the jars, vials, and medical devices to smithereens. A botched job. The work of someone looking for morphine or, more likely, a junkie who knew where to find opiates. I'm not surprised. It must be hard to score some horse these days.

I rummaged through pieces of broken glass for a vial in good condition, mentally repeating the list: antiseptics, antibiotics, gauze, painkillers (no opiates, since Prit had already maxed out on morphine), sutures, bandages, sterile needles.

I felt a jabbing pain in my hand and yanked it back. I'd sliced my finger with a sliver of glass as thin as a knife. I swore under my breath and put my finger in my mouth. The salty blood ran down my throat. I wrapped my finger absentmindedly in a butterfly suture and went back to searching, in a worse mood, piling my booty on a shiny aluminum tray.

That tray saved my life. When I turned around to set down a roll of tape, I saw movement behind me reflected in the metal mirror. I turned around like a snake and clumsily raised the AK-47. The bitter taste of fear rose from my stomach.

A decrepit old man, completely naked, with some of his intestines hanging out, was rocking back and forth, less than two yards from me, the right sleeve of his hospital gown rolled up. He opened his mouth in a mute roar as he stumbled toward me, stepping on the glass barefooted, feeling no pain. I was paralyzed with horror. The old man had no eyes. Although his eye sockets were empty, and two bloody streams slid down his face, he knew exactly where I was.

Everything happened in slow motion. I raised the AK-47 to his face. Curiously relaxed, I pointed the gun at his neck to compensate for the kick, something I'd learned from the Pakistanis. I let him get barely a yard away and pulled the trigger.

The bullet left a gaping red hole in the old man's forehead. Splinters of bone, brain, and blood splattered the wall behind him.

The old man collapsed like a sack with a wet, gurgling sound, dragging along a pile of folders as he fell. The smell of gunpowder stung my nostrils, and a piercing whistle rang in my ears from firing in such a tiny space. I'd have a headache in the hours to come.

Once again, I'd had a close call. But that shot would've been heard for more than a mile. Every being, living or not, in the hospital would know we were there. Jesus, what a day…

As I calmed my heartbeat, I cursed myself. How could I have been so stupid? The speargun hung over my left arm. If I hadn't been in such a hurry and as scared as a hysterical old woman, I could have taken out the old man with a silent spear instead of the noisy AK-47.

I'd had to act fast. I hadn't had the presence of mind to think about the speargun. The assault rifle was the first thing I got my hands on, and I acted instinctively.

Now I had other things to worry about. The shot triggered a wave of sound throughout the hospital. Doors banged, things crashed on top of each other, something fell noisily to the floor (a stretcher?), and there were dull, muffled thuds against the walls. It was one lethal symphony. And most of all, the fucking groaning. How could I forget that? It was an indistinct, deep echo, as if someone was trying to talk but had forgotten how to move his tongue. It was impossible to explain the sound if you'd never seen those monsters. It's a chilling roar, human and inhuman at the same time.

I scooped up all the drugs on the metal tray and ran back to where I'd left Prit. He was awake, sitting bolt upright in the wheelchair, his right hand cradling his left hand, which was covered in bandages. He was dazed by the morphine and white as a sheet, but otherwise fully conscious and alert. And scared. As fucking scared as I was.

He asked me what had happened and where the hell we were. Quickly, I brought him up to speed from the time he had the "accident" until I'd left him sitting in that chair in the middle of a deserted, dark room. Then I realized the tremendous shock he must've felt when he regained consciousness, all alone, wounded, in the dark, in a strange place filled with terrifying noise. If it'd been me, I'd have had a heart attack.

I hesitated about whether to tell him about his injuries. Hell, he's got eyes, he's not an idiot. I told him he'd lost two fingers on his left hand, and the ring finger didn't look good. The Ukrainian didn't blink. He coldly asked if he still had his thumb. I nodded. He seemed to relax a little. He matter-of-factly said that wasn't so bad, as long as he still had his thumb and two fingers to oppose it. "I've seen worse," he added. "You should've seen my friend Misha in ninety-five after his helicopter was hit with a thirty-seven-millimeter grenade. Now, *he* had a problem. So I'm okay. I'll make it. Now, pass me the AK-47 and stop making all that bloody racket, by God. Our ass is on the line here."

My relief was so overwhelming I nearly cried. I knew Prit's apparent calm was only a front, but just hearing his voice made me feel less alone. I handed him the heavy AK-47. The Ukrainian deftly crossed it over his wounded arm and felt for the magazine with his good hand. He seemed perfectly capable of defending himself with one hand.

I was already calmer. Knowing I didn't have to keep one eye glued to an unconscious Pritchenko was a big relief. And knowing that he had my back again was an even bigger relief. But as much as he played the tough guy, I could read fear and anxiety in his eyes. Plus, I couldn't forget that the guy needed urgent medical attention. More than I could give him. And he needed it now.

It was time to get the hell out of there before things got uglier. I left Lucullus in Prit's care (my cat looked distressed to lose sight of me) and walked back down the hallway to the ER. I had to find out if the path was clear.

The hallway was even darker than when we got there, lit up by only the lightning. The worst of the thunderstorm had passed, and there were fewer lightning bolts. But the rain was far from stopping. Sheets of rushing water fell from a dark violet sky. The wind was gradually reaching hurricane speeds. Broken branches, bark, and dozens of unidentified objects whirled around the parking lot. Swirls of rain reduced visibility to a few yards. That was the least of our problems, by a long shot.

Outside dozens of undead staggered in the downpour, taking up the entire parking lot, moving slowly toward the hospital. I was stunned by the scene. I hadn't seen such a concentration of those beasts since the early days of the plague.

There were men, women, and children of every age and condition. Some looked unscathed; others had terrible wounds that went far beyond what a normal human being could endure. The majority wore the clothes they'd had on when they mutated. Others were stark naked, or their clothes were in shreds due to the weather, accidents, or God knows what, making the sight doubly disturbing. A couple of them were scorched and blackened all over, as if they'd been set ablaze. The fire had disfigured their features to the point I couldn't identify their sex or age. Others had ghastly amputations, as if those body parts had been blown off by an explosion. The variety of horrors was endless.

From the huge multitude rose a chorus of creepy groans. The scraping noise made by hundreds of feet, in shoes or barefoot, dragging across the ground, was drowned out by the boom of thunder. Spectral rays of lightning lit up the scene.

Water dripping off the edge of the tunnel rolled down my neck, but I didn't feel it. Even hidden in shadows, I turned all my attention to the sea of humanity (not human, I corrected myself bitterly) that slowly encircled an area as far as I could see.

I racked my brain, trying to understand where such a crowd could have come from. The obvious answer popped into my head. The hospital environment, the scene of extensive carnage, must've had dozens, maybe hundreds, of those things. The roar of the engine as we approached had drawn them back here the way a light attracts moths. But instead of continuing our journey, we'd stopped, giving them time to catch up to us. And we were in no shape to get the hell out. Great.

ENTRY 82
April 20, 4:21 p.m.

The first monsters had already reached the SUV. I cursed my stupidity. When I got Prit out of the SUV, my arms had been full, and I'd forgotten to close the passenger door. Now, a couple of those things—a tall, thin man with a big gash down his back and a young boy about fifteen who was missing the calf of his right leg—had crawled inside. Maybe they were drawn by our scent.

It was just a matter of time till that multitude surrounded our SUV, making it completely inaccessible. And it would only take them a little while to figure out what path we'd taken into the hospital. There was no way we could shoot our way to the SUV and make our getaway. That'd be suicide. Even supposing all of our shots hit the target (doubtful in my case), it was too great a distance for Prit and me to cover at once. There were just too many of them.

I understood the pure terror the defenders of Safe Havens must have felt when they faced a flood of those monsters in even greater numbers. Trying to kill them is like trying to keep ants off your blanket at a picnic. You can step on dozens of them, but more keep coming...and coming. They're fucking unstoppable.

Their overwhelming numbers and the fact that they're dead make them a formidable foe. They don't hesitate, don't sleep, don't rest; they have no fear, and nothing stops them. They have one goal: to capture anyone who isn't one of them.

A huge weight lay on my heart. I tried to swallow, but my mouth was as dry as straw. I couldn't make a sound or breathe or think clearly. I'd never felt so much like prey. And I'd never been so aware of how hopeless our situation was.

The world is no longer ours. It's theirs. How long will this situation last?

A little jingling to my left me brought me out of my trance and back to reality. Pressed against the wall, propped up by one hand, a guy in his early twenties with long hair, wearing loose, baggy pants, inched along. A long silver chain with a bunch of keys hung from where his right pocket should've been. His keys dragged along behind him, bumping against his legs, making the jingling sound that had alerted me.

Like all these monsters, the boy's skin was waxy and transparent. Myriad small burst veins traced a grotesque map on his skin. His left arm hung limp, and he had an ugly gash on his bicep. He was wearing a dirty, stiff shirt. I could clearly see three or four bullet holes in his chest. One of the bullets had entered his heart, and the other bullets were in his lower abdomen.

That sight made my head spin. That creature had already faced a survivor, who'd shot him in defense. But the guy was still on his feet, so I didn't figure the gunman had survived. Now the guy was headed for me.

Instead of coming to the hospital by the access road, like most of those walking corpses, he'd entered through a side entrance. While the crowd was swarming over the sandbags, he was already inside the perimeter, and he'd found me.

A moan escaped his throat. He picked up his pace and rushed toward me. That time, I took things more calmly. When he was fifteen yards from me, I took the speargun off my shoulder and checked the bolt and the rubber band. I also checked the gun in case something went wrong. Then I leaned against an overflowing, smelly trash can to steady my aim. When he was just three yards from me, I pulled the trigger.

The spear entered above his upper lip, near his cheekbone. The tip went through his occipital bone, making a crunch like a dry branch breaking. The monster stopped suddenly. Putrid blood gushed from the wound as the guy wavered. The shaft of the spear was in his line of vision, and he tried to grab it. However, as with all the undead, his coordination left a lot to be desired. He swatted the air in front of the spear as black, smelly blood streamed down his face and chest, staining them a dark purple. His movements became slower and more erratic.

With a strange gurgle, he extended his good arm and fell forward. If it weren't such a lurid scene, I would've laughed at the way he fell. But this wasn't the time for joking around. I lunged toward the body to retrieve the bloody spear. Just as I was about to grab it, I froze. I remembered I had a cut on my finger, and I wasn't wearing gloves. I looked helplessly at the spear that stuck out like a flagpole from the back of the guy's head. So close, yet so far.

I vacillated. I only had three spears left in the quiver strapped to my leg. Leaving the spear behind was a huge loss.

I weighed the possibility of finding some latex gloves somewhere and coming back for the spear, but one glance at the crowd convinced me there was no time. Thirty or forty undead had broken through the defensive line and were headed in my direction. I stood out clearly against the white wall of the hospital. I had to get out of there.

After one last look outside, I ran full speed back down the dark corridor, my footsteps echoing in that cavernous tunnel.

A leak in the roof had formed a puddle in the middle of the hall. I'd seen the puddle before, but I was so crazed when I came back through, I forgot about it. I slipped and took one hell of a fall. I lay there for several seconds, the wind knocked out of me, trying to catch my breath. When I tried to get up, a sharp jab in my side made me scream in pain. I slumped back down, cursing a blue streak. Just what I needed—a broken rib. For sure I had a big, fat bruise. Fucking puddle! I was going to sue that fucking hospital.

Just the thought of a lawsuit, in this dire situation, made me double up with laughter, and that set off new spasms of pain. A lawsuit. What a joke! I struggled to my feet, whimpering in the pain, laughing hysterically, and kept going.

No doubt about it—my nerves were shot.

I pushed open the swinging doors with my good side and reloaded the speargun, still hiccuping with laughter. I took a quick look around me. Double doors opened in both directions. On one side of the doors were some steel hooks attached to two brackets on the walls. The hospital staff had used those hooks to prop open the doors to keep from having to constantly push them open.

I had a different use in mind for those hooks. Next to the door, on the floor, under a pile of discarded medical supplies, lay an IV pole with two empty IV bags hanging from it. I had to kick aside a mountain of gauze, boxes of tranquilizers, and used bandages to get to it. I slid that pole through the hooks to bar the door closed. I frowned, my heart heavy. It always worked so well in the movies. That pole wouldn't withstand the pounding for long. That crowd would be through the door in two minutes.

I was breathing hard when I reached Prit. He studied me with a worried face as I leaned on his chair and caught my breath. I brought him up to speed with the huge problem we were facing. It was impossible to leave through that door. Besides, I was pretty sure the undead would make it into the lobby very soon. We had to find another way out. A big complex like the Meixoeiro Hospital must have dozens of entrances and exits. That hospital was a maze of rooms and corridors that confused even the personnel who worked there every day. We had to find one on a different side of the building. To get on the other side, we'd have to go down into the bowels of the building.

We had no choice. I asked Prit if he could walk. The Ukrainian struggled to get up. Very brave, but futile. His legs failed him in a few seconds, and he collapsed back in the chair. The morphine still in his system and his blood loss, coupled with fatigue and not enough food for weeks, held him back. I'd have to push him.

I set Lucullus in Prit's lap. I held a flashlight in one hand and gripped the back of the wheelchair with the other, and off we went, just as we heard the first blows against the ER doors.

We set off down a corridor at the back of the room. I pushed open the door and paused. That hallway was dark as a well at midnight. Fluorescent tubes hung from the ceiling, covered in a thick coat of dust, useless junk without electricity. So little outside light filtered in, I could only guess where obstacles lay across the corridor.

I assumed that things would get worse, since we were headed deep into the bowels of the hospital. At least we were still fairly close to the outside. Some faint light from the lightning came in, and we could hear the rain. As soon as we stepped through the next door, we'd be in another world.

The smell, not the lack of light, stopped me in my tracks. The minute I opened that door, a pungent rotting odor smacked us in the face. Nowadays that putrid stench was everywhere, but I'd never smelled it that concentrated before.

That odor was heavy, like the smell that hung over the ruins of the Safe Haven, but ten times as strong, probably from being in a hot place with no ventilation. My eyes teared up, so I tied a handkerchief around my face. I coughed and tried to breathe through my mouth. I had a knot in my stomach and was getting more and more nauseated. Prit had screwed up his face, trying to keep from gagging. The hospital was full of dozens of bodies in an advanced state of decomposition. We were about to enter a mass grave.

We ventured into the hallway. Prit shone the flashlight into every corner while I pushed the wheelchair, veering around bodies. Our plan was simple. We'd cross the first floor, make a beeline for the front, and leave from there.

Before the pandemic, a nurse who knew the hospital could've made it down that long hallway in ten minutes, tops. In the dark, with no knowledge of that labyrinth, it would take us a lot longer.

For four or five minutes things went pretty well. As fast as we could, we got through several rooms and corridors, dodging tons of equipment and medical supplies. The hospital seemed to have been evacuated in a hurry, but the number of half-rotten bodies suggested the opposite. After evacuating the building, maybe the fugitives had retreated back into the building for some reason, and the undead had trapped them there.

Most of the bodies had bullet holes in their heads. Some of the remains were horribly disfigured and partially eaten beyond any possibility of resuscitation. Almost all of those bodies had on army boots: the defense forces making a last stand after everyone else had run off. Run where?

The jabbing pain in my side had gotten worse. White spots danced before my eyes, and my legs trembled. My breathing must've been labored, because Prit turned in his chair and looked at me with concern. "You're in bad shape. We can't go on like this. We'd better rest," he said. I agreed. I needed to catch my breath; I was hyperventilating.

A plywood door to our right opened into a dressing room; lockers lined the walls, with rows of benches in the middle. In the back of the room were a couple of couches. A bulletin board covered with notes and posters took up the entire wall. A huge plastic rubber plant stood guard in the corner. A woman's purse lay on the floor, its contents spilled out. In the light of the flashlight, I saw a lipstick, a wallet, and the handle of a hairbrush. A nurse's dressing room. Not a bad place to take a rest.

I closed the door and collapsed on a bench. Prit stroked Lucullus's head with his good hand, stoically enduring his pain. He's one tough guy.

I took off the top of the wetsuit. I was so thin I could count my ribs. I hadn't had a really nutritious meal for months in these subhuman conditions. My body was starting to pay the price. Vitamin C deficiency from a lack of fresh vegetables was the most dangerous. A huge bruise on my right side was slowly turning a dark purple. I touched it and choked back a howl of pain. I must have broken some ribs. That's a bitch!

I forced down some metamizole sodium, a powerful analgesic I'd found earlier, and picked up the purse. I rummaged around inside. A mobile phone with no battery in a cloth case, a crumpled pack of Lucky Strikes, a lighter, and a bent-up driver's license with a picture of a very pretty blonde with green eyes. She was smiling at me. Laura Viz. There was no hospital ID or document in her wallet. Thanks for the smokes, Laura. I wonder who the hell you were and what the hell you were doing here.

I stuck a cigarette in Prit's mouth, and he took a deep drag. Then I unwrapped the bandage so he could get a look at his wounds. The little finger was completely gone, and the middle finger was missing down to the second knuckle. There was a lengthwise gash in the ring finger that needed stitches. His palm had a deep cut, but fortunately it wasn't bleeding very much.

Prit looked up and calmly said it wasn't so bad, but he needed medical attention right away. He hadn't lost too much blood yet, but there was the risk of blood poisoning. But I was the only person around to tend to his wounds. With a first-aid kit.

Suddenly, something punched the plywood door hard, making a huge hole at the top. Sticking through the hole was a cadaverous hand, covered in splinters.

The hand pulled back out and hit the door again, nearly ripping it off the frame. Damn, that bastard was strong! I took a few steps back, holding the flashlight tight, while Prit cocked the AK-47 and aimed at the door. I could see the undead guy through the hole. He was young, burly, with a beard and curly hair. All he was wearing was a funny cartoon T-shirt that was way too big for him. A thick bandage covered his right calf. I bet a million euros I knew how he got that wound.

With one last blow, the flimsy door split in two, and the creature lunged forward just as Prit pulled the trigger. Blood and bones gushed out the gaping red hole where his left eye had been.

The guy collapsed like a sack in front of me. I kicked him to make sure he wasn't moving. There was something odd about the corpse. It took me a while to realize what it was. He was drenched. That thing had come in from outside not five minutes before. They'd found a way in. The front door had fallen, and they were on our trail.

April 21, 4:19 p.m.

I turned to Prit. Sweat ran down my back. The Ukrainian and I exchanged a look that said it all. Our situation had taken a turn for the worse. We were on the run—again.

After I'd wrapped his hand in a bandage I'd found in the first-aid kit, we crept out of the nurses' quarters. The hallway was empty, but the shot Prit fired had unleashed a furious assault on the hospital. We heard more groans and blows, only much closer. Dull thuds were coming from the locked room across the hall. I placed my hand on the wall and felt the vibration of enraged fists beating against it. I stepped back, terrified. I prayed that thing didn't find a way out of there.

Suddenly we heard the sound of breaking glass coming from a room we'd passed ten minutes before. Someone had tripped over a monitor, and it had shattered on the floor. The roaring was getting closer.

Prit placed Lucullus on his lap, clutched the cocked AK in his good hand, and motioned to me to head out with the other. I pushed his wheelchair faster. I had a huge knot in my stomach and cold sweat running down my back. I was scared, really scared, and I didn't mind admitting it. Anybody in that situation would've been scared to death. And anyone who says different is either a liar or brain dead.

The hallway went through a broken door and into a slightly wider room. A large white sign overhead read PEDIATRICS in big blue letters. Children's drawings of cows in meadows, clowns, and daisies hung on the walls, making the room look like a nursery school. I guess they'd made the young patients more comfortable. However, clumps of dried blood dotting the drawings ruined the decor. It looked like someone had turned on a giant meat grinder in the middle of the room. Prit gasped in anguish. I wiped the sweat off my forehead. It was oppressively hot in there.

Right in front of us was a drawing of huge clown with a big smile. He watched us from the wall, not realizing that a huge clot of dried blood streaked his face. He held a giant bouquet of balloons in a gloved hand. Blood had dripped down his yellow overalls, and dried brain matter was embedded in his teeth. He looked really evil. I shuddered. That sweet clown seemed poised to jump off the wall. With the bits of his victims in his mouth, he looked like a demented predator. That room was a nightmare.

We backed away from that scene and moved on, trying not to stare. You didn't have to be a genius to realize that someone had barricaded himself in that room to fight. Not hard to guess how that ended. Bullet casings carpeted the floor. Piles of stinking bodies were silent witnesses to the desperately fought battle. The dreadful scene we saw next stopped us in our tracks: the body of a little boy, no more than a year or two, lying crosswise in the hallway, facedown, with a gaping hole in the back of his skull.

Prit wept silently, nervously fingering the safety on the AK-47. I didn't say a word, remembering he had a son about the same age. The sight of that little body must've made him wonder about his family's fate, somewhere in Central Europe. I couldn't imagine the feelings torturing him.

A thud on our left got our attention. A plastic-and-glass partition sectioned off the Pediatric ICU. That was where the families of young patients could see them through the glass. Now, on the other side of the glass there was utter blackness.

I shone the flashlight on the partition, trying to light up the other side. The glass must've been polarized; the light bounced back off it, momentarily blinding us. I tried again, this time looking to the side, but got no better result. It was impossible to shine a light into the other side past that glass.

I was convinced I heard a sound coming from the other side. I pressed my face to the glass, cupping my hands on either side of my eyes. When my eyes adjusted, I could make out a bed covered with a plastic bubble that was open on one side. Suddenly a bloodstained hand swatted the glass right in front of my face, accompanied by a long groan. The waxen, enraged face of a girl about six years old glared at me through the glass, less than an inch from my eyes.

I jumped back and landed on Prit's lap. My heart nearly leaped out my mouth. She beat her palms on the glass and let out a monotone howl. A four- or five-year-old boy, dressed in hospital pajamas, joined her. They pounded harder and harder.

I stood up, white as a sheet. The glass trembled with each blow, but the kids didn't seem to have enough strength to break it. I got a good look at them. The little boy's bald head was as slick as a cue ball. He must have been undergoing radiation when this tidal wave of madness reached the hospital. I saw no wound on his body, but there must have been a cut or scratch somewhere. The little girl had a deep gash in her neck. Her attacker had severed her carotid artery with one bite, killing her almost instantly. Her little body was covered in dried blood. I prayed it was just her blood.

That devastating scene seemed to crush Prit. He stared glassy-eyed at the partition, his hand hanging limp on the AK-47. Out of his half-opened mouth came an unintelligible sound as he shook his head from side to side. The fur on Lucullus's back bristled. He yowled angrily, adding his voice to that symphony of moans and thuds.

I leaned down and whispered some reassuring words to Prit. Then I cocked the gun and set off again. If those things got out of there, I'd be the one who'd have to deal with them. Prit couldn't shoot a child, even one of those monsters.

That hallway seemed to stretch on forever. The two little monsters walked along beside us, behind the partition, howling and hitting the glass; fortunately it didn't break. My attention was divided among the hallway, the glass, the undead, and Prit, who was still muttering under his breath. The Ukrainian's nerves were starting to unravel.

At the end of the hall, I stopped a moment, unsure where to go next. The glass curved behind us, preventing the little creatures from continuing alongside us. They knew they couldn't follow us and let out a string of frustrated howls. I was pretty sure the glass wouldn't give, but I didn't want to stick around to find out.

There were two doors in front of us: the one on our right had been kicked in, and there were bloodstains on the frame. The one on our left was closed and intact. The push bar was on our side and couldn't be operated from the other side. A priori, the intact door offered greater security, but I had the feeling it led back to the main section of the hospital. Hoping I wasn't all turned around, I decided on the shattered door, headed in the direction we'd just come from.

A slight breeze was coming through from the dark room behind the broken door. That tipped the balance. After flipping the bird to the raging little monsters, I opened the door on the left, hoping that would confuse our pursuers if they made it this far, and pushed the wheelchair through.

Again, I felt the breeze. Air was coming in from outside. We walked about ten minutes in total darkness. A couple of times we came to a dead end and had to retrace our steps. Prit was starting to worry me. He was now lethargic and indifferent to everything. At one point we passed a couple of steel fire doors that shook violently. A horde of undead was crowded on the other side, uselessly beating against the doors. Someone had nailed some wedges into the door frame to keep the doors from opening. Not even that aroused the slightest interest in the Ukrainian. He was struck dumb.

We rounded a couple more corners and reached an area with some light. The breeze was stronger, and we could hear the rain. My mood lifted. We had to be close. Damn close.

When I opened one last swinging door, I couldn't contain myself—I shouted for joy. A huge lobby stretched out before us in the shadows, lit up by lightning we could see through a long glass wall. The room overlooked a huge park and weed-covered gardens, silent in the downpour. The lobby was deserted. A pole with a tattered, scorched Spanish flag stood guard next to an identical pole lying on the floor. I didn't see a single creature in the rain, human or otherwise. I smiled with relief. We'd made it. We were saved.

The lobby floor was littered with papers, medical files, and flyers in every color. On one end was a closed café, waiting for employees who'd never open it up again for medical staff that no longer existed. At the other end was an empty reception desk crowded with phones. Some of the headsets were off the hook, hanging by their cords, mute and motionless.

In the middle of the lobby stood a newsstand, like an abandoned monolith. Stacked against it were magazines and newspapers still in bundles. Out of curiosity I picked up a copy of each publication. They were dated four months ago. Their front covers announced the creation of Safe Havens and asked the public's cooperation in addressing "this crisis of epidemic proportion whose origin is still unknown." Safe Havens. Yeah, right. And unknown origins. What a load of shit!

I've always been an avid reader of the press, so out of habit I began to flip through the pages. The international section was down to the bare minimum; the sports and business sections didn't exist. Some newspapers had no more than thirteen or fourteen pages, all devoted to the pandemic. The articles must've been written by a skeleton team of journalists, the ones who dared to keep going to work.

I smiled at the foolish ideas and nonsense I read. The public was blind right up to the last minute. Arrogant, foolish sons of bitches.

I looked up to discover that Prit was not in his chair. Dropping the newspapers, with my soul on tenterhooks, I scanned the lobby and spotted the small figure of the Ukrainian, silhouetted against a wall by lightning. He was absorbed in something on that wall. When I figured out what had caught his attention, I felt my stomach shrink.

In a bright flash of lightning, I got a good look at that wall. It was covered with hundreds of messages and photos that had one thing in common. They were all notices of missing persons. Family or friends had stuck them up there, hoping for news of their loved ones. Photos of smiling people gazed down at me. Heartbreaking notes. Anyone knowing the whereabouts of Little Johnny, please call this number right away. Mr. So-and-So disappeared three days ago. Little Susie and her entire school bus vanished a day and a half ago. If anyone has seen our child, please contact us at this number. "Missing" was written in bold letters with a red marker below the picture of an older woman sitting at a table decorated for Christmas. The photograph of an entire family smiling in a garden, in summer, with "disappeared" written over it with a cell phone number. "Javier Piñon, we're at your parents' house. Meet us there." "Luisa Sabajanes, if you see this note stay where you are. I'll come by every day till I find you. I love you." "If anyone has seen this man, please contact this number." And on and on.

It was a sickening sight. I took a couple of steps back, stunned. Of course. A hospital was the logical place to look for a missing person. Thousands of missing people, in fact. You got a feel for the magnitude of this chaos. Fuck. It was chilling. I could feel pain and anguish oozing out of that wall. I was staring at pictures of thousands of people who were dead. Or worse.

I jumped when I felt a hand on my shoulder. I turned and looked into Prit's infinitely sad eyes. "Let's go," he said. "Let's get out of this place right now, or by God, I'll go crazy. Doctor my wounds someplace else, anywhere, just not here. We gotta go. This place is bad, very bad. Come on. Please."

He didn't have to ask twice. The Ukrainian wasn't the only one on the verge of a nervous breakdown. I wanted out of that macabre place, too.

I went to the door, with Prit leaning on my arm, limping, and a rather cowardly Lucullus tangled around my legs. As we approached the door, an alarm went off in my head. Something wasn't right. What was wrong with this picture? I couldn't figure out what until we were standing right in front of the door.

Of course. Those ultramodern glass doors slid open on rails. There must be a sensor nearby. With no electricity, the doors remained obstinately closed.

Yet there we stood, Prit and I, like fools, expecting the doors to open by magic. When it dawned on us that those doors wouldn't open by themselves, we calmly thought through the problem. Pritchenko said that kind of door had an emergency backup system. There should be a lever located on the door frame that could be activated manually in case of a power outage.

Nervously I felt around the edge of the doors, until my fingers found a recessed compartment on the floor, next to the door. I pulled off the cover and froze. All I found was the symbol for emergency and a diagram explaining how to use the lever. That was it. That and bare wires. Someone had ripped off the lever.

Fearing the worst, I rushed to the other two doors, but those levers were ripped off too. Someone had turned that sector of the hospital into a fortress and wanted to make sure those doors couldn't be opened, even by accident.

I felt Prit's eyes boring into me. I had a look of shock on my face. I picked up a heavy red fire extinguisher. I reared back and threw it as hard as I could against the glass. A loud *Bam!* echoed through the lobby, sending a million more echoes throughout the building, but the glass held fast. Only a slight scratch marked the spot I'd hit with the fire extinguisher.

Seeing red, I threw the container against the glass again and got the same result. Choked up, unable to swallow, I cocked the pistol and, holding it with both hands, shot into the glass. The weapon kicked savagely and almost jumped out of my hand. A tiny hole opened two feet above where I'd aimed. I fired again. And again.

Prit rested his hand on my arm, forcing the barrel down. "It's useless. That's security glass, nearly three inches thick. It wouldn't break if you ran a truck into it."

I punched the glass, enraged. So close, yet so far. We were just a few inches from getting out of there. We could see the way out…and we were still trapped. Damn it to hell!

Calm down, I told myself, think for a moment. On the way there, we'd felt a breeze, right? That gust of air came in somewhere. I just had to find where.

I dashed across the lobby and stood in the middle of the room, on top of the Galician Health Service shield engraved in the floor. I closed my eyes and stretched out my arms, trying to detect any puff of air. A slight breeze ruffled my hair. I opened my eyes. It was coming from the left, behind the reception desk.

I hooked my arm through Prit's and dragged him over to that point. The Ukrainian seemed to draw strength out of weakness and despair. He contemptuously refused to use the wheelchair anymore. "If we're fucked," he said very seriously, looking into my eyes, "I want to die like a man, standing up, not sitting in a fucking chair."

Despite his brave words, I noticed that the glow in the Ukrainian's eyes had faded. Something had broken inside him when we walked through that room with all the children's bodies. Seeing that boy's body lying in the hallway had been the last straw. Under so much emotional pressure for months, he'd snapped. His nerves were shot. That tough soldier who'd survived the slaughter at the Safe Haven, the cold-blooded guy who slowly hacked off a woman's neck without blinking, was falling apart. I'm sure any psychiatrist would've diagnosed PTSD. What good would that diagnosis do now?

There was a narrow corridor behind the front desk. Large metal cabinets were lined up silently against the walls, half-hidden in the shadows. Internet servers, I concluded, when I noticed the huge bundle of wires that ran along the baseboard.

The corridor led to a square room. At the back of the room was a big red door with EMERGENCY EXIT painted on it. Thick chains crisscrossed the two push bars. I rattled the door but couldn't open it with my bare hands. I'd need an acetylene torch (before all this happened, I wouldn't have even known what that was). Since I didn't have one in my backpack, we were screwed.

A staircase disappeared into the shadows to the floor above. The flashlight's beam reached the next landing, but no farther. I could only speculate where those stairs went, but that's definitely where the breeze was coming from.

Cautiously, we started up the steps. Prit carried the AK-47 across his chest, strapped to his belt. I held the gun with one hand and the flashlight with the other. Lucullus skittered along, half-strangled by the cord tied to my wrist, glued to my ankles.

We had to climb three more sets of stairs before we reached the next floor. Before us was a cavernous, gloomy room. A row of overturned beds formed a bunker. Someone had tried to mount a defense there, but it mustn't have worked. The left half of the row was completely pushed to one side.

A strange, watery slurping sound coming from behind one of the overturned beds put us on alert. We approached quietly, Prit on one side and me on the other, trying not to make any noise. I tied Lucullus to the leg of a chair so I had both arms free. Then I swapped the pistol for the speargun. We'd made so much noise on the ground floor, I didn't want to make any more noise here.

Prit was already alongside the bed, waiting for me, looking disconcerted. He nodded. For so long, he'd seemed to be in another world. Now he was ready.

I took a deep breath and shone the light on the other side of the bed. Crouched on the floor, an orderly or a nurse (I couldn't tell which, but it was wearing a hospital uniform) was bent over something I couldn't see. I focused the flashlight on the thing's head. When he noticed the light, he whipped around, and I saw two things. First, his face was covered with burst veins, his skin was a dead, yellow color, and fresh blood trickled down his chin. Second, a huge black rat lay on the floor, ripped open, its guts spilling out. The monster glared at me with bloodshot eyes. He'd been so engaged in his prey, we'd taken him by surprise.

I squeezed the trigger about eight inches from his forehead. The spear pierced his skull cleanly, splashing putrid blood all over my face. Sick to my stomach, I set the flashlight and the unloaded speargun on a bed and frantically began to wipe myself off with the sheet.

I was so absorbed in what I was doing, I didn't see the second undead guy rush me from behind. He was a young guy with a horrible haircut that reminded me of an ashtray. He wore lots of gold chains around his neck like a Latin Kings gang member.

A weak cry from Prit, who watched the scene, glassy-eyed, warned me, but it was too late. Ashtray Hair grabbed me by the armpit as I turned around and sank his teeth into my shoulder. His bite couldn't penetrate the thick neoprene, but I got a close look at those teeth. I needed to keep him from scratching me with his bloody hands.

I held tight to the undead's waist and tried to push away from him, but the beast was very strong. We spun around the room, colliding into everything in our path. I screamed for help, but Prit was curled up on the floor, moaning, rocking back and forth.

The undead guy and I struggled furiously, linked together. We looked like a couple dancing cheek to cheek, all the while trying to rip each other's throats out. I was in trouble. If I let go to grab the pistol hanging from my waist, that monster would overpower me and finish me off. If I didn't, sooner or later he'd succeed in biting me, and that would be the end of me.

I don't know when we bumped into the flashlight, but it smashed to bits on the floor and plunged us into total darkness. That's when the situation became really desperate. We were now wrestling in silence. The beast kept trying to bite me through my wetsuit. I tried to wrap one arm around his hands, grab his neck, and immobilize his head with the other hand.

We stumbled against something hard and lost our balance. I teetered around like a drunk, desperately waving my leg around to regain my balance, but inertia was unstoppable. I realized we were falling, still cheek to cheek. A sharp edge drove into my bruised side. I screamed in pain, but that was all I had time for. Our mortal dance had brought us to the edge of the staircase, and we tumbled down those stairs at top speed.

For several minutes, I didn't know what happened. I don't even know how much time elapsed. I just know I woke up in a haze. Pain spread over every inch of my body. I had a salty taste in my mouth. Blood. I gingerly touched my lips and found I'd bitten my tongue. I tried to sit up, but a stabbing pain on my bruised side coursed through me like an electric shock. The pain was bad before, but now I was on fire.

Gradually my mind cleared. I remembered Ashtray Hair. Where the hell was that bastard? I groped around in the holster strapped to my leg and pulled out the Bic lighter I'd found in the nurse's purse. That lighter felt like it was running low on fluid. When I clicked it, a faint blue flame weakly lit the scene. The creature was lying on the landing, his head smashed against the wall. At my feet lay his body in the throes of strange seizures. Between bursts of pain, I managed to sit up so I could take a look.

That son of a bitch had gotten the worst of it in the fall. I surmised his spine was broken, since he couldn't move his arms or legs. The bastard jerked his head from side to side, his teeth snapping like a trap. He looked at me with hatred in his dead eyes. Fuck you, you dumbshit, I thought. You're no threat to me now.

I kicked him hard and sent him rolling down the next flight of stairs, hoping his head would split open on a sharp corner. Sore and exhausted, I stood up. My right ankle was swollen to a size that didn't bode well. Every time I breathed, I felt a knife in my side. My mouth was bleeding, and I had a colossal headache. I was a mess.

I hobbled up the stairs, leaning on the railing to steady myself. The lighter was burning my hand, and the blue flame was fading. My backpack lay on the ground, right where I'd left it to switch the pistol for the speargun. I dug down in it and found the spare flashlight.

I swept the beam across the cavernous room. It looked like a tornado had hit it. Prit was curled up right where I'd left him, unscathed. Suddenly, my heart sank. The chair I'd tied my cat to was upside down. Lucullus had disappeared.

I shook Prit's trembling body. The Ukrainian shrugged me off, muttering gibberish in Russian. He couldn't take the stress any longer. I draped one of his arms around my shoulders and helped him stand up. My mind was racing. I couldn't leave without Lucullus, of course, but finding the cat with Prit in tow would be really difficult. I had to find a safe place to leave him while I looked for my cat. Then I'd come back for him, and we'd get the hell out of that hospital.

I spotted a huge, heavy, carved wooden door at one end of the room. Its intricate engravings and huge brass handles looked like something from a Rococo mansion, not a supermodern hospital that was all angles and straight lines.

Intrigued, I nudged the door carefully with my foot. It was locked, but a heavy old key dangled from the keyhole. After a couple of noisy turns, the lock opened and the door swung open wide.

Soft light filtered through tall, narrow windows, covering the floor with green, blue, and red dots. At one end was a small nave with a double row of wooden benches on each side and an altar on a raised platform. Above that was a large wooden cross, hanging on thick steel cables. We were in the hospital chapel. It was too ironic.

I let Prit collapse on to one of the pews. I was exhausted, so I rested for a second, then prowled around the chapel, peering into every dark corner, making sure we didn't have any company. I braced myself and then kicked open a confessional. The disgusting image of an undead priest leaping out terrified me. But I breathed a sigh of relief. There was nothing in it or the adjoining sacristy.

Out of a little closet built into the wall, I grabbed a couple of stoles worn to celebrate mass. I draped them over Prit, who'd fallen into a deep, restless sleep. Bundled up in those warm robes, the Ukrainian made a strange picture. I shook him by the shoulders. I needed twenty seconds of his attention. He stretched, a lost, glazed look in his eyes. A tremor shook his left hand uncontrollably.

"Prit, I need you to listen for a minute. I have to leave you alone for a while. Lucullus has disappeared, and I have to find him. Understand?"

The Ukrainian nodded without saying a word. He was almost catatonic. I tucked the stoles around him and wiped his forehead. I unclipped the canteen, which had gotten dented up in my fall, gave him a sip, and set it beside him.

I had to sit there for a good twenty minutes till my legs stopped shaking. The twenty minutes turned into almost an hour. Every time I thought about going back out the door, an uncontrollable panic screwed my feet to the floor with the force of a hydraulic drill. I knew I had to control that fear. I was a goner if I let panic get the best of me. And Prit along with me.

For a moment, I weighed the idea of abandoning Lucullus to his fate, but I discarded the idea faster than it took to write that.

Lucullus was not just my pet and constant companion. That cat was the last link to my former life. If I lost him, I'd lose part of my soul. The memory of that life would scatter like sand in the wind. I had to find Lucullus. The poor guy must be scared shitless, hiding under a pile of trash.

As I stood up, my knee cracked ominously. That wasn't a good sign. I was beaten up worse than I thought. I'd take the speargun, the remaining two spears, and the pistol with the seven rounds we had left. I took the flashlight, too. Enough light was filtering into the chapel so that Prit could see without it.

Prit sank back into a restless sleep as I ventured back out of the large room in the dark. I closed the chapel door behind me. Those massive, heavy oak doors were probably the most solid ones in the entire hospital. It was the safest place to leave my friend. I studied the huge key in the lock. Then I gave the key a couple of turns and hung it around my neck. I'd be back in a few minutes, I thought.

I didn't have the faintest idea where to start looking for Lucullus. He must have been scared to death by the fight. He probably took shelter in some quiet corner. At home, during a storm, he'd burrow into the back of the linen closet until the worst had passed. I realized that finding my cat in that vast hospital with thousands of dark corners could be a desperate mission, made worse because my frightened cat might not want to be found.

I had to try. I know it sounds crazy. He's just a cat, but I felt a moral obligation to find him. After all the time we'd spent together, losing him would break my heart. Anyone with a pet understands what I'm saying. Whispering his name, I crossed the room till I came to another very steep stairway, heading deeper into the darkness.

I shone the flashlight on the ground. A huge puddle of water spilled down the stairs. The steady dripping echoed everywhere in the dark.

A couple of drops fell on my head, startling me. I looked up at the ceiling. Seven or eight stories above my head was a huge skylight that had originally flooded those stairs with light. I was standing on a staircase that connected all the floors. Liters of rainwater filtered through that shattered skylight and trickled down the stairs, soaking everything.

Again I felt a gust of wind whipping across my face. My heart sank when I realized the wind was blowing from the broken skylight. That was not a way out. I was starting to think I'd never find a way out.

A soft whine, faint but unmistakable, pulled me out of those bitter thoughts. My ears perked up. There it was again. It sounded like a crying child—or a meowing cat. It was coming from the bottom of the stairs, which were shrouded in shadows.

I cursed under my breath. The hospital basement was the last place I wanted to go. For some reason that escaped me, Lucullus had hidden there. I had no choice. I screwed my courage and started down the stairs.

ENTRY 83
April 22, 3:30 p.m.

The pool of water at the foot of the stairs spread out like a lake. I stood on one of the last steps on "dry land" and scanned the area with the flashlight. Its beam lit up the water that stretched out to the end of the dark hallway. Rainwater had poured in through the broken skylight and accumulated down there. Iridescent oil spots and some empty boxes floated in the water like swimmers on a pond.

It was highly unlikely Lucullus had gone down there. Aside from the deep-seated hatred all cats have for water, there was no way my Lucullus would have deigned to stick his aristocratic paws into this dark, murky pond.

I started to head back up the stairs. Then I heard that whine again, and I froze. The sound had been faint at the top of the stairs; now it was crystal clear. It was a cat's meow. MY cat's meow. My Lucullus. I was 100 percent sure. After two years listening to that furry playboy yowl at the neighborhood cats night after night, I knew his voice.

The meow quivered with fear. It sounded like it was coming from directly across that dark expanse of water. It was growing weaker, as if he were going in the opposite direction. I had no time to consider how Lucullus got across that little lake. I descended the remaining steps to ground level.

The water was up to my waist. Part of my brain told me that a cat wouldn't go through that lake on his own. Something or someone was dragging Lucullus along. Normally fear would've made me head back the way I came. But another part of my brain turned a deaf ear.

I splashed noisily as I waded down the long corridor. There were piles of water-logged stuff as far as the eye could see. I spotted a sheet of black plastic floating along with all the other trash. I hooked it with the tip of my spear and shone a light on it. When I discovered it was a body bag, I shuddered out of fear and disgust. I took a deep breath, trying to control my fear, and made sure the bag was empty. It looked like it had never been used. But finding it there could only mean I was dangerously close to the morgue. Not exactly the best place to prowl around in the dark.

The slamming of a metal door echoed like a cannon through the basement. I gripped the speargun with sweaty hands, thinking it would be great to have a flashlight on the end of the gun. Duct tape would have done the trick, but the only roll I had was in the backpack in the chapel with Prit.

I cursed under my breath. My mobility was limited, since I had to shine the flashlight with one hand and fire a gun with the other. The speargun wasn't the problem. When you're under water, you usually shoot it one-handed. But the pistol was a different story. I needed both hands to control the weapon's powerful kick and aim with some accuracy. It'd be no laughing matter to shoot a hole in the roof trying to kill a hungry undead monster ten feet from my face.

I missed a step and nearly fell face-first into the water. The flashlight swung wildly in every direction, sending iridescent glimmers across the oil-slick water. I leaned against the wall to get my balance. The pungent smell of oil saturated the air.

That step was the top of another short flight of stairs up to where the water only came up to my ankles. Splashing down the hallway, I walked the last few yards to a completely dry room. A heavy steel door in the back of that room stopped me in my tracks. The door had no handle or doorknob. The dark keyhole was recessed, with no screws to remove it with. It stared at me mockingly. I furiously kicked the door. Without the key, I'd come to a dead end. Devastated, I punched the door over and over, muttering a string of curses, heaping shit on the heads of all the saints.

My angry outburst stopped abruptly when I spied damp footprints glistening near the door. There were two sets: one set was my size, and the other set was much smaller and looked like tennis shoes. The smaller footprints came up to the door and turned left.

In the flashlight's beam, I followed the stranger's footprints, speargun in hand, ready to beat a hasty retreat if I discovered that one of those beasts had left those footprints. The tracks turned a corner behind a janitor's closet and trailed off to the end of the hallway. Adrenaline pulsed through my veins as I plunged into the darkness. Beads of sweat slid down my temples. My mouth was dry as a desert.

I swept the light across the footprints, which were growing fainter. Suddenly, the light shone on a pair of bright red sneakers. I slowly raised the light. Dirty, faded jeans, a wool sweater—a young girl, barely more than a teenager. Huge green eyes framed in a perfect oval face. A scared but determined look on her face.

Glowing, smooth skin.

Living skin.

A living human being.

I was speechless. I blinked a few times to make sure she wasn't an optical illusion. No, she was a real girl. Right in front of me. If I stretched out my arm, I could almost touch her face. Her breath kept time with mine. A huge sense of relief washed over me. I felt like screaming for joy. But, I didn't. The barrel of a gun was aimed at my chest. I'd have to keep my shouts of joy in check.

She squinted, trying to see me better in the shadows. I realized the light from my flashlight was blinding her. Cautiously I set it on a table. I raised my hands from the speargun and showed her my empty palms. The girl swallowed hard.

"Hello," I greeted her.

The girl jumped when she heard my voice. For one horrifying second I thought she'd shoot me.

"Hello," I repeated. "What's your name?"

The girl hesitated. Her gaze swung nervously between my face and the narrow corridor to my right, toward the metal door. She was scared. Of me, I thought with a shock. I tried a third time.

"Take it easy. I won't hurt you," I said, soothingly. "My name's—"

The roar of the girl's rifle drowned out my words.

Something white-hot passed close to my face, crashing into the wall behind me. Plaster rained down on me. The bullet left a gaping hole in the wall.

I cringed, terrified. That lunatic was going to kill me. "What the f*ck're you doing?" I shouted in a panicked voice. "Don't shoot me, damn it! I'm alive!"

The girl was trembling like a leaf. The huge army-issue assault rifle looked like a cannon in her hands. Judging from the way she held it, she'd fired by accident.

I stretched my hand toward the gun and pushed it aside. The green-eyed beauty didn't put up a struggle. Chalk one up for me, I thought. Just don't screw up.

A long, plaintive howl broke the silence. The pack hanging on the girl's back started moving frantically. Something inside was struggling to get out. A half-closed zipper gave way, and out peeked a furry orange head with bristling whiskers and a very angry look on its face. A look I've come to know so well over the years.

"Lucullus!" I cried excitedly. I breathed happily. I'd found my lost pet.

My cat struggled to get his fat body through the broken zipper. He kicked like crazy till he hung out of the pouch like a sack of potatoes. His rear end and tail were still trapped inside the backpack. He launched himself forward one more time and got completely free, leaving behind tufts of orange fur. Once on the floor, he licked his sides for a few seconds and recovered some of his feline dignity.

A huge smile spread across my face. Same old Lucullus. A leopard never changes his spots. I should've known where I'd find him—in the company of some female, even in this nightmare!

Lost in thought, I stroked my cat and then looked long and hard at his new friend. The astonished girl just stood there, still speechless, her rifle pointed at the floor.

Now I could study her calmly. She was sixteen or seventeen, at the most, but she was very tall. Her startling, catlike green eyes shone brightly now. A few freckles decorated the harmonious features of her face. Thick, dark hair spilled over her shoulders. Her slim body looked supple as a reed. I detected perky breasts under the enormous faded sweater she was wearing. Her entire body was tensed as she watched every move I made. She looked like a panther about to bolt.

"My name's Lucia." Her voice was warm but shaky. She was clearly frightened. "What's yours?"

I repeated my name and introduced her to Lucullus. I added sarcastically, "But you two've already met."

A deep blush spread across Lucia's cheeks. "I thought he'd been abandoned. I heard gunfire and went up to investigate. I found your cat in the hall and picked him up without thinking. I wasn't stealing him," she added defensively.

"I believe you," I answered with my best smile, as I scratched Lucullus's ears. "What the hell're you doing here?"

A dark shadow veiled Lucia's eyes, and her whole body shivered. "I shouldn't be here," she shook her head and repeated in a monotone. "I shouldn't be here."

"Well, if it's any consolation, I shouldn't be here either." I wheezed as I struggled to stand up. "None of us should be here."

"Is someone else with you?" There was terror in her voice.

"Well, I left a Ukrainian pilot resting in the chapel. He's missing two fingers on one hand, and all this is starting to get him down." I saw the surprised look on her face, so I added, a bit cocky, "But he's a good guy. I'm taking care of him. He just needs some sleep."

I couldn't believe what I was saying. Five minutes before, I'd been scared to death in a dark hallway, praying to find a way out of there. Now I sounded like a teenager strutting around like a peacock in front of that gorgeous girl. Granted, it's been months since I've seen a live woman, but the way I was acting was over the top.

Lucia didn't seem to notice of any of that. She laughed delight-edly, relieved like me not to be face-to-face with the undead. And, like me, pleased to have some company.

"Where were you?" I asked. "How long have you been here?"

"Nearly three months." She looked me up and down, taking stock. "You're not part of the rescue team, are you?" she asked skeptically.

Imagine the picture I made: a rail-thin guy in a filthy, ripped wetsuit, a speargun slung across his back and a pistol at his waist, Pancho Villa style. The stethoscope around my neck added a sur-real touch. At least I'd shaved at the Mercedes dealership before we left. I may have looked like a beaten-up, crazy bum, but at least I was clean shaven.

I cleared my throat, uncomfortable under such intense scru-tiny. I asked her what she meant by "rescue team."

"The *army* rescue team, of course!" She must've thought I was touched in the head. "One of these days, they'll assemble a team from the Safe Havens and rescue those of us who stayed behind. Sister Cecilia says it won't be long."

I shook my head with a heavy heart. Three months cooped up there, cut off from the outside world. She didn't have a clue.

"No one's coming," I muttered. "There're no more Safe Havens. Everything's gone to hell. You're one of only a handful of survivors I've come across in three months."

Lucia looked at me, dumbfounded. I think if I'd said we'd eaten roasted baby for dinner, she couldn't have had a more hor-rified expression.

"What?" She wrung her hands nervously. "That can't be." She was talking more to herself than to me. "Someone has to come. There's got to be someone in charge!"

"I don't think so," I replied. "I've roamed around the entire area for several weeks. I've only come across a handful of survivors." I lit a cigarette. "And they weren't very nice people. The Safe Havens are a graveyard. Lack of food and disease weakened all the refugees. And," I added, noting how the color drained out of her face, "those monsters overpowered the defense forces and finished everyone off."

Lucia's legs buckled. She fell back against the wall and slid to the floor, staring into space, in shock. "No one left," she murmured. "No one…what'll happen to us?"

"Us?" I looked at her, puzzled. Then I remembered she'd said something about a Sister Cecilia. "Is there someone else with you?"

She nodded as tears welled up in her eyes. She pointed to the metal door I'd kicked a minute before.

I helped her to her feet. Her skin was soft. For a split second, I got a whiff of her scent. It wasn't perfume. It was a soft, warm human fragrance with a pungent female undertone. She smelled like a woman. Six months of abstinence had made my sense of smell very keen.

Lucia looked me in the face. For a moment I thought I'd drown in her eyes. They were like vast green lakes. My head was buzzing. I felt dizzy. Lucullus's scratches brought me back to reality. My cat was trying to get my attention. He was determined to climb my pant leg, pissed off that we weren't paying any attention to him.

We retraced our steps across that expanse of water from the basement to the foot of the stairs. Although we'd just met (or maybe because of that), we splashed along side by side without saying a word. Occasionally one of us tripped on something hidden underwater and leaned on the other to get our balance, muttering "Thanks" or "Watch out." That was it.

Funny. I was convinced that if I found another survivor, someone besides the laconic Ukrainian, I'd talk up a storm. But now I didn't know what to say. I was as tongue-tied as a teenager on a first date. Maybe she felt the same way.

Actually, I think it's easy to explain what happened. After months of isolation and silence, after all the stress and danger, we'd painfully learned the value of silence. There were things we didn't need to talk about. The presence of another living being was one of them. We were enjoying that rediscovered experience so intensely we thought (or at least I thought) talking might break the spell.

We made it back to the chapel in just a few minutes. What had seemed to take an eternity was surprisingly brief on the return trip. It helped that we hadn't run into a single undead. The monsters had the run of the place, but this girl knew the building very well. We moved down closed-off corridors where no one had walked in months. It was all a blur to me. I was still in shock at finding a survivor who spoke my language, who didn't try to put a bullet in me, and who seemed even more freaked out than I was. I needed some time to reflect.

With the key I'd hung around my neck, I unlocked the chapel. My first thought was—Prit's dead. His head hung down at an unnatural angle, and he didn't move a muscle. He was slumped over on the pew where I'd left him. His body was as limp as if he'd been in that chapel for a million years.

I rushed down the aisle, braced for the worst, sure the stress had gotten the best of the Ukrainian. All those months on the edge had taken their toll. I realized I was crying. No, Prit, please. Please.

When I got to his side, I found that the Ukrainian was breathing. A huge sigh of relief emptied my lungs. I cradled his head against my chest. Not yet, old friend, not yet. Hold on a little longer.

Pritchenko may not have been not dead, but his condition was alarming. His glazed eyes peered off into space. Drool trickled from the corner of his mouth, making him look helpless and fragile. I said his name over and over but got no answer. Prit was catatonic. Completely gone.

Lucia stood a few steps behind me, watching me with a puzzled expression. She just had to take one look at him to wonder how on earth I got there, dragging along an invalid—a short guy with a big mustache, one arm in a blood-soaked sling and a thousand small cuts on his face, who seemed to be on a different planet.

I felt her questioning gaze on my back. I got really mad. How the hell could I explain everything Prit had been through? How did I explain the horrors he'd braved to reach that lousy abandoned room?

Lucia didn't ask any questions. She just spoke in a soft voice as she slipped an arm under Prit and helped him sit up. I was surprised how tenderly she treated him. She looked like a little girl nursing a baby duck with a broken wing.

We headed slowly back down to the metal door in the basement. Clearly Prit was in no condition to leave. Oh sure, I could go it alone (that is, Lucullus and I could). We'd probably make it, but I ruled out that option.

I couldn't leave Prit behind. Not that girl either. And just thinking about going back out there alone made my stomach churn. No, for better or worse I'd stay with them. If I could endure all those ordeals, I could deal with whatever lay ahead.

When we reached the metal door with no lock, Lucia knocked a few times (two quick, three spaced apart, and finally a loud kick) and waited. After a few seconds, someone turned the lock from inside, and the door opened. Light streamed out through the open door, blinding us for a second.

Light.

Electricity. Somehow they had electricity.

I took a couple of steps toward the door. I smelled something really delicious cooking. I glanced back at the gloomy, damp tunnel and hesitated. I'd had bad experiences with other survivors. I didn't know who or what I'd find on the other side of that door. Under the circumstances, I decided it was worth finding out. Bottom line, I had no choice. Not hesitating any longer, I stepped through the doorway. The heavy metal door closed behind us with a thud, leaving the hallway dark again.

Whatever came next, we were part of it.

ENTRY 84
Mid-July, 3:40 p.m.

I've spent four magical months recovering my sanity and putting some distance between me and the cornered animal I was becoming. Those months helped me remember I'm a human being, not just prey fighting to survive.

I've recovered physically, too, thanks to the rest, good food, and attentive care of my new friends. I'm back to the shape I was in before all hell broke loose. But not everything has healed. Part of me has grown hard and bitter, like a war veteran. My values and my idea of what's important have changed. That shouldn't be a surprise. The whole fucking world has changed.

Now we're a group of four, not counting Lucullus. Prit and I have joined forces with Lucia and Sister Cecilia. I couldn't believe my eyes. A fucking nun in the middle of this madness. As I write this, they're working away at the stove, their backs to me. It's great to have a hot meal every day.

Our refuge is fantastic. Behind the metal door and up a short flight of stairs is a subbasement that's completely closed off from the rest of the hospital. This was the hospital's huge kitchen, which turned out thousands of meals for staff and patients daily.

There are only three ways to gain access to the place: the freight elevator that carried supplies to the top floor, the stairs that connect to the rest of the hospital, and the emergency staircase we used to get in. The elevator was disabled by a piece of metal that held the doors open. The main staircase is cut off from the next floor by thick doors that are chained shut. The only possible way into the basement is down the emergency stairs. A single entrance and exit, protected by a fire door. Completely safe and impossible to get through.

But that's not the best part. To our relief, the hospital's emergency generators are still running, supplying power to this sector. The giant freezers in the kitchen, filled with enough food to feed an army, are still operating. Since there're only four of us (and a cat who eats enough for two), I calculate we have enough frozen food for two years.

The hospital has its own water supply. Years ago, when they were digging the building's foundations, they discovered a huge aquifer. So water's not a problem.

All we have to worry about is the generators failing or running out of fuel. We don't know exactly where they're located or where the control panel is. We ration energy as much as we can, but we know that the generators' reserves of diesel fuel aren't infinite. Sooner or later we'll have to face that situation.

Sister Cecilia Iglesias is an exceptional human being. She's a small woman in her fifties, bubbly and plump with an intelligent twinkle in her eyes, from a remote village in Avila, like Spain's patron saint, Saint Teresa. For the last fifteen years, she'd worked in a hospital run by her order a hundred or so miles from Nairobi, Kenya. She'd come to Vigo to give lectures at several religious schools but got trapped by the turmoil of the pandemic at the airport. At first she was housed in a crowded hotel in town, waiting for things to blow over. When it was clear that the situation was out of control, this energetic woman refused to be a passive refugee.

She learned that Meixoeiro Hospital was still caring for hundreds of people, but had an acute shortage of medical personnel. Most had fled or were dead. She didn't hesitate to show up at its door, offering her services as a nurse. She spent the final weeks of civilization in a whirlwind of exhausting work that kept her from learning news of the outside world. While I was comfortably holed up in my house, Sister Cecilia was tending to a constant, heart-wrenching stream of wounded refugees.

Meixoeiro Hospital was the only medical center that was operational until almost the end. That's why so many ambulances and cars kept making their way to its door to drop off dozens and dozens of injured people.

Sister Cecilia told me that a couple of army doctors sorted through the wounded at the entrance of to the ER. Those who had bites or scratches or had had some contact with the infected creatures were escorted by a platoon of soldiers to another "specialized medical center" nearby.

I didn't have the heart to tell that pious woman that that "specialized" center never existed. The overwhelmed military must have applied their own brand of "final solution" to the injured for whom there was no hope. In some field nearby, there're probably hundreds of dead with a bullet in their head, slowly rotting in a mass grave. That's how terrible the situation had gotten.

Not counting those unfortunate people, there were still hundreds of sick and wounded that the overloaded hospital staff struggled to administer to. Traffic accidents, people injured in rioting and looting, stroke victims, patients with appendicitis…the whole spectrum of illnesses and accidents poured in. Meixoeiro Hospital reached crisis mode as the situation outside unraveled.

One day, the order came to evacuate everyone to the Vigo Safe Haven. Authorities could no longer secure the perimeter. Out of all the ambulances that responded to emergency calls, only half returned. The rest were mysteriously swallowed up.

A BRILAT armored unit appeared one morning to organize the evacuation convoy. Hundreds of sick and wounded were crammed on to the open beds of army trucks and into ambulances, taxis, private cars—anything with four wheels—along with tons of drugs and most of the medical staff. They had to leave behind about a hundred patients who were too sick to be moved. A small group of volunteers, Sister Cecilia among them, chose to stay to care for those poor doomed people so they didn't have to suffer a slow, painful death alone. Maybe it would've been better if they had.

The group included three doctors and five nurses, counting Sister Cecilia. A small conglomeration of soldiers and policemen were stationed there as protection. Their mission was to hunker down in the hospital and wait for a larger rescue team that would come "at a later date." Obviously, the rescue team never came.

While the medical team struggled to keep their critically ill patients alive, the soldiers systematically fortified the entrances. That accounts for the locked doors we encountered. The basement we're in was christened "Numantia" by a sergeant with a macabre sense of humor, a place to reenact the Spaniards' famous resistance to a Roman siege in the second century. If the defenses fell, everyone was to take refuge in this sector. The generators were set on automatic. They cut the power to the entire building except the kitchens. Once they'd done that, all they could do was wait.

That was when Lucia showed up. She's a baby, just seventeen years old ("almost eighteen," she never tires of saying), but she has a sexy, grown-up body. She lived with her parents in Bayona, a small tourist town about twelve miles from Vigo. When the order came to evacuate their town to a number of Safe Havens, the authorities attempted to carry it out in an orderly fashion. Somewhere they found a fleet of buses to move the people. While thousands of people waited at an inn on a small peninsula, buses tirelessly made the short trip over and over between Bayona and the Safe Havens.

In all the confusion, Lucia got on one bus and her parents got on another. Trusting she would easily find them at the Safe Haven, she made the trip without protest, overwhelmed by the situation like everyone else. However, the bus Lucia's parents were on never reached its destination. Along the way, it mysteriously disappeared. Everyone feared the worst. Back then, attacks on the Safe Haven were getting worse as the undead swarmed everywhere.

Lucia nearly went crazy with despair. Alone, not knowing her parents' fate, she was enveloped by the quagmire at the Safe Haven, crammed into a frozen-food warehouse along with three hundred other people. She decided to find her family. She reasoned that if they weren't at the Safe Haven, the only other place they could be was Meixoeiro Hospital. So as rations dwindled and they recruited volunteers for reconnaissance groups, she was one of the first to sign up.

They issued her a camouflage jacket several sizes too big and heavy combat boots, but no weapons. There weren't enough to go around, ammunition was getting scarce, and her frail appearance didn't inspire a lot of confidence in the officer in charge. So she served as a porter. When the team reached its objective, one group secured the perimeter while another group raided the place. The porters had to drag out many pounds of nonperishable food and any other useful items they came across.

Lucia spent three grueling weeks cheating death on every outing. She saw half a dozen members of her team die. She was nearly caught once by an undead crouched down in a warehouse. But she still went out, day after day, waiting for her chance.

Finally, she got that chance. When she calculated that that day's objective was relatively close to Meixoeiro Hospital, she slipped away from the group and started walking down the road toward the hospital. That was the most frightening forty-eight hours of her life. At night she hid anywhere that was high and inaccessible. At first light she started out again, dodging the undead, forced to spend long stretches of time in hiding, waiting for her predators to move on.

When she finally reached the hospital, the soldiers were dumbfounded. For weeks they hadn't seen a single soul in the area, apart from the throngs of undead that wandered their way. The sight of that young girl, dressed like a soldier, walking up in search of her parents was disconcerting.

That brave girl was devastated to learn the hospital had no record of her parents. She realized she was completely alone. She didn't know what to do next.

But the worst was yet to come. The presence of a pretty young girl among a group of isolated, brutalized young men created sexual tension. More and more fights broke out among those soldiers, whose nerves were on edge. One night, one of the soldiers got drunk off his ass and tried to rape her. Fortunately, one of the doctors stopped the guy just in time with a well-aimed blow to the head, but the situation was out of control.

The lieutenant in charge ordered Lucia and Sister Cecilia to remain in Numantia. They weren't to leave for any reason. Outraged protests from the sister and Lucia did no good. The lieutenant was old school. He didn't want women fraternizing with the men under his command. End of story. For a couple of weeks, they worked as cooks and helped out the doctors on the upper floors. Meanwhile patients died one by one of their grave illnesses, since the doctors lacked specialized drugs and couldn't perform any kind of surgery. All the defensive team could do was wait.

But not for long. A couple of nights later, they lost radio contact with the Safe Haven. Hundreds of undead began to gather around the hospital. Instead of trying to fly under the radar, the lieutenant, an empty-headed, power-hungry idiot, ordered the soldiers to fire at will. The *clackety-clack* of automatic weapons drew an even larger crowd of those creatures like a magnet.

In the end, the undead managed to get in. Neither Sister Cecilia nor Lucia could explain how. They were entrenched in the basement as the drama unfolded above their heads. All they knew was that one of the soldiers, a very young, scared boy with a strong Andalusian accent, stuck his head in to Numantia and warned them to lock the door from inside.

For a couple of hours they heard shooting outside, explosions around the hospital complex, and then a bomb. The shooting soon ringed the interior corridors of the hospital. Then it stopped altogether. For two hours, the nun and the girl waited for someone to come tell them the fighting was over. No one ever showed up.

Steeling herself, Lucia took a risk and left Numantia to find out what had happened to the soldiers. She saw what Pritchenko and I found months later. Empty corridors, evidence of fighting everywhere, and not a single living being.

Since then, the two women have lived in that basement, protected from the outside. They had light, water, and food, and were safe from the undead. What they didn't have was a clear idea of what the devil to do next. They knew the odds were not in their favor on the outside. On their own, they wouldn't get very far. They concluded that their best option was to wait for the rescue party.

But all that showed up were two tired, injured, hungry, disoriented survivors. And a cat. Our arrival and the news from outside brought a mixture of horror and hope—horror at discovering there was nothing left of the civilization they knew; hope that, because of us, there was finally a solution to this complex situation.

Prit is a whole lot better. The minute we walked through the door, Sister Cecilia took him under her wing like a mother hen shelters her chick. Not only did she mend his shattered left hand with remarkable skill (although there was nothing she could do about his missing fingers), she also drew the Ukrainian out of the debilitating depression he'd sunk into. She diagnosed both of us as being shell shocked. It's curable. Normally, a couple of weeks in a safe, quiet, stress-free environment alleviates it, but sometimes the sufferer never recovers.

Fortunately, Prit wasn't one of those cases. His zest for life is too strong for a little thing like a nervous breakdown to get the best of him. I've seen his outlook slowly grow more positive. I'm sure the long talks he's had with Sister Cecilia well into the night have contributed to his recovery. The nun and the Ukrainian have forged a close friendship based on trust.

Like many Slavs, Prit's a devout Christian. Although Sister Cecilia's Catholic and he's Orthodox, her presence has comforted him deeply. During those long talks, he must have tried to make sense of this hell. Why did he lose his wife and child? Why did God unleash this catastrophe? I don't know if he found any answers, but his search has been a balm for his wounded soul. Something inside his heart is broken forever, that's for sure. Now at least he's learning to live with the pain.

For my part, I prefer not to ponder it. Every minute of the day, I wonder what happened to my family. Damn, I never thought I could miss anyone in such an intense, hopeless way. It's highly likely they're mutants, I know, but I refuse to accept it.

I've had the same nightmare for weeks. I'm walking down a dark corridor. I can hear the sea splashing against one wall, but it doesn't smell like the sea. It smells like something rotting. The corridor is littered with trash and shell casings. The walls are stained with something that looks like shit, but I know it's dried blood. Suddenly, my sister and my parents come out of a door. They've been turned into those things. They walk toward me with blind eyes, after my blood. I'm armed in my dream, but I can't raise my gun, and then,... then I wake up, deeply upset, with an urge to throw up.

Undoubtedly, those who have changed into those creatures are in hell, but we survivors are living pretty close to that hell.

ENTRY 85
Mid-September, 9:45 a.m.

Yesterday afternoon, Prit and I were standing in the elevator shaft, discussing the fastest way to reach the SUV. We agreed we should drive it around to our exit in case we needed it in an emergency. Moving it from time to time would also keep it in running condition. Winter was coming, and I was afraid the cold weather would damage the starter.

In the middle of our conversation, the Ukrainian straightened up suddenly, sniffing the air nervously like a retriever, with an intensely focused look on his face.

"Smell that?" he asked.

"Smell what?" I said. After nine months surrounded by trash and slowly rotting corpses, my sense of smell wasn't as keen as it used to be.

"Fire," Prit said as he closed his eyes and sniffed the air eagerly. His eyes flew open, boring into me.

"Fire? A fire? Here in the hospital?"

"Not in the hospital. A fire out there! In the forest! I'm sure of this." Prit's voice caught in his throat.

I trusted my pilot friend. After years of fighting wildfires, he could detect the faintest hint of a fire, fires the average person wouldn't notice. I didn't smell anything, but if the Ukrainian said he smelled smoke, that was the end of the discussion. The question was how it would affect us.

"It's blowing in on the wind. Come here," the Ukrainian continued.

"We should go take a look."

"Yes."

We stared at each other. The Ukrainian shook his head, and I cussed under my breath. We both knew what came next.

Shit, I thought. We had to get back out there. We had to stick our nose out of our little hole, whether we liked it or not.

After we'd made that decision, we headed back to Numantia to bring Sister Cecilia and Lucia up to speed. The look of dread on Lucia's face when she heard what we were planning was almost comical.

As she helped me get into my patched wetsuit, she nervously chattered away nonstop, reminding me of a thousand things not to do. "Don't take any chances, don't go into dark places, don't go near anything suspicious, don't wander too far from Prit..."

I tried to calm her down, for my sake as well as hers. I was getting more nervous by the minute. Lucia isn't a hysterical person, but the possibility that something would happen to us outside that refuge really got to her.

Finally, Prit and I were ready. We were armed with assault rifles the army had left behind. I was also carrying the speargun across my back, with a spear loaded and two more strapped to my right calf. The Ukrainian, decked out in an awful fuchsia tracksuit so bright it hurt your eyes, had a huge hunting knife tucked in a holster. He chewed some gum mechanically and was surprisingly calm.

We agreed that the best way out was through the elevator shaft. We wouldn't have to go back through the dark hospital, plus it was the fastest way out. Once we were in the storeroom on the top floor, all we had to do was open a window to get a view of the entire valley surrounding the hospital.

We soon discovered that climbing up the elevator cables was harder than it looks in the movies. They were covered in grease, and the noise we made as we climbed should've attracted a legion of those monsters. But as far as we could tell, things were going our way. At least for a while.

After struggling to the top floor, Prit eased the elevator door open, ready to duck back inside at the first sign of danger. I kept the cable as taut as possible. If there was trouble, we could slide back down to the ground floor.

Prit slithered behind the door like an eel and disappeared out on to the upper floor. For fifteen long seconds, I didn't hear a sound. Just when I thought my nerves would snap, the Ukrainian slipped back behind the door and signaled that the coast was clear. Strangely clear.

For the first time in months, I felt sunlight directly on my skin. It felt so good that I stood stock still for a moment, enjoying that wonderful sensation. We were standing in a warehouse on the top floor. From there we'd ventured out into the ambulance garage. Sunlight was streaming in the heavy metal gate trucks used to drive through, which had been left wide open during the evacuation. That discovery made my stomach clench. With that door open, there was nothing to keep the undead from wandering around this huge room. But there wasn't any sign of them.

Prit and I peered out. It was a beautiful late summer day. Although the sun was shining brightly in a cloudless sky, the windchill from a strong north wind made it very cold. That wind also carried the strong smell of burning wood. Even I could smell it now.

My gaze swept nervously from side to side as I tried to detect any suspicious activity, but there wasn't a soul in sight. Only dozens of birds darting everywhere, completely disoriented. The air was so charged with electricity it almost crackled.

Suddenly Pritchenko elbowed me in the ribs. I looked in the direction he was pointing. Over the hills at the end of the valley, about a mile away, rose a thick column of smoke. Enormous black spirals twisted and turned with a fury. An evil glow dyed the horizon orange, adding a sinister, surreal touch to the landscape.

I stood there, horrified at what I saw. A fire. A huge, uncontrollable forest fire. A couple of days before, a strong storm with a lot of thunder and lightning but no rain had hit in the area. Maybe lightning from that storm started that fire. Or a gas cylinder left out in the sun for months. Or a hundred other damn things I could come up with. No way to say for sure.

All I knew was that with no one to fight that fire it was reaching terrifying proportions, destroying everything in its path. As if someone had read my thoughts, a powerful explosion shook the air. A huge orange fireball rose over the horizon. The fire had just devoured a car, probably more than one, given the size of the explosion. That fire was becoming a monster.

Then I suddenly remembered the strange lack of undead in the area. I wondered if something had warned them to escape the flames. Wouldn't surprise me. Those creatures seemed to be driven by the same basic instincts as animals. One of the most basic impulses of nature is self-preservation.

Somehow the undead had perceived the danger and left for safer areas. Or maybe the flames had trapped hundreds, maybe thousands, of them. Even so, there'd still be millions of those lost souls wandering around. No, the fire wasn't the solution to the problem. It posed an even greater problem. And we survivors certainly didn't need any more problems. We could hardly keep our heads above water as it was.

A couple of wild boars ran out of the tangled patch of weeds the front garden had become and raced across the deserted parking lot, fleeing the wall of flame. Prit and I looked at each other. The animals were following their instincts and getting the hell out. We should follow their example. You didn't need finely honed instincts to figure that out. One look at the edge of the fire and the direction the wind was blowing told us that the hospital would be engulfed in a couple of hours, four at the most. There was no time to lose.

We quickly rounded the southern wall of the hospital toward the parking lot, where we'd left the SUV months ago. I remembered I'd left the passenger door wide open, and a couple of those things had gotten inside. We didn't know what we'd find, but we were pretty sure the SUV's battery would be completely dead. I wasn't sure I'd turned off the headlights when I dragged Prit out of the car. Just in case, at the bottom of my backpack was a brand-new battery we'd scavenged from the ambulance repair shop.

As we rushed around, switching the new battery for the old one, I felt a strong sense of déjà vu. It was the same situation we'd lived through months before, when we landed at the port of Vigo. Only now we weren't flying blind like before. And we didn't have a bunch of armed Pakistanis hovering over us. That made a huge difference. I wondered what became of the crew of *Zaren Kibish*. As far as I was concerned, they could burn in hell.

The motor coughed a couple of times, hesitated, then started up. Just then, the first flames broke over the hills near the hospital. The sky was bright orange, and the smell of smoke was getting stronger. The wind had picked up, and the temperature had risen a couple of degrees. The situation was getting uglier by the minute.

We drove around the building without seeing a single one of those monsters. Crunching on the dry gravel, we pulled the SUV up to the tunnel leading to the storeroom. Prit waited in the car with the engine running while I shot down the greased elevator cable to the bottom floor.

Sister Cecilia and Lucia were waiting near the elevator car, looking really worried. You could smell the smoke in the basement now. Maybe it was my imagination, but I thought I saw wisps of smoke floating in the light of the magnesium lamps.

I quickly brought them up to speed. A huge fire was approaching the hospital. There was no way to contain it; it would reach us in about an hour and would burn the place to the ground. Even the undead had fled as fast as their battered bodies would take them. We had to get out now, or we'd be burned to a crisp.

Their reaction was more serene than I'd imagined. I'd had a mental image of a meltdown or even an outright refusal to leave the safety of the basement, but they took the news in stride. Lucia went to retrieve the emergency backpacks we'd packed. The nun asked if there was a way to unlock the elevator and get it back in operation. "There are many things this nun can do," she said, "but climbing up a cable covered in grease is not one of them. So move your butt, my son, or you'll have to take me out the long way, and that would take too much time."

I smiled, shaking my head, too impressed to speak. Those two were made of strong stuff. They had to be to have survived on their own for so long and endured that hell without getting devoured. Where big, hairy-chested men had collapsed like a broken spring in the face of difficulties, those women just gritted their teeth and kept on going. They were definitely not delicate, prim, and proper ladies. Just the opposite.

Just then, Lucia came back around the corner, piled high with two huge army backpacks and another one in tow. We'd packed everything we thought we'd need when it came time to leave— dozens of freeze-dried army ration packets, a huge first-aid kit that could treat a regiment, ammunition, flares, my shortwave radio (with no batteries, since a sailor on the *Zaren Kibish* had decided he needed them), liters of water, and God knows what else.

I heaved the heaviest backpack on to my back and helped Lucia put hers on. Despite Sister Cecilia's indignant protests, I didn't let her carry the third backpack. Lucia and I dragged it and the box with Lucullus in it. Things hadn't gotten so bad that a woman her age had to carry a backpack that weighed as much as she did.

Before we got in the elevator, I took one last look around and felt a twinge of nostalgia. I'd lived an almost normal life there for months. It might've been the only safe place with electricity, water, food, and comfort for many miles. Not only did we have to leave, but it would be engulfed in flames in minutes, and there was nothing we could do about it. The thought that such a wonderful place was going to vanish made my heart sink. I smiled, bitterly aware of the strange irony underlying that thought. To us a dark, locked basement, full of food smells, the walls covered in damp condensation, seemed wonderful. That was fucked up.

I stuck the ivory rosary the nun had left on a table into my pocket and walked slowly to the elevator, where the women were waiting for me. I didn't bother to turn the lights off. What did it matter? The *Titanic* had gone down with all its lights on too. And the orchestra playing on the deck.

After a quick inspection, I realized the elevator would be surprisingly easy to unblock. I just had to remove a huge soup ladle someone had wedged into the gap that allowed the door to close. When I pulled it out, the door snapped shut with a deafening metallic screech. Almost immediately, the cabin started to rise slowly, with very unsettling jolts.

Our ascent was slow and tense. Smoke filtered through the vents, drying our throats. Its acrid smell became more intense. I kept picturing dozens of those things waiting patiently at the top for the special of the day. I pictured dozens of eager mouths, outstretched arms reaching into the elevator to tear us apart and devour us.

I squeezed my eyes shut; I was breathing really fast. I couldn't do a thing, not a damn thing...

A hand rested on my arm. I opened my eyes and saw the calm look on Lucia's face. She squeezed my arm affectionately and whispered warmly in my ear, "Take it easy. Everything'll be all right." Then she gave my earlobe a playful, not-so-innocent nibble that almost sent me through the roof of the elevator. Naughty girl.

The elevator came to a stop with an even stronger jolt. The door was stuck, after not being used for so long. It wouldn't open all the way, so we had to push on it. Once outside, we stopped, overwhelmed by what we saw.

Clouds of smoke enveloped the grounds and the parking lot, reducing visibility to about an eighth of a mile. Everything glowed an unhealthy red, like a scene out of hell. We could clearly see the flames moving over the hills. When the fire breached the hills, it flew downhill, devouring everything in its path. A huge stand of eucalyptus trees was engulfed by the flames. The heat was so intense, they exploded like matches thrown into a fireplace. Thousands of sparks flew everywhere, carried by the wind whipped up by the fire. Some of those sparks fell on highly combustible dry underbrush, starting new fires. The situation was much more chaotic than we'd foreseen. The gusting wind had pushed the fire along even faster than we anticipated. In less than fifteen minutes, it would be licking the hospital's walls.

Our eyes tearing from the smoke, we reached the SUV. Even though its lights were on, it was almost invisible in all the ash and fire. A restless Prit was waiting for us next to the SUV, beckoning for us to hurry, all the while monitoring the entire area. I noticed he'd taken the safety off his rifle, something that hadn't occurred to me. Once a soldier, always a soldier. Those precautions must be etched into his subconscious.

While everyone stuffed packages into the trunk, I slipped into the driver's seat. In this situation, I preferred to take the wheel. I'd had enough of the Ukrainian driving experience—the last thing we needed was an accident.

When everyone was aboard, we sped away in a cloud of dust, sending gravel flying in all directions. The scene was right out of Dante's *Inferno*. A huge red cloud enveloped everything as far as the eye could see, which wasn't very far, just forty or fifty yards ahead of the headlights. The roar of the flames was punctuated by explosions and the crackle of burning dry wood. I crossed the parking lot in the dark. At the last second, I dodged the abandoned wreck of a bloodstained Peugeot.

I finally found the exit, framed by two monstrous pieces of concrete, and then crossed through fifty yards of barbed wire fence. With a jolt that drew shouts of protest from all my passengers, we ran over a rotting corpse crawling with maggots that lay in the middle of the road.

We'd only been on the road for a mile or so when a huge explosion reverberated in the air, shaking our vehicle. The flames must've reached the oxygen tanks stored on the hospital grounds. The explosion was so violent I was sure it brought down half of the front wall. For the next fifteen minutes, we heard a series of explosions, one right after another, as flames devoured abandoned vehicles in the parking lot.

Finally, a massive explosion, considerably more powerful than the rest, made us jump out of our skin. It was either the fuel for the generators or the furnace. The flames had made it into the building.

Blessed Christ. We were on the road again, with no shelter, but with two more people. What next?

We drove the rest of the way in silence. Lucia and Sister Cecilia must've wondered where the hell we were going, but they refrained from asking. Maybe they were thinking that the first order of business was outrunning the fire. We'd decide our fate once we reached safety.

Nothing was further from reality.

Prit and I hadn't forgotten the little metal part in the Cyrillic-covered package, stashed in the pocket of the Ukrainian's back-pack. That part was all that ensured that the helicopter would still be there, waiting for us.

The helicopter. A temporary solution to our problems. Prit and I had talked about it so often over those long, wonderful months. The forestry heliport where Pritchenko had parked his helicopter was less than eight miles as the crow flies from Meixoeiro Hospital. We'd plotted the best way to get there on a road map, combining the Ukrainian's and my memories of the area. It was feasible to get there via secondary roads and aban-doned firewalls that didn't appear on maps. We wouldn't be in much danger, since we'd be traveling through unpopulated areas. We'd planned to make a run to the helipad in October, when the rain would hide our movements from the undead, and then fly the helicopter to the hospital and fill it up with supplies. But that fucking fire had forced us to move up our plans.

In theory our plan didn't seem too complicated, especially since the fire wasn't moving in that direction. But a sudden shift in the wind could change all that. For now, we were driving in an area that seemed safe. Meanwhile the fire was devouring the huge hospital complex, reducing it to rubble that glowed in the distance as flames leaped out the windows on the upper floors. That fire was moving through the valley at an amazing speed. I could make out the backlit shapes of the buildings on the outskirts of Vigo. If the fire wasn't stopped, it would devour the city, burning it to the ground in hours. And the only thing that would stop it was a heavy downpour.

The old world of mankind was definitely over. The new world, the world of the undead, the Cadaver World, had taken its place, gradually destroying every trace of our presence on earth. I had a terrifying thought. We scattered survivors were the last of our race.

There weren't any obstacles in our path until the last mile, where a landslide had blocked the road. We traveled the rest of the way along an old firebreak that ended near the boulder where I'm sitting now, writing this. From the top of the hill, about two thousand feet above sea level, we have a rare view of the entire Ria Vigo, part of the Ria Pontevedra, and several miles inland. There are no signs of life anywhere. Human life, that is.

The base was completely deserted and had been for several months, judging by the thick weeds growing up to the door. It took a good five minutes to hack our way to the fenced-off area.

ENTRY 86
Three Hours Later

To our relief, Prit's helicopter was still at the base. It's an enormous PZL W-3A Sokól with an elongated nose. Its body is painted red and white, its blades black and white. It rested on its oversize tires with all the doors open. On top of the cabin was a huge hump in which, Prit explained, were located the two monstrous turbines that drive the thing. The interior is spacious and wide. In addition to the pilot and copilot, it could fit ten people, although usually the fire brigades had only nine members, to give them more leg room.

Using a small tractor, we rolled the huge machine on to the tarmac. From where I'm sitting now, I can see Prit perched between the blades. He's got the turbine housing open and is tuning up one of the motors. I'm glad the Ukrainian's here. Not only has he proven to be a great companion, but thanks to him, we can get out of here.

The fire is now devouring the area north of Vigo. With high-powered binoculars, I've spent the last three hours scanning the horizon all the way to the city limits, about ten miles away. I can't see many details through the thick black smoke. There are frequent explosions as the fire devours vehicles, service stations, gas pipes, and the thousands of flammable things in a city that size. I'm so glad I'm not there.

Smoke also keeps me from getting a look at the port, which is wrapped in a dense cloud of ash and soot. I wonder if the *Zaren Kibish* is still anchored in the bay or if they managed to get out.

Wherever I point the binoculars, I can see them. The undead. Thousands of them, swarming everywhere. I imagine the fire will force them out of the city, and they'll roam the fields and small towns and suburbs, looking for something to sink their teeth into. God knows what they'll find. I'm sure the fire trapped many of them in the maze of Vigo's streets, but from what I can tell, most got out in time. On the way, we passed a few of them at a safe distance, but it's only a matter of time before they make their way here.

So we'd better get the hell out of here. And go far, far away.

We've chosen a destination—Tenerife in the Canary Islands. It's the logical choice. Anywhere on the European continent, we'll have the same problems as here. These days, this part of the world is no place for humans. We're sick of it. I'm tired of living like a cornered animal. We need a place where there's peace, food, electricity, and, most importantly, people. Man is a social animal; he needs to be around other humans. We'll go crazy if we don't have new faces, new people, new ideas. If we don't find a bigger group of people, I'm afraid we'll lose part of our humanity.

On the helicopter's radio, we picked up some very weak transmissions, full of static. We're sure they're military transmissions regarding air traffic at Los Rodeos Airport in Tenerife. That airport is still operational, so we assume there's an enclave of people. Lucia reminded us that the sea and airspace around the islands had been closed to keep more people from fleeing there. But that was months ago. They might welcome a new group of survivors now.

I kept going over the one problem I foresaw: the enormous distance we'll have to travel. Over a thousand miles from this part of the peninsula to the Canary Islands. The range of a helicopter like the Sokól is around 250 miles, so we ruled out flying in a straight line. Our only alternative is to fly over the peninsula, across the Strait of Gibraltar to Tarfaya, Morocco, the town closest to the islands. Then, just a couple of hours' flying time separate us from the island of Fuerteventura.

Refueling along the way will be a problem, to say the least. We have no idea what to expect at airports and airfields along the way, or even if they'll still be there. You can't get helicopter fuel at a gas station. It has to be the kind of fuel you can only get in refineries and airports. I've racked my brain, but haven't come up with a solution.

This morning, Prit and I pored over the map and debated all the possibilities our limited range allowed. The Ukrainian was in favor of flying south along the Portuguese coast, refueling in Oporto, Lisbon, Huelva, Tangier, Rabat, and Casablanca, and then heading for the islands.

After our experience in Vigo, landing on the outskirts of a metropolis like Oporto that once had hundreds of thousands of inhabitants sounded like a nightmare. I was in favor of heading for the interior, to unpopulated areas, filling up at heliports and small airports like this one. I realized that the chances of finding "dry" airfields without a drop of fuel were considerably higher than in a large airport. Even so, I thought my plan was preferable to negotiating a big city.

Either option involved a lot of risks. To put it bluntly, a journey full of horrors.

The solution, once again, came from Lucia. While Prit and I went on and on about the plan, she was listening, gazing thoughtfully at the bottom of the helicopter. Suddenly, she interrupted us.

"Prit, what's that?" she asked, pointing to a strange basket bolted on to the belly of the giant Sokól.

"That?" said the Ukrainian. "That's the bambi."

When he saw the strange look on our faces, he explained. "The bambi is what we call the bag we fill with water to put out fires. I usually carried crews to the fire and then unfolded the bambi, filled it in a nearby river, and emptied it on the flames. I repeated the process over and over." He smiled. "It was my job, you know?"

"How much does it hold?" Lucia asked, with an intelligent gleam in her eyes.

"About five hundred gallons. I don't see what the hell difference that makes," Pritchenko snapped.

"Wait! I think I know where she's going with this," I chimed in. "Five hundred gallons are—"

"Of course! Two tons! Instead of carrying water, we carry fuel. Our range would be…"

Lucia looked inquiringly at Pritchenko, but he'd already turned his back on us, grabbed some paper, and made some quick calculations. After a few minutes, he gave a couple of satisfied grunts, turned, smiled, and winked.

"I think it'll work. We fill the tank to the brim. With a five-hundred-gallon tank of fuel hanging below, we could get there without refueling anywhere. It'd be close, especially if we run into a headwind. But we just might make it." He stopped and stared into space and did more calculations in his head. "We just might make it," he repeated with a sparkle in his excited eyes. "Yes, it might work."

My chest swelled with joy. We were getting out of here. I couldn't believe it.

So now, while Prit puts the finishing touches on the Sokól's turbines, a shiny mountain of barrels filled to the top with helicopter fuel are stacked neatly on the edge of the track, inside a huge, superstrong transport net. The plan is to hang that huge bag from the belly of the helicopter, where the bambi would normally be. Each time we need to refuel, Prit'll land the helicopter in a clearing and pour some of those barrels into the helicopter's tank. A piece of cake after all we've been through.

The helicopter is loaded with our belongings, and everyone's ready to leave at first light. Lucia and Sister Cecilia are resting inside the hangar. Prit just closed the hood of the turbines, looking very satisfied.

I'm sitting on this huge rock at the end of the heliport. Lucullus is curled up at my feet, chewing on my shoelaces. The sun is setting over the river, casting golden sparkles on the water. It feels strange to think I may never see this landscape again.

We're the last train leaving the station. If there's anyone left in this area, I'm afraid his chances are slim to none.

Chances are slim that someone will come here in the future. But just in case, I'm leaving a copy of my journal in a plastic envelope on a table in the hangar. What if everything goes to hell and something happens to us along the way? At least if someone reads this, he'll know that for nine long months a group of people fought hard for their lives. We never surrendered. We always kept in our hearts the most noble, beautiful feeling that sets human beings apart: hope.

Okay. I'm going to take a nap. Tomorrow will be a crazy day.

ABOUT THE AUTHOR

Photo © Pablo Manuel Otero, 2012

An international bestselling author, Manel Loureiro was born in Pontevedra, Spain, and studied law at Universidad de Santiago de Compostela. After graduation, he worked in television, both on screen (appearing on Televisión de Galicia) and behind the scenes as a writer. *Apocalypse Z: The Beginning of the End*, his first novel, began as a popular blog before its publication, eventually becoming a bestseller in several countries, including Spain, Italy, and Brazil. Called "the Spanish Stephen King" by *La Voz de Galicia*, Manel has written three novels in the Apocalypse Z series. He currently resides in Pontevedra, Spain, where, in addition to writing, he is still a practicing lawyer.

ABOUT THE TRANSLATOR

Pamela Carmell's publications include Matilde Asensi's *The Last Cato* (HarperCollins), Belkis Cuza Malé's *Woman on the Front Lines* (sponsored by the Witter Bynner Foundation for Poetry), Antonio Larreta's *The Last Portrait of the Duchess of Alba* (a Book-of-the-Month Club selection), and the short-story collection, *Cuba on the Edge*. She is also published widely in literary magazines and anthologies.